In the Scattering *of* Light

Charlotte Geringer

Copyright © 2022 Charlotte Geringer
All rights reserved
First Edition

NEWMAN SPRINGS PUBLISHING
320 Broad Street
Red Bank, NJ 07701

First originally published by Newman Springs Publishing 2022

ISBN 978-1-68498-651-4 (Paperback)
ISBN 978-1-68498-652-1 (Digital)

Printed in the United States of America

For Lisa
who insists on nourishing my creative parts

*The future belongs to those who believe
in the beauty of their dreams.*
—Eleanor Roosevelt

The fears we don't face, become our limits.
—Robin Sharma

Chapter 1

August 22 blew in like the harrowing storm that it was, right on cue. It was an hour before midnight on a cloudy August evening in the city as Danni rushed across the cracked pavement. Her steps were deliberate, but the familiar fear in her mind choked her heart. The warm wind tugged ruthlessly at her long, tangled strands of hair. Just as expected, she received the dreaded phone call from her mother, calling her to the house. She performed this ritual every year, without fail. Her apartment was within walking distance, which was by design. She could never pry herself away from the immuring history of her family. Her mind swirled through the sad memories of the past as she approached the front door of the home where she grew up. Its paint had slowly been chipping away for years. She hesitated there, trying to catch her shallow breath. The houses on that street stood crammed together. Their solemn windows stared hopelessly at her, harboring their mournful secrets. It was a tormented street in Devil's Pocket, where the people endured life under its spell.

She looked at the number on the door. Two twenty-two. She instinctively added the numbers up to six and cringed at its malice. The house kept her parents hostage inside. Two souls, blown to pieces by the shot that came in the dark one night. They've been swept up in its current for over twenty years. Dragging their remaining children down with them. Danni was pained by the harm they have done. She has lived under its yoke for most of her life. But she has never been able to let go.

The door was still locked. She fumbled nervously around in her bag to find her key for the house. She took another long, deep breath. Counted to four before she exhaled to temper her escalating anxiety. Earlier, when she came home from work, she paced in front of her fridge like a caged animal. Her appetite withered as time stretched into the evening. It was the twenty-second day of August, and she feared that unrelenting, historic night would never loosen its grip on them.

She turned the key and opened the door. It was quiet inside. Her airway constricted as soon as she stepped inside. She coughed loudly, trying to force her breath through. Then, out of nowhere, her mother's footsteps rushed toward her like an avalanche racing down the mountain.

"Thank goodness, you're here," her mother said, squeezing her hands tightly.

She looked as if she had lost more weight. There was more gray in her hair.

"What was it this time, Mom?" Danni asked as she tried to squirm out of her mother's grip.

"He went out to the bar of course. I expected him to. I went to bed early, but woke up when I heard the crash. He was lying on the bathroom floor. I couldn't get him up."

Her mother finally let go of her hands, and Danni rushed up the stairs toward the bathroom. Her mother chased after her.

"We should call the paramedics," Danni said, hesitating in front of the bathroom. She reached into her bag for her phone.

"Don't call them," her mother cautioned. "He won't go the hospital."

"He could have broken something."

She pushed the bathroom door open and saw her father on the hard floor next to the toilet. His leg was twisted awkwardly under his body, and a swollen goose egg was already forming on the side of his head. Her eyes darted around him, looking for traces of blood, but luckily, she couldn't find any.

"We need to get some ice for that ankle."

Her mother looked relieved to have someone take charge and quickly turned around to get ice from the kitchen. Danni looked at her father on the floor, contorted and out of breath. He was thin and bony. She hunched over him to get closer and smelled the sour stench of alcohol on his breath. She pushed the sweaty strands of hair out of his eyes. Her fingers stroked his rough, stubbled cheek, and she pinched her eyes to fight back her tears.

"Are you all right, Dad?" she asked, unable to keep her voice from quivering.

"Am I?" he asked with a soft, raspy voice.

"Your ankle is very swollen, does it hurt?"

He nodded, opened his eyes and reached for her hands.

Her mother returned with a ziplock bag filled with ice. Danni pulled her father away from the tight space where he was trapped. She repositioned his legs and laid his head on her lap. She had no idea how she was going to get him up.

Her mother draped the bag of ice over his ankle and then sat beside them on the edge of the tub, gripping her head in her hands.

"Your brother should have been here," she huffed into her hands.

Danni's brother made his great escape when he was barely seventeen years old. He chose the streets over living at home with them. A girl and her father from a local church found him and whisked him off to New Orleans with them. They haven't seen him since. He told Danni once that he was suffocating at home. He had nightmares that the walls were clawing at him, like sharp fingers, scratching at his eyes. She thought he has gone crazy. She wasn't mad at him, like her mother. She envied his freedom.

She looked at her mother, slumped over on the edge of the tub, wallowing in self-pity. Blaming her father, as usual. Unwilling to reach out. She was still blind to any of his needs or the needs of her children. Always adding more fuel to her anger.

Danni pushed her body forward to scoot her dad farther away from the wall. She then lifted his head off her lap and wiggled out from under him. She took the ice pack off his ankle and placed it in the sink. She crouched down over him and grabbed his hands.

"Dad, we have to get you off this floor," she said loudly, trying to keep him awake and focused.

"Mom, come stand here behind him," she ordered as she pulled her father's body up into a sitting position. She rested his bony body against her mother's legs. She was sure it was the most physical contact they had between them in years.

Danni looked again at her father's swollen ankle and bent his other leg at the knee so he could help to stand when she pulled him up.

"Okay, Dad, I'm going to pull you up. Mom, push him from behind when I pull, okay?"

"I'm ready," her mother said.

"I'm going to count to three and then we should lift him. One. Two." Danni took a deep breath to muster all her strength.

"Three!" she called loudly and pulled him up. He was lighter than she anticipated, and with her mother's help from behind, they hoisted him up to stand on his healthy foot.

"Keep the weight off that swollen ankle, Dad," she said as she moved in beside him and draped his arm over her shoulder to support him. They stood there, side by side, while her mother braced his back. The bathroom was too small for all three of them.

"Let's get him over to his bedroom," Danni said.

She started walking with him as he hobbled gingerly beside her, unable to put weight on his ankle. His room was right across from the bathroom, so they didn't have far to go. She swung the door open and walked through the door with her father hanging off her side. Her mother stayed frozen on the other side of the door, as if she couldn't allow herself to enter his space.

Danni laid his frail body down on his bed and draped a blanket over him.

"It's late, get some sleep. You'll feel better in the morning," she whispered. She stayed next to him on the bed, until she was sure he fell asleep.

She looked around the room. The moon shined its soft light into the window, through the clouds hanging in the sky. The light shimmered off the floor next to the table in the corner, highlighting what looked like wood scrapings scattered across the floorboards. She tiptoed over toward the table slowly and saw a set of carving knives and wood chisels laid out. She knew she was invading his privacy, but she couldn't contain her curiosity. She missed him so much. He rarely left his room, and when he did, it was mostly to go drink himself into oblivion. She looked at the carvings made by him. Tiny wooden sculptures. She turned the small table lamp on to shed more light. Her eyes rushed over to make sure he didn't wake up from the burst of light into the room. His body stayed still.

She inspected the carvings on the table again. There were several small wooden boats with fine detail and polished wax. The same construct repeated over and over like a perseveration. Next to the boats laid a scattered collection of small figurines. Young, faceless boys carefully carved to life. Some of them were mutilated with deep, angry lashes cut across their bodies. She stood at the table, facing her father's demons. She placed a faceless boy inside a tiny waxed boat and remembered. Her brother Matthew was only five years old when her father took him out on that boat with some of his friends. It was the twenty-second day of August that year. He sobbed when he talked to her about it once, many years ago. He said the wind picked up and the waves grew bigger. The boat was tossed around, and somewhere in the dark, Matthew was thrown from it. His lifeless body wasn't found until the next day. He struggled himself out of the life jacket that must not have been tight enough around him. The darkness of that night swooped in and covered him like a heavy cloak. Her mother's anger raged on like a never-ending fire. It devoured them, and Danni and her older brother, Robbie, became invisible to them.

She reached down for one of the faceless boys and raised it up to the light. She filled it with the image of Matthew's face as she remembered him again. His careless face, joyful and adventurous even at his young age. He was her mother's favorite, always under her feet in the house. Danni, instead, mostly stayed close to her father. Attached to him like one of his limbs, anytime he wasn't working.

She felt the salty sting of her tears rolling down her face and she clenched the wooden boy in her hands. The image of her brother's rosy cheeks flushed her mind. She remembered how his blue eyes shined like diamonds. She could imagine her father's shock when he realized that Matthew was flung out into the dark water. He must have sunk quickly under the weight of the water as soon as his life jacket slipped off his terrified body. Waving his arms in vain while the water pushed him down relentlessly. And when he took his final breath, her father was knocked to the ground. The life seeped out of him as he stayed curled in a ball in his room. He was drowning in despair.

Their house turned cold, and the walls turned their back on them. They lost the grip they had on each other and turned into strangers, trapped under the same roof. Her father sentenced himself to solitary confinement. Her mother found work for every waking hour. She was too angry to be home. Robbie found refuge at troubled friends from school. The air in their house grew stale and drifted through the halls like menacing ghosts.

She turned the light off and snuck out of the room. She found her mother, still standing in the hallway. Leaning against the wall with her arms folded across her chest. Her body was stiff and anxious.

"Can you stay over tonight?" she asked without making any eye contact.

Danni nodded. Her mother kept her bedroom untampered with when she moved out a few years ago. She stared at her mother. Saw the pain in her eyes. She took a leap, stepped over to her, and pulled her away from the wall into her arms to warm her body with her own. To soften her angles.

"We made it through another year, Mom."

Her mother nodded and relaxed her head on Danni's shoulder.

She felt her breathing slowing down, and Danni could not remember the last time she was that close to her. It seemed as if time was breaking down the walls between them.

Chapter 2

It was quiet at the music store that Monday morning. Danni had a chance to drink a cup of coffee and scroll through the news headlines on her phone. No one had ventured in, and Peter wasn't expected until the afternoon. She enjoyed working at his music store immensely. He only hired her because she was dating his favorite nephew, Jake. Peter inherited the store from his father after he died. He wasn't the most willing candidate to manage it, but in time embraced the responsibility and transformed the store into a popular haven for music students in the area. Jake worked as a bartender for his other uncle, Mark, in his bar on the opposite end of the neighborhood. Both his uncles made it clear to Jake that they would do anything for him. They made a pact to keep him off the path his father chose. Danni simply wanted a job that would allow her to move out of her parents' home. She didn't have any aspirations beyond that. She didn't have a yearning for a career of any sort. Peter's wage afforded her a small apartment on her own, but it all hinged on an inevitable marriage to his nephew. It was implied that she would become part of their family, and Peter invested in her because of that. He told her that family was most important to him. He wasn't married with kids of his own, but Jake was always his most treasured nephew. Jake was a dreamer. He wanted to run his uncle's bar eventually, and he dreamed about all the luxuries that life could offer when he did. He was adamant that she wouldn't have to work once they were married, despite her protests and arguments that working was important to her. It wasn't easy to convince Jake of anything he didn't believe in. She, however, had enough turmoil with her own parents and didn't want any strife with Jake added to her life. She went along with him to keep the peace. Anytime she tried to carve out a dream for herself, the gears in her mind would come to a sudden halt. Jake's mind moved as fast as white water when he talked about their future. It was easier to let his dreams roll over her than to be the rock, obstructing his path.

Danni heard the door chime, announcing the end to her time in solitary. She moved over to the sales counter and watched a tall, slender woman walk past the racks of sheet music toward her. Something on the shelf caught her eye, and she stalled to page through one of the books. Danni was sure she hasn't seen her in the store before. She would have remembered her. She had shiny brown hair flowing softly down to her shoulders. She wore a turquoise tank top with spaghetti straps and a lively flowered pencil skirt that hugged the shape of her body perfectly. Her bare shoulders looked soft, and Danni studied her as she inched closer toward her. She stalled again as something else on the shelf captured her attention. Danni finally pulled her eyes away, feeling like a stalker. She returned to her desk and scrolled over the headlines on her phone again.

The woman finally reached the sales counter. Danni stashed her phone away in the drawer and approached the counter to help her. She clearly harbored a question. The reason for her trip to the store that day. Her eyes were a soft blue that lived in perfect harmony with the turquoise palette of her shirt.

"How can I help you today?" Danni asked cordially, forcing her shoulders back.

"I hope that you can help me," she said.

Her hands rested on the counter between them, and Danni noticed her long, slender fingers. They looked like the fingers of a piano player. Peter had the same agile fingers.

"I am looking for Peter Dunne. I believe he is a piano teacher here."

Her eyes felt like water, holding Danni's attention.

"Yes, he is. He won't be here until one o' clock this afternoon. Are you interested in taking lessons with him?"

Danni could easily think of ten more questions to ask to keep her from leaving the store.

"Not for me. For my daughter. I am looking for a local teacher for her. We moved here recently, and I cannot be her teacher and her mother any longer."

Danni's heart sank into a puddle of relief. She had a family. She was most likely married. Of course, a beautiful woman like her would be.

"Peter is a great teacher. How old is your daughter?"

"I looked him up on the internet. The reviews are all five stars. My daughter is twelve," she said with a smile even softer than her eyes.

"Perfect. Are you married?"

Danni wanted to kick herself as soon as she uttered the words, and she noticed the equally surprised reaction from the woman in front of her.

"I'm so sorry! That was not what I meant to ask. I meant to ask where you moved from, of course."

It was a frantic attempt to rectify her embarrassment.

"Don't beat yourself up!" she said, as her surprised reaction softened back into her smile.

"Yes, I am still married, even though I'm not entirely sure it's a good thing. We moved here from upstate New York. Peekskill, to be more precise."

The blue of her eyes turned a shade darker, like clouds deepening the sky at the very start of a storm.

"What do you mean?" she asked with piqued curiosity.

The woman hesitated, and Danni warned herself to ease up on the prying.

"I don't know. I feel miles away from him these days. Like we live in separate worlds. He is not as curious about me as you are," she teased, her face opening slightly.

"I'm probably crossing a boundary with these questions."

Danni tried to revive her sinking heart.

The woman squeezed her hands together as if she was trying to snap her thoughts back to the present. She gave Danni a faint smile.

"It's good to be curious sometimes. People should talk more, don't you think?"

Danni's eyes rested on her face. She abandoned an immediate response, but the silence between them felt comfortable. She took the chance and lowered her gaze to her full lips and then slowly up over her delicate nose and back up into her blue eyes, which has changed back to their lighter shade. More like sapphire. Danni was used to recording the finest details of people. She often stared at people from any distance. To record their features and feed it into her memory bank. She wasn't as comfortable talking as she was looking and listening. It was something she learned to do with her father when she was young, before the accident. Through the years, she became painfully aware of everything around her.

"If you needed someone to talk to, I can. I mean, I am good at listening," Danni said, surprising herself for acting so completely out of character.

The moment was interrupted by the sound of the door chime as another customer entered the store and disappeared between the shelves. They both were slow to refocus on each other, suddenly treading more lightly.

"You said Peter should be in after one?"

"If you give me your name and telephone number, I could have him call you."

She hoped the woman was more willing than she would be to give her particulars out to prying strangers.

"My name is Simone, but I think I would rather come back here to meet with Peter in person. Could I make an appointment?"

"I think I saw that he had a free hour this afternoon at four. Could you come back then?"

Danni thought her name fit her perfectly.

Simone looked at her wristwatch, and Danni saw a slight frown as she mulled over the offer.

"When does your day here end?" she asked, pushing her chest out just slightly.

"I'm done at five today."

She watched Simone take a deep breath.

"I will come back at four thirty. To meet with Peter and then I would like to take you out for coffee. When you are done working."

Danni's tongue stuck to the roof of her mouth. It was a bold move and it couldn't have been easy.

"I'm Danni. It's nice to meet you," she said and reached her hand out to Simone, compelled to match her act of courage. "I would love to go for a coffee with you. Since you are new in the area," she added.

Simone's hand felt soft. Almost like holding a butterfly.

"You said you played piano as well?" she asked, scared to let the fluttering fingers go.

"I do. Not as much as I used to."

"You have the fingers for it."

The browsing customer finally made it over to the counter with two pieces of sheet music in her hands. Danni let Simone's hand fly out of hers, holding her breath for an instant as she watched the moment flutter away.

"I'll see you later today then," Simone confirmed.

She turned around quickly and left the store. Danni's eyes followed her until the door closed and she could no longer see her.

"Just these two books?" she asked the customer in front of her.

"Yes, but I was also looking for a book called *Mozart's Favorite Piano Works*. I couldn't find it on the shelf anywhere."

"I don't think we have that one, but I can order it and have it here within a few days."

She willed her mind to stay focused on the woman, away from the memory of Simone.

"That would be wonderful, thank you!"

"Just fill in your information on this sheet here." Danni pushed a yellow notepad over to her.

When she left with her two books in hand, Danni stood alone in the store, feeling like a beehive, buzzing with emotion.

She sank down and chastised herself quietly. It wasn't strange for her mind to entertain such irrational notions. She remembered getting infatuated easily with pretty classmates and teachers in school. Sometimes, random women in the park would catch her eye. She has never acted on those feelings. She would simply entertain them for a while before blowing them away like smoke rings. Watch them vanish into thin air like they never existed.

She assured herself that this time would be no different. She could admit that she was pleased with her heart's vibrancy when her eyes rested on Simone's splendid face, but she contended that her interest was as fleeting as always.

Danni reached for her phone in the drawer and composed a text to Jake.

"Sorry, I cannot make it to dinner tonight. I am working late to help Peter with inventory."

She tensed as she waited for his response, hoping that he would let her off the hook easy.

"Sure. Donnie asked me to go to the gym with him, so I will go do that instead."

"Have fun!" she responded back, but felt the sting of her deceit.

She pushed her excitement away from her. A string of customers entered the store as if they were on special order, and she happily starved her memory of Simone's image for the next few hours.

Chapter 3

Simone waltzed back into the store at exactly four-thirty, after Danni had been watching the clock like a hawk for an hour. She hurried over to Peter's office to let him know that Simone arrived for her appointment.

Peter tagged along to the sales counter with her, where they found Simone waiting. She looked calm. Unlike Danni's heart, which was jumping out of her chest like a wild mustang.

"Hi there," Peter said and shook her hand gently. "I'm Peter."

"It's so nice to meet you," she responded with a warm smile. "I wanted to come talk to you about piano lessons for my daughter."

"Let's go to my studio in the back."

She watched them walk off to the back of the store, and her mind sneered that Simone wouldn't be up for coffee anymore. That she probably regretted her invitation the moment she left the store. She scrolled around nervously on her phone while she waited. Alex was scheduled to arrive at five to relieve her and cover the evening shift. She was desperate for a distraction and found her mother's number.

"How's Dad?" she texted, but she knew her mother often ignored her texts while she was at work.

It's been a week since her dad fell and twisted his ankle, and she felt guilty for not going back to check on him since.

"Still hobbling around."

Her mother's response came surprisingly quick.

"Is he doing the stairs yet?"

"No, not yet."
"I can come over later this evening to see if he can do it."
"I can't tonight."
She was surprised again.
"Plans?" she pried.
She didn't know her mom to have evening plans usually.
"I'm going to visit a friend this evening. Just to get out a bit."
"Do you need a ride?"
"No."
Her answer seemed deliberately vague.

She decided to let her mother off the hook this time. She was simply meeting a friend, and it was good for her to get out. It was not as bad as herself accepting an impromptu invitation to go out for coffee after work with a total stranger.

"Maybe I will stop by tomorrow night instead."
"That will be good. I should be home then."
"Have fun tonight, Mom," she added.
"Sure. I should get back to these customers now, Danni."

They signed off, and her eyes searched for the clock again. It was a quarter till five and there was still no movement coming from Peter's office. She assumed that their meeting was going well. Hoping that it was.

Ten more minutes passed before Peter and Simone finally emerged from his studio, both their faces revealing that they had reached an agreement. They shook hands, and Peter told her he was looking forward to meeting Billie, who Danni assumed was her daughter.

"Can you schedule her daughter, Billie, for her first session next week?" Peter asked.

"Sure," Danni said as she opened her scheduling program on the computer.

He looked again at Simone, and his face beamed. He was always so excited about meeting new students.

"See you next week, Simone."
"Yes, I look forward!"

Peter walked back to his studio, and Simone stayed back at the sales counter. Alex walked into the store, right on cue.

She clicked around on the scheduling program to find an open slot for Billie.

"He has the same hour available next Monday. At four. Will that work for you?"

"I will make it work," she said.

Danni added her name into the program and then looked up into the bluest eyes, seemingly fixed on her.

"Do you want to walk over to that coffee shop down the street?" Simone asked.

"Actually, how does the Wine Loft next to the coffee shop sound?" Danni countered spontaneously.

Simone raised her eyebrows and smiled.

"Are you trying to get me drunk?" she asked, teasingly.

"Not at all. We should celebrate your daughter's new budding career with Peter. Besides, if I drink coffee now, I will never sleep tonight."

Danni hoped Simone would fall for her pushy sales pitch. She knew that a glass of wine filled to the brim was her only hope to calm her nerves enough.

"The Wine Loft it is then," Simone agreed enthusiastically.

They walked down the busy street, side by side. The noise of the traffic made a conversation impossible, but their strides fell into an easy sync. They were very similar in height. Danni caught a few quick glimpses of her bright blue eyes and full lips and was relieved that she still had all her features stored accurately in her memory.

The Wine Loft wasn't packed yet, even though happy hour started at five. Jazz music filled the background and dressed up the soft lighting. A friendly hostess guided them to a table in the far corner of the restaurant and looked at them for approval. They nodded and sat down, and she left them with menus.

"Have you been here before?" Simone asked.

"A few times. I come mostly for their delicious cheese boards," Danni confessed. She wouldn't tell her that she frequented the place by herself mostly to satisfy her voyeuristic addiction.

"It looks like a great place to unwind after work. Is there a certain wine you usually like here?"

"I usually go for any of their Chardonnays here. What are you in the mood for?"

"I usually pick something red. Maybe I will go with a Malbec today. Do you think it will match up with any of the cheese boards you have in mind?"

Her pick of the Malbec certainly matched the depth of her eyes.

"Let's get the strawberry cheese and olives then."

The waitress came back, and they placed their order. Danni could feel her hands shaking, and she prayed the wine would be airlifted to their table.

"It looked like the meeting with Peter went well?" she asked, trying to get the conversation going.

"I was very impressed with him. I'm sure Billie will agree when she meets him next Monday."

"You said she was twelve now?"

"Yes. She loves the piano as much as me. Although she is quite different from me in her approach to it."

"Is that why you found it hard to be her teacher?" Danni asked.

"Yes," she said. "We have different styles, and I think I frustrate her. She needs a teacher of her own."

"What is her style like?"

"She is very precise. Doesn't allow herself to make any mistakes. She'll practice for hours and hours every day, obsessing to get every note right. I tend to play more freely. And not as much."

"She sounds perfect for Peter. He really pushes his students and begs them to put a lot of time into practicing. He had a few students take first and second place in some of the competitions last year. Do you think she would be interested in competing?"

"She probably should. I'm not sure how she would handle the stress of it. When we lived in Peekskill, she didn't have those kinds of opportunities available. Plus, she couldn't stick with any of the teachers."

"She will like Peter," Danni reassured her.

'I really hope so. I know I like him."

"I will be meeting quite a few piano players over the next few weeks," Danni announced, hoping to raise her interest.

Simone's eyes engaged as she took the bait.

"Why is that?"

"Peter is going to interview for a new piano accompanist for the upcoming season. Mostly for the violin students Marius teaches. He is a very good friend of Peter. Teaches mostly out of his home."

"Who did they use last year?"

"Some guy named Stefan. But he was not the best, and luckily, he ended up moving to Seattle."

"Maybe I should apply," Simone said, flashing her flare for boldness.

Danni was curious to hear her play as her eyes cornered her agile fingers again.

"Do you think you would like it? I can certainly put in a good word for you with Peter," she teased.

"Don't you think I should have to earn the job fair and square?" she asked with feigned seriousness.

"Peter is a tough critic," Danni countered.

"I only have to be better than Stefan," she argued back.

"I'm going to slot you into the schedule. But we should surprise him and not tell him it's you. We could use an alias."

"Surprise him?"

"Yes. You could blow his socks off."

"What makes you think I would be able to do that?"

"My psychic abilities to predict the future, of course."

Simone pondered her exaggeration.

"Are you sure he won't be upset? He may think we played him for a fool?"

"Not if your audition blows his mind."

"That is a lot of pressure, Danni," Simone said, but her skin flushed with a warm glow of excitement.

"I can send you the list of pieces he would like to hear. So you can practice. I think you only have to pick two."

"You have me so excited now. I think it would be a lot of fun, and it would get me out of the house and back into the music world. It's perfect."

"Why have you exited the music world?"

Simone took some time to adjust to the change of intensity of the conversation.

"My daughter," she said finally.

"I don't understand."

"I got pregnant in college with her. It ended my musical aspirations very abruptly. I got married instead and gave up on those dreams."

Danni didn't expect her answer, but found it full of sadness.

"How did you end up moving here?"

"My husband moved us here."

"The same husband that you feel miles away from now?"

"The very same one, yes."

Her eyes darkened almost to a deep ocean blue. She seemed instantly troubled after mentioning him.

The waitress appeared at the table to take their order. Danni ordered the California Chardonnay and strawberry cheese board and Simone pointed to the Argentinian Malbec on the menu.

"Would you rather not talk about your husband?" Danni asked as soon as the waitress stepped away.

"Do you think that I asked you to come here with me to talk about my husband?"

"Friends should be able to talk about anything."

"Do you think we could be good friends?"

"I don't see why not?" she asked, ignoring the doubt she had that she could ever think of her as just a friend.

"My husband, Bill, is a real estate broker. So we have very little in common as you can imagine. Other than Billie. He came here to take over a brokerage, convincing me that there was opportunity for him here to make more money."

"Has he?"

"Made more money? I think so. He is also very busy now. I hardly ever see him, but he bought a really nice house and pretty much anything we could ever want."

"Are you happy with the move?"

"I haven't been. Everything is so much bigger here. It's been harder for me to meet friends. So I would say until now, I haven't liked the move here."

"But now you have made a friend," Danni said, smiling like she was the biggest catch east of San Francisco.

"Exactly. I think I found a pretty good friend today."

"You should probably take me for a longer test drive before you render a verdict on that. I could be a cold-hearted serial killer," Danni teased.

"I have already looked deep into your soul, Danni, and there is nothing about you that even whispers serial killer."

Danni laughed at her assessment.

"How has the change been for Billie?" she asked another one of the countless questions she had for her.

"I'm not sure. She has been practicing more than ever, which has me a little concerned. She will also start at a new school soon. Which has her very nervous."

"She practices piano as a way to cope?"

"Exactly. She has an obsessive mind. All her teachers in Peekskill urged me to get her tested, so that she can be started on the right medications," Simone said, sounding irritated.

"Did they think she had OCD?" Danni asked.

"I think they wanted to label her with that."

"And you don't agree?"

"I don't know. I would love to know what the best thing to do is. Right now, I'm just keeping an eye on it. She has found a way to deal with it. Even if it is incessant practicing. Sometimes, I have to physically drag her away from the piano."

"Still, it counts for something. Moving was most likely very stressful for her on top of now also having a new school to go to. I'm sure she needs a hefty dose of music if that is how she handles stress."

"That is why I wanted to get her in with a new teacher right away. So she can be guided to practice constructively. She also misses my parents already. We were able to see them much more when we lived in Peekskill. How do you know so much about troubled teens?"

"I think I was a troubled teen myself, if you listened to the many counselors at school who tried to take a crack at me. The healthiest coping mechanism I developed was stalking people for hours. I still use it to this day. Some of them called it obsessive and wanted to give me the same hard-hitting medications. Luckily, my mother never had the budget for that," she explained, hoping that her own experience would help Simone's troubled heart about her daughter.

It wasn't as if she was usually open about her life with anyone. She preferred to operate from a distance. Even with Jake, she kept a certain armor on. But she noticed that her hands were no longer shaky, and she was able to keep her gaze steady on Simone, slowly tracing the outlines of her face. She knew she would be able to remember and reproduce every contour of her face perfectly on paper later that evening if she cared to.

"I was very brave today. Asking you to come here with me," Simone said, changing direction.

"It was a beautiful act of kindness," Danni said, matching her honesty.

The waitress interrupted again and put the two glasses of wine with the accompanying cheese board down on the table between them. She didn't linger, likely sensing that they were engrossed in their conversation. The food looked delicious, and Danni raised her glass, inviting Simone to join her.

"I will toast to a brave offer of friendship," she said.

Simone clinked her glass, and they both took sips as their eyes stayed on each other.

"To us," Simone said with a relentless smile.

"To you. Coming out of nowhere," Danni added.

"Peekskill, Danni. That is not nowhere."

"I've never been outside of Philly."

"Philly is certainly big enough to not ever have to leave."

"I should never say never, but right now, I'm still very tied up here."

"What is anchoring you here?"

Danni didn't feel the need to keep her distance, the way she usually felt around people.

"My father mostly. My mother. And Jake."

"Jake?" Simone asked curiously.

"The old ball and chain," Danni said and chuckled.

"Must be a boyfriend. I didn't see any rings."

"Yes, thank goodness. Jake is Peter's nephew. Which is how I landed the job at the music store."

"Ah, interesting, I was wondering how you ended up there. Do you think you will make him a husband?"

"Maybe. He wants to. I'm not always so sure I want to be a wife in the sense that he would want me to be."

The words rolled so effortlessly off her tongue. Simone was easy to talk to.

Simone leaned forward and rested her elbows on the table. She looked like she was about to reveal the secret of life to her.

"What is it?" she asked eagerly.

"Don't, rush, it," she said, pausing between each word for extra emphasis.

"Don't rush it? That is your mind-blowing advice?" she quipped as she sipped on her Chardonnay.

"How long have you been together?" Simone asked.

"A lifetime, Simone. We are to the point where we are synonymous. We grew up together. Started dating in high school as soon as our hormones were ready. It's always been an easy thing. I don't know if that is the best way to be. We just never pushed back."

"So it seems very settled then?"

"I suppose so."

Simone chuckled and took a big sip of her wine.

"My relationship was full of contradictions. We were complete opposites," she offered.

"You rushed into it?"

"Like a whirlwind," she explained.

"Did it last?" Danny asked cautiously.

Simone hesitated while she grazed on some cheese to collect her thoughts.

"Like I said, I got pregnant in college. We desperately wanted to keep that fire going, even though we were both scared out of our minds. He suggested that we get married. I jumped in headfirst. I didn't want to raise a baby alone. No way."

"And now your advice is to not rush in?"

"The fire dwindled, and we were left with just a lot of responsibilities."

"Do you doubt the decisions you made?"

"I quit college to raise Billie. I have sacrificed a lot, and on top of that, it was a very difficult birth, I nearly died. My parents were devastated. But I can't say that I regret having her. She turned us into an instant family and changed our lives forever."

Danni watched her take another sip of Malbec as she pondered all her confessions.

"I love her more than anything," she continued. "And I am grateful that Bill has been able to give us so much comfort. Even though the fire between us cooled. He thrived in the role of provider for us."

The light in Simone's eyes dimmed again. She clearly felt neglected by her husband, compelling her to reach out for a friendship instead.

"We both seem to be in some pretty uneasy situations with the boys in our lives," Danni surmised.

"It seems that way. Maybe we can endure them together."

"I agree. I confess that making friends have been way too low on my to-do list. But I'm really happy that you reached out."

"It was very spur of the moment. The way I used to be."

Her smile widened.

"Did you study music in college?" Danni asked.

"You got it."

Danni could easily picture her as a music major.

"What did you hope your career was going to be like? Before you got married?"

Simone's eyes filled with nostalgia.

"Me and my family thought I could be a concert pianist. Things were heading in that direction. I was consumed by it. Playing all day without end. I didn't pay enough attention to the birth control pill cycles, with my head in the clouds with Mozart and Beethoven. Along with that fire that Bill stoked. I really think he was an outlet for the passion the music evoked. I should blame Mozart for all of it."

"Is he your favorite?"

"Composer?"

"Yes."

"I'm in love with the Beethoven piano concertos. But Mozart is fantastic too. There are too many extraordinary composers, really."

Danni had no idea what any of the Beethoven piano concertos sounded like, but she promised herself to listen to each one as soon as possible.

They both finished their wine and most of the cheese on the cheeseboard. Danni knew she could comfortably stay in their conversation all evening. Simone was the most intriguing person she has met in a long time, if not ever.

"We probably have to continue this conversation some other time?" Simone said, tuning in to Danni's thoughts.

"We should. I'm sure you have to get home soon. Don't forget that I will send you the suggested pieces for Peter's audition."

The waitress seemed to have picked up on their cues. She rushed over and asked if they needed the check. Danni felt bold.

"Yes. Just one check."

Simone raised her hands in protest, but Danni wouldn't hear of it.

"I'm paying for this round. To make sure that we will have round two for you."

Simone surrendered.

"I like the way you think, Danni."

Simone fumbled in her purse and found the pen that she was looking for. She reached over to a small napkin on the table and started to write down a telephone number. She pushed the napkin over to Danni.

The waitress walked by them as she placed the check next to Danni. She gave Danni a wink before she walked off. Danni placed her credit card into the billfold and intended to leave a more generous tip than usual. She felt big-hearted about the way her day has turned out.

"Do you think you will give me a call then? To get together again?" Simone asked.

She still has not lost her nerve.

"I will. Did you name Billie after your husband?"

Simone chuckled.

"Yes! Can you believe it? I thought it would help them bond. And I wasn't sure I could ever go through the ordeal of giving birth again."

"Did it help their bond?"

"She loves him very much. But she has a hard time to convey that. She writes little songs for him sometimes, but ends up playing them mostly for me. He finds it just as hard to connect with her."

"She sounds like an extraordinary kid."

"I would love to not have to medicate any part of her."

"I can understand that. As her mother, you would probably love for her to be exactly who she was meant to be," Danni said it, realizing that her own mother didn't know a whole lot about how that worked.

They got up when the waitress brought the credit card back and headed out.

"Where did you park?" Danni asked as a light breeze kissed her face as soon as they pushed through the door.

"Are you planning on walking me to my car?" Simone asked playfully as the wind lifted her hair off her shoulders.

"Oh, definitely. These streets are too dangerous for a talented musician like you to be strolling around alone," Danni teased.

"It's down toward the end of the block. I found a wonderful parking spot when I came. Couldn't believe my luck!"

She stayed close to Simone as they strolled leisurely towards her car.

"Do you live far from here?" Danni asked.

"I live in Queen's Village. Bill found a great place there."

"It pays to have good connections," Danni confirmed.

"How about you? Where is your place?

"I have a very small apartment in Fairmount."

"That is not too far from me."

"I pay just about everything I earn to rent there."

"And yet you picked up the bill today."

"I wanted to. Remember? To hold your feet to round two."

"The next one is definitely on me. No excuses!" Simone bumped her gently in the side, and Danni warmed from her touch.

"My face hurts from smiling so much today," Danni confessed.

Simone pushed the button on her key remote and the car next to them chirped as she unlocked the doors.

"My face hurts too."

They turned to face each other.

"You still have my phone number?" Simone asked.

Danni realized she didn't offer her own number to her.

"I am going to call you for sure. Do you want my number?"

"I will get it when you call me."

Simone blinked quickly and then pulled Danni in for a close hug.

"Thanks for coming out with me tonight," Simone said as she kept Danni close to her.

"Thank you for asking me."

Simone finally let go, and Danni watched her get into the SUV. She kept her eyes on her as she set her purse on the passenger seat and started the car. She waved and then drove away down the street.

Danni felt that beehive inside buzzing again.

She walked briskly back up the street to the music store parking lot and tried to bring her head out of the clouds. She reprimanded herself again. Tried to blow the memory away like it was just another one of those pesky smoke rings. Tried to shrug it off as nothing. But the memory lingered. And her smile returned undeterred.

Chapter 4

Danni found a bench under a large oak tree to sit in Rittenhouse Square Park. There wasn't a cloud in the sky, and it was her day off. She focused on her usual routine of scanning through the crowded park, trying to find something unusual to focus on. She brought her sketchbook today as an extra tool to keep her mind occupied, but her mind's eye seemed to glaze over everything she looked at. Whenever she tried to focus on someone walking toward her, her one-track mind dressed them in a turquoise top with spaghetti straps. Her eyes were playing tricks on her all afternoon. She recognized Simone's shadowy eyes in everyone. She opened the sketchbook and put her pencil on the paper. A woman holding the hand of a young girl walked toward her. The girl tripped and the woman kneeled to tie her shoelaces. Her shiny brown hair laid on her shoulders. Her expression tempered. She saw Simone in her, raising the young girl instead of following her dreams.

Her hand stayed frozen on the sketch pad. She closed her eyes and replayed the conversation they had. She imagined Simone seated in front of a piano. Swaying with the music as she played. She saw a three-year-old Billie walk up to tap on the keys with her, playing over her. She saw her lift her hands and shift over to make room for the young girl on the bench instead. Letting her pound random notes with her small fingers. Encouraging her instead of continuing to play herself.

She opened her eyes only to watch the woman with the young girl fade out of her view. Then she closed her eyes again and steered her mind further into the past. Beyond when she sat across from Simone in a cozy wine loft. She steered her mind well into the past, to when she was about eight years old, sitting in the park on a bench next to her father. On similar cloudless days when they listened to the plethora of sounds emulating from the park. He would instruct her to look around and take it all in. They would spend hours playing their little "I spy" games. He would ask her to find the man with the red Phillies ball cap. Or the old man in a suit reading the newspaper over in a far corner. He would ask her why he was sitting alone. She loved those years with her father. Completely engaged with him. It felt like he was teaching her all of life's big secrets, and she was his most eager apprentice. He would spot someone and ask her what they were doing in the park. She would inspect their outfit carefully and try to make an assumption. She had to let her imagination run wild. He would find someone else and ask her what kind of work they did for a living. He was full of questions about everyone. Was that woman with the young boy still married? What was she doing in the park on a Tuesday afternoon? He wanted her to paint the details and create the stories around ordinary people. He had her young imagination working overtime. They would switch and she would get to ask the questions about anyone she could find in the park. Learning to ask the right questions, he said, was very important when talking to people.

Some days, he would just want her to focus on descriptions. To describe the color of their hair and the shade of their eyes of any person who walked by. She would guess how old they were. How tall. Some days, he asked about their feelings from what she could see. Were they sad or angry or worried? He assured her that good people could do the worst things you would never expect. That even the worst person could help an old lady cross the street just the same. You could never judge a book by its cover, and always expect the unexpected. He was full of little lessons and quotes to drill into her developing mind. She remembered that he had a knack for creating detailed stories filled with intrigue, and she tried to follow suit every step of the way.

Danni steered her mind back to the moment. Sitting in the park under the big oak tree. She opened her eyes and focused on the people around her. She needed to find a person who could steady her fleeting mind. She scanned around and finally settled on someone pacing over to the right of her about fifty feet away. She paused as she recognized the familiar posture. The blond scruff and muscular frame. She squinted and refocused, but then clearly recognized him. It was Jake. The last person she expected to find at the park. She fumbled around in her backpack for the baseball cap that she brought. She felt around for a hair tie and was relieved to find one in one of the side pockets of her bag. She quickly pulled her hair back into a ponytail and pulled the cap over her head to try to make herself inconspicuous. She held the sketch pad in front of her face to hide herself even more. He told her he was scheduled to work a double shift at the pub, which would have started at eleven. It looked like he was waiting for someone as he paced back and forth, looking at his wristwatch a few times. A man she did not recognize from anywhere walked up to him. He was taller than Jake, with very broad shoulders. He was dressed in a gray tailored suit. Jake looked nervous as he handed him a stuffed envelope. The tall dark-eyed man grabbed the envelope and reached into his inner suit pocket for a small notebook. He scribbled something down and placed it back in the pocket along with the fat envelope Jake gave him. He looked Russian to her. With dark eyebrows and deep lines cutting into his forehead and all along the sides of his nose. His dark hair was cropped very short to match his neatly trimmed beard. They continued a short conversation, and she noticed Jake's tense body. She could feel her suspicion take flight as she tried to piece together the puzzling scene that played out in front of her. Danni reached for her phone to text Jake.

"Are you at work yet?" she texted and watched his reaction.

He took his phone out and looked at the screen. He quickly shoved the phone back in his pocket, ignoring the text from her.

She assumed that Jake's anxiety was a result of owing the man money and he was only able to pay part of what he owed. They ended their conversation, without exchanging as much as a handshake. The Russian man simply turned around and walked away at a relaxed pace, having completed a successful or partially successful transaction. Jake slumped down onto a park bench, gasping for air and tapping his foot nervously. He looked at his phone's screen again. Then started to text a message that she received almost instantly.

"Sorry I missed your text. Was busy at the pub, setting up," she read his blatant lie.

She didn't respond back, but her eyes followed him as he got up and walked off at a brisk pace. She followed him, staying some distance behind him. He wasn't looking around, probably in a hurry to get back to the pub for his shift. As soon as he exited the park, he pulled out his phone again to start texting. Her phone buzzed again.

"How was dinner with your parents last night?" she read his text.

She was reminded that she was deceiving him as much as he was deceiving her.

"It was good. My mother made sausage and mashed potatoes as usual. Dad's ankle is starting to feel better."

She felt guilty for lying to him so easily. Danni turned around and walked in the direction she saw the Russian man take when he left Jake. She exited the park and looked up and down the street to see if she noticed him somewhere. She recognized him some distance down the street and ran to see if she could catch up for a closer look. She stopped within easy viewing distance and noticed he was talking to another man, dressed very similar to him. He pulled the envelope out of his pocket and showed it to the man, then placed it back inside. They both walked toward a black luxury SUV parked on the street.

Danni was certain that none of Jake's friends could afford that type of car. Her mind spun around a series of wild assumptions. She would need to find a way to get more information from Jake without letting him know she caught him in the park. Even though she spotted him by complete accident, he would still accuse her of spying on him.

The two men in the SUV drove off, and she decided to head back into the park to process what exactly unfolded in front of her. She wanted to capture as much of the Russian's facial features while she still had it fresh in her memory. She found a bench, took her sketch pad out, and started drawing his face as she remembered it. She remembered the harsh look in his dark eyes vividly, the dark lines around his nose, his trimmed beard. She filled in as much details as she could. It was a hardened, ruthless face, and he reminded her of a man she once saw in a television show, nicknamed the Butcher. He looked too old to be in Jake's close friendship circle. He looked like a mobster to her, shaking people down for money. She was certain that envelope was filled with cash. She had no idea how Jake would come up with so much of it. She shuddered at the possibility that he stole it from his uncle's bar.

An hour later she was still sitting in the park and decided to call Jake again. She could tell that he was back at the pub and the place sounded busy. She kept the conversation short. She didn't want to make him suspicious of anything. She wanted to invite him to her place for dinner. A chance for her to ask him some questions and a chance to catch him off guard. His only night off during the week was Thursday evenings, and he sounded excited about her invitation.

"I will see you at seven," he responded eagerly.

She already started to prepare a series of questions for him. Danni looked at her final rendition of the Russian on her sketch pad. She was satisfied that it was a close depiction of the man she saw taking money from Jake.

She looked at her watch and noticed time was well on its way to five o' clock. She started walking the couple of blocks to get to her parents' home. She needed to get some eyes on her father, and she promised her mother she would see if he could do the stairs on his own two feet.

She found her mother in the kitchen, sitting at the table with a very decadent cake in front of her.

"That looks amazing," she said and stared at the cake, smothered in creamy vanilla icing with a decorative chocolate drizzle.

"It's one of Max's latest masterpieces. Sarah left the bakery, so I've been getting a chance to help with the cakes more."

"That is great news, Mom," she said and took a seat across from her mom at the table. "How is Dad?"

"In his room as usual," she said, rolling her eyes in frustration.

"I'll go up to see," she said and started to walk to the stairs. She didn't want to stay too long at the house. The hairs on the back of her neck always perked up every time she visited.

She climbed the creaking stairs slowly and stopped in front of his bedroom door. She placed her ear up to the door to listen for any sounds coming from inside. All she could hear was a soft scraping sound, and she remembered the set of chisels on his desk. She assumed he was carving more boats and boys, reliving his pain for the millionth time. It made no sense to her, but if it helped him drink less at all, she was not going to judge his obsession.

The scraping stopped, and she supposed he realized someone was casing his door. An unwelcome intruder, trying to breach his protected fortress. She stayed at the door, quietly. She slid down and sat on the floor, next to the door, trying to think of a way to communicate with him. She took the sketch of the Russian man out of her bag. It resembled a type of police sketch of a crime suspect. Something drawn with the help of an eyewitness. She added a few more shadows and details as she sat on the floor next to her father's bedroom. She wrote "Wanted" at the bottom of the sketch and smiled.

She pushed the sketch under the door into her father's room and waited. She finally heard him get up and walk over to the door. He picked up the paper, and she heard his footsteps fading away from the door. She could hear him sit on the chair next to his desk. She placed her ear close to the door again and listened to the silence. She waited patiently for him to respond. An uncomfortable silence stretched out between them, but she kept her ear to the door. She finally heard what sounded like a pencil, scribbling on paper. Then she heard the chair move as he stood to walk back to the door. The sketch was pushed under the door back to her. She picked it up quickly and held the paper with trembling fingers, eager to read his reaction.

"Russian gangster?" she read his question under her own "Wanted" inscription.

She felt pride in the accuracy of her own assumption. She wrote back on the sketch, "I thought so too. I saw him at the park with Jake," and pushed it back under the door.

Her dad was still at the door, and she could hear him groan softly as he bent down to grab the sketch. She could hear the limping shuffle of his gait as he walked back to the desk again. Then the silence filled the space between them again.

"Strange. Any tattoos on him?" she read on the paper he slid back under the door.

She scanned her memory, but he was dressed in a suit that covered most of his body.

"Couldn't see tattoos," she wrote back on the back of the sketch. "Only swollen knuckles," she reported as she remembered some bruises on the man's right hand when he tucked the envelope into his inner pocket.

"Money collector. Jake is probably in trouble," her father responded.

He confirmed her gut feeling, and her heart swelled with warmth for the connection she still felt between them. She hoped that he felt it too. She remembered the games they played so well.

They could spend hours unraveling the imaginary lives of the people around them. He played those games with her because he was a police officer who was just promoted to be a young detective. He was constantly investigating everything and everyone. And she was his very own protégé. His attention meant the world to her. Instead of reading her bedtime stories, he would test her memory by asking her about the people in the park. He was training her young mind to develop into a detective's mind. She thought he had big aspirations for her.

Their fun together ended abruptly after her brother lost his life, and her father surrendered himself to the four walls of his bedroom. He stopped being a detective and started to drink instead. Instead of remembering details, he worked diligently on forgetting all of it.

Danni walked back downstairs. She walked away from their memories together, but she could still feel the spark between them. Their connection kept echoing through her mind.

She found her mother still sitting at the dining table, paging through a recipe book.

"Still thinking about cakes?" she asked, looking over her mother's shoulder at a recipe for a beautiful raspberry cheesecake.

"Max asked me to look for something new. He likes to try something new at least every week. Sometimes even every day. Hates to get bored baking the same cakes all the time."

Her mother's eyes filled with a peculiar lightness.

"Didn't you tell me before that eating cake every day would make you fat?" she teased.

Her mother laughed. "Maybe eating cake every day would make you sweet!"

'Sweet, my dear mother, is so much better than bitter. You are right."

Her mother just looked at her in a puzzled silence, but Danni knew that she caught her drift. She focused on the recipe book again, paging through the colorful pictures of irresistible deserts. It seemed like her mother's promotion was having a positive effect on her. Every week something new. She knew her mother to be strict and regimented. It was something unusual for her to say.

She looked at her mother closely. As if she was someone in the park she had to describe to her father. She wore makeup today, making her cheeks look warmer than usual. There was slightly more shine to her hair and a softness was trying to break through the usual harsh look in her eyes. The changes were miniscule, but to Danni, they were undeniable. It reminded her of tiny cracks in an egg.

The funny thing was that she could relate to her mother suddenly. Unexpectedly faced with a person of interest at work. Like a gust of wind that blew in off the water, out of nowhere. The encounter with Jake would have bothered her a lot more before in the same way her mother was far less bothered by her father's latest drunken escapade. Instead, she was thinking about constructing a list of audition pieces Peter requested for Simone, while her mother sat calmly, paging through a magazine filled with beautifully decorated cakes. Something was brewing in the air.

She walked over to her mother and kissed her gently on her forehead and then sat back down and watched her surprised reaction.

"I'm glad you are having fun at the bakery. A new cake every few days sounds exciting," she said softly. "I'm cooking dinner for Jake on Thursday," she continued. "Would there be a new cake you could bring over? Or I could pick up?"

"I'll ask Max to make his famous Death by Chocolate cake on Thursday," she suggested.

"It's only because you know how much he loves chocolate."

Her mother smiled at her knowingly.

"I do. Jake will most likely eat the whole cake by himself. That boy just works too hard. He deserves something special, don't you think?"

"He is up to something, I think," Danni said.

"Working on saving for a ring for you, I'm sure."

"I hope not!" Danni objected.

"It's inevitable, my dear daughter. No sense in fighting against it."

"I have decided not to rush it," she said, remembering Simone's advice at the Wine Loft.

"Young people today think they have all the time in the world. You won't want to chase children around when you're too old."

"I'm not old!" she yelled. She quickly smiled, because she didn't want to start any arguments.

Danni got up from the table and started gathering her things so she could head to the sanctity of her apartment. She knew a brisk walk in the warm August air would help clear her mind.

"How's your father? You didn't say," her mother protested her inkling to leave.

"He's not ready for the stairs yet. I would give him a little more time to heal up more," she fibbed, wanting to cut him some slack for a few more days.

Her mother kept paging through her magazine quietly. Danni wasn't sure if she really wanted an answer when she asked.

She left her parents' home after she kissed her mother's forehead again and reminded her to bring a cake over on Thursday evening.

Her mother nodded and started ripping a page with a recipe she liked from the magazine.

"I'll bring it, Danni. It would be good to see Jake."

Danni enjoyed the walk home. She thought about Simone's eyes and their many shades of blue. She planned to listen to one of the Beethoven piano concertos when she got home. A perfect time to replay their conversation in her mind. She would keep her feelings secret and bask in them. She would enjoy them only briefly before she would inevitably push them away again. Blow them off into thin air and render them inconsequential. Exactly like she has done many times before without any harm done to anyone.

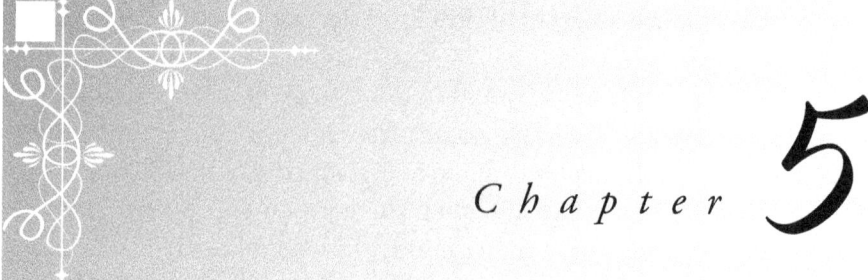

Chapter 5

"Are you still interested in that audition?" she texted to Simone.

She was filled with excitement about making a connection again. She wanted to reach out earlier in the week but held off. She had to restrain herself on many occasions, and finally, on Thursday afternoon, she decided she had waited the appropriate amount of time.

"Definitely," Simone responded back quickly.

She looked at the list of piano pieces that Peter asked the candidates to play. She had no idea what any of them sounded like.

"He gave suggestions. But it says here that you can choose any other pieces of your liking if you didn't want to play any of the suggested pieces."

"Let's hear the options," Simone texted, sounding interested.

"Beethoven's violin sonatas no. 1 and 5, or Brahms violin sonata no. 1. Four romantic pieces by Dvorak, or Mozart's violin sonata in D."

She hoped that the list made more sense to Simone.

"That is a great list. I am familiar with all of them."

"How much time would you need to prepare?"

"A couple of weeks. I have worked on some of them during my college years. They are great pieces for violin players for contests and auditions."

"I will let Peter know that Katya is going to do four romantic pieces for him!"

Danni laughed as she texted her response.

"Katya?"

"Your alias. We don't want him to know it's you that are scheduled for the audition."

"I don't think Peter would want to hear four romantic pieces from Katya."

"You are very right about that."

"The romantic pieces are beautiful though. Maybe I could do them."

"I have not listened to anything romantic in a long time," she wrote and ended with a sad-faced emoji.

Danni felt sorry to admit that even though she worked at Peter's music store, her knowledge of classical music fell terribly short. There was just so much of it that it made her feel lost in an unfamiliar landscape. But she has vowed to expand her knowledge this past week.

"I thought you would pick one of the Beethoven pieces," Danni said, recalling her love for his music.

"Well, you said I could pick two. I could also just surprise you."

"I will add your name on the schedule then?" Danni asked.

Danni opened the calendar of Peter's audition schedule on her computer.

"He has an opening in two weeks on Wednesday at one in the afternoon. Will that give you enough time?"

"I think so."

"It's good that you're confident. It's a good strength to have," Danni said.

"I noticed that you notice things," Simone responded.

"Old habit of mine."

"What are you doing tonight?" Simone asked.

Danni's heart sank. She had those dinner plans with Jake and no way to get out of them. Her mother was bringing a cake, and she was determined to see if she could corner him about his encounter with a Russian operative in the park two days ago.

"I'm cooking a steak dinner for Jake," she texted.

"Lucky is the man with a woman that can cook."

"Anyone can cook steak."

"My steak is very often overcooked."

"Probably because your head is in the clouds with Beethoven and the romantic pieces."

"You already know me so well!"

"Not even. Not yet," Danni argued.

"All we need is more time."

"You know where to find me. Stop in anytime."

"I also have your number now."

"Feel free to use it."

"I will."

"Customer coming. Talk later?"

"Yes. Later then."

Danni put the phone down and helped a woman at the cash register pay for a portable music stand.

When she left with the stand in a bag, Danni picked her phone up to scroll through the conversation she had with Simone again and chuckled about their easy exchange.

She opened Peter's audition schedule and typed the name Katya Petrov into the schedule, at the one o' clock slot. She knew he would be intrigued when he saw that name, and she would tease him that Katya flew all the way from Russia to do the audition with him. The last piece of the puzzle would be to find a way to insert herself into the audition. There was no way she could miss it.

Chapter 6

Danni rushed to the grocery store on Thursday after work to pick up some steak and fingerling potatoes for the dinner she wanted to make for Jake. She picked up some fresh broccolini to complete the menu. It was his favorite vegetable. She expected her mother to bring dessert. She stopped at the liquor store for her backup plan, which was two bottles of anything that would get him to talk more freely. She had many questions lined up for him. She also had a few bottles of his favorite Guinness beer already cold in the fridge. She was determined to get answers.

When she got home, she jumped in the shower and slipped into a pair of skinny jeans with a black low-cut top. She picked gold loops for her ears and high-heeled sandals to finish the look. She spent extra time and added makeup to her face. She never applied makeup for work, but she usually felt compelled to dress up for Jake. Even after they've known each other for a lifetime. She has read countless headlines on the cover of fashion magazines while waiting in line at the grocery store to keep your man by not letting yourself go. That type of message inevitably lodged into the subconscious. How could she not be hypnotized into thinking that jewelry and gym memberships were the secret to a lasting relationship?

After getting all dressed up, she started to cook. She worked systematically and confidently. Starting with the roasted potatoes first. She timed the dishes perfectly in order to finish everything at the same time. She set the table with two plates and glasses for her wine and his beer. She added some flowers on the table to convince him that she had good intentions for the evening.

The soft knock on the door came a few minutes before seven. She yelled out from the kitchen that the door was open. He joined her in the kitchen, dressed in jeans and a comfortable t-shirt. She noticed that he hasn't trimmed his beard for the evening.

"Dinner ready?" he asked, heading over to the fridge.

"Just about. I was waiting for you to get here before I start the steak. It will only take a few minutes. There's Guinness for you in the fridge."

"You look very nice tonight." he said after he changed direction and headed toward her instead. He walked up behind her and pulled her close to him.

"Is there something I should know?" he asked softly in her ear, and she could feel his smile against her skin.

"Like what?"

"Oh, I don't know. Maybe you would blow me away and propose to me. Something crazy like that?"

She pulled away from his hold on her. She needed to start searing the steak.

"I can see how you would think that with all this fanfare. But no, I just wanted to do something nice for you tonight. You seem a little stressed out lately," she said, but doubted that he heard her over the sound of sizzling steak hitting the hot pan.

He must have realized that she was going to hit him with all her usual objections and made his way to the fridge. His phone buzzed just as he reached for a bottle of beer. He seemed peeved as he read the message on the screen and took the bottle into the living room.

Danni had a suspicion that his change in mood had something to do with his money troubles, and she was still undecided about how forceful she should confront him over the situation.

The steak was seared perfectly, and she pushed it into the preheated oven. She set the oven timer for ten minutes. She checked on the roasting potatoes and tossed them around, added more oil and spices, and slid them back in next to the steak pan. She reached for her phone and texted her mother.

"Are you bringing that cake soon?"

Her attention shifted to the broccolini. She washed them and prepped another pan with oil and garlic. She had just added the mushrooms when her phone buzzed with what she expected to be her mother's response.

"I should be there in five minutes."

Everything was working out perfectly. After she added the broccolini to the other dishes in the oven, she walked quietly over to the living room and watched Jake on the couch. He was still busy texting on his phone. He shifted around on the couch and scratched his bearded cheeks. She saw the empty beer bottle on the table beside him and went back to the kitchen to grab another Guinness for him.

"You must be thirsty," she teased.

He forced a smile as he took the bottle from her and put the phone back in his pocket. He stretched his neck from side to side to release some of the tension.

"Uncle Mark was just asking me to work extra shifts this weekend. I wanted a weekend off, but he can't seem to find anyone to cover them."

She peered into his eyes to gauge the level of truth in his explanation. She has become so short on trust for him.

"My mom will be here in a minute. Can you open the door for her when she gets here? I'm just finishing up with the food in the kitchen."

"Sure," she heard him say as she walked back to the kitchen. She glanced back at him quickly before she entered the kitchen and noticed that he was already back on his phone again.

She checked all the dishes in the oven and heard the doorbell ring. Moments later, she heard her mother's voice raised a notch from usual, most likely from her excitement to see Jake. Her mom adored Jake, and she would no doubt be giving him a big hug as soon as she put the cake down somewhere safe.

A few minutes later, her mom entered the kitchen with the cake. Her eyes still had the same lightness to them as when she saw her at the house.

"It smells so good in this kitchen, Danni. You seem to have the same knack for cooking as your father used to have."

Her mom hugged her shoulders just before Danni reached into the oven to pull the pans out to get the meat ready to rest.

"Dad used to cook?" she asked surprised.

"Oh yes, he loved it. Way back, of course. These days, he is happy with whatever I bring him, but it wasn't always like that. I used to be the one booted from the kitchen most days."

"That is wild, Mom. I would have never guessed that."

"Oh, well, things have changed so much. You look beautiful tonight, Danni," her mom said, and Danni was surprised again at her mom's generosity.

"What do you think of the effort he made tonight?" Danni asked, trying not to sound blatantly irritated.

Her mom chuckled.

"Maybe he was in a rush, honey. You know how guys are."

"I guess," Danni replied, but she couldn't hide her disappointment.

"Well, I can't stay, honey. Have fun with the dinner and let me know how you liked the cake. We put a lot of effort into that one today," her mother said, admiring her and Max's creation displayed on the counter.

"Say hi to Dad."

Her mom was already on her way out of the kitchen and didn't respond. Danni let it go, and she started to plate the food on a large serving dish so she could bring it to the dining table.

The table was already set, and as soon as she set the serving plate down, she called Jake over. The second beer clearly seemed to relax him more, and he walked over to the table with a big smile on his face.

"It smells amazing! I still don't know what I did to deserve this, but I'm going to enjoy every minute."

She went to grab another beer for him and poured herself a glass of Merlot before she joined him at the table. Jake started serving his plate immediately, eager to start eating.

"You must be starving!" she said as she watched him starting to slice his steak before she had a chance to serve herself.

"Sorry. I should wait, I know."

"Take a sip of beer. I'm trying to catch up with you. I thought we could reconnect tonight. We've been like strangers lately."

He looked puzzled. She wanted to discern his tolerance level for what she wanted to broach with him. She had a habit of pushing too hard, and he often had a low tolerance for any kind of prying.

"You have been working a lot more lately."

She finished serving herself and nodded over to him so he could start eating.

"Just trying to make extra money, Danni," he said as he immediately continued to slice into his steak.

"Are you saving up for a big-screen TV?" she teased, before taking a sip of wine.

He smiled as he tried to figure out what she was getting at.

"I want to get things ready for us, you know that."

"I know that you are putting yourself under a lot of unnecessary pressure."

He took another bite as she could see the gears of his mind turning. She was sure he was trying to get to his infamous white flag.

"You are a very good cook. Everything is delicious," he said.

Changing the subject was a tactic he often relied on.

"Those two semesters at the culinary school paid off, I guess," she explained.

Years ago, she entertained the idea of becoming a chef, but she dropped out after she realized what long and late hours she would have to work as a chef. Jake was not supportive of her aspirations. He complained endlessly how they would never see each other with him being a bartender and having long work hours already. They negotiated some, but mostly argued for a short stint, and ultimately agreed that it would be an unpractical lifestyle for them. She did manage to learn a few things and at least now knew her way around a stove.

"They sure did. Remember how we almost never saw each other when you were in school there?"

"I know. It's something you remember clearly."

They ate in silence again. Danni could feel the tension brewing under the surface between them.

"I like things the way they are, Jake," she said, taking her turn to change the subject back to their original argument.

He rolled his eyes as soon as he realized that she was steering them back into the minefield.

"We will need a house, Danni. We need a down payment. We will need money for when the kids…" He stopped himself abruptly.

He looked up at her to gauge her reaction. They often chose to skim over the specifics.

She kept her eyes on her meal. His words washed over her like heavy water. She finally managed to pull her eyes back up at him.

"We have plenty of time. There is no need for you to get stressed out about any of this."

"Uncle Mark told me that for fifty thousand, he would let me buy into the bar. Once I can do that, there will be such a better future for us. I could eventually even own the place all by myself, you never know."

"How many shifts will that take? To get your hands on fifty thousand dollars?"

She wiggled the line again, hoping that he would take the bait.

"I don't know, Danni. I have some other plans in the works too. You just have to trust me."

"Other plans?"

She saw an opening and wanted to pressure him a little more. She was sure the man in the park factored into his other plans.

"I actually have many things in the works."

He seemed to think that he could deal with Russian gangsters and get away unscathed. Often flaunted a sense of bravado, bragging about his intentions to get rich.

"I guess there are many ways in this city people make extra money."

She knew she was harping, but she couldn't resist.

He looked at her, and she could tell he was getting more irritated. He stayed quiet for a while. More careful with his words.

"It's nothing to worry about, Danni. Sometimes, you just have to know the right people."

He took a sip of beer, peering at her from the corner of his eye. But she could tell he wasn't completely ready to surrender yet.

"The city is full of dangerous people. Of course, I would worry," she countered.

He gave her a curious look. Tried to calculate his next response. Maybe he wondered why her remarks didn't heed to his reassurances. Maybe he started to realize that the steak dinner and flowers were more of a trap that she set for him. He finished the last bite of his meal and pushed his plate away. He kept his expression neutral, but she could tell that he was clenching his teeth.

"You have to take risks sometimes, Danni. Take hold of any opportunities coming your way. How else would you get ahead?"

"Risky business doesn't always pay off in the long run."

"I'm not asking you to take any risks. That is for me to do. I will find a way to get my slice of the pie, you will see. Get my share of the bar. I'm going to make that happen for us."

Danni watched the passion return to his face as he tried to pitch his dreams to her. She knew he took it all on himself. He didn't expect any financial contribution from her. He was hungry for a better life than what his father handed to him.

"Speaking of pies. Are you ready for a slice of that cake my mother brought?" she asked, sensing that they would just end up going in circles with their argument. It wasn't as if she was upset about him taking risks. It was that he wasn't honest with her.

"Sure, I'm ready for something sweet. Your mom made it?"

"Yes. She has been so excited about her promotion at the bakery. Helps the owner now more directly with the cakes, it seems."

"That's wonderful! She got an opportunity and accepted it."

She knew what he was insinuating, but ignored him. She got up instead and walked to the kitchen to get him a piece of cake. The plates and utensils were already set out on the counter. She turned the coffee maker on. She realized that despite having the evening well planned, it still felt like a disaster. They were talking completely past each other. She watched the coffee drip slowly and wondered if she would ever change Jake's mind about their roles in the relationship. She was unable to convey to him that it has started to feel like a cage to her. She was weary of his stifling expectations. She pictured him at the table, waiting for her to serve him while he boxed himself into a pile of worry. Trying to make a house with a picket fence a reality for them. She was in the kitchen in a box of her own. Pushing against the walls closing in on her. It was a fence she didn't want around her.

She suddenly felt like she was suffocating. She wanted their evening to be over. She wished she could fabricate a text from the Russian to pull him away. He would feel compelled to take a hold of his opportunity and leave, all in the name of making more money.

She wasn't ready for the future he conjured up for them. Frustration boiled up into her throat as she poured the coffee and sliced two pieces of cake. The cake was beyond decadent, but her appetite for it had vanished.

She served the cake and coffee for them once she joined him again at the dining table. She took a deep breath before she sat down across from him, unsure of where their conversation would go next. She felt the start of a headache as tension grabbed the muscles in the back of her neck.

She watched him dig into the cake without any hesitation, while she pushed it around on her plate. The silence felt uneasy between them, and she decided to take a leap. She needed to jump into the deep end, instead of wade around aimlessly in the shallow water. It was the only way to get him out of her apartment.

"I read on the internet that they found a guy in a dumpster last weekend. Killed," she said.

He looked at her without any reaction, waiting for her to elaborate.

"Lots of people get killed in this city," he finally said when she didn't.

She couldn't find any regard from him for the concerns she had. He was like a stubborn mule, just barreling ahead, no matter the tornado clearly brewing in the distance.

"I read the guy owed the Russian mafia money. He couldn't pay them. They killed him to send a message to all the other suckers thinking about not paying their debts."

She didn't care if he knew she was lying.

"Did the article say why he owed them money?"

His eyes stayed detached from her dramatic tale.

"For what it matters, Jake, next we'll probably read that his wife and kids joined him in the dumpster because the debt has to be paid somehow."

She could feel her anger flare up more as she tried to break through his indifference.

"He lost a card game. He owed them thousands," she kept speculating, taunting him, while she silently dared him to get up and walk out of her apartment.

Jake looked at her, offering his best poker face, but she noticed how he struggled with that. Which only infuriated her more that he was trying to gamble without enough control over his facial expressions. His eyes blinked several times, and she could see the twitch in his left temple.

"The Russian mafia? You really think they waste their time with silly card games?"

"I do. They probably also enjoy tormenting stupid people who think they can get rich off them."

"I'm not involved with anything like that, Danni. I feel like you are accusing me of something so baseless, you almost sound crazy."

"People who are desperate for money will get themselves in all sorts of predicaments. It's not crazy. Maybe the guy in the dumpster didn't even know he was dealing with the Russian mafia."

"So this is why you lured me here tonight?"

He pulled his shoulders back, and she noticed his hands tensing up.

She leaped again to pour gasoline over the fire.

"You are up to something, Jake. On your phone all the time. Lying to me about where you are."

"You are letting your imagination run wild, Danni. I'm not lying to you. Here I thought you were trying to help me relieve stress tonight, not add to it," he said, clearly trying to reel the situation back toward a more manageable level.

"I'm not imagining anything."

She got up and started gathering the plates from the table. She closed the book on their dinner and tried to convey the message to him.

Her feelings about their relationship had become a tangled mess that on most days she didn't want to think about. She was losing her grip on them, but she noticed a strange sense of relief to see it all unravel.

"Why are you pushing me away? Can we not just enjoy the evening?" he asked, once she came back from the kitchen.

He reached out to her hand. His grip was soft and warm on her hand, and his eyes softened and pleaded with her to join forces with him. To stop pushing back.

"Jake, I have to protect myself. And I don't like the lies."

His eyes continued to shield the truth.

"Don't worry so much, Danni. You have nothing to be scared of."

She looked at him swimming in false assurances. He refused to speak any truth to her. The image of the Russian mobster he handed an envelope of money two days ago was permanently etched in her memory. She had his face drawn in great detail on her sketch pad. She could easily point him out in a crowd or a police lineup.

"You cannot assure me of that," she said as she let go of his hand. Her face stayed stone cold as he looked off, obscuring his true self from her.

She walked over to the sink and started the water to wash the dishes as sharp resentment spilled over her. She was unable to get him anywhere near a confession. Which was almost as frustrating as his lies to her. He was committed to keeping her in the dark, and she kept fretting about a body in a dumpster. And not just his body. She believed that she could be the one ending up dead just as easy. Guilt by association. She would work fine as collateral for his indiscretions. She contrived that story to draw a reaction from him, but it has evolved into a concerning reality for her. She focused on getting every dish clean to scrub the lies of the evening away. She didn't rush back to the dining room.

She reminded herself of her mother, who likewise spent years in front of the sink to forget about the anger welled up inside. It was the worst way to reach her father, but it was an effective escape from what their lives had become.

When she finally walked back to the dining room, she was glad to find that Jake had left. She checked both the bathroom and the bedroom to make sure he wasn't there. She fell into the couch, relieved that she had managed to push him away. She walked over to the front door to make sure the lock and the deadbolt were engaged, but she still imagined several dead bodies piled up in a dumpster right off an abandoned highway.

She was trying to break out of the mold they set for themselves years ago, but she feared that she was merely growing tired of hiding from her true feelings. It was getting harder for her to ignore that reality. The whole reason for turning on Jake was filled with ulterior motives. She turned out the lights and sank deep into the soft couch in the living room again. She was alone, and she could feel herself expand with every breath she took until she finally spanned the entire room. She took her phone out and opened her iTunes app. She found the Beethoven violin sonatas that she had just saved in her library. She closed her eyes and let the music flow into her mind. She imagined Simone sitting at the piano, closing her eyes as she played. She watched the ceiling above her open, and she floated into the night sky. She kept floating higher, until she reached the stars that shined their lights brightly around her. The music filled the entire universe around her as she kept floating upward. She floated above the stars before she finally looked down on her life, far beneath her, and she was relieved that she could not see her childhood anymore.

Chapter 7

She's been grinding through every slow moving hour since the last time she texted Simone on Thursday. Through the disaster of a dinner on Thursday night. She needed all of Friday to recover from the gut-wrenching blow of the event and the guilt that consumed her for pushing him away so forcefully. She went through the motions at work, counting the hours to get back home, only to get into bed and sleep the rest of the evening away. She cancelled her dinner plans with her parents because of an ill feeling on her stomach. It spread to every part of her body eventually, and all she could do as remedy was to push herself into a deep sleep in order to numb the sick feeling that inhabited all her organs.

Her thoughts were a tangled mess and angry. She knew Jake for almost a lifetime and realized now it was as if she never knew him at all. She needed movement and fresh air by Saturday and spent most of the day in the park close to her apartment. She needed to get back into her routine. She forced herself to sketch detailed renditions of anything she set her eyes on. She took cover and snapped photos of unwitting people. She escaped into the bustling energy at the park, glad to get out of her head. She needed to avoid anyone that was related to her or intimately acquainted with her.

Sunday's hours were the steepest uphill climb. She listened to music. She listened to all the Beethoven sonatas for piano and violin over and over. She discovered Dvorak's romantic pieces and started listening to the first piano concerto that Beethoven wrote. It soothed every strand of her short-fused nerves.

She was forced to make a trip to the grocery store before going to work on Monday, after finally acknowledging her hunger, only to discover empty shelves in her cupboards.

The day stretched out in front of her. Her eyes guarded the clock as time inched slowly toward the much awaited four o' clock hour.

She was in the last stretch, when Peter emerged from his studio and walked over to her with a bounce in his step.

"I'm excited about Billie's first lesson!" he cheered.

Danni's own body was crawling with nervous energy that took great effort to conceal.

"Simone said she practices all the time."

"A dream for any teacher, yes."

He still could not stop smiling.

"Did she tell you much about Billie?" Danni asked, wondering if he was aware of Billie's level of anxiety. She would assume that was why Simone insisted on meeting him in person.

"Just that she is a very serious twelve-year-old that plays piano obsessively."

"Should be interesting, right?"

"They are both very interesting." Peter said, shooting Danni a prying look.

She didn't take the bait, opting to stay vague about their connection, especially since she hasn't made sense of it herself.

"I wanted to ask you about Jake though. If you thought he was all right?" Peter asked, changing the subject and dulling her mood instantly.

Talking about Jake was not on her wish list. The mix of anger and guilt made her feel nauseated.

"I'm not sure. We had a bad evening on Thursday. I haven't seen him since," Danni explained reluctantly, knowing that it would spark further inquiry.

"Something is different with him lately," Peter confirmed, but he looked hopeful that she would have some answers for him.

"I haven't noticed," she deflected.

"I was visiting my mother on Saturday night. He came over, obviously intoxicated, asking for rent money. Did you know he has not been able to pay his rent?"

"He hasn't said a word about that to me," she said, figuring that his rent money was most likely stuffed in the envelope he handed the Russian.

"He said his car broke down, and he needed all the money he had for the repairs," Peter continued.

Jake was also lying to his family.

"He never mentioned any of that to me. He usually does the repairs himself on that car."

Jake worked in a mechanic shop all the way through high school to make money. He would never let anyone but himself work on his most prized possession. She would have thought that Peter knew that about him.

Peter looked puzzled.

"Did your mother give him the money?" she asked.

"We both did. He said his landlord would show no mercy for late rent."

Danni was aware of the changes in Jake over the last month. He was less available and more nervous. More defensive. Drinking more, but she would have never expected him to go to his family to ask for money.

"Has he ever asked you for rent money before?" she asked, hoping to get a more accurate timeline of his trouble.

"No. Which is probably why we trusted his story."

"How about Mark? Do you know if he has asked him for money?"

Peter was quiet as he pondered her question.

"I will have to ask him. Mark hasn't mentioned anything to me about that."

Danni connected the dots and decided that this was new behavior from Jake, which meant that his trouble started recently. She didn't want to tell Peter about the Russian man in the park yet. She needed to gather more information first since she couldn't rule out the chance that she was not completely objective about him. She wasn't sure that the Russian man in the park was indeed Russian or part of a gang at all. For all she knew, Mark could have sent him to the park to pay someone who fixed his freezer at the bar. She was making wild assumptions, she knew that. Things would have been easier if Jake simply confirmed her suspicions while slicing through that tender steak she carefully prepared. But he was a closed book on the matter.

"Have you noticed that he was drinking more?" Peter asked.

Danni remembered the three beers he had on Thursday evening, but it hardly signaled any cause for alarm.

"Jake is a bartender, Peter. He is always around alcohol, but I don't regularly see him getting drunk."

She felt compelled to defend him, even though she knew Peter's concerns were valid. She still considered herself on Jake's team. She had a habit of going to bat for him. Jake has essentially taken her under his wing when they were both very young, and she didn't have her own family to rely on.

"He was very drunk when he came to the house. As in stumbling drunk. He took an Uber to get there. We were really bothered by it. It looked like he had lost some weight too."

"He has been working a lot more for the past few weeks. He told me that he is trying to get money together to buy into the bar. Apparently, Mark told him he could buy in for fifty thousand. He said that was his sole focus now."

"Mark hasn't mentioned that to me," Peter said.

"Jake's goals are set on the idea that he needs buckets of money to get married and start a family, but he shouldn't feel any pressure for that from me."

"It's not your goal for the two of you?"

"Not right now, no," she said with certainty as she saw more confusion settle into Peter's expression. "I'm not in need of buckets of money," she added.

"So what do you think we should do?" he asked, clearly feeling overwhelmed by the problem.

"You know him better than most people, Peter. He is a bit of a mystery to me, even though we've known each other for a long time. He's been portraying something other than who he really is, I think."

"Maybe we should just keep an eye on it then for now. If you notice anything worth mentioning, you can just let me know."

She felt as if she was asked to do surveillance. She nodded haphazardly, but didn't give him an actual agreement. He clearly didn't understand the full dynamic between her and Jake.

Their conversation was interrupted by a familiar voice coming from the front of the store. She checked the clock again and saw that it was five minutes before four. She would recognize her voice anywhere. Her stomach fluttered immediately in reaction to Simone's close proximity. She was eager to meet Billie. Peter's eyes tracked along with hers toward the front of the store and his excitement was spilling over.

Simone smiled generously as she looked slowly from Danni to Peter. In contrast, Billie's face was without expression and her eyes only made contact in short bursts. Danni took a deep breath and hoped her face wouldn't noticeably burst into flames.

The girl was tall for a twelve-year-old. Her blond hair was cut in a layered bob with bangs that framed her quiet blue eyes. It was the exact same blue as Simone's. Billie's frame was thin, with lanky arms and legs. She had Simone's long, nimble fingers. It looked as if she was born to play the piano. She wore skinny jeans and a blue striped rugby shirt, making her look a bit like a tomboy, even though she shared many of Simone's feminine features. Her hair was much lighter that Simone's, which she must have inherited from her father.

"So here we are," Simone said. "Billie could hardly wait today."

It looked like Simone shared Billie's sentiment.

"I have been just as excited to meet you," Peter said as he offered his hand out to her, but Billie did not accept.

"Billie is shy when it comes to handshakes," Simone said apologetically.

"I don't blame her," Peter said quickly, pulling his hand away.

"Billie, this is Danni. She works in this wonderful store that I'm so glad to have found," Simone continued the introductions.

Danni offered Billie a smile and a nod. She would have wanted to offer her a big hug, but held back for obvious reasons.

"It's nice to meet you, Billie, your mom has told me what a good piano player you are."

Billie looked at her, and Danni noticed the attempt at a smile from her. She changed quickly to just offer a shrug instead and then looked to Peter.

"My mom said you had three students compete in the Albert Greenfield competition last year." Billie had a hard time maintaining eye contact even when she was talking directly to Peter.

"I sure did," Peter said. "It was a very good year for three of my most dedicated piano students. It took a lot of hard work, but we were very happy with the results there."

Billie finally looked straight into his eyes, and Danni could tell that she was pleased with his answer.

"Were you thinking that you would like to play at that competition?" Peter asked.

"I have watched it on the internet."

Peter smiled at her, and Danni could tell his curiosity was growing.

"Are you ready to go to the piano for your lesson?" Peter asked her.

She looked at her mother, somewhat hesitant. Simone smiled at her and nudged her along.

"Go with Peter. I will be right here waiting for you."

Billie followed Peter to the studios in the back of the store, and Danni looked at Simone's watchful eyes, glued to them until they disappeared into the doorway.

"Do you want to hang out in the store while she has her lesson? I can give you a tour," Danni offered.

"How was your steak night with Jake?" she asked instead of accepting the tour.

Danni was impressed that she even remembered.

"It started off lovely, but it took a bad turn somewhere in the middle and ended way down in the dumps," she chuckled as she reported on the dreadful evening for the second time that hour.

"Oh no! He didn't like your steak?" Simone teased.

"No, he totally scarfed up the steak. We made it all the way to my mother's Death by Chocolate cake. It killed our night."

Danni tried to be earnest, but there was no way she could feel solemn about anything while talking with Simone. Not even a tumultuous breakup with her lifelong boyfriend. She was more focused on Simone's radiant skin and her blue eyes shining like crystals.

Simone could not keep from laughing about the dramatic report Danni delivered.

"I'm really sorry! Maybe your mother is secretly sabotaging your relationship," Simone teased again.

"My mother adores Jake. Or so she tells me, but I'm coming to find out that things aren't always what they seem."

Danni basked in the joy that radiated from Simone.

"How is your preparation for the auditions coming along?" she whispered, deciding to change the subject away from her drama with Jake.

"I have very little time to practice, with Billie practically glued to the piano these days."

"So you're not practicing?"

"I have mostly been listening to the music. I haven't found an acceptable way to pry Billie away from the piano. By the time she is done, it's time to make dinner or do laundry. It's a struggle to be a housewife," Simone said, still seamlessly playful.

"You don't seem worried. I'm thinking it's because you said you already know the pieces you will play."

"By heart."

"Maybe you need another piano. We do sell a few of them," Danni said, congratulating herself for pulling off an opportunistic sales pitch that would make Peter proud.

Simone waved her hand in the air in a demonstrative show of opposition.

"Oh no! Bill would have a fit," she said laughing.

"You can play when he is not home," Danni suggested, true to her habit of solving every problem.

"You are determined to get me back on stage, aren't you, Danni?"

"Are you afraid the bug will bite again?"

Simone's eyes lost a bit of their spark instantly. She didn't answer. Instead, she looked elsewhere around the store for a distraction. Danni sensed that she hit a nerve.

"I'm sorry, I didn't mean to upset you," Danni apologized. "Should we just do that tour I promised you?"

"No need to apologize. I do have regrets about the way things turned out, but I try not to focus on them. For Billie's sake. I never want her to feel like I sacrificed anything for her."

"Being an accompanist here would be a perfect compromise."

"I agree," Simone said.

"You said moving to Philadelphia was another big change in plans for you."

"Definitely, my family was my main support with Billie," she said, then paused, as if she was counting before making a leap. "But to tell you the truth, I have changed my mind about the decision lately."

Danni told herself that Simone was referring to the pending audition she had at the store.

"I am sure that it has a lot to do with finding a good piano teacher for Billie," she explained to herself, more than Simone.

The mischief settled back into Simone's eyes.

"Of course," she concurred. "I have been overjoyed about finding Peter."

Danni's heartbeat still raced at an unmanageable pace, no matter what she told herself.

"Marius is the violin teacher, whose students will need the accompanist. He mostly gives lessons out of his home though. He plays in the symphony from what I hear."

Simone gasped.

"That is impressive," she said in a more serious tone. "I have heard really good things about both. It would be a dream to work with them."

"I have been hoping for the exact same thing," Danni said, elated about the prospect of seeing Simone at the store more frequently.

"You haven't even heard me play yet."

"I know. I've only pictured it. I gave you a standing ovation, so you must be very good."

"Will it be the three of you listening at the audition?"

"I will definitely be there, so I suggest you drag that girl of yours away from the piano even if it's kicking and screaming."

She touched Simone's arm briefly and noticed a faint redness permeating her cheeks.

"I will have to find a way," she said.

"I have the day off tomorrow. Maybe I can take her somewhere so you can have the day to practice?" Danni offered spontaneously and then watched Simone's stunned face turn speechless.

"I could not expect that of you, Danni!" she finally said.

"I would be happy to do that for you," Danni interrupted her objection quickly.

"I would have to ask her if she would go do something with you. She can be so hesitant when it comes to people she doesn't know. I mean, sometimes she can be downright reluctant. Maybe if you took her to the movies, she would be agreeable."

"A movie would be easy. We could do two movies back-to-back to give you more time," she said, suddenly filled with bravado.

"That is an amazing offer, Danni. I wouldn't know how to thank you!"

"Let's see if she agrees first, before you start taking your checkbook out," Danni said jokingly.

"You are probably right," Simone said.

She touched Danni's arm, letting her hand linger on her skin, drawing all of Danni's attention to the warmth spreading all the way down to her feet.

"I have listened to the Beethoven sonatas, and none of them sound like a walk in the park."

"No, it is not. I really lucked out, though. I worked on a few of them in college. The first one especially."

"Are you going to do all three movements?"

"It's too long. I'm sure the first two will be enough to sell them on me."

"They may just not be able to get enough of you," Danni quipped.

A customer came to the counter to check something out, and Simone stepped aside, then pointed in the direction of the sheet music rack. She walked off toward that section. Danni forced her focus to the man in front of her buying guitar strings. She asked him if he found everything that he needed out of habit. He assured her that he did and mentioned that his guitar strings always broke at the most inopportune times, and he was just happy to be walking distance from the store. She placed the strings in a small bag for him and completed his credit card transaction. He walked out of the store with long, purposeful strides. She wanted to adopt his style and transport herself over to the sheet music rack.

Fortunately, another few customers approached her with more items to check out, keeping her mind stranded in reality. It helped that they offered lesson material right at the store for the students. Most of them took advantage of the convenience and kept the store busy.

As soon as she had everyone checked out, her eyes glanced over to Simone, still browsing the sheet music. She restrained herself to give her some space. She noticed that she was inching toward the back of the store where the lesson studios were. She was likely curious to hear how Billie's lesson was going. Simone turned to her and signaled for her to join her. Danni looked around. She didn't spot any immediate customers that needed her attention. She placed a sign up on the counter that asked to ring the bell for help and then rushed over to Simone.

She followed her to the back of the store to Peter's studio. They stopped at the door and placed their ears close to it. They could hear the muffled sounds of the piano through the mostly soundproof door.

Simone's face lit up as she listened to her daughter play. Her eyes were beaming with sheer joy.

Danni tried to listen along, but she was distracted by Simone's close proximity. Her eyes were drawn to Simone's neck. She wore a gold necklace with a round diamond pendent. Most likely one of

Bill's lavish gifts. Her eyes moved lower. She pretended to listen to the music, but her ears felt as if they were on fire, and she was unable to distinguish any sounds.

She closed her eyes for a moment to redirect her thoughts back to Billie's playing. When she opened her eyes, she noticed Simone's gaze, resting unapologetically on her mouth, moving slowly up to her eyes. They stood motionless there. The sound penetrating through the door competed for their attention, but Danni was lost in the blue sky of Simone's eyes. She sank deeper into the pale blush of her cheeks, slowly reddening as their eyes found each other again. Danni could hear the echo of her heart beating in her ears. Simone's mouth pulled into a gentle smile, and the expression of her eyes eased as she continued to hold her gaze. She noticed the sweet smell of jasmine circling the air around them.

She pulled herself away abruptly. She had to close her eyes to calm the intoxication that filled her head. She stiffened her shoulders and scorned herself again for validating such an unrealistic fantasy. She pulled the darkness behind her eyes over the soft image of Simone. Her apprehension stepped aside when she felt Simone's warm fingers fold softly around her wrist. She opened her eyes quickly as the sensation of her touch buzzed through her like electricity.

She met Simone's smiling eyes resting on her.

"Are you all right, Danni?"

She nodded hastily.

"She sounds good, right?" Danni stammered, even though her mind has not registered much of what she heard.

Simone nodded. Her smile was persistent. She kept her fingers around Danni's wrist.

The familiar sound of the bell echoed from the cashier's counter through the hallway. She looked down at her hand.

"Saved by the bell," Simone said softly.

"Indeed," Danni said as she took a deep breath. Her other hand wrapped around Simone's fingers and gently lifted them away from her arm. She pulled her hand away from Simone's slender fingers reluctantly, before she turned around and walked toward the check-out counter, while her thoughts swirled like a flock of blackbirds in her chest.

Back at the counter, she focused intensely on the customer, in spite of their eyes ricocheting nervously away from her gaping eyes. She needed to stay in the moment.

"Did you find everything you were looking for?" she asked the woman in front of her, reminding herself to blink.

"Can you recommend a good metronome to me?"

"They are all in aisle 3, I will go show you."

Danni knew the store like the back of her hand. She talked about the differences and helped the woman decide which one to get. After she checked her out, she sank into the chair behind the counter, exhausted from her heart racing through most of the past hour. She looked at her watch and saw that it was close to five. Billie's lesson would be winding down soon. She was excited to see Simone and meet Billie today, but she was capsized by the flood of emotions that accompanied their encounter. The intensity between them was already palpable at the Wine Loft, but somehow, it had heightened even more this afternoon. She pleaded with her heart to stand down. She urged her rational mind to take charge of the situation. It was not the first time she had to implore her pining heart, but this time, she would need a miracle.

Billie, Peter, and Simone finally strutted down the aisle toward her.

"Danni, can you put Billie in for next Monday afternoon again? I think I saw an opening at three?" Peter asked.

"Sure thing. I think Tyler cancelled, so we do have that slot available next week," Danni said as she clicked on her keyboard to open the scheduling program on her computer.

"Nice work today, Billie," he said, turning to Billie with a big smile. "I am so impressed by you already!"

Billie kept her bashful guard tight around her, and it was clear that it would take more time before she would lift it. She reminded Danni so much of herself at that age.

Peter walked back to the studio, and Danni was left with the musical duo in front of her.

"So what's next on the docket for you lovely ladies today?"

She hoped that her charm would mask the trepidation she felt. Simone's gaze, on the other hand, seemed open and free.

"I promised Billie some ice cream after her lesson. To celebrate what we hope is a long and prosperous journey with a wonderful new teacher, right, Billie?' Simone said, still looking at Danni, almost invitingly.

Billie nodded and started to walk off after her mother's reminder of a sweet reward. But Simone grabbed her arm gently to hold her back.

"Sweetheart, how would you like it if Danni took you to go see that movie you wanted to see at the IMAX theatre tomorrow?"

"*Journey into Space*?" she asked keenly.

"Yes, you've been asking to go see it."

"I thought you were going to take me?"

"Danni told me that she really wanted to see it too, and she has some free time tomorrow afternoon."

"Are you coming too?" Billie asked, looking stumped.

"I can't tomorrow, love. I have to go do something, but I know you would have a great time with Danni."

"We can have some burgers afterward if you want," Danni offered, joining forces with Simone to clinch the deal.

Billie paused for a minute, looking around the store, then shrugged nonchalantly. "Sure," she said, and started to pull her mom toward the exit of the store.

"I will text you later, Danni," Simone said as she let Billie lead her all the way to the door.

Danni smiled as she watched them leave the store.

She took her phone out and searched for the showtimes of the movie that Billie wanted to see at the IMAX theatre at the Franklin Institute. She found a two o'clock start for *Journey into Space*. The theatre was close to Logan Square Park, and Danni could see them grabbing some burgers before heading to the park, to give Simone more time with her piano.

Peter approached her, and she quickly stashed her phone away.

"What did you think of Billie?" she asked.

"She has excellent potential," he said, his face beaming with excitement.

"Simone says she plays piano constantly."

"I can tell. She is a little tense, so she will have to work on relaxing more, but she has good technique and a sharp mind for her age. She picked up everything so well today."

"It will be good for you to add yet another outstanding piano student," Danni said. "Your reputation is going to explode!"

"I have been lucky with a good batch. Billie seems to have natural talent. Like she was born to do it."

Danni stayed quiet about the source of her talent. She didn't want to ruin his surprise in any way.

"Remember that I'm off tomorrow," she reminded him.

"Yes, I have Nathan coming in to help out in your place."

Peter often gave his willing older students an opportunity to make extra money on the side.

He lingered around, obviously still with something plaguing his mind.

"I hate to be a broken record about Jake."

Danni could feel herself tense up instantly. She still has not spoken to him after he left her apartment on Thursday night and didn't want to make the first move. She couldn't be the one to go crawling back to him. Not while he was the one caught in a lie.

"I don't know, Peter, you are probably rightly concerned, but I'm the one totally in the dark here. He didn't tell me about having car troubles, and I didn't know he was struggling to pay his rent."

"I'm just wondering why he would hide that from you."

"I'm guessing that he needs money for something else, and the story about his rent troubles was just to swindle money out of you."

Peter looked bewildered at her direct analysis.

"He would just deceive us like that? I mean, do you know him to be such a liar?"

"He's been making more excuses and rationalizations. I don't know him as an outright liar, no. But he has been more defensive. Plus, he has been working just about every day."

"If you can just try to get more information from him somehow. It's important to our family to keep him from ending up like his father. If he is in trouble, we would most definitely find a way to help him."

She didn't want to tell him that they weren't even on speaking terms. That she was considering not getting back together. Despite being riddled with curiosity about what he was up to. She couldn't quiet the nagging desire to find out if her suspicions were accurate. And she wanted to keep her job at the music store, now more than ever. Realistically, she knew she was going to have to swallow her pride and contact him.

"Maybe showing up on your doorstep drunk, asking for money was a cry for help."

"That or one heck of a manipulation."

"That would depend on the extent of the trouble he is in, I guess."

Danni was convinced pleading for money from his family was connected to the money he handed to the Russian in the park. He owed money to the wrong people, and she needed to find out who those people were.

"You know the kind of trouble his father got into."

Danni knew only what Jake told her, and Jake only knew what his uncles told him. According to them, his father had to leave Philadelphia all together to get away from people who wanted him dead. He was involved in a robbery gone wrong and didn't have enough protection to deescalate the situation. He could never set foot in Philadelphia again, and he couldn't tell anyone where he was. He was essentially dead to his family in order to protect them. Jake was in turmoil over it with a lifetime ahead of him to agonize over it. He would either lift himself up from it or let it eat him alive. They were all still waiting to see which way he would turn. Right now, it seemed as if he was getting devoured.

"I will see what I can do. He has been guarded, but I will figure something out," Danni said, not able to resist Peter's pleading heart reaching out to her.

"Thank you, Danni. Just be our eyes and ears. His mother is worried also. Terrified that she will end up losing Jake the same way she lost his father."

Danni's knew that she would have to ask Jake's forgiveness and pretend to forgive him to get their relationship back on track. She would have to get to the bottom of Jake's charade. She needed Peter to stop worrying about Jake. To focus on his students and the auditions for a piano player. For him to pick Simone, so that she could get a fresh start on her abandoned dreams.

Danni thought about her movie with Billie the next day. Her unhinged emotions around Simone. Her father's ongoing self-induced confinement. She didn't even know what to make of her mother's capsized personality recently. She closed her eyes and felt the weight of it pressing down on her shoulders. She thought she would have been crushed. But she could sense herself pushing back this time. She felt the swell in her chest, as she held everything above water, and she started to feel stronger for the coming days

Chapter 8

Danni went home that Monday evening and fixed a quick salad to eat. She turned to her computer and browsed through some available options for GPS tracking devices she could use to track Jake's car. She was developing a plan. If she wanted to keep track of Jake's location to follow him in order to get information to Peter, she needed the right equipment. She researched the multitude of options available to her while she crunched on her salad, eyes glued to the screen. She finally settled on a magnetic tracker that would connect with her phone. She expedited shipping so she would have it within two short days.

She was reluctant to contact Jake, but she knew making the first move was inevitable. And she would need to handle him in an entirely different way to get him off his back feet. Her confrontation on Thursday was too strong. She would need a much softer approach if she ever wanted to pull her mission off. She needed to follow him without raising his suspicions.

She could use her camera to capture evidence for Peter. She had binoculars to keep a safe distance. What she really needed were night vision devices. She was sure the bulk of his indiscretions occurred at night. A camera flash at night would only draw attention to her. She searched the web and found a pair of night vision binoculars with video recording capabilities. She ordered them right away, and her excitement about the operation was climbing ten stories high.

She squelched her reluctance and grabbed her phone. She scrolled to his contact information. She clicked on the message icon and stared at the empty screen, searching for the right words. Her mind came up empty. She wanted her words to be authentic, but finally landed on the sad realization that she was just going to have to fake it.

"I'm so sorry about the other night," she typed.

It was a good enough start. She knew he would be relieved that she took the first step. He would be even more relieved that she took responsibility for the argument between them.

She sent the message and waited. He would still be at work and wouldn't check his phone as often. She could wait patiently. Patience was one of her virtues.

She scrolled to her phone's music application and found some of Haydn's piano music to play in the background. She started to plan her movie outing with Billie. It was out of her comfort zone. A rather spontaneous proposition that wasn't in her wheelhouse normally, but meeting Simone this past week and agreeing to their friendship wasn't normal for her either. She was faced with the predicament because she tried to impress someone, who incidentally seemed far out of her league. She has never spent an afternoon with a twelve-year-old, much less one overran with compulsive anxiety. Billie would have no piano available to help keep her calm. There was a mountain of pressure on that movie. Hopefully, it would hold her attention for the hour. She was betting on help from the sun for the rest of the day.

She planned to pick her up around one. The movie would end around three thirty. She crossed her fingers that there would be previews. They could walk down to a park and find a bench. Danni could talk to her about New York or her grandparents or Bill. Hopefully, the fresh air would keep her anxiety at bay. If things went sideways, they could simply get back to the car and she would bring her back to her piano. Despite feeling nervous about it, she considered her plan bulletproof.

Her phone buzzed. She checked the screen and saw the message from Jake.

"I should be the one apologizing. For leaving like that."

"I shouldn't have pushed so hard. I know you have been under a lot of stress."

She offered him a way out on a silver platter. A way to put the evening behind them and move forward to the next phase in their relationship. She could be equally mysterious to him.

"It's for us."

"I know. I completely support what you are trying to do."

"It's busy over here. Have fun on your day off tomorrow."

It slipped her mind that she had told him about that.

"Thanks. I will."

She didn't want to leave any room for him to insert himself in her day.

He left it at that, and she praised herself for ending the conversation on a good note to ensure that they get back on speaking terms.

She suddenly wondered if she should get her hands on a firearm. She knew her father would most likely still have his service pistol, but getting her hands on it would require explaining a crazy tale of gangs and robbers that even he would reject. She knew she couldn't underestimate Jake's new friends. Direct confrontation with them would be very detrimental. She resigned herself to the fact that it would be better to keep her distance and scrapped the idea of the gun.

The phone buzzed again. She tensed up, knowing it was probably another message from Jake.

"What are you doing tomorrow?"

She fumbled quickly for an appropriate lie to keep him out of her day. She was dead set on taking Billie to the movie.

"I'm taking my dad to the doctor for his ankle."

She felt guilty for raising a smoke screen that easily.

"Okay, I hope it's good news. I should really get over to see them."

"He's been in a funk. Mom seems better though, for some odd reason."

"I thought so too. She looked happy on Thursday."

"Maybe the tides are turning for her. We'll see."

"Yes, we will. Shoot, it's getting busy here again."

"Okay. See you soon."

She surely dodged a bullet. She put her phone down and turned the television on. A rerun of an old police drama popped up on the screen, and she stayed on the channel. It was bound to be filled with tips that she could use. About the nature of criminals and the incredible courage required of the people trying to stop them.

Chapter 9

Danni woke up early on Tuesday morning. She grabbed her phone off the nightstand, feeling tempted to send a text to Simone, but she knew no one liked receiving messages from anyone at five in the morning. She put the phone back and closed her eyes. She thought about the day ahead of her. There were many details to go over with Simone. It would be better to call and talk to her about it. She implored herself to be brave and call as soon as the sun was out.

She couldn't fall back to sleep and got up to go make some coffee instead. She sat at her dining room table with the warm cup and looked at the map of the Franklin Center with its surrounding areas on her phone. The movie theater was within easy walking distance from Logan Park. She found a deli on the map where they could stop for sandwiches. She reminded herself to take a blanket for them to sit on, in case there were no empty benches available. She designed a list of questions she could ask Billie to fuel the conversation. She decided to start off with her grandparents and Bill. She remembered about the music competition she seemed interested in and did a web search of all the music competitions offered in Philadelphia. She added the Albert Greenfield competition to her list of topics. Danni knew that Billie was probably not all that social. Sitting outside on a blanket, watching people without twenty questions from Danni would most likely be easier for her to handle.

The morning developed slowly as she watched the sun's light pour in through the window. She was on her second cup of coffee and found herself sketching on the drawing pad she kept on the dining room table. She would usually sketch something inspired by a picture she took at the park and see how close she could copy it. The picture she used that morning was of an old man slumped on a park bench with his head in his hands. She remembered the day, earlier that summer, when she took the picture. She found him there, looking lost and grief stricken. He was sobbing while oblivious people all around him paid no attention to him. She finally walked over and sat beside him. She placed her hand on his back and asked him if he was all right. He told her that his wife passed away two weeks before and that he was still completely heartbroken. They used to sit in the park together, and although he wanted to relive that memory, it was painful for him to experience it without her by his side. He finally sat up and looked out at the people in front of him. His breathing calmed down. Danni held his hand, and they sat there, together in silence to experience his grief together. She stayed quiet next to him. He finally got up and said he was ready to go. She gave him a hug before he walked away. She had the picture to remember their encounter. She wanted to sketch him to recreate the feeling of the connection they had. She seldom reached out to people. She preferred to be alone with her thoughts, but that experience reminded her how valuable it was to extend yourself to people sometimes.

By the time she finished the sketch, she had a song stuck in her head. Her thoughts were a broken record, stuck on the lyrics that cried about how people who needed people were the luckiest people in the world.

She looked over to the clock on the microwave and saw that it was already close to nine o' clock. Time always flashed by like lightning when she sketched. She always got lost in all the finest details. She knew that she had waited long enough. Not calling Simone started to feel like procrastination.

She picked up her phone and scrolled to the number that she saved. She realized she didn't even know her last name yet. Her palms felt clammy as she waited for her to answer.

"Hello, Danni."

Her voice was full of energy.

"Am I calling too early?" she asked.

She put the call on speaker so she could dry her sweaty hands on her pants.

"Not at all. I just finished my coffee, so you have perfect timing."

"I wanted to go over the details for today, so you could plan the rest of your day."

"I still don't know how I got so lucky. Are you sure you want to do this?"

"Of course. It would be good for all of us, don't you think?"

"How is that?"

"Well, you will get to practice, Billie will get to see the movie, and I will get to do something out of my comfort zone."

"And you getting out of your comfort zone is a good thing?"

"Yes, I should make an effort to connect more with people."

"I promise to make the most of the time here on the piano."

Danni could hear the smile in her voice.

"The movie starts at two this afternoon. I think we could grab something to eat after. To give you some extra time."

"Are you sure? I will make sure she has enough money."

"Do you think Billie will be all right with that? Please don't send any money."

"If she gets to be too much to handle for you, just bring her back. But I think she will be all right. You can let me know what I owe you when you bring her back."

"How will I know if she is uncomfortable? I mean, what are the signs?"

"She would pace. Or wring her hands. Or snap her fingers and count."

Danni let the words sink in. She suddenly questioned whether sitting in the park filled with people would be a good idea. She would have to pay close attention to her if the park was crowded.

"Are you still interested?" Simone asked after Danni's pause.

"Of course. I will keep an eye out and adjust the day as needed. I promise to bring her back if she is uncomfortable."

"She will love the movie. She hasn't done anything like this since we moved here, so we will just need to see how it goes today."

Danni was relieved that Simone trusted her enough to do it.

"I will pick her up at one at your house. Can you text me the address?"

"Yes, I will. What time do you think you will have her back?"

"Let's shoot for between five and six?"

"This is really so kind of you."

"Are you going to work on the Beethoven Sonata?" she asked to shift the attention away from herself.

"Yes. The first one. To refresh my memory of it."

"Peter was very impressed with Billie, so I am sure he will love you too."

"You haven't heard me play a single note yet," Simone teased.

"Billie must get her talent from somewhere, and you haven't mentioned anything about your husband having any musical talent."

Simone giggled.

"That is true. He is put together very differently."

"What is he like?"

Danni was curious about the man who managed to capture her heart enough to get married. She tried to ignore the hint of jealousy brewing just under her skin.

"He is more serious. Likes to be in charge of things. It's probably the reason Billie wants to control everything so much."

"That makes sense. Are you usually drawn to people who like to be in charge?" Danni didn't want to be too forward, but Simone was easy to talk to.

"When you're in college with your head in the clouds, it's easy to gravitate toward someone that will steer you somewhere."

"You said things ended up differently from what you planned though."

"Yes. I had big dreams, but no road map for any of them, and where Bill was going was miles away from where I wanted to go. I think I'm ready to make some plans of my own now."

Sadness for Simone's life washed over her. Life didn't always lead you to where you wanted to go. It was true for her parents and for Jake. Her brother in Louisiana. They were all kicking around in unfamiliar waters. Working in a music store never crossed her mind growing up. And yet, it brought her to this moment.

"Maybe you are at a crossroad now."

"I just want to take a little bit of control back. I regret giving so much of it away. I want to be braver than I used to be."

"You were brave when you asked me to go to for coffee. And even braver when you decided to do this audition."

"That is the point. I wouldn't have found out about the audition if I didn't ask you to go have coffee with me."

"It makes you wonder, doesn't it?" Danni asked. She knew very well how frustrating it was to be out of control in your life. She looked at the light streaming in through her window and felt the warmth of the air around her. She relaxed into all the revelations of their conversation. The ease between them.

"That day, I was strangely compelled to do something I wouldn't normally do," Simone said, and Danni felt the words burrow into her heart.

"You will probably do well at the audition then," Danni said.

It was because of the growing comfort between them that she had to constantly remind herself that Simone was married. A permanent fact that would never change.

"When I visualize the audition, I see you sitting in the room with Peter, listening. Is that crazy?"

Danni was surprised. She felt Simone lean ever closer to her. Making her even more leery.

"You probably want someone familiar in there to help calm the nerves."

"I feel like I could skip practice and come with you and Billie to the movie instead."

"Your music is the only thing you need to focus on today."

"What if we met for more than reviving my music career?"

Closer and closer, she leaned.

"I told you I will spend as much time as you need with Billie so you can have more time for yourself."

She could hear Simone take a deep breath. She knew she was frustrating her, as much as she was frustrating herself.

"Very well then. I will focus on the music," she said after pausing.

"Simone, you should know that I'm not blind to what you're saying. I am just a little blindsided by it."

She wanted to be truthful, and where Simone was heading was a steep hill with nothing but loose rocks under her feet.

"I like the way you say my name."

Her feet kept slipping as she followed Simone down the hill.

"What's your last name?"

"Bradley. It's Bill's."

"What was it before?"

"Laurent."

"French descent?"

"Yes. An artistic lot we are. Both of my parents are musicians. They were my biggest fans growing up."

"How did they handle your detour?"

"They love their granddaughter, not my marriage."

"And the move to Philadelphia?"

"It was devastating to them. They would be at my doorstep today to move me back to New York if I let them."

"You have options!" Danni teased.

"You mean, I had options."

"What do you mean?"

"Two weeks ago, I had options. Then I met you and everything changed."

"Yes, this audition is going to change everything for you."

"We will get to see a lot of each other."

"Don't say it."

"Yes, we won't speak of that at all."

"I will see you at one today. Text me the address," she reminded her.

"I will have her ready to go."

The conversation left Danni feeling like air, floating out of herself. She was forced to crawl back in bed to ground herself, to find solid footing. She pulled the covers over her head and focused on breathing slowly in and out. All she could see was Simone's eyes, her mouth, and her slender fingers. She pulled the covers even tighter to keep herself from getting lost in the images. She pushed herself to focus more on her breathing. Inhaling and exhaling slowly, until she finally drifted off to sleep.

It was close to noon before she was awakened by traffic noise outside her apartment. She realized she would have to move like the wind to make it over to Simone's by one. There was no time to think about their conversation, much less how much fate was weaving itself into her life recently.

Chapter 10

She made it to Simone's address at exactly one o' clock. The house was part of a series of brick homes, typical for the neighborhood of Queen's Village. Five steps led up to the black painted front door and a tree provided greenery and shade in front of the second story windows. A few potted plants lining the steps helped to add a welcome feeling to the home. Danni took a deep breath and thanked her lucky stars for finding a parking space practically right in front of the door. She bounced up the steps and pushed the doorbell. She shoved her nervous energy down and only pressed the doorbell once. The door swung open, and she once again stood in front of the beautiful woman that has stepped into her life so effortlessly. Her hair framed her face. It glistened with shine, always accentuating her striking blue eyes.

"Right on time, Danni!" she said, smiling at the sight of her.

"I am following a strict schedule today, wish me luck," Danni said, as Simone swung the door open wider to invite her in.

"Come on in for a second. I will tell Billie you are here."

She was casually dressed, in jeans. A dark green summer shirt hugged her curves. Danni stayed close behind her as she followed her into the house.

The front room was large and open, with white walls to make it look even bigger. The furniture was arranged around a modern fireplace. The back of the room opened into a large dining room, which in turn opened into a very modern kitchen with granite countertops and stainless-steel appliances. There was a great deal of financial comfort on display throughout the home. She tried to ignore the contrast between her own humble apartment and Simone's lavish home.

"Are you ready for some magical blood, sweat, and tears on the piano?"

"It's your generosity that is magical."

"I think I should be able to get a sneak preview before the audition, don't you think?" she suggested boldly.

"That will surely make you late for the movie."

Simone stepped closer to her and looked into her eyes. Danni forced herself to hold her gaze. Simone took another step closer, which surprised Danni, and she drew her breath in loudly. She could smell the familiar smell of jasmine radiating off Simone's chest.

"I should have told you to come earlier. For a sneak preview," Simone said.

"Maybe when we get back?"

"If Bill works late today, perhaps."

"He doesn't like to hear you play?"

"He doesn't like to be confronted with the sacrifice of my life."

"Maybe the sacrifice was just temporary."

'We haven't really talked about that in detail."

"But you have told him what you are planning, right?"

Simone looked at her without saying anything. They were still standing so close to each other, Danni could hear her taking each breath.

Simone reached out to her and took her hands in hers. Her touch was warm and electric. Danni willed herself not to resist.

"I have only discussed this plan of mine with you," Simone said, holding on to her.

"So it is our secret?"

Simone nodded.

"It is a very big secret. Just between us."

Danni raised her eyebrows.

"Should I be flattered?"

"Maybe."

Billie walked into the room, and Simone dropped her hands instantly.

"There you are," she welcomed her daughter, reaching her hands out to her instead. "Are you ready?"

Billie nodded and smiled in her direction, but she didn't offer Danni any eye contact.

She was dressed comfortably in jeans and a t-shirt with canvas sneakers, and Danni was relieved since she had planned plenty of walking after the movie.

"Let's go see that journey into space."

Billie continued to look hesitant and looked at her mother.

"Are you sure you don't want to come along?" she asked with pleading eyes.

"I cannot today, sweetie. You will have fun with Danni. She planned a nice day for the two of you. I will be right here when you get back."

She nodded and then started to walk toward the front door. Simone smiled at Danni.

"I hope you guys have fun."

"I'm sure we will," Danni reassured her and then followed Billie out the door.

She was relieved to find that the Franklin Institute was not very busy, most likely because it was a weekday afternoon. Danni wasn't sure how comfortable Billie would be around crowds, but she seemed relaxed as she absorbed the scenery at the Institute. They walked past a giant statue of Benjamin Franklin on their way to the IMAX theater and into the short ticket line. Danni offered to buy popcorn at the food counter, but Billie declined and opted for a lemonade instead. The theater was filled sparsely, and by the time they got to their seats, the lights were already dimmed, and the previews on the screen.

Danni noticed Billie taking two polished rocks from her pants pocket, rolling them around in her hand. She was most likely using them to fidget as another coping strategy.

With that, Billie stayed focused on the entire movie and barely took a sip of her lemonade. Danni stayed quiet herself, not wanting to interrupt her attention. But she was curious about where her interest in the stones would have originated.

Danni remembered seeing a rock store not far from the Franklin Institute on the map. She decided to surprise Billie and let her browse around inside for a while.

After the movie ended, Billie stayed in her seat while most people rushed out of the theater. She placed the rocks back in her pocket.

"Did you like the movie?" Danni asked.

"Very much!"

"It's amazing to think all of that is out there, right?" Danni said, trying to draw her into a quick conversation.

"Maybe one day everyone will just be able to go anywhere into space any time."

"Is there anywhere specific you would want to go?"

"I would like to visit all the planets to see for myself what they look like."

"Do you think they look anything like earth?"

"No, I think each one is different and not like earth at all."

"They would be interesting to see."

Billie just nodded quickly and started to look around nervously. She got up as soon as everyone cleared out of the theater.

Danni followed her out of the dark room back into the Franklin Institute.

"Are you ready to walk over to Logan Park for a while? We can get something to eat on the way."

"Sure," is all she offered, looking eager to stay on the move, which Danni assumed was yet another coping mechanism.

Danni had their route pre-mapped to get to the park, but she wanted to add the detour to the rock store. She looked at the GPS on her phone to find the quickest way to get them to the store. They started to walk, and Danni was grateful that the sun was out in full force.

They reached the storefront and Danni stopped and pointed her gaze up to the sign that said "Earth Rocks." Billie's eyes followed hers to the sign, and they widened when she recognized what kind of store it was.

"Have you ever been to this store?"

"Not this one. We used to go to a rock store when we lived in New York all the time."

"Is that where you got the rocks you keep in your pocket?"

She nodded, turning her eyes down, as if she was embarrassed.

"It's good to keep something of the earth close by," Danni quickly reassured her.

"Mom says it helps to keep me calm."

"Do you think it helps?"

She nodded again.

"I also like to read about rocks. There are so many different types. When I play piano, I imagine walking in the mountains."

"Mountains have a lot to explore," Danni said, hoping to temper her insecurity about her interest. An interest in geology should be admired. Even if it was simply a way to ground your nerves.

"Mountains are metamorphic rocks. They change because of heat and pressure. Kind of how people change all the time too. Like rocks."

Danni looked at the twelve-year-old in front of her, and it was clear to her that she was not an ordinary child her age.

"Do you want to go see what they have inside?" She pointed to the entrance of the store.

Billie's smile was the only answer she needed, and Danni pushed through the door with the young girl following close behind.

Billie seemed like she wanted to get lost in the store. There was a lot to see, and Danni had no knowledge of any of it. To her, it was like looking at a foreign language. Billie immediately started to wander down one of the aisles, looking at the rocks displayed in rows of glass cases. She moved slowly, looking at the rocks carefully. Danni let her roam to take it all in. It felt like they were walking through an art gallery. They spent over an hour in the store, browsing countless amounts of crystals and stones, showing themselves off like hidden treasures.

Danni's intention of getting something to eat and spending time in the park faded quickly, but she decided to adapt. Billie was obviously enthralled with the turn of events. It wasn't quite how Danni envisioned their afternoon, but Billie nailed it when she explained that people were all different. For Billie, wandering around in a place filled with rocks and minerals showcasing the metamorphosis of the earth were fascinating. Danni preferred to look at people. To her, people were all uniquely morphed from different elements of life and personal encounters.

The young girl finally came to a halt in front of a case holding a collection of bright blue rocks.

"Ultramarine!" she called out with more enthusiasm than Danni had seen from her in any of their encounters before.

"They are beautiful" Danni said and walked over to the glass case where Billie stood, mesmerized.

"I have read about these," Billie's eyes were wide and filled with wonder. "It's a metamorphic rock made of lazurite, pyrite, and calcite. They are beautiful."

"Where are they from? Do you know?" Danni asked, surprised that Billie could recite so much information.

"They are mostly mined in Afghanistan. They also used to be very valuable to the Egyptians."

The price tags on the rocks were steep, most definitely rendering them more suitable for observation, but Billie still seemed exhilarated by her discovery.

"They used it for the ultramarine blue pigment that was used in some famous paintings."

"I will have to read up more about them," Danni said, impressed with the extensive knowledge Billie displayed. She seemed to have a photographic memory for facts she was interested in.

Billie finally managed to pull herself away from the blue treasures and continued her exploration down the aisle. She seemed to be on the prowl for something familiar that she learned about before. She was very different from the day before, when they first met. That encounter was brief and didn't prepare her at all for what she found today. She was in her element, surrounded by geology of all things. She saw that while they were in the movie theater a few hours earlier, and it was evident again in the store. Her musical talents seemed so different from this side of her. She was forged from two very different elements. A scientific mind fused with the creativity of music. It would explain her practice habits, as Simone explained it. Constant and grounded as she explored the ever-changing world of artistic creativity.

By the time they finally left the store, it was nearly six o'clock, and she remembered that she agreed to have Billie home by six at the latest. She tried to orient herself as to where they were in relation to where she parked as her phone buzzed in her pocket with a text message. She retrieved it, fully expecting a berating message from Simone asking if she had kidnapped her child.

"I made dinner. Please join us when you get back with Billie."

"Are you sure? You guys probably need some family time," she responded, feeling as hesitant as ever to be around Simone for too long.

She instinctively reacted against every true desire in her heart and didn't know what frustrated her more. Her feelings or her inability to acknowledge them.

"Bill is working late. It would just be the three of us."

"Are you ready to go home? Your mom made dinner," Danni asked Billie.

Billie nodded again. She seemed relaxed. As if she had been recharged with positive ions all afternoon.

Danni texted with fluttering fingers.

"We are on our way back now."

They left the store and started walking in the direction of her car. Billie followed blindly, her mind clearly still elsewhere. Danni pondered if it was normal to have a mind infatuated by rocks and facts at such a young age. She was clearly a rare specimen. She wanted to get to know Simone's family better. Especially her parents. She was completely enamored. She followed Billie's suggestion and compared them to the stones of the earth. Individually forged and unique. She smiled all the way down to her heart, knowing she would welcome the journey.

They reached the car, and she opened the door for Billie. She made sure that her seatbelt was clicked.

Billie turned into an ordinary twelve-year-old when it came to daily life.

Just before Danni started the car, she suddenly remembered that the great Leonardo da Vinci himself painted extraordinary works of art, while his mind was filled with rocks and fossils. She looked at Billie and imagined a young Leonardo, most likely intrigued by all the mysteries of the world at the same young age as her. With that in mind, she drove to Simone's home extra carefully.

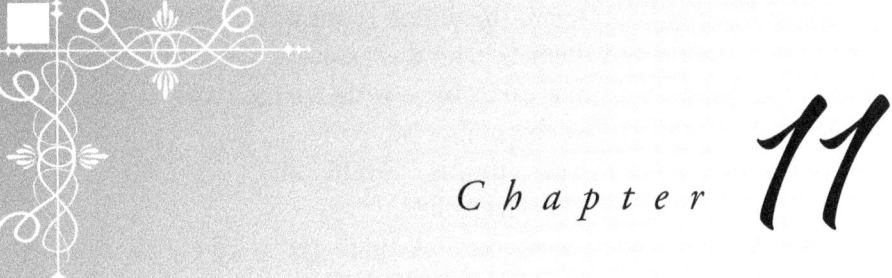

Chapter 11

"How was it?" Simone asked Billie as soon as they walked through the front door of the home, her face beaming with joy.

"We went to a rock store!" Billie announced, equally excited.

"Really?"

"We passed that store called Earth Rocks after the movie on the way to the park. She seemed so eager to go in there," Danni explained.

"You have discovered her second passion in life very quickly, Danni." Simone sounded impressed.

"She may have given me a slight clue during the movie," Danni said, knowing that her ardent ability to pay attention to detail paid off that afternoon.

Simone looked puzzled.

"She carries a few polished stones with her, so I figured that she might have an interest."

Billie's hand fumbled around in her pocket again.

"It's that keen sense of observation you possess."

Danni shrugged, but she was happy that Simone noticed.

"Are you guys hungry already? I made a big chicken salad for us."

Danni nodded along with Billie. She has not eaten anything at all that day. Her nerves wouldn't let her come near any breakfast or lunch. She was relieved that Simone made a light meal and begged her stomach to tolerate it.

They followed Simone to the dining room where the table was already set. She invited them to take their seats as she went to the fridge to get the salad. She came back with a large bowl of fresh greens, topped with grilled chicken.

"You really went all out with this," Danni said.

Simone looked proud as she smiled.

"I was just so happy that you took Billie out to have some fun today."

Simone and Billie sat next to each other, while Danni picked the chair across from them.

Simone jumped up again as soon as they all sat down.

"I forgot the iced tea," and headed back to the kitchen.

Billie took a big scoop of salad and piled it up on her plate. She doused everything lavishly with ranch dressing.

Simone returned with a glass jug filled with iced tea. She poured a glass for Billie, and then for Danni, keeping her eyes fixed on her.

"Say when," she said.

"When," Danni said when the glass was halfway filled.

Simone finally switched her gaze to Billie.

"So how was the movie?"

Billie was already devouring her food without pause.

"Great," she finally said without making any eye contact.

Her mind was elsewhere. Most likely still in the store full of rocks, if she ventured a guess.

"How was your afternoon?" Danni asked Simone, eager to find out if Simone got to work on her audition pieces.

"Very productive," Simone said.

"Yes, Mom, what did you do this afternoon?" Billie asked between bites.

"Believe it or not, Billie, your mother worked on a piece of music on the piano this afternoon," Simone stated boldly.

Danni remembered that she has not shared her audition plans with her family yet.

"Believe it or not? I don't believe it," Billie said and laughed.

"Peter is looking for someone to play piano for the violin students at the studio."

Billie just kept staring at her, looking puzzled. They were both waiting for Simone to elaborate.

"I have decided to see if he likes my skills enough for the job," she continued, testing the waters. She must have plotted her confession between the flight of melodies over harmonious chord progressions earlier that afternoon.

Billie's eyes abruptly turned back on her food, and she fell quiet.

"What a wonderful plan!" Danni offered after an awkward silence stretched out between the three of them. She was hoping that her encouragement would sway Billie's muted reaction.

"You think?" Simone played along with a wink.

"He really needs someone this year. His trusted piano player from last year moved away," Danni explained and winked back at Simone.

Billie looked at Simone again.

"What piece are you going to play?" she asked, and Danni quietly sighed in relief.

"One of the Beethoven sonatas for violin and piano. The first one, actually."

"Why not the fifth?" Billie asked. "More violin students would be playing the Spring sonata."

Danni was again floored by the twelve-year-old's maturity and knowledge.

Simone pondered Billie's suggestion.

"I agree with you. The fifth is a much more popular sonata, but I like the first one better."

"I definitely disagree. The fifth would be more popular with the violin students."

Danni was amused by their exchange.

"Do you know what the fifth sonata sounds like, Danni?" Billie asked.

"I have to admit that I have not heard it before. I promise I will listen to it very soon."

Billie continued to take stabs at the remaining pieces of salad she had left on her plate.

"Do you know what the first one sounds like?" she asked again.

"I have listened to that one, but I wouldn't say I know exactly what it sounds like. They are pretty intricate."

"Three, five, seven, and nine."

Danni looked confused at Billie.

"My favorites. Of the violin sonatas. Just like his symphonies."

"When did you start listening to them?" Danni asked the young girl.

She thought about it for a while.

"Probably in my mother's womb," she finally said and chuckled.

Simone laughed along with her answer.

"That is the truth. I did listen to them a lot when I was pregnant. They really helped me get through it."

Billie finished her salad and took a big gulp of iced tea.

"You can remember that?' Danni asked Billie.

She laughed.

"No. I wasn't born yet. But I have liked Beethoven's music ever since I can remember."

"You have that in common with your mom then?"

Billie didn't answer, and Simone just looked at her daughter, her face gleaming with pride.

"So what is tops for you? Beethoven or the rocks?" Danni asked, excited about being able to keep her engaged in the conversation.

Billie shrugged.

"I like it all the same."

"She will just have to become a musical scientist," Simone said.

"A rare specimen," Danni added.

Billie laughed at their word play.

"Rock me, Amadeus!" she added to their banter, making them all laugh again.

Danni lifted her glass in a toast.

"To Billie. With a future as bright as all the stars in the universe."

Danni noticed Billie's cheeks turn a bright pink from the compliment.

"Can I be excused?" she asked abruptly.

Danni was certain her urge to escape was prompted by the unexpected physical reaction of her face. Simone warned her about the challenge social interaction posed to Billie. Danni could relate to her need to escape, and she admired Simone's intention to not medicate that away.

"Yes, sweetheart," Simone said, sensing that Billie's had enough interaction for one day.

Billie quickly pushed her chair back from the table and got up to head to her room. She walked away, staying on the tips of her toes and with her hand fidgeting in her pocket.

"You didn't think she was too much to handle today?" Simone asked, once Billie was out of earshot.

"Not at all. She is an amazing kid."

Danni wanted to ease Simone's anxiety about her daughter's quirks.

"I wish her teachers at school felt the same way."

"Was she in a gifted program?"

"Heck no!" Simone said quickly. "They thought she was completely unable to pay attention in class."

Danni looked at Simone. Without Billie present at the table, there was no buffer between them. She watched the color of her eyes, as striking as the first time she saw them. She looked at her hand, lying across from her on the table. She struggled to resist the temptation to take her hand in hers.

"She may be bored in class. I heard her ramble off plenty of facts about a stone she recognized in that store. She is no doubt able to pay attention to things she has interest in."

"Yes, she is just not that good at conforming to a teacher-directed class routine. They told me she was obsessive compulsive, way too rigid and uninvolved. It rips your heart out when people say things like that about the child you love more than anything."

Danni noticed a sadness rolling in across Simone's face.

"She is going to blossom once she goes to college. I wouldn't be surprised if school is just not challenging enough right now. I bet you she is already way ahead of her classmates, and they are just jealous."

"I hope you are right. I hope the teachers at her new school will be more understanding. I want her to have a normal childhood, but she doesn't seem too interested in that for herself."

Simone's face had turned solemn. Danni could see how dealing with Billie's struggles would keep her light-years away from her own aspirations.

"She is going places, that kid. She is unusual, and I think she will thrive once she can follow her own path. She is smart and very talented. It sure beats a kid with no interests. My parents could tell you what that is like," Danni explained.

She had very little confidence growing up, after her brother's death. Mostly because her parents never really reached out and encouraged her anymore.

"Are you referring to yourself?" Simone asked.

Danni could sense her heart reaching out.

"I am twenty-seven years old, without any real direction and no idea of how to find it. I see Billie and all of her certainty. She has clear interests that will guide her throughout her life. That is admirable."

Simone's face softened again, and it looked like she found sustenance in Danni's encouragement. She noticed her fingers relax on the dark wood of the table. She was so still, and Danni could see her mind turning inward.

"And here I am. A thirty-two-year-old, trying to figure out how to get back to the place where I lost it all," Simone lamented softly.

Simone's disclosure nestled down into her body. She abandoned her resistance and reached out to her. She placed her hand on the slender piano fingers and melted into her soft skin. She tried to call it a gesture of friendship. Simone did not pull her hand away. Words evaporated into silence that stretched out between them as wide as a canyon. Danni was unable to breathe truth into her feelings and stayed quiet instead. She watched idly as the moment drifted off into the horizon.

Simone pulled her hand away and got up. She started to clear the empty plates from the table as if they were all of her bad intentions.

Danni berated herself for making Simone feel ashamed and determined that it was time for her to go home.

"Can you bring the glasses to the kitchen?" Simone asked, mustering half a smile.

The return of sound between them was a relief. She changed her intentions and followed Simone into the kitchen with her hands full of dishes. Her eyes fell on the sway of Simone's slender hips. She watched the curve of her back and her soft hair bouncing off her shoulders. She slowed her pace to gain some distance between them, but her feelings rushed in like a tidal wave.

She quietly snuck in next to Simone and placed the glasses in the sink. She was already rinsing the plates under the gushing water.

"Are you upset with me?" she asked softly, trying to get an account of Simone's feelings. She could feel the conflict of their emotions working their way to the surface.

Simone set the plate down and turned to Danni. She grabbed her hands quickly, as if she wanted to act before she could change her mind. This time, there was no table between them. She let their fingers entwine. The nervous energy between them lit her skin on fire. The seconds ticked loudly in Danni's mind again, trying to distract her. It was a loud beating drum, deafening her to anything around them. She was aware of the rhythm of time and the feeling of fire on her skin. Her heartbeat chased after her quickening breath. It wasn't anything she could allow herself to feel unrestrained. There was a mountain of hesitation in front of her, with seemingly no way to get beyond it. Her muscles became hard as rock, and she couldn't shift her mind even an inch.

"You seem nervous."

Simone's words finally registered.

Danni's eyes were stiff as she stared into Simone's eyes. She couldn't make herself move an inch closer.

"It is because this is a nerve-racking situation, don't you think?" Danni finally said, willing a smile at Simone.

Simone nodded. Danni could feel her tug at her arms, trying to pull her closer, but she stayed back.

Simone took a step and moved closer to Danni. She stepped closer again until her lips were less than an inch from hers. She challenged her to take the final step, and Danni saw the longing in her eyes. It fell on her like rain, like a soft melody drifting through the air.

She met Simone's lips with hers, softly. She pulled her closer into the warmth of her body. She sank deeper into the softness of Simone's lips, trying to find a way to agree to the journey.

But her paranoid mind jumped back, warning her that Billie could walk in on them. Or worse, Bill. She pulled her lips away. She damned herself for her lack of judgment. Pulled the alarm for the consequences they would face for giving in to their desires. She rested her forehead on Simone's for a moment, to collect her thoughts.

"That was probably not the right thing to do," Simone said without much conviction.

"Probably not," Danni said, with an equal amount of uncertainty. "The right thing to do is not always the right thing to do."

Simone nodded.

"I know what you mean."

"We have to consider Bill. And Billie."

They both took the difficult step back from each other. Their separation felt awkward.

Danni heard the front door open.

"See?" she said.

"That is probably Bill," Simone suggested, and she started to walk out of the kitchen. Danni followed her, and they found Bill, walking into the dining room.

He was a tall man with blond buzzed-cut hair. He had a full beard and was neatly dressed in gray suit with a black button-down dress shirt. He looked more like a CIA agent than a real estate agent. He was carrying a large duffel bag uncomfortably. It was weighing his shoulder down. He looked surprised to see Danni there and seemed reluctant to engage in introductions.

"Hi, honey," Simone said. Her words made Danni cringe.

His face remained serious. Not overly thrilled to see his beautiful wife. His eyes were trying to evade hers. He offered them both a quick hello, then started walking toward the kitchen.

"Can I introduce you quickly to our guest?" Simone asked, challenging Bill to stop. He turned around and placed the duffel bag on the floor.

Danni had to force herself to look away from it.

"Hi, I'm Bill," he said. He was soft spoken, but she could tell he just wasn't all that interested in meeting her.

"I'm Danni," she countered and placed a fake smile on her face.

He looked puzzled, probably since no one explained to him why she was in his house.

"Danni took Billie out to the movies today, and I asked her to stay for dinner to thank her."

It seemed as if Simone could read Bill's mind as well as hers.

His mysterious eyes still questioned the explanation she offered.

"I wanted to offer Simone some time for herself," Danni said in reply.

He turned to Simone.

"Do you need time for yourself?" he asked, the question dripping with sarcasm.

Simone's eyes walked back and forth between Bill and Danni, but she kept her demeanor light and gracious, ignoring his cutting undertones. Danni looked at the bag on the floor again.

"Everyone needs time for themselves sometimes," Simone explained.

Bill used her statement as a lead to get back to his bag and a way to get out of their way.

"I need to get out of these clothes," he said.

They both watched as he muscled the bag back over his shoulder and headed to the stairs.

"It was nice to meet you, Bill," Danni called out after him.

He turned around briefly.

"Where do you know my wife from?" he asked.

"The music store. Where Billie is taking piano lessons."

He nodded halfheartedly and seemed eager to avoid the topic. He rushed toward the stairs. It looked like he was trying to get rid of a body, and her curiosity about its contents increased exponentially.

Danni quietly watched him disappear from their view. She picked her words carefully.

"Handsome guy," she settled on.

Simone rolled her eyes and grabbed her hand quickly. She pulled her back into the kitchen.

She whispered urgently, not letting go of her.
"I'm not sorry about what happened between us in here."
"You should be, it was wrong," Danni whispered back.
"You don't mean that."
"There is no room in your life for that kind of thing."
"I know that. But I won't regret it."

Danni could barely believe her ears. Simone was going to force her to be the sober one.

"You can't mean that, Simone. I had a wonderful day today with Billie. Please tell her that. And dinner here was so kind of you. I'm going to head home though. We both probably need to clear our heads a bit."

Simone finally surrendered and let go of her hand, but her face couldn't hide how disappointed she felt. Danni felt like a lying thief.

"Can I walk you to your car?"

She wanted to object strongly to her request, knowing what an unwise decision that would be. But she went against her better judgment and nodded.

They left the home and bounced down the steps toward the sidewalk. She fell in step next to Simone, walking close to her to let her know how hard it was for her to leave. When they approached her car, Simone reached for her hand again. Danni looked up and down the street. Surely her neighbors knew she was married.

"Do you know any of these people?" Simone asked with a smile, pointing down the street with her eyes, sensing Danni's concerns.

"We may end up as front-page news, if you keep this up," Danni joked.

"Keep what up," Simone teased, squeezing her hand.

"My offer to be your babysitter still stands," she said to change the direction of their conversation. She wanted nothing more than to pull her close and kiss her without hesitation, but the situation they were in would not afford her that luxury.

"You are going to ignore your feelings then?"
"Of course. That is what we both should do."
"You have my phone number," Simone said.
"I do."

"Don't be a stranger."

Simone pulled her close to her and hugged her, and for a moment, Danni lowered her shield and relaxed into her.

She got into her car and smiled at Simone.

"See you soon," she said through the open window before she pulled away to drive home.

When she passed Simone's house, she looked up at the second-floor windows, just to see if she could see Bill, looking down on his wife and her friend on the street. But she could find no trace of him. He was most likely dealing with the contents of the bag, somewhere in his house, away from the prying eyes of his wife and child.

She managed her way to her apartment, even though her thoughts stayed deep within the kiss with Simone in her kitchen. She was whisked away, swept up in a current. Curious to explore the new landscape in her heart. But she found it littered with flashing warnings all pointing to the exit sign.

She unlocked her apartment door and picked up the package that was delivered. It was most likely the GPS tracker she ordered. She sliced the package open and found the little device, beckoning her. She smiled and imagined herself a famous detective, hot on the trail of murderous gangsters. Like her father used to be. Her head swelled with a sense of purpose. She felt its strong pull, like a calling. She could see herself stepping into the dark night with long strides and the sole purpose of uncovering the truth. Shining a light on the treacherous underworld to bring it to justice. The exact life that her father sacrificed for the sake of the memory of his lifeless son. A penance to his wife for her enormous loss. The price he could pay, however, would never be enough.

Chapter 12

That Thursday evening, Danni was ready to put her plan into action. She had a dark outfit ready. The GPS tracker was packed. Earlier in the day, she had studied the instructions repeatedly and watched at least six YouTube videos. She was certain that she could install the device on his car and track his location on the program she installed on her phone. It was close to eleven o' clock. His shift at the bar would be winding down, and her plan needed to be fully executed before he made it back to his car.

Her mind switched to autopilot as she drove to the bar. She found a parking spot nearby where she could gather her thoughts and calm her nerves. She looked up and down the street and found that, as expected, very few people were out. It was a cloudless evening under the stars. They looked down at her as if they were cheering her on. The moon played along and shone only half of its light, knowing she needed a cover of darkness to pull this off.

Her heart was beating fast, and her mind was firing on high alert. She started the engine and started to circle the block, looking for Jake's car. There was no dedicated parking lot for the bar, so his car could be parked anywhere on the street nearby. She circled the block again and then spotted his beloved forest green 1972 Buick Skylark, parked along the street next to a lush tree. It was the only thing his father left behind when he took off. It wasn't running at the time, and Jake had been restoring it since high school. He turned it from an abandoned, stranded piece of metal into a thunderous, eye-catching beauty. It's what inspired him to work at a neighborhood auto shop part time as a teenager.

He learned everything he could about cars and how to repair them. She thought he would make a career of it. To him, it was merely a way to revive his father's presence in his life. He often boasted that when his dad came back, he would be amazed to see how he transformed the car. Jake has never been able to experience that day, but the hope for it was always somewhere in his eyes.

She couldn't find a parking spot close to his car, which meant more time on foot for her. A bigger chance to be noticed. She parked her dark gray Honda Civic on an adjacent street. She turned the lights off and checked the time. It was eleven thirty. She was fast approaching closing time. She sent a prayer up into the stars above and stepped out on to the street. It was as if the curtain lifted, and the spotlight was on her.

She took long strides and made it to his car in just under seven minutes. She looked up and down the street again. There was still no one in sight. She kneeled by the wheel well of the left back tire and shined her flashlight to find a suitable spot for the tracking device. She quickly unzipped her backpack and felt around for the little device. It was equipped with a strong magnet and could be attached easily to any piece of metal on his car. She reached into the wheel well and attached the tracker to the inside, well out of sight. She checked the phone app quickly to make sure it detected the tracker's location on its map.

Danni rushed back to her car, relieved to have part one of her mission completed without being noticed by anyone. Part two of her plan was to follow him after his shift, to make sure the tracker worked. She crossed her fingers that he wasn't planning to go straight home that night.

She sat in the car. It was midnight, which brought the end of his shift. He would need time to close the bar up and get the stragglers out. She pictured herself on a stakeout, and she regretted not bringing coffee. She watched too many police dramas as a child. In reality, she knew coffee would make her need to use the bathroom, which would certainly complicate things. There was no director calling "Action!"

and "Cut!" and her mission was far from a made-for-TV movie, complete with bathroom breaks and time in the makeup chair.

A half hour later, she detected movement on the tracker's phone app. She watched the green dot on the screen move up the street, and she started her car. She followed in the same direction, feeling exhilarated that the chase was on. She made sure to keep her distance, especially with the sparse traffic out on the streets at that hour. She followed him through quite a few neighborhoods, relieved that he didn't just go straight home. He finally parked his car in the neighborhood of Bustleton, in the northeast part of the city. The only thing she knew about that part of town was that it was home to plenty of Russian immigrants. Surely, it wasn't just another coincidence. She drove by his car to make sure he was not sitting in it. The car was empty, but she had no idea where he went. Most of the businesses on that street were already closed. About two blocks away, she finally drove by a place that looked like it had some lights on. The sign above the door said, "Red Square Tavern." She drove another two blocks down and found a place to park. She felt exposed, sitting there on the street in an unfamiliar neighborhood. She didn't have a view of anyone coming in and out of the tavern. She did a quick Google search of the place. The only information she could find was that it had a Russian owner, which did not surprise her. The menu consisted of Russian food, and they served plenty of Russian vodka. Jake never mentioned a particular love of pelmeni to her, so he certainly wasn't there because he loved Russian cuisine. She was assuming a lot, but it was the only place near his car that was still open. She remembered the ruthless eyes of the Russian man he met in the park and decided it was too risky to be a sitting duck out on the street. She opted to keep moving instead and started to circle the block. She also wanted to see who was coming in and out of the place.

The first time she circled, she saw a man dressed in a suit go in. No one was coming out. A few lights were on inside, and a stocky man came to unlock the door to let the man in. He locked the door behind them, and they both disappeared out of sight. She circled again and noticed that there was no one sitting at the tables visible through the windows. No one was there to eat at that hour. It was already close to one thirty in the morning. She drove around the block again and saw the doorman lead another suited man inside. People were going in, but not leaving. The lights were on, but the tables were empty. She looked up to the second floor of the building, but saw no lights on. They must have gone to the basement of the building then. She imagined that whoever entered that restaurant did so by invitation only. In the middle of the night. For some reason, Jake was invited to go to the basement of a Russian tavern in the middle of the night. Jake, a twenty-seven-year-old half-Irish kid from Devil's Pocket.

She finally decided to head home. He could be in there all night, and she had to go to work in the morning. He was involved in something peculiar. It's been her gut feeling ever since she saw him in the park and ever since he tried to convince her that he would pounce on every opportunity coming his way. She couldn't confront him about it again. Not without concrete evidence. She knew Peter's worry about his nephew was justified. Especially after what happened with Jake's father. Both Peter and his older brother Mark were forced to choose more responsible paths to save their family's legacy. Peter jumped ship on his dreams in New York and returned home after his father died and his youngest brother, Jack, became inaccessible to them. Mark followed suit with an equally responsible life, agreeing to keep a close eye on Jake at the bar he opened. And now this was transpiring right under their noses.

Jake turned out to be the spitting image of his father. Peter showed her a picture of his father, once while they were talking about him at the store. The resemblance between them were stark. It worried Peter. He worried that their likenesses would be more than physical. They were all just holding their breath around him. If Danni told Peter that he was frequenting a Russian bar in a Russian neighborhood in the middle of the night, where people only entered with a proper invitation, it would crush him. It was eerily similar to the life his father picked. Jake assured her countless times that all his plans were for her sake. For their future together. Marriage, kids, and a house. She felt sick to her stomach thinking about her own convoluted part in his derailment.

She arrived at her apartment well after two in the morning. She sat in her car in the parking lot, while a sea of sadness washed over her. Her premonitions were accurate, and Peter was right to fret. She didn't have anything tangible to offer him yet, which meant her mission was far from over. So far, she sensed that Jake was reenacting the sins of his father, while convincing himself he was doing it for her.

She locked her car and walked up to her apartment. She checked her phone app again and saw that his car hasn't moved an inch from where she left it.

Chapter 13

"Hi, Mom, how are you?"

Danni found her mother sitting at the kitchen table. She kissed her on the cheek and noticed her hiding her phone quickly, face down on the table.

"Hi, Danni. Why the happy face today?" her mom asked.

"Oh, my sad face took a sick day," she fibbed. There was no way she could admit that the real reason for her flushed face was the unexpected text she received from Simone right before she walked into her dreary childhood home.

"I miss you already," the text said.

Her heart bucked up instantly before she could pull the reigns.

"I know the feeling," she wrote back, picking her words carefully, pulling back.

The dinner at Simone's lingered in her mind. She had to temper her heart in favor of friendship, but the kiss they shared in her kitchen was difficult to ignore. Her guilty conscious raged on about Simone being married with a child to raise. She urged herself to stay focused on Jake instead. Mend their relationship somehow. Forget about the feeling of Simone's lips on hers and heed to the multitude of warning signs lighting up the sky around them.

"What are you doing?" Simone asked.

"I just arrived at my parents' house for dinner."

"You're a good daughter, Danni. I want to meet them some time," Simone responded.

Danni had no idea how she would ever make that leap in her life. She pictured a far-off day in the future, walking into her childhood home, holding Simone's hand. But the dream quickly turned sour as they found Jake and her parents sitting at the table, pounding their fists with sneering eyes. She couldn't fling the chilling image away quick enough.

"Maybe one day," she said, despite feeling hopeless about their prospects.

"I'll hold you to it."

Simone had way more courage.

"I know you will."

Wanting something she couldn't have was demoralizing.

"My daughter's happy face makes me wonder," her mother said, pulling her back to their conversation.

"I don't know what you're talking about," she teased.

"All right then, I can tell you don't want to clue me in. You have always been such a secretive child," she said, easing down.

"I can ask you the same thing, you know," Danni said.

She knew she should have accepted her mother's resignation, but she had a nagging feeling that something was brewing with her. She quit her second job last week and transformed her tired gray locks into a youthful sea of caramel. It surely wasn't aimed at getting her father's attention.

"Whatever do you mean?" her mother teased back.

"That color looks great on you. Very impressive."

"New hairdresser over at Fabio's. He said he couldn't stand old ladies with gray hair, and he was on a mission to dye every gray head of hair that came across his station."

She wished her father could follow suit and allow a makeover of his own. Or at least just come out of his room for a different reason than going to the liquor store. She wished they could sit around a table for a meal again. Hold hands and say grace for the blessings in their life. She has been nursing that pipe dream for over twenty years.

"Are you sure that is how that happened?" she pushed.

Her mother's eyes turned away. They weren't used to debating the mechanics of her inner life. They've spent years filling the rooms with quiet mystery, keeping the walls between them dense. The bonds between them were just loose strands of obligation. And yet, she came back there every week, hoping to find a way to reconnect. To her, it was a rescue mission of people taken hostage by their past. The door to her father's room has remained shut. Bolted down actually. With many different locks and combination codes. None of which she had the answers to. At least her mother was seated at the kitchen table in plain sight. An easier target, but no less elusive.

She looked over to the kitchen counter and saw another scrumptious chocolate cake on display. It's become a trademark of her new life these days.

"I hope that cake is on the menu tonight!" she said, pointing her eyes to the cake.

"It's an absolute hit at the bakery. It's literally flying off the shelves, but I managed to snatch this one right before we opened this morning."

"What is in it?"

"Lots of sugar and chocolate. Mostly everything that is bad for you, but people simply can't get enough of it."

Danni recognized her mother's depiction of life itself.

"You guys can call it life as a cake," Danni said and laughed.

Her mother answered with a puzzled face.

"You seem to really like your job there," Danni detoured, still fishing for clues.

She remembered the years that her mother stopped by the house just long enough for a quick change of clothes. Her jobs have always been the perfect escape for her.

"I love having just one job to go to."

"Whatever will you do with all your free time now?"

"Spend time with my children finally. If only my son didn't move light-years away."

Her mother has been scorned by her brother's decision to flee the wrath of their existence. She was also jealous of his good luck, but today, regret spilled out in her gaze. She surely has never been blind to her role in their family's destruction. Danni would not walk away from forging a bridge to her somehow. She decided not to challenge her mother's sneering remark.

"Do you need help with dinner?" she asked instead.

"No, I have pork chops resting in the oven and mashed potatoes on the stove. I just need to put some veggies in the microwave. I'm keeping it simple tonight."

"Do you want me to see if Dad wants to come down?" Danni asked. It was mostly out of habit, and she knew it would take more than a miracle to get him to the table. Her mother looked at her, unable to conceal the guilt she felt.

"You know he won't, Danni."

It was her usual response, and Danni sensed that she had no hope for him to change.

She backed down again. She wanted to keep the air light and focused on her mother instead. She sensed that it was where the real mystery was unfolding.

Her mom got up and walked to the freezer to get the bag of vegetables out. She ripped it open and emptied it into a glass bowl. She pushed the microwave door shut and tapped hard on the keypad to set the timer for six minutes. For her mother, thinking about her father has always petrified the softness right out of her face and turned her nimble culinary fingers into sharp sticks.

Her mother's phone buzzed, and she rushed over to the table to pick it up. She looked at the screen keeping a cool face. She didn't respond to the message. She simply tucked her phone away in her apron's pocket and walked over to the stove to stir the potatoes. Danni, however, didn't miss the slight upward pull at the corners of her mouth while she busied herself in front of the stove.

"Can you get some plates out?" she asked. "I will make a plate for your father so you can take it up to him."

She willed her legs into action to get out of her head. She dialed her disappointment down to a less painful level, to where she could accept the reality of it and ignore the anger boiling under her skin.

She went to her father's room with the food her mother plated for him. She made no attempt to coax him out. She didn't add any garnish or spices. She didn't even include a slice of the chocolate cake. Danni listened to the creaking floorboards under her feet in the hallway. She was taking a prisoner his meal in an old, abandoned castle with ghosts hiding around each corner. The doors whined, and the wind rattled the windowpanes. The haunted house whispered constantly like it was angry. Like her mother used to be. She never knew if it was real or if it was simply her perception of it. Sometimes, the house felt downright wicked, slamming doors to rip through the quiet. The wind would rush through the walls and bring a chill into the hallway. The house bottled its misery and poured it over all of them.

She remembered her older brother's life while he lived there. He relied on the kindness of strangers most of the time, but for short stints, he would come home on a drug binge. Confined to his room for days, infected with anguish. Consumed by anger for their parents and addicted to it. Eventually, in a quiet daze, he would disappear into his pain. A weathered ball of weakness that made him look exactly like his father. It infuriated their mother. She would call him worthless and throw him out countless times. They wouldn't see him for weeks, but he would inevitably return, because her mother kept money in the tin on top of the kitchen cupboard. It was a foolproof way to lure him back. She was just as addicted to her anger. Their cycle of abuse carried on for years until the universe finally sent him a savior. Sarah pulled him out of the burning wreckage of his life. She found him homeless on the streets. She picked him up and whisked him miles away to New Orleans, along with her father's ministry group. It left her mother without her favorite punching bag.

Danni knocked on her father's door. There was no movement coming from the room. She knocked several more times, but didn't hear a sound. She turned the knob, and to her surprise, the door swung open. He lay on the bed, curled up in a ball, and asleep. She saw the half-empty bottle of whiskey on the floor next to the bed. Her heart fell to her feet at the sight of him. It looked like he hadn't bathed since she last saw him. She looked over to the table and saw none of the wooden carvings out on display. She walked over to the empty table and opened the drawer. The figurines and tools were carelessly shoved inside. She closed it quietly, careful not to disturb him. The room smelled stuffy, but the noise from the street through an opened window would interrupt the rest he clearly needed.

Tears welled up in her eyes, and she wiped them away quickly with the back of her hand. She looked over to the small table in front of the window. It held a camera with a long zoom lens. Next to it was a pair of binoculars. She looked at her father again, defeated and hazed. She wondered if he saw something. Something that pained him. She turned around and walked out. She didn't leave the plate of food for him. From experience with her brother, she knew he wasn't in a place where he would nourish himself. She closed the door quietly behind her and tiptoed down the steps back and walked back to the kitchen.

She found her mother, engrossed in a texting conversation on her phone. She put the phone down as soon as she saw her come in. She questioned the plate still in her hands.

"He's not hungry?"

"Apparently not," she said and shoved the plate into the fridge.

"You should have left it there."

"Should we be worried about him drinking so much these days?"

"These days?"

"It seems more now."

"I don't have the answers about your father, Danni."

"He needs help though. He looks like he's down as far as you can go."

"In the end, people have to help themselves."

Danni sat down at the table feeling defeated. Her mother's words were as merciless as it was true. She couldn't remember seeing her ever trying to help him. She was different with her father than with Robbie, but equally as destructive. The cold apathy toward her father was just as damaging as the blazing fire spewed at her brother. She used to be so different when Mattie was still alive. Before her pain turned into anger. She would never admit it, but it transformed all of them. In the same way her father's guilt did. They still lived under the spell of it.

Her mother dished the pork chops into their plates. She served herself some mashed potatoes and then handed the bowl to her. Danni looked at her arm stretched out to her across the table. Like a peace offering for all the years of pain she caused. She accepted the gift and settled into her gaze, searching for a way to connect. A place of honesty to start healing the broken bond between them.

"I met someone very interesting recently," she said after she scooped the potatoes onto her plate.

"Really? Where?"

She didn't have any idea what else she expected her mother to say.

She took a deep breath.

"A pianist from Peekskill. She came into the store, looking for a piano teacher for her daughter."

Her mother placed her fork down on her plate and pondered Danni's announcement. She shifted around on her chair.

"Is she interesting because she is rich?"

"No. She is just very charming. And beautiful."

Her mother glared at her.

"Lessons for her daughter? Is she also married?" she finally asked.

"Unfortunately, she is."

She stayed quiet again and took a few more bites of her vegetables.

"I feel like you are trying to tell me something without telling me," her mother said cautiously.

Danni suddenly felt lost in her own confession. She didn't have a road map for it. It was a desperate, foolish attempt at honesty and connection. It left her stranded in a foreign place, riddled with landmines. She remembered the anger her mother was capable of, crushing Robbie under her sharp insults. She searched frantically for the exit sign.

"It would have been easier if she weren't married," she said finally. She begged herself to stand tall against her mother's reaction. She didn't avert her eyes. She didn't collapse her shoulders.

"I could have sworn you wanted Jake in your life as a partner. Was I wrong?"

"I'm not sure about that anymore."

"He knows this?"

"No. It's a recent development."

Her mother started eating again as if she needed time to absorb the blow. Danni was surprised at how calm she remained after the bombshell she dropped.

"Still, you said she was married," her mother said as if she was slapping a trump card down on the pile.

Danni decided to raise the bet.

"Marriages are complicated, as you know," she offered while keeping her poker face intact. It was not a good time to back down or show weakness. Her mother was known to be emboldened by any signs of weakness.

Her mother stared at her inquisitively. Surely checking her face for any signs of fear.

"Yes, they are. You have never mentioned to me before that you were interested in women in that way. So I'm just surprised."

"We don't usually discuss personal matters."

"And yet you decided today, over a plate of pork and potatoes, that you would bring this to my attention?"

Danni couldn't help but laugh at her mother's counterattack.

"Seeing all that trouble that you went through with the meal, I figured, what better time to fill you in about the calamity that I'm dealing with. The perfect way to make small talk."

"You think this is making small talk? It's nothing?"

"I should have brought a bottle of bubbly to celebrate my coming out, but I know how you feel about alcohol."

"Danni, you can make fun all you want. But I don't know what to say. I probably can't blame you. Me and your father made such a mess of our marriage. You're probably terrified to get married yourself. This could simply be a way to avoid getting into a similar mess."

Danni was surprised that her mother opted for a reasonable explanation, instead of merely flinging insults.

"Women can get married these days, you know?"

"Not if one is already married."

"I don't think I want to marry Jake, regardless of how things turn out with Simone."

"Simone. It's a nice name. I hope she doesn't break your heart, Danni, because that name will be hard for you to forget. Is she showing the same interest in you?"

"I think so. She even kissed me."

"Then you better hope her husband is not a jealous jerk."

"I met him, and I won't say he is a puppy dog."

"She won't get out of her marriage easily. And you said she has a child to consider in all of this."

"Speaking of marriage, Mom, do you think there is any way yours could be mended?"

Her mother's face hardened instantly. Danni knew it was a low blow.

"Danni, a marriage can be ripped to pieces and still be hard to get out of. Sometimes impossible. You need to realize that. Just because she smacked lips with you doesn't mean she wants a divorce."

"Did you have any doubts before you married Dad?"

"Not an ounce of doubt. But we took our marriage for granted. We choked the life out of it and turned it into the nightmare that it is today. We did that. Chose that, among all the better choices we had available to us."

"Why not just end it then?"

"You can only walk away when you are ready to. It's the pain of it that is hard to leave. Have you seen how many people in this world are hopelessly addicted to pain? Pain comes very easy, and it's just as easy to inflict. And that is powerful."

Danni sat and looked at her mother in silence. She pushed back as she felt her words strangle her heart. She would never want that way of life for Simone. Or herself.

"Maybe the best thing you could do would be to set each other free."

Her mother seemed battered from the honesty between them. As if she suffered over-exposure. She got up and took a direct escape route to the cake on the counter as if it was a safe house. Danni has lost her appetite for it, but she didn't want to ruin the effort it took to get where they were.

She came back with two slices of cake, looking as proud as if she baked it herself. Danni would grant her the much-needed reprieve from their conversation.

"The special cake," Danni announced, when she placed the plate down in front of her.

"It's a Max special," her mother said, unable to hide the burst of light shooting into her eyes as soon as she said his name.

It hit Danni all at once. The light in her eyes when she looked at the cake. The curl of her lips when she stirred the potatoes at the stove. She undoubtedly had feelings for Max. Danni's brain compulsively connected the dots. The recent raise, the new hairdo, and the secretive texting. She drowned in disbelief as she thought about her father, lying upstairs in a river of despair. She remembered the camera and the binoculars near his window. He must have noticed the change in her too. His suspicious mind surely hasn't completely ceased to function. Her mother has left the marriage. Not legally, but she has checked out of it. If she fell in love with Max now, it would surely slam the nails into the coffin.

Danni needed time to comb through the details of her discovery and decided against bombarding her mother about it.

She took the first bite of the cake and knew exactly why it flew off the shelves. The cake was perfect. Sweet, moist, and full of flavor, enticing her to visit the bakery to meet Max. She was curious to see if he was anything like the desserts he made. To see if she could sense any chemistry with her mother. For all she knew, her mother's crush could be completely unrequited. Pining for love and just harping on him to find it.

"Do you think you would be willing to meet the pianist?" she asked, remembering Simone's request and subconsciously at least, she strived to make all her dreams come true.

Her mother laid her fork down, her mouth still sweet from the cake.

"About you and the pianist, Danni. Nowadays it's not that unusual anymore. I see that kind of thing all the time at the bakery.

All kinds of couples come in there. The trouble is not that she is a woman. The trouble is that she is married, and most husbands are jealous. She also has a child. If it's a woman you want in your life, I think you should look for one that is available to you."

"I didn't go looking for anything like this. It came looking for me."

"It still sounds like trouble to me."

"At least you know now that a marriage between me and Jake would be doomed from the start. I know you like him a lot."

"If you tend to fall in love with girls, you will never be faithful to Jake. You should save him the agony of going through that."

Her mother was right; she could feel it in her bones. Even more since she has met Simone. She could never stay faithful to him if she was honest with herself. The failure of her parents' marriage was loud in her ears, and it never faced any of the red flags she was dealing with. Being married to Jake would feel like being buried in quicksand.

She took a breath, then took the last bite of her cake, and she realized that her mother has already escaped to the sink to start washing the dishes. Her hands moved deftly, as if she was eager to go somewhere else.

"Are you going somewhere?" she asked, realizing that her mother has reached her limit.

"No, baby. I have to get to the bakery early. Max reminded me that we're baking for a big wedding order tomorrow. It will be a long day on my feet, so I need to turn in soon."

"The cake was delicious. He'd be inundated if he doesn't stop baking cakes that delicious."

Her mother's face brightened again, and Danni was more in tune to it now. If he could soften her eyes like that and put the warmth back in her veins, she would love to remind her that her marriage was only paper thin.

"I'm learning a lot there. I don't mind the long days now."

"I'm happy for you. It seems like a good fit."

Her mother kept rinsing the dishes as she stared out of the window. The image of her eyes in the window reflected all that was good in her. So different from the stark eyes spewing venom at their family for as long as she can remember.

When Danni left the house, she glanced up at the second floor to see if her dad was guarding his window. He could easily see anyone close to the house from there. He could see far in either direction up the street, even farther if he used the binoculars. She wouldn't expect her mother to be careless enough to meet Max close to the house. But then again, Simone found a way to lure her into her house despite all the warning signs. She orchestrated it masterfully. Where there was a will, there was a way, and people in love don't see the forest for the trees. People in love would often risk swimming in shark-infested waters. The way that she blindly risked following her boyfriend into a lion's den.

Her life was hard to recognize. As if she was trapped in a video game, challenged to conquer countless obstacles in her quest to win it all. In the game of love, there was no room for crippling fear or hesitation.

Chapter 14

Danni was at her usual post at the store, sitting at her desk behind the sales counter. She was engrossed in the Beethoven piano concertos that streamed through her headphones. She was captivated by Simone's most cherished music. She was just starting to enjoy the soothing string lines of the Adagio un poco, when Peter approached her. She pressed Pause and removed the earbuds.

"How is it going?" he asked, his body resembling an overly taut string. She assumed he wanted to talk about Jake.

"It's quiet out here. I was just enjoying Beethoven's fifth piano concerto."

"That is a new interest for you?" he asked, looking puzzled.

She offered a candid smile.

"One of many these days."

"That is what I wanted to ask about. Not the music. I wanted to ask about Jake. Were you able to find some answers?"

She was torn about how honest she wanted to be with him.

"Still piecing things together."

"Anything promising?"

His eyes became more insistent, backing her into a corner. She ventured carefully, trying to sidestep his line of questioning.

"He goes to a place after work for a few hours sometimes. I don't know exactly what for yet."

"Where? I mean, this would be after midnight, right?"

"I'm not a hundred percent sure, but I think he went to a bar in Bustleton."

The lines between his eyes deepened. He chewed on the side of his lip.

"That is odd. I can't think of anyone we know in that neighborhood."

"Maybe he met someone at the bar. He probably meets new people every day there."

"He hasn't mentioned anybody specific to you?"

"No, nothing specific."

"He goes to the same place all the time?" he asked. His mind was knee deep in drawing conclusions.

"As far as I can tell."

"Do you think we should just point blank ask him what he is doing in Bustleton every night?"

"He would be upset that we were spying on him. And I think he would lie to us."

"What do you think we should do?"

"I think we need to be patient. If he simply keeps this up, there's no harm done. He may just go there every night after work to blow off some steam."

"Why would he be so secretive about it if it's nothing?"

"I don't know. I have a hunch that he's gambling there and losing money."

Danni was far more intrigued than bothered by his recent pattern, but it was clear that Peter didn't share her indifference.

"Has he come by again to ask for money?" she asked.

"No. I assume his car has been fixed and the rent has been paid."

"All is well then," Danni said flippantly, hoping to put him at ease. She didn't plan on letting Jake off the hook, but she needed more evidence before she could close the book on him. He was always a risk taker, and trouble had a way to multiply the longer you entertained it. She had an inkling that he was mingling with a menacing group of people. He made it clear that he wanted to get his hands on more money. She wasn't sure if there was any truth to his uncle's offer to buy into the bar, but she knew he was craving a more comfortable life at least. A life different from the life he had growing up. And he's had plenty of luck landing him on his feet, a fact that has only ever encouraged him.

"Let's do it your way then. Keep an eye on him for a little while longer. Maybe I'm just paranoid."

"I will let you know if something changed with his routine."

"Thank you, Danni. I really appreciate your help. If there is any way I can repay you, please just let me know."

Asking Peter for a favor regarding the auditions has crossed her mind, but she has placed a bet with herself that it wouldn't require a favor from Peter for Simone to land the accompaniment position.

"How has it been going with the auditions?" she fished.

"Average. Painfully average so far."

"It can only get better then," she joked to lift his mood.

He finally calmed the frown etched between his brow and grinned at her.

"You have clearly been in better spirits these days. I need some of your vibes," he said and smiled at her.

His charm amplified tenfold when he smiled.

It was clearly obvious to everyone then. According to those who knew her best, her cheerless disposition has wavered inexplicably. It wasn't because she was nearing a decision about picking a career for her life. Her parents' marriage was still a complete failure. Jake was still spiraling down into a life of crime according to her rich imagination. Yet somehow, she felt as if her life was ignited by a warm light. She wasn't blind to the reason for it, even though she wasn't brave enough to call it out. Except strangely, to her mother.

"I'm counting my blessings these days," she said, hoping that he would ease his prodding.

He looked at her with a softness in his eyes.

"I should do the same, I suppose. I should let this anxiety about Jake go and focus on the good things that are going on."

"Yes. There is a lot of good stuff going on. A whole season of young, budding artists right under your nose."

He sighed.

"The season for them can be so nerve-racking. What would really help is finding a good piano player for them. Or this whole season is going to be a nightmare."

She looked at him. He was more nervous than Simone. Yet he was able to push his students to do better than they ever expected. She attended one of the local music competitions for a day last year where two of his students performed, and she was astonished at how well they played. He was a basket case the entire day. Simone could bring a calm presence that would benefit him and his students immensely.

"You need the Yin to your Yang," she said, making him laugh.

"Are you saying I should look for a female piano player this year?"

"Someone to balance out your edginess, maybe."

"You know me very well, Danni. And nothing passes by your watchful eyes."

She considered it a compliment, even though she didn't know many edgy people who would like to be under anyone's watchful eyes. She has developed a very meticulous personality. Spending hours studying people and memorizing their distinguishing features. Turning the memories into a hard copy on paper. She could only attribute it to her mistrust in people. She felt safest at a distance. Amid her father's seclusion and her mother's busy work schedule, she became a very lonely child. Passively, painfully observant. Now, when she thought about her late-night excursions to track the whereabouts of her boyfriend, she was exhilarated by the courage it took to allow herself to push the boundaries. She felt like a moth drawn to a flame.

Danni's eyes moved back to Peter. He was still standing in front of her, watching her. She felt embarrassed for letting her mind wander off.

A customer approached the counter with a few items, and Peter tapped his fingers on the counter.

"Like I said, keep me posted with any new developments," he said and turned toward the studios at the back of the store.

Danni looked at the items the young woman in front of her picked out. She usually would have stayed cordial and checked her items out in silence.

"Are you taking lessons with Marius here?" she asked, trying to connect this time.

She just nodded. She was shy, and Danni knew it would be to her detriment as a musician.

"He is a great teacher, don't you think?" she asked again, trying to break through some of the ice.

"Yes, he is."

Her response was still reserved, and Danni pressed one more time.

"What are you going to work on this year?"

"I really want to get a spot in the youth orchestra. I'm going to do an audition for that soon, and I hope I get in. I have a friend that already got a spot, so I hope I make it this time."

"What do you think you'll play for the audition?"

"I don't know. Marius suggested I do a Bach or Mozart concerto."

"You're buying the Brahms sonatas here."

The girl flashed a big smile, proving her weakened defenses from Danni's persistence.

"I know. It's not for the audition. They are just so beautiful. I can't wait to work on them."

"They really are beautiful. Who is your favorite violin player? Other than Marius, of course," she asked, glad that the girl had abandoned most of her bashfulness.

"I like Hillary Hahn."

"What do you like about her?"

"She never makes any mistakes," she said after contemplating an answer for a while.

Danni smiled and placed the books carefully in a paper bag and handed her the change.

"Good luck with your audition. I really hope you get in. Although I'm sure you will."

She smiled and put the change in her wallet.

"Thank you," she added.

She turned around and walked away, but not without Danni noticing the nervous bounce in her step. It was the same bounce Billie had when she walked. These kids needed confidence and a belief that they could make it. With the right guidance, the future was full of possibilities for all of them.

Chapter 15

Danni did not expect anyone to visit her that Saturday morning. She had gotten up early, thinking she would seize the day. She had big plans to follow Jake that evening and into the night. She was cleaning a few dishes when, unexpectedly, the doorbell rang. Simone didn't know her address, so it could only be one person. She hasn't seen Jake in a while. They've exchanged apologies for the dinner disaster, but after that, they have walked on eggshells, resorting mostly to texts.

When she opened the door, she found him standing there, shoulders pushed back and wearing his most confident smile. He held a bouquet of flowers out to her while his eyes begged her to accept his offer of truce.

She opened the door wider to let him in. He obviously rushed over, not even taking the time to shave. She was getting used to the constant stubble on his face and considered it a side effect of all his late nights in Bustleton. She remembered Peter's plea to keep an eye on him and didn't want to start an argument. She gave his scruffy mouth a kiss and took the flowers from his hand. He followed her to the kitchen sink to rescue the flowers with some water. He seemed relaxed, and there was more bravado in his step. He must have had a good night at the tables. And he probably also noticed the white flag she raised.

"I didn't think you'd be up this early."

"You wanted to give me flowers in bed?" she teased.

"That was the plan," he said with a mischievous grin.

"I figured you had a reason for buying them," she said, but she regretted the sarcastic tone that snuck into her voice. She pleaded with herself to go easy on him.

He walked up behind her at the sink while she filled a vase with water. She could smell alcohol and cigarettes on his breath when he threw his arms around her waist and pressed his muscular body into hers. She realized that he probably came over straight from the Red Square Tavern.

"I just wanted to show you how much you mean to me."

"Thank you, Jake. I really appreciate them."

She wiggled out of his tight embrace and walked over to the dining table to set the flowers on display.

"How about we crawl back in bed for a while?"

His request was direct. She would have a difficult time to evade his advances that morning. He obviously came over with the intention to reconnect physically. She was grateful for his busy work schedule, keeping the sexual encounters between them to a minimum. She had no confidence that she could finagle out of it that morning.

Her brain left her body as she smiled at him and started walking over to the bedroom. Halfway to the room, she threw her shirt off. He picked up his pace to keep up with her all the way to the bedroom. He wrestled her playfully onto the bed, and they fell into their old, familiar routine.

Danni's mind wandered off throughout, while Jake seemed more focused on the act than on her. Her mind meandered around her plans for that evening. She was determined to see where he went when he left the Tavern, which meant that she was in for a long night. She has been wired with anticipation since waking up just past the crack of dawn that morning.

Jake picked up the pace, and Danni sensed that he would finish up soon. Sweat dripped off him onto her skin, and she flinched from the smell of beer on his breath. He moved her head to face him and willed her to look into his eyes. He stopped abruptly when she closed her eyes to avoid his eye contact.

"Danni! Can you look at me?"

She opened her eyes and saw his face, inches away from her.

"What are you talking about? Why did you stop?"

"Are you with me?"

His question frustrated her. She was right underneath him, breathing heavily. Trying to sound as convincing as he did. It was hardly the best time to strike up a conversation.

She looked up at him and smiled.

"Yes, baby, I'm right here. Keep going."

He started rocking on top of her again, and she let out a silent sigh of relief. She forced herself to keep her attention on him since he seemed unusually diligent that morning.

When they finally finished, him into his condom and without the eye contact he demanded, she pushed him off her body. She was mixed with satisfaction and relief. She stayed silent and listened to his breath slowing down as he lay next to her. Neither of them said anything as the sound of traffic outside her window filled the air.

He finally looked over to her.

"I love you, Danni," he said softly.

"I love you too, Jake."

"For real?"

"Nah, I usually hop in bed with any old stranger off the street," she teased.

"It's just, you haven't been in touch a lot lately. I've started to worry, you know? About us."

"There's nothing to worry about, Jake. Nothing at all. I've just been busy, the same as you."

"You still think we'll get married some time?"

Danni cringed. She hated these overbearing conversations with him. It was not as if she could admit to him that she never thought about getting married. That she was content with the way things were. That she didn't even trust that he could keep himself out of prison for the rest of his life. To her, he has started to resemble his father so much. The real kicker was that she couldn't admit that she has developed feelings for a woman who wandered into her life out of nowhere. That she wanted to explore those feelings instead of having sex with him. She would spare him the gory details and spare herself the temper tantrum that would follow.

"Of course, we'll get married. When the time is right, you know?"

"I know. I know. It takes a lot of money for all the things that come with marriage. But I'm working on it. Making progress, you'll see."

"I know, Jake. You have been working a lot. It's good."

"Things have been good there. I make a lot in tips, and I'm saving every penny."

"Are you sure you haven't just been spending it on that flashy car of yours?" she joked.

He smiled. Jake possibly loved his car more than he loved her, but he would never say it.

"I'm saving for a ring just as flashy as that car."

"I don't need anything that flashy."

"You'll want a house, I'm sure of that."

"Maybe just a bigger apartment."

"We need room for kids, Danni. An apartment won't do."

"I'm sure kids won't be for quite a while."

"You're not getting any younger. We don't have all the time in the world."

"I think we have plenty of time."

He looked over at her again. She was sure he was used to her rebuttals by now.

"Why are you fighting me so much?" he asked, keeping his tone soft.

"I'm just being realistic. You have such big dreams. I like to keep things simple."

He smiled.

"Good then. You keep things real down here and leave the dreaming to me. If we land somewhere in the middle of that, we should be good, right?"

She nodded. He seemed satisfied with the compromise.

They laid in silence again, and she gave in to the temptation to get real with him. She considered it a minor retribution for the sex.

"Peter said you had a hard time paying your rent last month."

IN THE SCATTERING OF LIGHT

She made sure to breathe slowly and stay close to his reaction. She didn't want things to spin out of control this time. His smile disappeared instantly, and his eyes filled with the same suspicion she saw the night of the dinner.

"What?" he said finally. "Why would he tell you about that?"

She could tell that he felt cornered.

"I don't know. He said he was worried about you. That you went to his mom's house drunk, asking for rent money. He said you looked very stressed out and that you told him that your car broke down, which took all the rent money to fix."

She stayed calm, breathing slowly in and out as she gauged how much further she could push.

He shook his head slowly, and his face was covered in disbelief. He fell silent, scurrying around his mind looking for an alibi. She had obviously blindsided him.

"He just wanted to know if I knew anything about your car troubles," she said carefully.

He glared at her, giving her time to elaborate. He didn't offer an explanation.

"I fibbed and told him I knew about your car, but nothing about the rent issues."

He suddenly sat up at the edge of the bed. He squeezed his head between his hands. She expected him to shut down as usual, but she was satisfied that he was at least made aware that he underestimated her level of awareness about the details of his life. She couldn't let him think that she was totally oblivious.

"It took a lot for me to go to him for help. He used to be way more helpful to me, but he has gotten so stingy. Probably really loved to see me grovel."

"What was wrong with your car?"

"Huh? My car? I don't know, Danni, it needed a new muffler. What's all this questioning again?"

"It didn't have anything to do with your car then?"

"It doesn't matter what I tell you, really. You won't believe me anyway."

"How about just telling the truth?"

"Okay, detective smarty-pants. A friend needed money. I helped them out, so I figured Peter could help me out in return. I'm sure he makes a fortune at that store my grandfather left him."

Danni could sense his blood seeping into the water. She wanted to close in on him, but she doubted he would surrender more. All she had was rumors from Peter. And assumptions based on the few times she followed him. It wasn't enough.

"What friend, Jake? What's his name?"

"What makes you think it's a guy?"

His answer surprised her. He has never insinuated infidelity before, but clearly, he was desperate to get her off his back.

"So your lady friend needed money. That is what you're going with this time?"

He just stared at her, looking for the right words to hit her with.

"Yes. That is what I'm going with," he said with raised eyebrows and a squared jaw. Words have never been his strong suit.

"What for? Is she saving up for a ring for her boyfriend as well?"

"Very funny, Danni. No. She needed money for rent. Is that complicated enough for you? Or are you going to keep digging?"

Danni just kept staring at the ceiling. She pulled the sheets up over her chest. He gave her another glimpse of how short his fuse has become every time she challenged him. He has changed into something far different from the schoolboy she fell in love with. He used to be a good kid. He used to work hard at being different from his father.

He looked back at her, as she kept her eyes fixed on the ceiling, a white canvas on which a different world could unfold. His eyes softened and pleaded with her. He reached out to her hands and loosened her grip on the sheet.

"I feel like you don't trust me anymore, Danni."

She looked over at him. He was right. She couldn't uncouple him from his lies. She felt less willing to oblige his deceptions. She didn't believe that he was just dreaming big, no matter how hard he tried to convince her. To her, he was becoming who he has been all along. He was finally coming into his own, and she didn't recognize him.

"Do you want me to tell Peter that there's no reason to worry about you?"

"There is no reason to worry about me. I have everything under control, I swear."

She could imagine his father saying the exact same words to his mother, right before he was chased out of town by a group of gangsters.

"What's your plans for the rest of the day?" he asked, changing the subject deliberately.

He lay back down next to her to see what captured her eyes on the ceiling.

"Laundry. Maybe going to the park."

"Which park?"

"Rittenhouse. To get some sun. Have you been there recently?"

"No, you know I don't hang out in the parks. Way too crowded these days. I don't know how you stand it."

She wouldn't confront him with the fact that it was the same park she caught him settling his debts. Questioning him bared no fruit.

"Sometimes, a crowd is just the place to go unnoticed in."

"Why would I want to go unnoticed?"

He smiled and waved his hand from his chin all the way down to his knees. "This body is way too good-looking to go unnoticed."

She smiled, rolled on her side, and reached out to his chest. She stroked his skin lightly, finally waving her white flag. It was getting late, and she needed to change the mood between them. They have become too comfortable waging war. She was happy that for once, he was telling the truth. Jake was indeed a very handsome man. He sensed what she offered and leaned over to kiss her mouth again, slowly this time. She closed her eyes and surrendered. She met his lips with her tongue, inviting him into her warm mouth. He shifted closer to her. She kept the kiss going, glad to put the disagreement behind them. He moved on top of her, and she pulled her legs up around his hips, giving in to his heartbeat quickening and the rhythm of his hips as he pushed inside of her again.

Chapter 16

As soon as Jake left, Danni felt restless. She wanted to erase their encounter from her mind. She opened the fridge. Her eyes found the beers instantly. They were usually in there for Jake, but today, she needed them to dull the swell of guilt thrashing her mind. She reached for two of them and went to sit on her couch. She could feel her leg muscles twitch as her heart accelerated to push adrenaline into her bloodstream. She scowled at the flowers on the dining table. She had to squint to stomach their biting intensity. She poured the bitter liquid down her throat as if she was trying to douse a fire. She finished the first bottle in one swoop and uncapped the second. She savored the bitterness of it on her tongue. Took another couple of swigs until she finally felt the numbing sensation saturate her veins. She tried to refocus her gaze on the blaze of color emanating from the flowers on the table, but her eyes skidded off. She could still feel her nerve endings scrape against their brashness, making her gulp more of the bitter brew in her hand.

She kept guzzling from the bottle to dampen her senses. Her stomach felt as if it wanted to burst, and she set the bottle on the table next to her. Her jaw clamped up, and she felt the sting of disappointment rising from her belly into her throat. It turned into a wave of disgust, rushing upward, trying to suffocate her. She walked over to the vase on the dining table. Her breathing rushed forward as she glared at the galling gift from Jake. She grabbed the vase and shut her eyes, gripping tight around it as if she wanted to strangle it. Every time she opened her eyes, a jarring, penetrating light shot into her skull. Her head started to throb. She lifted the vase high over her head and spiked it down hard. She watched the porcelain shatter into a sea of tiny shards. The water splashed out over the floor and rushed into the cracks between the floorboards. Her eyes filled with tears at the sight of her crushing anger. She clenched down hard on her teeth and collapsed down to her knees. She let the sobs rip through her and lay her head down on the floor among the broken pieces. Tears streamed down her face and dripped down on to the floor. She counted five shallow breaths going in and out of her lungs, racing away from her. When she couldn't catch them, she stopped breathing. She held her breath in and pushed herself down into the floor. She pursed her lips shut as tight as she could and pinched her nose hard. She held her breath and counted slowly. She clenched down even harder on her teeth. She made it to thirty before she finally took a big gulp of air in defeat and allowed her lungs to fill. She had hoped that she would pass out, but her adrenaline-filled body wouldn't let her get there.

She would need to find another way to expunge her memory. She reached out and picked up one of the broken pieces of porcelain in her hand. She squeezed it hard into the palm of her hand. She could feel the sharp edge of it cut through her skin. She pressed harder, letting the pain of it flow into her mind. She let up for a moment, moved the shard to a different position and tightened her grip around it again. She kept slicing her skin, feeling more and more relief as the pain pulsed through her hand and fingers. She kept splitting her skin open to let the blood drain out of her, as if she was releasing toxins. She opened her eyes and watched the blood drip down onto the floor. She panicked suddenly and flung the bloody weapon into the far corner of the room. She curled her fingers into a fist to stop the bleeding and settled her mind deep into the throbbing pain pulsing through her hand. An airy feeling of joy washed over her as she sank further into the burning refuge. Her breathing finally slowed down, and she felt a warmth spread through her whole body. Her hand relaxed into the ache of it as it lay heavy on the floor next to her, and she slowly drifted off into sleep.

When she woke up, her eyes slowly tracked around the room. She scanned until she found the clock on the cable box. It was just past noon. She looked at the display of anger scattered around her on the floor. She looked at the dried blood in the palm of her hand. The drops of blood smeared into the floor. The feeling of joy she remembered right before she fell asleep was gone.

She got up slowly and dragged herself to the kitchen sink. She ran cold water over the cuts, thankful that she didn't escalate and cut into her arms the way she used to. She wrapped a clean dishtowel around her palm, then grabbed the dustpan under the sink cabinet. She walked over to face the mess she made. She didn't have anyone to clean up after her like her father did. She scooped the broken blooms and shattered shards of porcelain into the pan and tried to ignore the discontent that towered inside her.

She thought she had conquered this weakness and distanced herself from it. But as soon as she let her guard down, it would strike at her like a viper. Her anger rolled in like sudden fits of rage, blindsiding her. There was no limit to the level she could sink to.

She needed to kill the hours before she would go out that night to follow Jake. She didn't want to abandon ship now, but she would need to stay busy. She could employ her usual routine and go to the park to watch people, but she was still too wired to be tied to a bench. She needed movement to keep herself from exploding. She settled on a bike ride to the bakery where her mother worked. Sweets would keep her going during the long night she had ahead. Plus, she could catch a glimpse of her mother's new love interest.

She pedaled her bike hard the entire way to the bakery. Getting out of breath was a good way to grind her heightened senses down. She pushed her limits and smoothed the jagged edges out of her system.

She pushed through the doors of the bakery, uncertain if her mother would even be at work that day. Something outside of herself steered her there, and she was merely going along.

She browsed around the many pastries and breads in the glass cases around the perimeter. There were countless splendidly decorated cakes and cookies on display behind glass by the cash register.

Her mother was manning the register, talking to a customer. She looked at home at her post.

Danni fell in line to move toward the cakes laid out in front of her mother. She locked eyes with her almost immediately. It was as if her mother had a sixth sense that one of her own was nearby. It wasn't as if her mother was ever overly warm toward her. Still, they shared an irrefutable biological bond. Along with many physical attributes. She had her mother's green eyes and full lips. She was taller, but they shared the same thin frame. Danni never had a good appetite and could often go for days without anything but coffee. Food often caused an upset stomach for her. Today's sugar splurge was unusual. She was used to an emptiness in her body. Sometimes, she even craved the pain of hunger that gnawed at her insides. She preferred it to drawing blood from her arms. She was supposed to find more constructive ways to deal with her rage by now. She had many sessions with the school counselor, teaching her to rely on more productive ways to cope. She was pretty sure sugar would not be one of his recommended strategies. She silently cursed at Jake again.

She finally reached the front of the line, not any less indecisive about what she wanted. The line was moving slowly, since most of the customers were equally overwhelmed by all the choices on display. She greeted her mother and noticed the apprehension in her eyes. She obviously didn't expect to see her there that afternoon.

"What do I owe this surprise to?"

Her tone carried a hint of suspicion.

"I know. Very spur of the moment today. I was struck by a very uncomfortable sugar craving, and this place came to mind. You have been talking it up quite a bit recently."

Her mother's eyes were fishing for an ulterior motive from her, but she noticed the bandage wrapped around her hand instead.

"What happened to your hand?" she asked, clearly concerned. She'd never forget Danni's tumultuous teenage years when she was often called to the school by the counselor. She never attended those sessions though.

"It's nothing. Just a dumb cooking accident."

"I could have had something ready for you. You didn't have to stand in that line, sweetheart," her mother said, probably relieved that Danni minimized her injury as usual.

"It's okay, Mom. I don't mind hanging with the common people," she smiled, trying to lower any suspicions she may have had about being stalked.

Her mother's face remained perfectly choreographed, which only confirmed Danni's suspicions. She was hiding something. They both kept their feelings masked. Danni's mind conjured up an image of her father standing at his window, peering through his binoculars. Finding her mother standing intimately with a strange man on the street below.

"Do you know what you want yet?"

Danni was still treading water in the sea of options.

"I'm going to need suggestions today. My head is a mess. I was just looking for something sweet, but that doesn't really narrow it down enough here."

"You can't go wrong with the cupcakes. I could give you an assortment if you can't nail down exactly what you're in the mood for. They are like mini samples of the large cakes we sell here."

"That sounds exactly what I need today. An assortment of things."

"You can pick a few today, and then come back another day for a different sample. The only way to really find out which one you love the most is to try them all."

"This place is the antidote for real life, isn't it?"

"Or it's the metaphor for the perfect life," her mother countered with a smile.

Danni pondered her mom's argument. Flexible and open contradicted what she knew her to be like. A handsome older man approached them from the back of the bakery with a big tray of cookies. He opened the display case and started adding the freshly baked batch to the few remaining stragglers left over.

Danni noticed her mother's face tensed while he stood next to her. His face, however, boasted an easygoing smile. His eyes were soft when he looked at her mother. Her reaction was most likely only tempered because she was trapped under Danni's watchful eyes.

"More of the chocolate chips for you, my dear. Let's watch these little birdies fly off the shelves some more."

He had a calm, deep voice with a thick European accent. Danni realized that it had to be Max. The baker that gave her mother a raise so she could quit her second job. The man who likely spurred the welcome change in her. The man who now got to call her "my dear."

"Max, this is my daughter, Danni," her mother said with a crackle in her voice. She looked unprepared for the situation she was faced with.

Max looked straight into Danni's eyes. His blue eyes felt as comfortable a soft blanket. He reached his hand out to her across the counter.

"It's so nice to meet you, Danni. Too bad, we are so busy today. I would love to stay and talk for a while, but if I stay out here, something back there will start to burn."

Danni met his generosity with a soft grip and shook his hand.

"I will definitely come back soon, when it's not so busy."

She could see why her mother liked him. He looked strong and wide open. Very different from the curled-up ball that her father has become.

He rushed back to his ovens in the back of the bakery, leaving her mother behind to face her. Her face was flushed. She looked around the store as if she was looking for the easiest way out. Danni realized that they were causing a bottleneck in the line behind her.

"I'll take a dozen of the cupcakes. You pick." Danni said quickly, eager to prevent a riot by the frustrated customers.

There was no time for her to analyze the exchange between Max and her mother's nervous energy. There was no time to weigh the consequences of what she perceived. She dulled her mind's conclusions, while she watched her mother prepare a box of assorted cupcakes for her. She glanced at her wristwatch, realizing that time still towered like a mountain between where she was and where she needed to go that night. She would need to orchestrate yet another way to bridge the divide.

"Are all of these for you?" her mother asked when she handed her the box.

"I have to find someone to share it with. No way I could consume all that sugar and survive."

"How about your new lady friend and her daughter?"

"I remember you asking me to resist that temptation."

"I thought about it again. The odds are stacked against you for sure, but something tells me that you really like her."

Danni was not primed for her mother's change of heart and the line behind her simply grew too restless to continue their exchange.

"I'll come for dinner soon," she said as she turned around and walked out of the store without making eye contact with any of the people that snaked around the gallery of confections.

She sat on a bench out on the street a few doors down from the bakery. She pondered her mother's demeanor around Max, which redirected her straight to her father. Her heart ached for him. Buried alive in the cocoon he spun for himself. Removed from his family and the world. She had no clue how he has managed to survive it for as long as he has. She felt a strange charge in the air when she called up his image. She could feel that his pain was at a breaking point.

A tall, lanky woman with shoulder-length hair walked by her. She was getting used to noticing people who resembled Simone. It was as if her eyes were catching her features in everyone. She looked at her watch again. It was a quarter to three. She was at a crossroad, tasked to pick a direction. Her mood has brightened from the exercise. It was after all on the list of remedies recommended by her school counselor. Along with sketching, lifting heavy things, and breathing mindfully. Strange that he never suggested falling in love as a remedy for stress. Maybe love was more complicated. The love her mother felt for Max could easily destroy her father. The love she felt for Simone could similarly destroy her marriage. The love Jake had for money would destroy his life. And yet, how could one not answer its call? To deny love would rob your soul and leave nothing but an empty shell behind.

She looked at the box of cupcakes. She recalled her mother's voice. As if she gave her permission to fall in love and ignore all the odds against them. She got up and walked to her bike. She fastened the box to the carrier rack and followed her instincts without giving it a second thought. She could be at Simone's front door in less than thirty minutes.

Chapter 17

All the nerves in her body tingled as she walked up the three concrete steps to the large front door of Simone's house. The bright blue flowerpots on each step beckoned her closer. Her lightened mood propelled her there, but she still felt fluttery and unsure about showing up unannounced.

She rang the bell and crossed her fingers that Simone would be home and happy to see her. She couldn't hear any footsteps approaching. She started to get cold feet as the unanswered minutes stretched out. A sinister voice popped up in her mind, urging her to leave, mocking her for taking the leap. It hissed cunningly what a fool she was. Yet her feet remained frozen in front of the large entrance. She continued to wait. Rang the bell again. Her cooler head argued that Simone simply wasn't home. That she was out somewhere with Billie, but then she heard the second story window open.

Simone's head peeked through the window. Danni looked up and found the aquamarine of her eyes.

Simone cried out in surprise at the sight of her.

"Danni!" Her face was filled with excitement, and any sinister doubt in Danni's mind evaporated.

She waved up at her, reassured about her hunch to make the trip.

"I'll be right down," Simone yelled, and her head disappeared out of the window.

Soon after, the big door swung open.

"What a lovely surprise," Simone said, but smiling as if she had her fingers crossed all day for a visit from her.

Danni felt self-conscious, standing on the porch with her heart pounding in her throat. She was certain anyone walking by could see her blood pulsing through her neck. As if on cue, Simone grabbed her hand and pulled her swiftly in through the door. Danni was caught off guard and fell into her. She felt the heat rush through her face and down the skin of her neck, certain that she was blushing a fiery red from being so close to her.

Simone steadied her, and she managed to hold on to the box of cupcakes. Dropping them would have negated her last-ditch effort to rescue the insanity of her day.

"Are you falling for me again?" Simone teased.

The flush in her face showed no signs of fading.

"Are you okay with me just dropping in on you like this?"

"Why wouldn't I be?"

"Most people prefer a call before someone just barge in."

"Normally I do," Simone said with an unrelenting glimmer in her eyes.

"And yet, here I am, and you don't seem upset."

"I don't think there's anything you could do to upset me."

"You make it sound like we're on a blissful honeymoon," Danni bantered.

Simone looked at her with utter bemusement.

"I brought gifts," Danni said, extending the box out to Simone. "Just in case you had misgivings about my visit."

Simone took the box and walked toward the dining room table. Danni followed close behind, happy to get out of the doorway.

Simone opened the box. Her eyes widened at the sight of the decadent cupcakes.

"These look delicious!" she said without taking her eyes off them even an inch.

"They are from the bakery where my mother works," Danni explained proudly.

"How did you know cupcakes were my favorite dessert?"

"I might have known it from a previous lifetime."

Simone looked up at her. Her face radiated as warm as the sun. Danni was stunned by how easy those gutsy words rolled of her tongue. She barely recognized herself around Simone.

"Tell your mother I'm beyond impressed."

Danni nodded.

"She was the one who suggested that I share them with you."

"You told her about me?"

"I did."

"I'm very proud of you, my friend of many lifetimes."

"Well, our reconnection is a big deal, and I couldn't help but enlighten her. I'm not sure that she was ready, but she seems to be working through it."

Simone walked around the dining room table toward her. It looked like she floated over on air, like a dancer. She stood in front of her, so close, she could feel her breath touch her face. Her eyes pierced right through her, but Danni couldn't look away. She pushed her shoulders back and held her gaze. A thousand butterflies buzzed through her head. It felt as if they were drawn closer magnetically, neither of them able to resist the attraction. Danni feared that they would merge into each other if she didn't force herself to step back.

Simone stayed close. Her breath warmed Danni's face, penetrating her skin and flowing down into the rivers of her blood vessels. A golden light spread through her, lifting her like a balloon. Her hands fluttered like hummingbirds. She wanted to pull Simone into her body with reckless abandon. With one step, they could join hands and jump off the cliff they had been edging and never look back.

Danni's body, however, didn't move. Except her eyes, which travelled from Simone's sapphire blue eyes down, over her fine nose to her full lips and soft chin. Her gaze rolled further down her neck to her chest that was rising and falling under her breath. She imagined her hands reaching for the rest of her shirt's buttons, working deftly to expose more skin. Her arms, however, stayed heavy as stone. She couldn't lift her hands to reach out. Her mind was yet again thrown back into reality, where anything more than a friendship between them would be impossible.

Simone seemed to be caught up in the same daydream, but without the same trepidation. She took the leap and pressed her lips softly on Danni's, waiting for permission to proceed.

Danni was caught off guard. Her brain exploded into a sea of light breaking through her barriers. She opened her mouth slightly to Simone's lips in agreement. Simone welcomed her weakened resolve and circled her lips with her tongue gently before she pushed the warmth of it slowly into her mouth. Danni's response took flight, and she abandoned any remaining wavering thoughts. She welcomed the warmth that radiated into her mouth from their kiss, and she joined her in lighting the fire between them. The kiss seemed to last a lifetime, and the fire spread into Danni's hands. She reached around Simone's lower back and pulled her body closer into hers. Her mind was filled with light that intensified from a soft yellow glow to a pulsing blood orange red. She pushed closer into Simone, getting lost in her. There was no room between them for any of the real-life consequences. Her hands moved over Simone's curves, and she noticed how different her body felt from Jake's. She sank into her softness, melted into her warmth, not knowing where the boundaries of it were.

They finally released each other, both gasping for air. Danni could feel the fast pace of Simone's heartbeat next to her own chest.

"Oh my, oh my, oh my, Danni," Simone finally whispered close to her ear. "What is this trouble we are getting into?"

"I wish I knew. I'm somewhere, lost in a wilderness with you."

"I like you," Simone said, her lips smiling against Danni's cheek.

"I like you too."

Danni finally felt her heartbeat slowing down as she relaxed into their embrace. She has never afforded herself that much emotion toward anyone.

Her stubborn mind managed a way to drift out of her body, and she watched from above as they stood in the middle of the room, tangled up like knots. Anxiety drifted in, driving a wedge between them. She pulled away and watched the warmth drain out of Simone's eyes.

"Where is Billie?" she asked nervously.

"She went to a movie with a friend she met at school."

"She is seeing a friend behind my back?" Danni took another step back and crossed her arms over her chest in a mocking display of jealousy.

"I'm so sorry, Danni. This kid came out of nowhere. She moved here from New York recently. You know, the kind of kid that is filled with confidence. She struck up a friendship with Billie as if it was the easiest thing to do. Her first day at school. Plays the trombone of all things."

"It looks like I'm going to have to pick up an instrument."

"My heart strings are up for grabs," Simone said.

The sparkle ran back into her eyes.

Simone took her hand and placed it over her heart. Danni kept her gaze on the movement of her chest under the feel of her hand.

"Your heart is beating so fast. It's vibrating like a string all through me," Danni whispered.

"We should get out of this room."

Danni looked around the big space surrounding them. Filled with large paintings on the wall and high-end furniture. There was obviously great care put into its decoration. She wondered if it was Simone's taste or Bill's. She pulled her hand abruptly away from Simone's chest as soon as she felt the sound of his name roll off her thoughts. There were so many obstacles between them. The futility of any pursuit of Simone overwhelmed her every other minute. She was terrified that it would end in heartache for both of them. Not to mention her whole family.

"Is Bill working?" she asked. The memory of their last encounter was still jarring.

Simone nodded and smiled mischievously. Danni sensed almost no reluctance from Simone to surrender to the reality of their circumstances. She seemed to allow herself the luxury of their fantasy. Danni urged herself to do the same. To surrender and run with her into their forest of make believe. A quick detour from the reality they were both tied to. It was the least she could offer this beautiful woman, with the sadness buried so deep in her eyes. Or was it frustration? About choices she made when she was too young to make good ones. Those choices, however, has led her to this moment, holding another girl's hand over her heart, asking to be revived. Danni couldn't willingly deny her request.

"When do you think he will be home?" Danni asked, looking over her shoulder one last time.

"Not until much later today. Maybe even later tonight."

"And Billie?"

"Don't be nervous, Danni. It's just us here for a while. Let's try to enjoy it."

"I want to."

"You worry endlessly."

"I know."

"What are you worried about?" Simone asked earnestly.

Danni hesitated. The thing that worried her most was the duffel bag that Bill carried around with him. She worried that he was involved in more than what he let on, making him far more dangerous. Getting involved with a woman with a dangerous husband was a reason to be concerned. However, letting Simone know about her suspicions wasn't an obvious choice.

"You don't want to know," she said, hoping to change the subject.

"I do want to know, absolutely."

Danni hesitated a while longer.

"I know this may sound crazy, but I wonder what he carries in that big bag he brought home the last time I saw him," Danni said, but regretted it instantly. She watched her words strain the intimacy between them and she wished she could erase them.

Simone didn't show any signs of panic. Or resentment. As if she meant it when she said Danni couldn't do anything to upset her. The sound of a loud motorcycle speeding past the house cut through the space between them.

"We don't discuss his business dealings," Simone confessed, shrugging.

"And you are never curious?"

"Not really." She looked at ease with her decision. "Bill has never responded well to questioning."

Danni could relate.

'Maybe it's for the best," she said, not wanting to turn into Simone's accuser at all.

"It is. I have tried to question him before and got nowhere with it. I decided to stop turning my home into a battlefield."

"Sometimes, Switzerland has a better view?"

"Something like that, yes," she said with a smile.

"I'm sorry that I brought it up."

"Don't be. Like we said, you tend to notice things."

"Where do you go to play your music?" Danni asked, sensing they needed a change.

"I have a music studio upstairs. Do you want to go there?"

"Without a doubt."

Simone's face relaxed as she took her hand again, as if it was the most natural thing to do and led her up the stairs.

Danni followed her into a large room that looked like a music sanctuary. It hosted a Steinway grand piano right in the center. The instrument filled the space with confident splendor. Its dark curves begging to be touched. The walls were adorned with framed pictures of musicians, composers, and music scores. There were built-in shelves that stretched the entire length of a wall, and it was filled with books. Danni assumed it was sheet music or books in some way related to music. A small couch dressed the opposite side.

"So this is where it all happens?" Danni said as her eyes scanned through all the details displayed in the room. It was a window into the person she has been so drawn to.

"The magic, yes. For Billie mostly."

"Oh yes, you mentioned how hard it was to wrestle her away from the piano."

"She is. I'm hoping this new friendship with the trombone player will make it a little easier."

"I doubt she would abandon her talent for a fleeting friendship with a trombone player, Besides, it's not Billie that's keeping you away from the piano today," Danni teased.

"Trombone players are a rare species, so maybe it won't be so fleeting. And you're right, I have encountered yet another distraction, but I'm finding out that it's more of an inspiration."

"I regret not playing an instrument more than ever."

"You already forgot how well you play my heart strings," Simone said, smiling. She sat down on the piano bench.

Danni decided to ignore her yearning heart and keep a safe distance. She took a seat on the couch.

"Do you want to hear what I've been working on?" Simone asked.

"I'm dying to hear."

"Come sit here with me."

Danni hesitated, but she felt exactly like a moth drawn to a flame. Somehow, against her own advice, she ended up sitting close to Simone on the bench.

"It's a piano sonata from Beethoven that I really like. The fifteenth sonata called Pastorale. Have you heard it before?"

Danni chuckled.

"Oh yes. It's the ringtone on my phone, don't you know?" she said with playful sarcasm.

Simone took a deep breath in, raised her shoulders, and placed her fingers on the keys of the piano. She looked serious, and Danni held her own breath in anticipation.

As Simone began to play, Danni soon caught on to her trick as she started to play Chopsticks. She heard that song frequently bellow through the walls of the music studios at the store, when the younger students came for lessons.

"That is no sonata by Beethoven. Even I know that much," she cried out.

"There is no fooling you," Simone said as she laughed at her own practical joke. "I was just seeing if you did your homework."

"I have been listening to all the piano concertos he wrote. I haven't explored the sonatas yet."

"It's one of my favorite sonatas by him. It's beautiful."

She started to play the theme of the sonata, and Danni realized she needed more space on the piano bench and moved back to the couch. Her eyes stayed fixed on her, watching her fingers run across the keys effortlessly to bring the centuries-old music to life. Her body moved along with the sounds that lifted off her fingers. She played from memory. Danni was mesmerized by its serene melody, slowly unfolding. The sounds rose like birds taking a majestic flight. The music slowly gained momentum, swelling steadily like waves under the crescendo of a strong westerly wind, until it finally spilled out into a climax, then faded off again, softly to the end as the bellowing wind died down.

"That was amazing, Simone," Danni said as soon as she finished.

She was born to play the instrument, there was no doubt in Danni's mind. She walked over to join her on the bench again.

"I could do that piece for the audition. What do you think?"

"I think he will love that."

"I haven't completely made up my mind yet. There are many other pieces I like as well."

"Do I get to hear some of them now?"

Simone smiled and shook her head.

"I will surprise you at the audition."

"You can blow me away again like you did today."

"I'm glad you liked it," she said as she took Danni's hand.

"I mean it. It was beautiful." Danni tried to keep the fire in her hand from spreading through the rest of her body.

"It's the only thing I was ever good at."

"I'm glad you are going for this. You should never give up on a talent like that."

"I've always hoped that my detour wasn't permanent."

"Being that the detour was for Billie, it was worth it. But I agree that it's time for you to get back to it. Especially now that the trombone player has made their timely entrance."

"You afforded me this opportunity. I don't want to pass up on it. What are you good at, Danni? Besides melting my heart?"

Danni squeezed her hand.

"That's just it. I don't know what I'm good at. I'm just ordinary, so I don't know how I would be melting your heart."

"Try telling the swarm of bees zooming inside me right now that you are just ordinary. I know you are good at something."

Danni's eyes got lost in her again. The glow of her hair, the shade of coffee moonstone. The color of her eyes, sparkling like topaz. Her skin as smooth as porcelain.

"I'm good at watching things. People mostly."

"I can believe that. Sometimes, I feel like you are looking deep down inside of me."

"I can watch people for hours and spend even more hours sketching my memory of them."

"Sketch them?"

"I grew up with way too much time on my own. It was a safe way for me to connect to people."

Simone's fingers travelled slowly up along the length of her arm. Her touch sent electric shockwaves through Danni's entire chest.

"Have you done a sketch of me?"

Danni looked at her with a guilt dripping off her face.

"I have. I hope you don't mind. I know people can be very protective of their privacy."

"If you promise to show it to me, I will forgive you."

"I have actually turned into a complete stalker, I'm sad to say."

Simone looked puzzled, and stopped moving her fingers abruptly.

Danni regretted spilling her secrets to Simone so easily.

"What do you mean?"

She hesitated, unsure of how Simone would react. "I have been stalking Jake."

Simone let go of her arm all together. The warm look in her eyes cooled off suddenly.

"Peter was worried about him. We both were, because some things didn't add up. I've been following him. Can you believe this?"

"You are actually physically following him?"

Danni nodded. She wanted to be truthful with Simone.

"In a way, I feel horrible about it, but I'm convinced he is up to something. I questioned him but got no answers. Just a series of well-rehearsed deflections."

"Don't you think it could be dangerous?"

Danni paused. The image of the Russian mob man was very familiar to her by now. Worry was not the only emotion his image conjured up.

"It's also thrilling in a way. The danger of it. It does come with an adrenaline rush."

Simone smiled.

"You're a spy junkie! And here I thought you were just a humdrum music store assistant."

"That is just my alter ego."

"So you are really a bona fide superhero?"

"My father was a police detective. I idolized him immensely as a child. I pretended we were the best crime-fighting duo in the nation. Summoned to solve every mysterious crime perpetrated on the people. He schooled me when I was young. Daily drills to train me how to tune into my surroundings. We would often sit at one of the parks, watching people, and create imaginary crime scenes for hours."

"Why didn't you become a detective yourself?"

"Things fell apart in our home. I think we are all still suspended, waiting for my father to come back to life. But it's been years now, and he hasn't shown any real signs of life yet."

Simone leaned in as she looked at Danni.

"Is that why you have these scars on your arms?"

Dannie jerked her arm away.

"What happened?"

Danni started to feel closed in. She could feel her lungs struggling to exchange the air that has suddenly turned thick. She wasn't sure she had enough strength to form the words to talk about her and her family's tragic history. She waited, to see if she could acclimate to the heaviness in the air.

"I am filled with sadness, Simone. I feel like I'm drowning most of the time. The loss of my father haunts me. It's like he is buried alive. My mother has checked out, even though she still lives under the same roof. My brother left, leaving me alone with the mess. Sometimes the pain I inflict on myself is the only way I know I'm not buried with him."

The words fell out of her mouth. They lay naked in front of her. She wanted to kick them away. Talking about her life never felt good to her.

Simone stayed quiet for a while. Danni knew how overwhelming her truth could be. She regretted putting anything but a smile on her face.

Simone's eyes turned soft as water then. She reached out and took Danni's hand. She leaned closer to her and kissed her mouth. Danni stayed frozen as she felt the warm sensation of Simone's lips on her, and she had to fight back the tears that were welling up behind her eyes.

"You are a superhero, Danni," she whispered when she pulled her lips away.

Danni smiled. She closed her eyes and pushed her chest out. She let Simone's words sink into her, down into her heart.

"Superheroes don't cry. I have to get my act together, you know? I shouldn't still be agonizing over what happened."

"You are putting a lot of pressure on yourself."

Danni knew she was right. She has created a lot of rules and coping mechanisms in response. Simone may have thought that she struck gold with her, but in Danni's head, she was often nothing more than fool's gold. But she hasn't been blind to the change in her recently. Something injected her with more courage, to emerge from the dark hole she has been hiding in.

"I was planning on following him tonight. After his shift ends at the bar."

"How are you following him exactly?"

"I installed a GPS tracker on his car so I can follow him from a distance in my car. To see where he goes. Peter usually wants a report of his whereabouts too."

"How did Peter get involved with this?"

"He told me that Jake showed up at his mother's place while he was there one night, very drunk, and demanded money for something bogus. It raised their suspicions through the roof, and he asked me to pry into it. Since I would have more access to him."

"So he wanted you to spy on Jake?"

"Exactly, but I didn't tell him that I have already started to spy on Jake on my own, before he asked me to."

"Why was that?"

"Because of his lies. I could just sense it. He would constantly lie to me about where he was."

"Do you think he is cheating on you?"

"No. I mean, who knows, but I think he is involved with some bad people. I'm sure he owes money to them for some reason. Someone who is putting pressure on him."

"See? This is dangerous, Danni. You should stay out of it. It's too dangerous to get in the middle of things like that."

"I can't turn a blind eye. I can't just act like it's not happening. He thinks we should get married and yet he is not honest with me."

"But you are also not honest with him. About spying on him, for one."

"You are right. There's no honesty in spying on anyone."

They were handling their situations with Bill and Jake so differently.

"Do you think it's best not to uncover the secrets of the person you're with?" Danni asked bluntly.

"It can be complicated." Simone answered softly.

"Sure it is. I have struggled with the decision myself, but if he is indebted to a group of dangerous people, I should know about that. It's risky not to know."

"So you're set on going tonight, then? To follow him?"

"Yes. I'm set on it."

"Then I will worry about you all night long."

"Don't worry."

Danni took her hand again to reassure her.

"I know Bill is up to something, Danni. You have caught on to that right away as well, but I think me and Billie are better off if we don't pry into it. I have to consider her in this."

"I don't know what is best. It's my instinct to dig, I guess. I have an unstoppable urge to shed light and solve the mystery."

"Let's see what you find out about Jake."

"Do you want me to tell you what I find out?"

"Of course. I'm hooked on you and everything you do."

"It's a riveting story about an unlikely superhero, remember? I would love it if you stayed tuned," Danni reported, smiling down into her chest.

"Am I in it?"

"I think so. Do you want to be the damsel in distress?" Danni teased.

"Oh god, no. I don't want to be a damsel."

"Sometimes, people don't realize that they need to be rescued." Simone pulled her closer to her.

"Maybe I'm rescuing you," she whispered.

Danni smiled at the irony of Simone's words, and just as she pondered the words, she felt Simone's lips on hers again. She couldn't stay frozen this time. She reached around the small of her back and pulled her close, responding to the kiss with the confidence of a superhero. She did want to rescue her, and at the same time, she could feel herself getting rescued by her every minute.

Danni's hands reached for the buttons on Simone's shirt. She fumbled to undo them to expose more skin for her hungry hands. She untucked the shirt from her pants and touched the soft skin on her back. Her hands could hardly keep up with her desire to explore all of her body. She felt Simone's hands reaching in under her clothes as well, and her breath was rushing ahead like a high-speed freight train.

They were both startled by a noise coming from downstairs and jumped away from each other. Simone got up on her feet and straightened out her shirt. She fastened the buttons in a flash and pulled her fingers through her hair. She swiped her hand over her mouth nervously and went to go sit on the couch. Danni watched her fumbling through her thoughts, looking for an alibi.

"It's fine, Simone. Remember? I came over to let you taste those cupcakes from my mother's bakery."

Danni noticed Simone trying to catch her breath and tried to direct her mind toward a more innocent train of thought. She didn't want them to look nervous and guilt stricken when Bill walked in. She wasn't sure they could avoid looking disheveled from the onslaught of their hungry hands, but she didn't want them to look guilty about it.

"Of course, yes. Nothing wrong with that. And to see if Billie wanted to go to the movies again, but she already left with a friend, right?" Simone elaborated nervously on the story they would agree upon if questioned.

"Definitely. I was all excited to take her to see the new Star Wars movie. Didn't that just come out this week?"

"That is the movie she went to see today," Simone said, laughing about the whole situation.

"See? I had a hunch!"

"Bill may frown on an adult wanting to spend so much time with a twelve-year-old, don't you think?"

"It's to give you time to practice for the audition, remember?"

"Don't say anything about that yet."

"Then let's stick with the cupcake story. We should keep it simple."

"He likes cupcakes as much as I do."

Danni laughed loudly, hoping to reveal her presence to Bill. She dared him to show his face to her again. He was probably busy hiding another duffel bag somewhere in the house before he would come to find Simone.

"Let's hope he eats one to sweeten him up before he comes up here," Danni said.

"I wish I could tell you that you have the wrong idea about him, but I'm just as leery about him these days."

"I'm sticking with ignorance is bliss today."

"Exactly," Simone said and then they both perked their attention to the sound of footsteps coming up the stairs.

He pushed the door open. Danni berated herself for not thinking about how suspicious a closed door would look to him. There was no one else in the house. She couldn't remember closing the door, so it must have swung shut on its own. Probably while their hands were busy ravishing each other.

"Hi there," he said as they both looked up at him looming in the doorway. His face looked stern, but turned surprised when he saw Danni, sitting awkwardly on the piano bench.

"Oh, hi there again," he said, once he recognized her.

"Hi, honey," Simone interrupted. "You remember Danni, right?"

"Of course I do. The one who took Billie to the movies to give you time to yourself, right?"

"Yes. She brought cupcakes today."

"Where's Billie?" he asked frankly.

"At the movies with a friend," Simone responded, matching his frankness. Like it was the most ordinary thing for Billie to do. It was clear that Simone enjoyed the charade between them just as much. Countering his secrets with careful insinuations of her own.

"Really?" he said with his eyebrows raised.

"True story. Our child is becoming more social it seems. Did you taste one of the cupcakes?"

"No, I will try one a little later. I'm going to finish up with some paperwork if you don't mind. I'll let you guys continue with your visit."

"That's all right with me."

Danni looked at her watch and noticed it was well after five already. There really was no reason for her to rush home, but she knew she wouldn't feel as comfortable visiting Simone with Bill home.

"Anything planned for dinner? Or should I order something?" Bill asked.

"Oh, I haven't thought that far yet. I'm sure you are hungry. Are you in the mood for something specific?"

Simone sounded uninterested in a meal with him.

"I can have Dino send something from the restaurant."

"Have him send something for you. I will make a salad for me and Billie later."

"Okay," he said as he left the room.

Danni and Simone were both quiet as they listened intently to the sound of his footsteps fading away.

"I don't think he likes me," Danni whispered.

Simone frowned.

"It's only the second time he has met you. I'm sure he's also convinced that I don't need any outside friendships."

"I'm sure he has many outside friendships."

"He would say it's mostly work related."

"Like Dino's restaurant?"

"He met Dino right after we moved here. He loves Italian food and I mostly just chop salads."

"I liked your salad the last time I was here."

"Do you want me to make you another one?"

"No. I'm not hungry."

"I know, me neither. I should be starving, for as much as my heart has been racing this afternoon."

"Shh," Danni said with her finger over her mouth, looking at the studio door that was now wide open.

Simone got up and walked over to the door. She gave Danni a seductive look as she shut the door and came back to sit close to her on the small piano bench.

Danni shifted to create more space between them, but Simone laid her hand on the bare skin of her thigh.

"Are sure that you want to go out tonight? Instead of staying here with me."

Danni laid her hand on hers, letting her fingers straddle Simone's. With Bill home, it would be like staying in the lion's den.

"Don't worry. I'm always very careful. And you know there is no way we could be here together, while Bill is doing paperwork in the next room."

Danni's eyes kept darting over to the door, expecting Bill to swing it open any moment.

"He gets very engrossed in his paperwork," Simone said as if she took a walk inside her mind.

Danni stroked the top of her fingers gently as she allowed herself to get lost in Simone's blue eyes.

"My audition is this week. On Wednesday," Simone said while looking at Danni's hand on hers.

"I will be there."

"Are you sure Peter would let you come in to listen?"

"I will find a way. I know you want me to."

"I really do."

"You wouldn't feel more nervous with more people there?"

"No, I played for many people all the time in college. It's nerve-racking, of course, but I got used to it."

"You are braver than most," Danni said, not letting go of her hand. Her skin was soft as silk.

"I wish we were still alone here," Simone whispered.

"Me too. I love it when we kiss," Danni whispered back.

"I should come surprise you some time at your apartment."

"I'm not always alone either, you know?"

"I'll text you first to make sure the coast is clear."

Danni squeezed her again hand softly. They both kept looking at the door.

Danni started to get up from the bench, knowing she needed to get going if she wanted to keep their desires from escalating again. She felt like a racehorse around Simone, always on the verge of busting out of the gates.

Simone pulled her back to the bench and pulled her close. She kissed her again, and Danni held her mouth on her soft lips for a while. Simone reached under her shirt to touch the skin of her belly. Danni felt as if the universe opened, and the stars rained down in a spectacular show of fireworks around them.

She finally pulled away, but she knew that she would have never stopped if they were alone. Her heart was bucking like a mustang, and she was going to have to find a way to handle the effect Simone had on her.

"I really have to get going," she whispered in Simone's ear, still close enough to feel her racing heart against her chest.

"I know. Sad, but true."

Danni untangled herself reluctantly.

This time, Simone followed suit and trailed her down the stairs to the front door. Danni touched her hand one last time, before she bounced down the front steps of the home to where her bicycle was tied up. The sun was throwing long, tired shadows down, she knew the light would soon bathe her in her pink glow to announce the start of sunset. She turned around again and saw that Simone was still watching her from the door. She winked at her as she unlocked her bike lock. Simone smiled and closed the door slowly. Danni's mind tumbled through the experience of the afternoon, and she found herself again on that steep hill under the loose rocks, slipping and sliding down.

She started to pedal home, keeping her eyes focused on the road in front of her. The morning's experience with Jake felt light-years ago and her aching heart felt completely mended.

Chapter 18

Danni slipped into a pair of black tactical pants and pulled a dark gray t-shirt over her head. It was a quarter after eleven, and she was ready to get her mission off the ground after finding time for a much-needed nap when she got home from her emotionally charged visit with Simone.

She gathered everything she thought she would need for her evening of surveillance. The most important item that she needed to pack was a pair of night vision binoculars. She purchased a pair earlier in the week, and she was eager to use them that evening. It had a nighttime mode, which would enable her to take pictures and video at night without the need to use a flash. She grabbed her phone and a flashlight and tossed an expandable baton she found under some clothes in a drawer. She remembered buying one a while back for self-protection, but had since forgotten about it. She didn't plan on any confrontations outside of her car, but she wanted to be ready to defend herself if her plans derailed.

She threw all the items into a small backpack and went to the kitchen to make coffee. She kept her mind focused, envisioning how the evening would play out. She was reaching for anything to wrestle her mind away from the earth-shattering afternoon she shared with Simone.

She was tempted to borrow her mother's car for the evening. She wanted to be as inconspicuous as possible, but she ultimately decided against it. Her mom's old Chevy probably hasn't seen an oil change in years. The last thing she needed was to get stranded on the road with an overheated engine that late at night. She settled for her average gray Honda Civic, comforted that the roads were littered with cars that looked exactly like it.

There was still plenty of traffic around when she finally pushed through the front doors of her apartment building. People heading home from a myriad of gathering places in the busy neighborhood. The air outside seemed charged with energy. She could almost hear it buzzing. Her heart was thumping against her rib cage. She took a few deep breaths to calm her nerves and then opened her phone to look at the GPS tracking app. She was easily able to locate Jake's car. He was parked a few blocks from the bar, in his usual spot. There was no reason to rush, since he seldom left the bar before twelve thirty. She hopped into her car and buckled her seat belt. She was ready for lift-off.

"Good luck, you crazy girl," she whispered to herself before taking another deep breath. She started the engine and joined the traffic down the street.

She arrived close to his car's location according to the app and found a parking spot on the other end of the street. She reached into her backpack for the night vision binoculars. She turned them on and tried them out, taking a few pictures to make sure there weren't any hiccups. She checked her phone app again to make sure his car was still in the same spot, then prepared to wait, taking more sips of her coffee. She felt exposed sitting in her car on the street. She wished she had her windows tinted, but she was already stretching her budget thin with all the camera equipment recently. It wasn't as if her earnings resembled any kind of professional spy money.

It was a quarter of midnight when she checked her watch and took another sip of her coffee.

The radio host announced the next song on his set list. She just needed some easy background music for company and turned into a jazz station. After the first few bars of an improvisational trumpet solo, she heard the pinging chime of a message alert on her phone.

"Be careful out there tonight," she read the message coming from Simone's number.

Her heart swelled instantly. It felt good to know that she was still on her mind.

"I will be. All is quiet so far, no movement yet," she reported back, hoping to calm her worried mind.

"What do you expect you'll find out?" Simone continued.

A conversation with Simone would make the time fly, even though her first priority was to keep an eye on the GPS app.

"Not sure. I think he is involved with a group of Russians, which is not good," she said after she checked the app again to make sure that his car was still parked.

"Russians?" Simone fired back.

"I expect he would go to that restaurant in Bustleton again, after he's done with work."

"What's in Bustleton?"

Danni remembered that Simone was not from Philadelphia and wouldn't be familiar with the different neighborhoods.

"He goes to a Russian place called the Red Square Tavern," she answered. "My gut says it's to gamble, but I don't know for sure," she typed, always surprised at how easy she opened up to her.

"So you can see exactly why I'm so worried about you?"

"Don't be worried. I'll keep a safe distance."

"Unlike me," Simone texted back.

"Yes, unlike you," she agreed, but added a friendly emoji to let her know that her advances were not totally unwelcome.

"Thanks for coming over today." Simone said and added a fireworks emoji of her own.

"Very spur of the moment."

"Unusual for you, right?"

"Very. As you can tell, I'm not my normal self around you."

The texting continued while Danni flipped back and forth from the GPS app.

"I'm not my normal self around you either."

Danni enjoyed the honesty they had with each other. She missed that with Jake. She's not sure they ever really had it.

She checked the GPS app again and saw that the dot on the map was finally moving.

"I have to go. He is on the move."

"Keep me posted later, okay?" Simone asked.

Her fingers fumbled around on her phone and ended up only responding with a thumbs-up emoji. She switched over to the GPS app on her phone and started her car. It was go time.

She placed the phone in a holder on her dashboard so that she could squeeze both hands on the wheel to keep the situation from spinning out of control. He wasn't going in the direction of Bustleton as expected. Instead, he was going straight toward Fairmount, the neighborhood where they both lived. She was disappointed. It looked like he was calling it a night. Just before her heart deflated completely, he suddenly took a right turn. Her heart sparked back to life, and she followed him as he winded through the neighborhood. It seemed like he was heading in the direction of Peter's music store.

Danni was completely confused when he finally parked in the back of the store where she worked. She pulled into a parking space farther up on the street, making sure it was far enough away to avoid being seen by him. She grabbed the binoculars to see if she could get a better view of what he was doing.

She brought the binoculars up to her eyes and focused in on him. He got out of the car and walked to the back door of the store, glancing nervously over his shoulder several times. She noticed sweat glistening over his temples. She snapped a few pictures for Peter. She knew that he would never believe her telling him that his most beloved nephew broke into his store way past midnight on a Saturday night. Her hands trembled as she kept the binoculars up to her eyes and watched him through the viewfinder. She was dumbfounded, watching him punch the codes into the keypads to first unarm the store alarm and then to unlock the back door of the store. Peter must have given him the codes at some point. She was sure she never did.

Jake disappeared into the store, leaving Danni stunned and confused. She never expected to be watching what was unfolding in front of her. Her imagination was jumping to wild conclusions. She cracked the window to ingest the night air deeply a few times to stay calm. Peter could have asked him to go there for some reason.

She scrolled through the pictures that she took so far to make sure that she captured him entering the store successfully. The pictures clearly showed him entering codes into the keypad and then pushing through the door to go inside. Danni looked around the street to make sure she didn't have any unwanted eyes on her. As the hunter, it was imperative not to turn into the hunted. She looked around in every direction. She couldn't detect any witnesses to her discovery. Most of the restaurants that were on the same street closed around midnight. She looked up into the sky and welcomed the thickening of the clouds. The moon and stars were under cover, giving her an extra layer of refuge.

She convinced herself to not follow him into the store. Her mind ran through different scenarios while she waited. She pondered her next move and summarized the events of the past month to attach a reasonable explanation for this development. At the top of her list was her eyewitness account of Jake handing the Russian man money in a thick envelope. Then there was him frequenting a Russian restaurant way past any reasonable mealtime hour, often staying until the early morning hours. She listened to her gut suggesting that he was playing cards for money in the basement of a Russian tavern, and he was losing. It was the most logical explanation she had so far. Judging by the fullness of the envelope he handed over, Jake was settling a big debt. She was trying to fathom a way that he could come up with that kind of money. There was Peter's account of him showing up drunk at his family's home, begging for money, but they didn't give him nearly enough to stuff an envelope as thick as what she remembered it to be.

She never knew Jake to be a gambler. She was unaware he even knew how to play poker, but of course, he hasn't been the most upfront with her for quite some time. He mostly just rehashed all the pressure he felt from having to save for their future together. While assuring her that he had it all under control. She was filled with doubt when it came to his assurances. His latest actions made very little sense to her. Her best conclusion of his presence at the music store was that he lost a card game and now owed more money. Breaking into his uncle's music store seemed like a desperate, haphazard plan to cover some of those debts. Peter had a safe in his office, but he faithfully deposited all of the contents in the bank on Fridays. If Jake did his homework like any competent burglar would, he wouldn't be looking for money there tonight.

The back door swung open again, and she watched as Jake walked out with what seemed like three guitar gig bags. There was weight to what he was carrying, so she was sure he was stealing actual guitars.

Danni took more pictures as she watched him walk to his car. He opened the trunk and placed the guitars inside. He looked around nervously, and she sank down in her seat a little more. The store carried many valuable guitars, which could easily be sold for a few thousand dollars. He went back to the key code, punched the numbers in, and looked around the neighborhood again before he disappeared back into the store. Danni had to restrain herself from running after him into the store. She wanted to shake him out of his delusion. He reappeared quickly with two more gig bags, presumably filled with two more high-priced guitars. He loaded those into the back of his trunk with the others and then walked back to the keypad next to the door. He punched the numbers in again, resetting the alarm. It was as if he was never there. Easy money for him.

Danni tried to remember if she had ever missed any of their inventory before. It just seemed too easy for him to pull off. Peter never checked his inventory very diligently, being more focused on his students than sales. Danni usually ordered inventory as needed, but seldom double-checked that they had receipts for every instrument that left the store. All the more reason to show Peter pictures of what transpired. He would have a hard time believing her without them. She couldn't blame him. This came out of nowhere, and without hard, physical evidence, she wouldn't believe it either. She would never have believed that Jake would resort to stealing from his family. He must have been pushed into a far corner. Stealing from his family was something she would have expected more from his father. Jake's entire family would be hard pressed to accept that he was following in his father's footsteps.

She watched through the binoculars as his car took off down the street. The dot on her map was moving away from her. Danni took another pause to process what she saw. She was tempted to call it a night. Her heart was in shock. The evidence she was able to collect was damning, but she wasn't sure she could crush Peter's heart with it. He was in the midst of auditions and preparing for the season's music competitions. Jake's sudden affinity to steal would certainly put a damper on everything he looked forward to about the upcoming semester. She doubted that he would ever involve the police. He would absorb the loss of inventory, but he would be devastated about Jake resorting to such a low level. She needed to find a way for Jake to get untangled from the people that had a hold over him.

She decided to press on. She followed the dot in her car as her mind buzzed with questions. This time she hoped he would simply drive back to his apartment. They were at least thirty minutes away from Bustleton, and it didn't look like he was following his usual routine that night. The street of his apartment building was fast approaching, and Danni wanted nothing more than to see him turn onto it.

Jake, however, passed right by the street to his apartment. Nothing so far went the way she had expected. She kept following him. She had to see it through. Worst case scenario was that her recently turned gangster boyfriend was going on some crazy crime spree. She pinched the back of her hand to make sure she wasn't stuck in a dream. She would have never imagined this turn of events that morning, when he laid beside her in bed, reassuring her of their bright future ahead.

She assumed that by now he was running on pure adrenaline. He had just pulled off the easiest heist in the history of heists. It was a breeze to steal from his uncle's store, knowing the codes and most likely knowing a good contact to unload the guitars.

She noticed him driving around the block a few times. He seemed aimless as he continued around the same block a few more times. He found a different block and repeated the same pattern. It was almost like he was casing the area, trying to find something or someone. He turned off onto a darker side street, where the houses weren't as closely stacked. She was glad that she filled her car with gas the day before, since it looked like he had all night to find what he was looking for.

He finally parked his car on a dark street and waited. It was a residential area where most of the homes had driveways and garages. She pulled into the empty driveway of a home without any lights turned on at the opposite end of the block. Her heart was racing out of her chest. She turned her car's lights off quickly. She couldn't shake the feeling that he knew she was there, watching him. She sank down as low as she could into her seat and watched the dot on the map of her phone. It wasn't moving and she tried to remain just as still. She could barely breathe as she sat in the dark, suspended in time, waiting to see what his next move was going to be. She reached for the expandable baton in her bag as her mind had visions of him sneaking up on her car, swinging her car door open and yanking her out on to the street.

Instead, she waited without any incident. She finally calmed down and loosened the grip on the baton. She was still too nervous to peek her head up to look through the binoculars. She stayed crouched down in her car for almost thirty minutes, talking herself out of leaving.

She finally heard another car drive past the driveway where she was parked. She could hear the brake pads squeal as it stopped in front of Jake's car on the street. She heard two car doors open. She perked her head up just enough to get a glimpse of what was happening. She looked through the binoculars, but it was hard to see them camouflaged in their dark clothes against the night sky. She activated the night vision feature, allowing her to discern the outline of their movements.

The man who joined Jake was wearing a dark cap and had a thick beard, making it difficult for her to distinguish his features. He was taller than Jake with roughly the same build. Jake looked around in every direction, but he didn't seem to recognize her car. She was likely too far away, and he was without the advantage of binoculars. She could see that his body was tense, like he was about to do a high cliff jump into shallow waters. The two men stood by Jake's car and whispered to each other before walking across the street to a house with a car parked in the driveway. The bearded man walked over to the house while Jake lingered back by the car. Danni watched the scene unfold through the viewfinder of her binoculars. She watched the man by the house wave a small device in his hand along the front wall of the house. He finally stopped near the front door and then nodded in Jake's direction. Jake waved a similar device at the door of the car. Within seconds, he opened the door of the car as if it was never even locked. Danni assumed they used the devices to disable the alarm of the Mercedes in the driveway. Once situated in the driver seat of the car, she could see Jake fuss around the steering column, and in under a minute, he got the engine started. He backed out of the driveway without turning the headlights on and then drove off down the street. The taller man rushed back to his car and followed close behind him.

Danni's mind was blown as she watched the two cars speed away from her. Her instinct kicked in again as she quickly started her car up, backed out of the driveway, and followed them down the street. She didn't want to get too close. There was very little traffic left out on the roads, and she didn't have the luxury of the GPS tracker.

She was certain that he was probably on his way to a chop shop with the stolen car. She came to a stop light and saw both cars take off in front of her. She realized she wasn't going to be able to continue her pursuit safely and forced herself to throw in the towel. After he delivered the Mercedes, his partner would probably give him a ride back to his car, which meant that Jake was much deeper entrenched into their operation than merely losing card games.

She had no idea what her best course of action would be after everything she witnessed that night. She only had one picture of Jake getting into the Mercedes since her fingers fumbled around nervously on the buttons of the binoculars. She shook with tension, paranoid that she was going to get caught.

She drove home. The best person she had available to talk to would be her father. He knew the law and would have ideas of how to rescue Jake from the mess he made. The only problem was that her father hasn't spoken to her or anyone else in years about anything related to police matters. They would have to travel back in time a long way, to get the young, eager detective Matt Whelan on the case, and that would take a miracle.

Chapter 19

The day settled well into the afternoon that Sunday before she finally woke up from a deep sleep. Her head was pounding as she remembered the events of the night before. She got up slowly to go to the kitchen, knowing that she could only blame a lack of caffeine for her throbbing headache.

She started to brew a pot and sat at her dining table, phone in hand. She opened the GPS tracking app to find out where Jake's car has been after she left it. She did a search of the locations listed and discovered that he made it back to his car shortly after three o' clock that morning. He went to his apartment, but was on the move again a little after eight that morning. He parked in the lot of a strip mall in Bell's Corner, the neighborhood next to Bustleton. She researched the mall and discovered that it hosted a small pawn shop. It was most likely where he was instructed to pawn the guitars he swiped from the store. Danni realized that no matter how mortified she was, she couldn't keep her findings from Peter. She vowed to tell him as soon as she saw him at the store the next day. She would have time to visit her parents today, and she wanted to approach her father about the situation. She had no idea where Jake took the stolen Mercedes, and she regretted not being able to keep him in her sights. She just couldn't risk being exposed. Her nerves were so rattled by then, and she was unprepared for a confrontation with him or any of his gangster buddies. The person she knew Jake to be had morphed into a thief. Stealing from his family. Stealing for the mafia for all she knew. It was nothing to take lightly. There was no way she could predict what his reaction would be. She needed guidance from a professional. Someone like her father, who at least at one time made a career of chasing criminals.

The coffee maker alerted her that it was done brewing, and she poured herself a cup. She gulped the first few sips down as if it was her daily fix. After she sat back down at the table, she watched the message flash onto her screen.

"How did it go last night? I just need to know that you are all right."

The text was from Simone. Danni was exhausted by the time she made it home and fell asleep as soon as her head hit the pillow. She knew Simone wanted an update as soon as possible, but she was too stunned to reach out to her. Besides, her brain pulled the plug on her after the constant barrage of adrenaline that assaulted her bloodstream for most of the night.

"Sorry I didn't stay in touch last night. I was beat by the time I got in."

"Did he go gambling again?"

Danni hesitated. She didn't want to worry her. Her head should be filled with music, not the crimes of gangsters.

"Yes," she lied, but hated herself for betraying the honesty that was growing between them.

"Can I call you?"

Danni hesitated again. It would be harder to lie in person, but she couldn't say no to her. She decided to agree to the phone call and see if she could somehow avoid the subject.

"Of course," she texted back and waited for the phone to ring. It did, less than ten seconds later.

"Hey there," she answered, her headache slowly relinquishing more of its barrage on her with each sip of coffee.

"Did you just wake up?"

"I did, and I'm waiting for the coffee to kick in, so I may not be the most talkative yet."

"I'm glad to hear that you made it home all right."

Danni didn't feel as if she was all right. Her paranoia skyrocketed. She now found herself in a relationship with a thief, working for the Russian mafia. She had visions of federal agents following Jake. Snapping pictures of him coming in and out of her apartment. It felt like she had eyes crawling all over her like ants, trying to find her connection to their crime syndicate.

She walked over to the window and looked out over the street, sure to find officers sitting in unmarked cars waiting for Jake's arrival at her building.

"Are you?"

She heard Simone's question as she peered out.

"I'm fine. It was mostly uneventful. I was hoping for more action, but it turned out to be just his usual routine, you know?"

She suddenly felt overwhelmed by a sense of panic. She realized that her phone could be wiretapped and wanted to end the conversation with Simone as soon as possible.

"I'm getting a feeling that you are not okay," Simone said.

"Maybe we should talk about it more in person instead, you know?"

"I was afraid that you wouldn't want to see me in person again."

"Why on earth would you think that?"

Danni was bending the truth to put Simone's mind at ease. Of course, she was afraid of seeing her again after the afternoon they had the day before. She sometimes imagined herself a superhero, but she was powerless against the train on the tracks between the two of them.

"You know very well why."

"Maybe we could talk about that more in person as well."

"Am I going to have to buy you a burner phone?"

"Not a bad idea. I need to get my hands on one for sure."

"What are you doing the rest of the day?"

"I'm heading out to see my parents, actually."

"No shenanigans tonight?"

"No shenanigans, I promise. I will see you on Wednesday. I look forward to that so much. Are you ready for it?"

"I should be. I'm bringing Billie for her lesson tomorrow."

"Then I will see you tomorrow. Even better."

They both stayed on the line, hesitating. Even though Danni was anxious about talking over the phone with her, she was reluctant to hang up.

"How was Billie's movie with the trombone player, what's his name?"

"Her name is Britton. She said they had a great time. Came home pretty soon after you left."

"A girl trombone player. Well, what do you know! If I remember correctly, all the trombone players in my high school band were boys."

"Times have changed for sure. She is a girl, but I'm not sure she is girly."

"I'm sure it takes more than a girly set of lungs to blow that thing, so it's probably good if she's not all that girly."

"Billie is not bothered by it. Young girls sometimes take a while to grow into their girly parts."

"So true. I was a late bloomer myself."

"Me too. My parents were very worried for a long time. They kept buying new dresses every week to entice me," Simone said, and Danni could hear the smile in her voice.

Danni became restless again, certain that the phone was tapped. She still stood at the window, watching.

"I wish your phone wasn't tapped, Danni. I would have liked to talk about things."

"I don't think the phone is tapped," she said, baffled by how Simone was able to read her mind so easily.

"I will have to find and train a pigeon so that I can send messages to you."

"Those pigeons probably get scooped up all the time as well."

"Goodness, Danni. This sounds serious. Am I really to believe that you are not in trouble? We should meet somewhere so we can talk."

"No, I will get the burner phone. People get followed all the time. Besides, I'm probably just being paranoid today, I need time to think things through a bit. I think going to see my parents will help."

"I will wait to hear from you then, from an unknown, untraceable number."

"I hope you're not disappointed."

"Not at all. There's nothing you could do that would disappoint me," Simone reminded her.

"I feel like I'm stuck in a maze. It's confusing, to say the least. Yesterday, at your house especially."

Simone stayed silent. Danni got up and paced over to the living room window. She looked down on the street again at the row of parked cars. At people standing beside lamp poles reading papers. Everywhere she looked were visions of peril.

"I feel the same way, Danni," Simone responded. "I am questioning everything too, but I want to find the answers we are looking for together."

"It's not safe for you to go where I'm looking."

"It's safer if we do it together, don't you think?"

"What do you mean?"

"You know what I mean. We talked about it yesterday, remember?"

"The reason why you are not looking into things?"

"Yes."

"Do you want me to look into…" Danni was taken aback.

"Yes, I do, but we should talk about it in person. Since your phone is tapped."

"Are you serious?"

"I am serious, Danni. I thought about it last night. Something is going on, and it's true what you said, not knowing could be the more dangerous option."

"That's what I thought too yesterday."

"We are on the same page then."

"We can talk about it when I get the phone."

"Fair enough."

"I will call you soon."

"Bye, Danni. Oh, and say hi to your mother. Let her know that everyone in the house fell in love with the cupcakes."

"She will be so happy to hear that."

"What did you tell her about me?"

"Not anything that should be disclosed over this line."

"All right, all right, we will talk later."

"I will tell her you said hi."

When they finally hung up, Danni threw her head in her hands to keep the room from spinning. She felt like she was trapped on a fast-moving carousel at a freakish fair. First, Peter asked her to spy on Jake, and now Simone practically hired her to investigate her husband. The universe was clearly trying to tell her something. She lay down on the spinning turn table and looked up at the sky. She saw a sea of stars peeking through the dark cover of night. She looked closer and felt the drops of light raining down on her skin. Tiny specks of scattering light, illuminating the sky, and holding the answers to many of her burning questions.

Chapter 20

Danni stood on the sidewalk a few houses down from her parents. She was unsure about what she wanted to accomplish there. She planned to question her father about his past experience with Russian gangs, but she had no idea if he would even be interested or sober enough to have that discussion. Then there was her mother, who was having an affair. She was sure of it, but she didn't want to confront her about it. She could tell that it was making her happy. The same way that Simone made her happy. Who was she to throw stones? She took a deep breath and started walking toward the home.

She noticed that the sky was darkening. Thick clouds gathered, getting ready for a summer storm. The wind started to pick up, and she increased the pace of her steps.

She knocked on the door, hoping that her mother would open the door before the first drops of rain fell. She didn't bring a rain jacket. She waited, but no one answered. She couldn't hear any approaching footsteps. She knocked again, and still no one came to rescue her from the impending waters about to be released from the sky.

She had an uneasy feeling as she watched a few birds circling high above the roof of the house, looking for shelter somewhere. She remembered that she had a key for the house in the glove compartment of her car and rushed back to it. Before she looked for it, she dialed her mother's cell phone to see if she was even home.

There was no answer.

She found the key at the bottom of the glove box in a small leather pouch. She kept an extra key there because she was often called over by her mother. Mostly involving her father, getting too drunk to stand. She rushed back to the home just as the first of the raindrops started to pelt down on her.

She quickly unlocked the door to escape the storm's fury. The sound of the rain hitting the roof grew louder, drowning out any sounds coming from the house. She hesitated and worried about the nagging feeling spreading through her gut. She felt the blood drain slowly out of her body, and her legs became heavy and unwilling to approach the inner part of the house.

She started to register voices coming from the dining room. She recognized her father's voice, rising above the sound of the rain, and she strained her ears to hear what he was saying. It was unusual for him to be out of his room.

She walked anxiously toward the dining room. She heard sobs coming from her father. When she finally reached the door, she peered in, reluctantly. She took another step forward into the room and was shocked by the scene that jumped out at her. Her purse slipped off her shoulder and landed on the floor with a loud thud.

Her father was seated at the dining room table. He had a gun drawn to his head as tears streamed down his face. In front of him sneered a half-filled bottle of vodka. Her mother watched from the corner, hunched over, her face as white as a ghost. It looked like her heart was barely beating.

"Dad!" Danni cried out, her voice unrecognizable from the terror that screeched from her vocal cords.

"Danni, stay back!" he yelled back at her, keeping the gun pressed to his temple.

She stopped in her tracks and looked over to her mother, standing like a statue, frozen in time.

She could hear the pounding of the rain, hailing down as if it was trying to wrestle her father away from his insanity, while in fact, it only escalated the panic in the room.

"What's going on, Dad?" she asked, trying to engage him. She knew she would need to get him talking. Her visit was unexpected, and she hoped that her untimely arrival would help to sway him away from his crazed intentions.

"Ask your mother!" he yelled, squeezing his eyes shut to stop the tears from running down his face.

Danni's mother was still stunned and speechless in the corner.

"Mom?" Danni asked, but she didn't trust that her mother would say anything that could deescalate him.

"Can you put the gun down, Dad?"

He just shook his head as he set his eyes firmly on her mother.

"Please tell me what happened."

"I saw her! With him," he said as he shut his eyes away from the unbearable truth.

Danni looked at her mom as she put the damming puzzle together. Her father was most likely referring to Max. He must have discovered her mother's new romantic interest. He must have seen them through his binoculars. That she has grown blind with love and, most likely, also very careless.

The rest of her blood drained out of her as she realized the gravity of the situation. The reason for her father pointing a gun to his head.

"Matt, I don't know what you expected me to do," her mom said softly, not looking directly at him.

"Was it too much to ask that you stay faithful to me? Your husband?"

He raised his voice to compete with the pelting rain.

Her mother looked up. Her hands were trembling under the weight of finding the right words.

"You have locked yourself away in your room for years."

"Because you have never forgiven me. I have never been able to face you."

"It's true," her mother said, somehow managing to keep her voice calm. "We have both been angry and hurt for years, but we haven't been good for each other."

"I haven't been good for anyone," her father said through the tears.

Danni held her breath as she watched her father's finger on the trigger. She needed to get the gun away from him. They were wading into uncharted waters, and she wasn't sure how much of it he would handle before squeezing the trigger to get away from the pain of it all. The rain suddenly softened and faded into a soft background drizzle. It cushioned the space between them.

"Please put the gun down, Matt," her mother pleaded.

"No!" he screamed out at her. "Tell me who he is. I want to know the name of the thief who stole my wife."

Her mother's shoulders tensed up as she looked over to Danni, her eyes begging for guidance.

"Dad, we can talk about it when you put the gun down. I'm sure we can sort everything out. Just put the gun down so that no one gets hurt."

Her dad sneered at her.

"You think I won't end it?"

"I'm scared that you would."

"Your mother wants to leave me, Danni. You already left. Your brother." He closed his eyes abruptly. She didn't know which one he was referring to.

"I haven't left, Dad. It's you that has left us. Years ago. I would love to know what to do to get you back."

Tears kept rolling down his face as her words registered with him.

"I have drowned. In that bottle," he said, pointing at the vodka next to him with the gun. "I am dead already. Along with Matthew. I can't find my way back," he said, and she could hear him slurring from the alcohol.

"We are still here. Waiting for you."

He looked at her, pointing the barrel back at his temple, regret poured off his face along with the tears from his eyes.

"And you?"

He looked at her mother.

Her mother looked away. Trying to hide the guilt in her eyes. Danni could strangle her.

"You see? She's not waiting."

"Not true," Danni intervened desperately.

"Everyone would be better off without me, and you know it," her father said, and she watched his hand getting ready to act on his soul's deepest desire. She knew he wanted to get away from himself more than anything.

The muscles of his hand tensed, and she saw his finger squeeze down around the trigger. He closed his eyes and prepared for the bullet to rip through his skull.

Danni's legs sprang into action, realizing the horror that was about to unleash on their lives.

"No, Dad!" she screamed as she leaped toward him, reaching for the gun.

She anticipated the deafening sound that would drench the moment in agony and change their lives forever.

Instead, there was only a suspending click. No bullet was discharged. Danni ran toward her father. His face appeared utterly surprised as he found the silent gun still heavy in his hand. Robbed from the bloody consequence he wanted.

Danni punched at his hand, and the gun dropped to the floor. She kicked at it like it was a venomous snake, to get it out of striking distance. Her mother dropped to her knees and cried loudly into the space between them.

Danni embraced her dad, holding him close as sobs ripped through his frail muscles.

They were frozen and stunned. The light through the windows faded, and they held the moment, listening to the sound of the rain outside while taking every thrashing of the storm that raged inside the room.

Danni's father dropped his head onto the table, tears still flowing down his face, rolling off the table and dripping onto the floor. She held on to him and draped her warmth over him while immense relief for the gun's malfunction washed over her.

He finally calmed down and raised his head. He looked over to the corner where the gun lay, then looked at Danni.

"I double-checked it. I made sure."

"The gun?"

He nodded.

"Ten bullets. Ready to go, I made sure of it."

"Just because you are ready to go doesn't mean it's time for you to go."

"It's this house, Matt," her mother said. She was still crouched down on the floor.

They both looked at her, puzzled.

"What are you talking about, Mom?"

"It's this house," she said again. "I have felt it for years. There's darkness in every inch of this place."

"It's not the house, Sandy," her father said. "It's us. I ruined us. God wants me to let you go."

Her mother looked at him in disbelief.

"What are you saying, Matt?"

"I thought today was my last day. I was hell bound on ending it. I have planned it since I watched you and that man outside on the street. I knew I was in the way, and I wanted to set you free. I thought the gun would be the way. But that wouldn't really set you free. It would just trap you and punish you all over again."

"I have been the one sentencing you for years," her mother said, relentless tears streaming from her guilt-ridden eyes.

Her dad took a deep breath.

"We have to stop hurting each other," he said softly. "I've known that."

Her mom nodded, wiping at her eyes.

Her father got up from the table and walked over to her mother. He reached out his hand to her. She took his hand, and he pulled her up from the floor and into his arms. She didn't resist and threw her arms around his frail body.

"I'm so sorry, Sandy."

Danni watched her parents, and she couldn't remember ever seeing them so close to each other. Tears rolled down her own face as she watched them. She knew in her bones that it was nothing short of a miracle that her father was still alive. It was an enormous, blessed miracle, and she stood in awe as she watched the miracle expand, pulling her parents toward each other, closer than they have been in years.

They finally released each other, and her father led her mother back to the table. They all sat down to face the uncertainty of where they would go from there.

"I will let you go, Sandy," her father said. "You have suffered long enough."

Her mother didn't respond.

"I'm going to move out," he repeated.

Danni and her mother looked at him in disbelief.

"Matt, you don't have to. I should be the one moving out," her mother objected quickly.

"No. It's only fair that I go. You have paid for this house all these years with hours of hard work."

Danni's mom took a breath.

"Where will you go?" she asked.

"I don't know. I don't know. I will figure it out."

"You can stay with me for a while, Dad," Danni said.

She knew she would worry about him endlessly if he went off on his own after so many years. She also wanted a chance to reconnect with him.

"No Danni. I could never impose on your life like that."

"There is nothing I would rather do than help you get back on your feet. I have an extra room that you can use until you can find a more permanent place. We just need to find a bed somewhere. In the meantime, I have a comfortable couch."

Danni's heart warmed as she let her plan sink in. Being close to her father again would heal her whole world.

Danni's father hanged his head down and pursed his lips together.

"It's settled then. I will stay with Danni until I can find an apartment and a job. Something to do with the rest of my life."

"When will you go?" her mother asked.

Her father looked at her with soft eyes. She hasn't seen so much life in them for so long.

"Danni, I don't want to be alone tonight. I think I will stay with you tonight. The couch will be fine for a while."

"Of course, Dad."

Danni looked at her mother.

"What about you, Mom? Staying here?"

She closed her eyes as she shook her head and Danni knew what she meant.

"It's good, Sandy. It's good. None of us should be here, alone tonight."

Danni watched as her dad got up from the table. He looked at them with quiet eyes.

"I'm going to pack a few things."

Danni watched him walk out of the room. As soon as he was out of sight, she rushed over to the gun in the corner.

She brought it over to the table. Lay it down in front of her and stared at it.

She picked it up finally and held it in her hands as her mother watched her intently.

She pulled the magazine off the grip and pulled the slide back to inspect the chamber. One bullet spiked out. The bullet that would have met her father's demise. She looked at the magazine, which was filled with bullets. She counted ten of them all together. She looked at her mother, puzzled.

"What is it, Danni?"

"That bullet should have been fired."

Her mom looked at her with grave understanding. They both understood the weight of what happened. It was a miracle, witnessed in slow motion by both of them. It lacked any rational explanation. She remembered hearing the distinct sound of an empty click, instead of the deafening blow that was expected. He squeezed the trigger all the way down, she saw it with her own eyes.

She emptied all the bullets out of the magazine and placed them in her pocket. She walked over to her purse and placed the gun inside. She vowed to lock the gun up in her apartment, somewhere he wouldn't have access to it anymore.

She walked back to the table and sat across from her mother.

"So you and Max?"

Her mother looked up at her, nodded, and she saw the flicker of light in her eyes at the mention of his name.

"You are going to move in with him?"

"No, Danni. I will stay with him tonight, but only because I don't want to be alone after what we have been through today."

"It feels as if things are changing for all of us. Do you feel it too?"

"God knows, we could all use a change in our lives."

Danni felt her mother's accord settling down in her belly. She could feel their truth coming to rest inside of her. When she took a breath, she could fill her whole body with air, deep down into her stomach, without any tightness pushing back.

When her father finally came back into the room, he clutched a small suitcase. He needed a shower and a shave, and she intended to talk him into doing that once they got back to her place. She got up to let him know that she was ready to go. Her mother got up and came over to stand in front of him.

"Let's try this, Matt," she said and gave him another hug.

He reached for her, and Danni could see the hurt on his face as he said goodbye to his wife.

They left the house, and she pulled the door shut behind them. They walked down the street to her car in silence. The storm has passed, and the rain has stopped. Still, Danni couldn't stop thinking about the loaded gun. About the magic bullet that refused to inflict the damage he had in mind for it. It was divine intervention, unlike what she has ever witnessed.

They got in the car, and as she drove off, she watched her father lean his head against the window, straining to close his eyes as if he was pushing through into an unknown world with the daughter he had given up on so many years ago.

Chapter 21

Danni welcomed the prospect of going to work that Monday morning. She has never been so relieved to see the end of a weekend. Her father was still asleep on the couch when she left the apartment. She watched his sunken face for a while before she finally pulled the door shut behind her. She tried to come to terms with all the changes the weekend has brought, but she felt as if she was trapped in a nightmare. She locked the gun away in the safe she kept in the corner of her closet. She was nervous leaving her father alone in her apartment, afraid he would lose his nerve for the new direction his life was taking.

She didn't expect Peter at the store until after one that afternoon. He had two new students and a few regulars to occupy his schedule, and she would have to pin him down before their arrival. She rehashed the dreaded report for him over and over in her mind. She had no choice but fill him in about Jake's eventful weekend. There were quite a few valuable guitars missing from the inventory, and she would be complicit if she didn't tell him what she knew.

It was still early. She had no customers yet, giving her time to take advantage of the quiet and call Simone. The store's phone would be safe enough to use. She could wait until she brought Billie in for her lesson later that day, or she could wait until she came in for her audition on Wednesday. But she wanted to hear her voice. She was still frazzled from the ordeal with her father. She dialed the number and waited, hopeful that Simone would recognize the store's number and answer.

"Hello?" she answered, and Danni sank into her familiar voice.
"Hey, it's me."
"Oh, Danni. It's so nice to hear your voice. How are you?"
"Going crazy. How about you?"
"What's going on?"
"How much time do you have?"
"All the time in the world. Bill is at work and Billie is in school."

Danni didn't know where to begin. She was unable to structure a back story and fight back her tears. The silence between them stretched out.

"How was your visit with your parents?" Simone asked, sensing Danni's loss for words.

Danni still couldn't find a suitable sentence for what happened.

"Danni?" Simone asked again, patiently.

"Let's see. I walked in on my dad having a complete meltdown. He wanted to end it all."

She rattled the words off quickly before they had a chance to evade her again.

"What? How?"
"He was going to shoot himself."
"Are you serious?"
"Yes. He didn't, though. But it was very close."
"Oh my god, Danni. I'm so sorry to hear that."
"He is going to stay with me for a while."
"That is good. Do you want me to go over and check in on him while you are at work?"
"Aren't you bringing Billie over here for her lesson?"
"Yes, but if you need me to, I can go over before."
"I don't think that would be needed, but thank you for offering that."
"Just let me know."
"The reason why I called you," Danni said, "this phone is probably not bugged."
"Why would your dad try to end it?"

Simone was not ready to move on from Danni's grim account.

"My mother is having an affair," she explained frankly.

"Oh my! He found out?"

"Yes. He saw them on the street together, kissing or something."

"And now he's moved in with you?"

"Yes, it's for the best, believe me. I will see if he can help me with your situation."

"What situation?"

"About Bill. If it's all right with you, we can discuss it more when you bring Billie over."

"You think he will be up for it?"

"Maybe something constructive like that could help him deal with what's going on with my mother."

A couple entered the store, and Danni watched as they walked over to the guitar section. She needed to go over to give them assistance.

"I got a few customers now, so I should go."

"Okay. I will see you later today."

"I look forward to it. Really."

"Me too, Danni."

Peter walked in, right around one. Danni felt her heart starting to race, knowing that she would have to face him soon. She could feel the sweat leaking through her palms. She wanted to corner him before she lost her nerve. She decided to tell him everything. She didn't have a chance to talk with her dad about any of it yet, but she couldn't keep Peter in the dark any longer. Not with the stolen guitars now at a pawn shop. The police would surely have to get involved. She wasn't sure if she should go as far as telling him about the stolen car. She would need to gauge how much of the news he could handle.

"Hey, Peter," she greeted him timidly.

He seemed tired. Something was eating at him. She kept her eyes on him, hoping he would sense that she had information. It was difficult for her to form the toxic words about Jake's demise. Breathing their ugly reality to life.

"Should we talk in my studio?" he asked, and she knew her tense body language has registered with him.

"Yes."

He looked at her, his eyes knew it was not going to be easy. He was about to hear something that he has been afraid to hear for years.

IN THE SCATTERING OF LIGHT

She grabbed her backpack with the pictures she took and trailed behind him as they walked back. His shoulders were hunched under the weight of the world.

She entered his office and watched him put his messenger bag on the table. He took his jacket off and hanged it on a hanger behind the door. They were both procrastinating.

He walked slowly to the stool next to the table, sat down, and looked at her.

"You have some news, I assume?"

"I'm afraid, I do."

"Let's just hear it. I'll never really be ready for it."

Danni took the pictures out of her bag and placed it in front of Peter on the table.

"I followed him on Saturday night. All the way to this store. I watched him walk out of here with five gig bags. I checked this morning. I'm missing three of the Pro Strat Fenders and two Les Paul's. That's more than five grand missing."

Peter just stared at the photos spread out in front of him. She could tell he could barely take a breath. He was suspended on a tightrope, and any movement of his body could throw him off and send him into a free fall.

"He took the guitars to a pawn shop yesterday morning. In Bell's Corner."

"Bell's Corner? Not exactly close to anything here."

"No."

Peter looked up at her. His face was pale, and he looked like was going to be sick.

"Do you need some cold water?" she asked.

He shook his head and reached for a bottle of green tea out of the bag on the desk. Opened it hastily and took a few large swigs. She watched him trying to catch his breath as her report sank in.

"Why?" he finally asked quietly.

"Bell's Corner is not too far from Bustleton. Remember, I told you that he has been going to that bar in Bustleton frequently after his work shift at the bar."

"I think so."

"The Red Square Tavern I think it's called."

"Russian?"

"Yes. I really think the place is a front for some sort of gambling operation. Or maybe just a place where they discuss their next business moves. People going in there are let in by a door man, so it looks to be by invitation only."

"Do you think he stole the guitars to settle a debt again?"

"Probably. Have you noticed money gone from the store before?"

"I asked him before to take money from here to the bank to deposit. He didn't deposit all of it. But I just thought maybe I counted wrong."

Peter held his head in both hands, squeezing around his temples, trying to keep his head from exploding. He pressed his eyes shut. She assumed it was to fight off the tears. She was just as devastated about how far Jake has fallen.

"Danni, what should we do? I don't know if I can call the police on him."

"I think he may be pushed into a corner. Maybe he got into a money-making racket with these people. They may have him on the hook now."

"Money making for what?"

"I told you that he wants to buy into Mark's bar. He wants to get married, have kids. I'm sure he is doing the math of his tips and not coming up with everything he wants out of life."

"Gambling is not the way to go. He should know better because of his dad. How could he forget what happened to him?"

Danni couldn't tell him about the car he stole. She didn't think Peter could handle the added blow, and she couldn't bear saying the words to him.

"I have a theory that he met these people at Mark's bar. I could have my dad investigate it. He could go hang out at there and see what he finds out."

"Your dad? I think Jake told me your dad was a hermit that's been stuck in his room for years."

"He finally came out."

"When?"

"Yesterday."

She averted her eyes, hoping he wouldn't pry any further.

"He used to be a cop, right?"

"Detective. He is staying with me now."

"Oh, wow. I'm so sorry that I'm bugging you with all my family drama. You obviously have a lot of your own stuff going on."

"It's fine, Peter. Jake is my concern too. I want to find out what he's involved with. To see if we can get him out of this trouble. If we knew who he was dealing with, it would be easier. I'm sure my dad can help in some way. And it will be good for him to get into something constructive."

"So you're thinking to send your dad to the bar to see if he can find out who Jake's involved with?"

"Can't hurt. I can't help but to think that's where he met these people. Who knows, if he stole money from you to cover debts, he's most likely stealing money from the bar also."

"My brother would fire him on the spot. Giving Jake a chance there was only as a favor to me, but it took a lot of convincing that his father's tendencies wouldn't manifest in the same way with him."

"The only way to help him is to find out who they are."

"You don't think he would get suspicious? Seeing your dad there suddenly?"

"He would go in disguise of course," she said with a smile.

"You have a knack for spying, Danni. You must really take after your dad in that way."

"Maybe."

"I really appreciate all your help. What a mess we are in with him."

"It's probably a good idea for you to change the store code and not give it to him again. It was a piece of cake for him to waltz in here and take whatever he wanted."

Peter just nodded. He wiped his hands over his eyes again, forcing them to stay focused.

"How are you going to focus on your students today? Do you need me to cancel your lessons?"

He shook his head. "No, I need to keep my mind occupied."

They both heard the store bell ring, alerting them to customers entering the store. Danni needed to get back to her post, but she felt an enormous weight lifted after sharing at least part of the devastating news with Peter.

She left Peter's studio, looking back at him one more time before she passed through the door. He sat on the chair hunched over, deep in thought. She had time this weekend to absorb the blow. Time was not a luxury he had with his full schedule looming over him. The first of which would arrive in less than thirty minutes, and Billie was scheduled for four o'clock.

Simone would bring her, giving her another hour with her electric eyes. These days, thinking about the light of her kept her buoyant. It was the change her mother spoke about. There were forces pushing down on her from everywhere, but when she focused on the sound of her piano, she felt completely shielded.

Chapter 22

The hours flew by like birds heading south to flee cold weather. She contemplated following suit. How easy it would be to pack her car with one suitcase and head to a less complicated place. Maybe she could transport herself to her brother's doorstep in New Orleans. Sleep on his couch until she could dream up an entirely different life. If only she could warm up to the thought of not seeing Simone again.

It was ten minutes before four. She looked up just as the door opened. It was as if their inner clocks have synced after that last kiss.

Simone and Billie walked over to where she stationed herself behind the sales counter. Danni allowed herself only the briefest luxury of Simone's crystal-blue eyes. It was too much like staring directly into the sun. She could sense her face was on the brink of bursting into a red blaze of fire.

"Hi, Danni," Simone said, her face as radiant as a silver moon.

"My two favorite ladies," she responded, sure to keep her eyes on Billie. "I heard you made friends with a trombone player at school," she said, trying to engage Billie right away. She remembered their day at the movies so fondly.

Billie looked at her, smiled, and nodded.

"Am I out of luck now for a movie pal?" she asked.

Billie shook her head.

"No? You will go with me again?"

"Sure. Britton isn't really into documentaries."

"I'm in luck then. Keep your eye out for one you'd like to see and let me know."

Billie nodded, gleaming from the offer.

"Mom, I'm going in for the lesson. You'll be here when I get back?"

"Of course, I'll be right here. Go have fun."

Billie walked off to Peter's studio in the back, leaving Simone frozen in front of the cashier's counter.

"Hi," Danni said, hoping her mind wouldn't crumble into a stuttering mess.

"You look beautiful today," Simone said boldly with a warm smile chasing her compliment.

Danni looked around the store, her eyes desperately trying to find something other than the shimmering face in front of her.

"You wanted to talk to me." Her eyes finally succumbed and settled on Simone.

"I was hoping we could. Has the store been busy today?"

"Not really."

Danni pulled one of the high stools over to the other side of the counter for Simone.

"Can I get you anything to drink maybe?"

"A chardonnay?" Simone said, smiling, and her request accompanied the sweet memory of their evening at the Wine Loft. It seemed like it was ages ago, but the memory still sparked vividly in her mind.

"Wouldn't that be nice? Should we head to the Wine Loft? Abandon ship and elope?"

"Elope? I like that you're dreaming big, Danni, but we should probably stick with something less daring."

Danni walked to the small fridge in the back office of the store and came back with two cans of 7 Up.

"How is this for less daring?"

"Don't tempt me like that again," Simone said with a smile, opening her can. She reached into her oversized purse and presented two straws, handing one to Danni.

"Now we are set."

"Look at you! Prepared for anything."

"The mother in me."

"I didn't get the prepaid phone yet. So I'm glad that you're here today."

"How's your dad? Did you talk to him?"

Danni didn't respond immediately. Her brain still tried to distance itself from the shock.

"I haven't spoken to him today yet. We will talk when I get home."

"Do you really think your parents will end their marriage?"

Her eyes drifted down the aisle of the sheet music for a while, but she couldn't focus on anything. Her eyes started to well up. She quickly pressed her fingers over them to keep control of her emotions.

"Their marriage has been over for years. They knew they had to take the next step, but we didn't expect it to happen the way it did."

"I'm sure it was a horrific experience for you."

"It was scary. I thought I was going to lose him. It was a miracle that we got through it unscathed. I hope him moving out will help them get some part of their lives back."

"My god. You are going through so much these days," Simone said, her gaze soft.

"I know. It seems like the universe is trying to scream something at me."

"Maybe it's given you an assignment."

"You see it too?"

Simone nodded. "Clear as day. We should answer the call."

"I'm trying. I have a crazy feeling now that my father was meant to get involved. The whole time I've been dealing with Jake, I kept thinking that he would be the one person that could help me."

Simone nodded.

"Maybe this will be a way for him to heal. To get back to who he really is."

"I think so too. People can't thrive when they abandon themselves," Danni said. She believed it more than ever.

"Still, uncovering secrets can be so risky, Danni."

"All the more reason I should recruit my dad to help."

"That would ease my mind too. If you had him to back you up."

Danni smiled. She basked in the warmth of Simone's care for her.

"So let's talk about Bill," Danni said.

She looked at her watch and felt the sting of the hourglass running out.

"Are you sure you still want me to?"

A customer arrived at the counter with a basket full of products. It felt awkward with Simone sitting there; she should have planned better. She should have set them up to talk in the back office, but it wasn't as if they could be alone together. She wasn't strong enough for that. Not while she was at work and with Billie right around the corner.

Danni checked the customer's items out while Simone stayed in the chair in front of the counter, scrolling on her phone.

"Did you find everything you were looking for?" Danni asked him, painfully aware of the time ticking away.

"I did," he said.

Danni sighed in relief the minute she finished his transaction and bagged his items.

They both waited to restart their conversation until they could hear the doorbell chime, sure that he closed the door behind him.

"Of course I'm all ears. For what you want to talk about," Danni said, hoping she didn't lose her nerve during the interruption.

"I've been thinking about Bill and what you said."

Danni remembered his suspicious eyes both times she was in his home.

"What do you think he is up to?"

"He's been away from home more than ever. He is more secretive about his work."

"Do you think that bag he brings home is filled with money?"

"I wouldn't be surprised. He bought a new car the other day. I've noticed new watches, expensive suits. He tells me to get anything I want. He buys Billie far more than she needs. It's almost as if he spends money on purpose."

"Let's just assume it's not filled with gym clothes then. I heard that the housing market is good these days though. Are you sure his business isn't just booming?"

"He sold houses in New York also. He became a broker here, but he doesn't have that many agents working for him. We never had this kind of abundance back in New York. Talking with you this past weekend made me question why I just sit by so idly."

"All I can think to do is to follow him around a bit. Before we jump to too many conclusions. It will be hard with my work schedule since he probably does most of his business dealings in the day. I can try to get a few days off during the week. I will see if Peter has someone available to cover for me."

Simone sat quietly, pondering Danni's offer.

"Make sure you ask if your dad can help."

"Do you want to meet him?"

"Your dad?"

"Who else?" Danni said, smiling.

Simone smiled in return and lightened the air between them.

"You want me to meet your father?"

"Maybe we could have you over for dinner? You and Billie?"

Simone's eyebrows raised.

"He could use some social interaction."

"All right," she agreed slowly. "How is Friday night?"

"Friday night is perfect for me, but I will check with him and let you know on Wednesday when you come for the audition."

Simone pursed her lips.

"Cold feet?"

"I haven't told Bill yet, but it's not cold feet."

"Wear your warmest socks on Wednesday. Just in case."

Simone laughed.

"I still can't call you?"

Danni shook her head. "I promise I will get the phone after work today."

"I can't shake the feeling that we met for a reason," Simone said softly, but her eyes shimmered with excitement.

"I know," Danni admitted.

They both steered their eyes down the hall as Peter and Billie walked toward them. Danni's heart sank, realizing the last of the sand has slipped through their hourglass.

"How did she do today?" Simone asked Peter as she got up from her chair.

"Marvelous as always. She is moving through the practice pieces very quickly. I think she is ready for grade seven pieces already. I don't want to rush things for her, but she picks up on everything extremely quick."

Simone looked proud. "She works very hard."

"I see no end to her potential," Peter assured her.

The four of them watched each other, like they were stranded at a four-way stop sign not knowing who should make the next move. The silence stretched out awkwardly.

"Danni, who else do I have today?" Peter finally jumped ahead.

"Ben is coming at seven for his makeup lesson."

"I have to drive to Bell's Corner, can you call to see if he can come at eight instead? I'm not sure I will make it back by seven with rush hour."

"I will call him. Alex should be here soon for the evening shift."

Simone looked for a chance to jump in.

She reached out and touched Danni's hand.

"Sorry to interrupt, Danni, but we should head home. Billie still has some math homework to get to."

"Sure, thanks for keeping me company. And let me know about dinner on Friday," Danni said as she could still feel Simone's electrifying touch buzz through her hand. Peter's eyes caught the gesture as well.

"Dinner?" Billie asked surprised.

"I'll fill you in, sweetie. Come on, let's get going," she said as they started to turn away from the group.

"Good to see you again, Billie," Danni said and then watched as Simone steered Billie out of the store.

Peter glanced at her, looking perplexed.

"Dinner?" he repeated Billie's question.

"My father could use some company," Danni answered quickly.

"I'm sure!" Peter teased.

"I swear!"

"Relax. It's good to see that you made a friend. I don't think I have ever heard you mention having any girlfriends to hang out with."

"Guilty as charged. I am the worst at making friends. Have always been."

"And yet you and Billie's mom get along so easy."

Billie's mom. His words stabbed at her like a sharp warning.

"She is very beau…easy to get along with," Danni stammered.

He tapped his fingers on the counter once and looked at her, still amused.

"I have to get going. Please tell Ben if he can't come at eight, I will have to make it up to him some other time. I want to go see if I can still find the missing guitars at that pawn shop."

"I really hope you can get them back."

"Probably for a small fortune."

He left the store with long, hurried strides. A man on a mission to verify that his most beloved nephew has matured into his most unbeloved brother. A fact that once substantiated would surely haunt him for all his days.

Chapter 23

Danni unlocked the door to her apartment but hesitated before she turned the knob to open the door. She was scared to face her father, not knowing what to expect. When she left for work that morning, he was still sound asleep on the couch in her living room. He looked as haggard and tired as the night before. She hoped the sun's rays through the window would light a spark in him.

Her eyes jumped to the couch first as she walked through the door. It was empty and her heart lifted. She could smell the savory aroma of meat wafting toward her from the small kitchen. She heard oil sizzling in the pan, giving her apartment an unusual homelike feel. She placed her purse on the coffee table and entered the kitchen. Watched her dad in front of the stove, drizzling herbed butter skillfully over two thick pieces of steak. He had two more smaller pots simmering on the stove. Her eyes came to rest on him, and she hardly recognized him. Cleanly showered, shaved, and dressed in a clean set of clothes. Her heart warmed at the sight of him. A new man, cooking a meal for them in her apartment.

"Do you want to eat at the table? I can set it," she offered.

"That would be great, Danni. It will just be about another ten minutes here for the steak to rest and to finish with the vegetables. I made a salad too and put it in the fridge."

"Wow, Dad! I didn't know you still knew how to cook," Danni said, surprised at the effort her father put into the meal.

"Hidden talents. I walked to the market today for some fresh air, and I remembered all the meals you and your mother made throughout the years for me."

"You didn't always eat them."

"I wasn't always sober enough to be hungry. Still, I was aware of the effort you and your mother made. I wanted to start returning the favor today."

"It smells divine! I will be right back and set the table."

She disappeared to her room to change into something more comfortable. She was glad that he still had his culinary interest since she had pretty much already invited Simone over for dinner on Friday.

After she set the table, he brought the food, and she served two glasses of Perrier sparkling lemon water. She needed to avoid alcohol for his sake, even though her nerves would have killed for a glass of Chardonnay.

"So what kind of work are you into these days?" he asked once they sat down.

He asked as if he was meeting her for the first time. The conversations between them over the years were so sparse, there was no way he could have kept up with the changes in her life. She remembered the drawings of people she pushed under his door to spark some interaction. Most recently, she used the drawing of the Russian to reconnect.

"I work in Jake's uncle's music store not too far from here, just on the other end of Fairmount."

"Jake's that boy you've been with since school, right?"

She poured a generous helping of vinaigrette over her salad as she pondered his question.

"Yes. We have been going together for years."

"Is he marriage material?"

Of course, he would join the rest of the world on the marriage bandwagon, she thought.

"I used to think so. Not so much these days," she answered, knowing that it was exactly the direction she wanted their conversation to go.

"You said he was in trouble."

She was surprised he remembered.

"Yes, I have discovered quite a few alarming things about him recently."

He stayed quiet as he hacked away at his steak.

"You cooked the steak perfectly, Dad," she said, while she tried to collect her thoughts, weighing how much to bombard him with.

"I used to cook for you guys all the time. When you were very young. Of course, your mother was difficult to boot out of the kitchen, always baking something with Matt twirling around her legs," he said, and she watched a graying sadness wash over his face as he scoffed at the gaping wound still center stage in their lives.

They were caught in the memory, sinking down into a place they have both been trying to escape, and she desperately tried to catch her breath, coming up for air.

"You remember the picture I drew of that Russian man and showed you, right?"

"Yes, the man with the dark eyes."

"Yes. I think Jake owes him money. I have been following him to get more information and caught him stealing a couple of expensive guitars from the music store where I work. It was just this past Saturday night actually. He stole a car right after that, which he probably took to a chop shop. Can you believe all of this?"

Her dad put his utensils down on his plate abruptly and stared up at her.

"You followed him doing all this?"

"I just happened to see him one day in the park, handing that Russian man a fat envelope. I assumed it was filled with money. So of course, it piqued my interest. I followed him a couple of times after his work shift at the bar. Caught him going to a Russian tavern in Bustleton, and I swear he must be gambling there."

"Most likely losing money."

Her father appeared interested.

"It seems that way, yes. He keeps telling me he is working on making money so that we can get married. But he is more likely stealing for money to settle gambling debts with the Russian mafia."

Her father seemed deep in thought, considering the theories she offered him. He continued to eat his steak as if on autopilot. His mind was occupied with the damning report of her once future husband.

"Those Russian gangs out of Bustleton are not people you want to mess around with. They like to send messages with body parts. How on earth did he get involved with them?"

"The only thing I could come up with was that he hooked up with them somehow at his uncle's bar, where he works."

"I thought you said his uncle has a music store, where you work."

"Different uncle. He works at his uncle Mark's bar. I work at his uncle Peter's music store. His father turned out to be the bad brother, who had to leave Philly because he shot the wrong guy. He would have been killed if he stayed in town. Jake hasn't heard from him since. Anyway, Peter got a hunch that Jake was getting into the same kind of trouble as his dad and asked if I could keep an eye on him and let him know what I found out."

Her father couldn't contain the smile on his face, as he listened to her account.

"You spied on him for your boss?"

"Sort of, but I was very careful so Jake wouldn't find out."

"Seems like policing is in our blood, kiddo."

"You left the force so long ago, I didn't know if you were still able to feel the connection."

"I surveilled your mother, you know. Discovered her affair with that baker man. Not that I handled it very well, but still."

Danni pushed the memory of the previous night down into her stomach.

"It's a miracle that you're still alive."

"Exactly, Danni. I keep thinking that maybe I was spared for a reason. I must still have a purpose here, or else. You know exactly what happened."

"You could help me figure out what is going on with Jake, for one."

He mulled over her request as he finished the last few bites of his meal.

"They must get something from him. They wouldn't just invite him over to come gamble at their tavern. He must be doing them a big favor in return."

"He is not telling me anything. Shuts down every time I poke around."

"Where's the bar?" her dad asked.

"Brewerytown."

"Maybe I'll go have some beers there and see what I can find out."

"You would?"

"How else will we get to the bottom of it?"

"Make sure he won't recognize you though."

"Jake hasn't seen me in years. I don't think he would remember me."

"He comes around here, sometimes very unexpected. And he would surely recognize you then if you've been at the bar."

"Good point. All right, I will hide my identity, don't worry."

"Don't you think we should call the police though?"

"No, no. Let's just dig into this a little more. See if we can help him get out without involving the police for now. These gangs don't like the police meddling in their affairs."

Danni felt as if the veil has been lifted. The reason for the miracle. She could feel her heart swell, knowing that his life was spared for the sake of their relationship.

"I've managed to get involved with another dilemma as well," she said, looking at his mind already constructing a plan to help Jake.

"I have missed a lot it seems."

"Should I put a pot of coffee on?"

"I bought some ice cream. Coffee and ice cream sounds good."

Danni sprang into action to clear the plates from the table and worked on brewing the coffee. Her father grabbed bowls for the ice cream. He bought chopped walnuts and chocolate sauce, and she considered it part of the celebration.

By the time she returned with two filled coffee cups, he seemed ready to listen. The ice cream was already served up in two bowls. She was ecstatic to have him there.

"Tell me about this other dilemma," he said, and she didn't waste any time to get him up to speed.

"I made a friend at work. A pianist. She brings her daughter there for lessons."

Her father's expression stayed neutral while she talked.

"I invited her over for dinner with us on Friday. I figured we could both use the company."

"How is that a dilemma?" he asked calmly as he scooped sweet bites of ice cream into his mouth.

"She thinks her husband is involved in some unsavory business here in town. All I know so far is that he is a real estate broker, but he has been coming into a lot of money. She said he buys expensive things constantly, as if he needs to get rid of it. I have seen him come home with a duffel bag full of cash twice now. At least, we are thinking that it's cash."

Her father smiled.

"Are you the new private detective in town?"

She chuckled.

"Looks like it. No, she just asked if I could help her find out what was going on. Just as a favor. I told her about Jake and what I found out by simply following him, and it got her thinking that maybe her husband should be looked into as well."

"You should follow her husband because he is making a lot of money?"

"I told her I would ask your advice first."

"I think it would be best to see what I can find out about him. There are so many dangerous people in this town, Danni."

"I enjoy doing it. Uncovering things people hide."

"Some things are better left uncovered."

"She's been thinking the same thing for years, but she realized that it could be just as dangerous not to know."

"We should get more information from her on Friday when she comes over. In the meantime, I will hang out at Jake's bar to see what I can uncover there."

"Billie will also most likely be here on Friday. Her daughter. So we probably can't discuss anything in front of her."

He nodded.

"I will be discreet."

"Yes, it's more of a friendly, social occasion. She wanted to meet you."

"What should we put on the menu?"

"How about shepherd's pie?"

"You got it. I'll go to the store again tomorrow and get what we need."

"I'll leave money for you."

"I have money, Danni."

"How?" she asked, realizing that her father hasn't worked in years and her mother did the shopping for the home.

"See how suspicious you are now?" he said, but his eyes were kind. She swore she noticed pride in his eyes, mostly likely because she has become so much like him.

She shrugged, but her eyes would not let go of the question.

"I'm still married to your mother, aren't I?"

"I can pay for the dinner stuff for Friday, Dad."

He looked at her, and his shoulders sagged.

"I pay and you cook," she offered. "Seems only fair to me."

His eyes sparked, and she felt relieved after she kissed him on his cheek and retreated to her room.

Danni laid in her bed later that evening. The meal with her father felt surreal. She has been dreaming about the day that they could have dinner together as a family, but never thought it would turn out the way did. She thought about all the years her dad was absent from their table, but she never expected that her mother would trade places with him.

She didn't want to lose hope though. Her father was reborn by some miracle, and she knew there was still a chance that her mother could see him for what he once was and what he could once more become. She held on to the hope that they would find each other again and repair the years of damage that they have inflicted upon each other.

Chapter 24

Danni was up early on that long-awaited Wednesday morning. She was busy brewing a pot of coffee, as usual. She tried to be as quiet as possible with her father, still asleep on the couch. The living room was practically on top of the kitchen, and he could clearly hear every little sound she made.

Simone was scheduled for the audition at one o' clock that afternoon. Danni felt anxious on her behalf, even though she was sure that Simone felt the exact opposite. When she listened to her play piano on Saturday, she played with such confidence. She doubted she could ever feel nervous to play.

She would have already called her, had it not been so early. She stopped at a pharmacy the night before and picked up two prepaid phones. She was going to give one to her father to use. She was eager to let Simone know she had the phone and could talk freely, without her FBI paranoia kicking in. She knew she should be leerier. That their connection could be dangerous. They just both seemed too raring to head directly off a canyon cliff.

The hours would stretch out like seasons, with the audition feeling light-years away. She was riddled with impatience. She scheduled it for a time that Billie would be in school, knowing that Simone couldn't leave her alone at home.

Danni looked at the pot of coffee dripping its dark liquid slowly, and her mind buzzed right back to the visit she had with her on Saturday. She was desperate to feel her skin under her fingers again. To kiss her lips and pull her close to her for another thousand years.

Her father walked into the kitchen, and she forced herself out of her dreamworld.

"You're up early," she said, watching him yawn and rub the sleep out of his eyes.

She prepared two cups to pour for them. They both took the cups, added cream and sweetener, and walked over to the dining room table. The morning sun started to break through the window to brighten the room.

"Were you at the bar last night?" Danni asked as she took sips from her cup impatiently.

"I was."

"He didn't recognize you, right?" she asked.

"I don't think so. I wore a hat and glasses. Even added a thick mustache."

"I wish I had a picture of your disguise!" she said and chuckled.

"You would get a kick out of it. Anyway, you would be happy to hear, I found the place crawling with Russians," he said with a straight face.

"I knew it! I knew that's where he met that guy."

His face broke into a smile, unable to contain his amusement.

"Seriously, though, I ran into quite a few Russians there, heavy accents. I think they are selling drugs in the place, and they obviously got your boyfriend on the hook to stay quiet and look the other way."

She pondered her dad's theory. The pieces of the puzzle fit perfectly. They must have hooked him after a loss in poker. He probably owed them money, forcing him to hand the bar over to their criminal enterprise.

"He must have lost a few too many card games over in Bustleton," she theorized out loud.

"Most likely."

Her dad looked calm about the situation. As if he's encountered similar scenarios countless times before.

"It didn't take you long at all to get to the bottom of that at all. See? You're still a natural-born detective."

"Some gangs operate that way. I had a suspicion when you said he was a bartender. Gangs like to stake their territories, and a bar like that filled with young people is a gold mine to them. All they need is the DEA to stay out of it."

"So how does he get out of it?" she asked. She siphoned through everyone he was putting in danger with his ignorance. People who could become collateral damage the minute he opted out of his obligations.

"Not easy. He seems to be in deep if they rely on him to keep the territory. Losing him means they lose the bar. You remember telling me that his dad had to skip town to get out of trouble?"

"You think it's going to come to that with him?"

"I will need to find out who these people are. I have a friend at the unit I can call. He may have information about just how dangerous this group is. You still have that drawing of the guy you saw with him in the park?"

"Yes," she said and went to her room to get the drawing for him.

She handed it to him, and he looked intently at it as if for the first time.

"It's a damn good drawing, Danni. He's really coming alive on the page. You have gotten so good with your sketches, I have to say."

Her heart ballooned under his compliment.

"I will keep going and see if this guy shows up there."

"What would you do if he does?"

"I have to find out how many guys he has in that place selling for him. Maybe I can talk to him about an exchange for Jake. It's a long shot. Maybe he would trade my silence for Jake's freedom. If Jake wants to be free, that is."

"What if they opt to silence you and Jake permanently instead?"

"I would need an insurance plan, of course. I'll inform him that his drug ring would be exposed to the police the minute I die. Something like that."

Danni shuddered at the prospect of her father getting killed as a result of being lured into a plot with the Russian mafia by her. She would never be able to live with herself.

"They must also run a grand theft auto scheme which they dragged Jake into. I don't know how we would safely untangle him from all of that."

"I don't know either, sweetheart. Just be careful when you see him. He could have a tail on him. They would need to know what kind of collateral he has to ensure his loyalty."

"I've been so nervous lately. That he was being followed or that his phone was bugged. Even that the FBI was involved somehow."

"You're rightfully concerned. The FBI is always looking for someone willing to snitch. That is an even more dangerous predicament. Very few survive it."

She placed her head in her hands, feeling trapped and framed for a crime she didn't commit.

"Our only option might be to get tangible evidence and then negotiate his freedom with it. I'm going to need a few more disguises," he said, smiling.

He looked as if he couldn't wait to get back to the bar, doing what has loved forever. It seemed as natural as breathing to him.

Danni was grateful for his help. For as much as she wanted to pry into her boyfriend's criminal predicament, his need for rescue couldn't have come at a more inopportune time in her life. She could very easily become collateral damage, along with anyone she associated with. Including Simone and Billie. She wasn't naive about the level of cruelty these gangs could resort to in order to keep someone devoted to them. Any message they would choose to send could end up being very costly for all of them.

"I need to get ready for work, but I'm absolutely stoked that you are helping me with this."

Her dad looked at her for a while, his eyes turning sad.

"I have neglected everyone for far too long."

"You did what you could. I knew you would get to a place of healing eventually."

"You have no idea, Danni. I haven't felt this alive in years. Since that day Matt died. I have only known myself trapped in darkness. I was in hell, and I couldn't see any way out. I know you were out there, and Robbie. I just couldn't see my way through to you. I can't even tell you the number of times I wanted to die."

"And then that bullet vanished. Like magic."

"It did. I finally squeezed that trigger. I have been obsessed with it for so many years, but instead of the pain I anticipated, I felt a powerful light bursting all through me. I felt so free right after that happened."

Danni walked over to him and threw her arms around him.

"I feel like I'm free again too."

He joined her embrace and held her close to him. She felt the earth, rock solid underneath her feet. Her life suddenly sprouted, and she felt like she could move forward. She contemplated all the options that has opened in front of her, feeling more ready for it than ever before.

She returned to her room to get ready for work. It was an important day. She still hasn't clued Peter in on the fact that Simone was coming to audition. As far as he knew, Katya Petrov was on the schedule. He did say that he looked forward to it and was surprised that he has never heard of a young Russian pianist with that name in the area. Peter has always been in the know about everything in the Philadelphia music scene. She couldn't wait to see his surprise as soon as her fingers took flight on the keys. She wouldn't miss it for the world.

She arranged for Alex to come in early for his shift to free her up for the audition. She pledged her undivided attention to Simone. The short moments they had together were the richest treasure to her. Despite having to hide their feelings from each other and anyone around. So much relied on their secrecy. Sometimes, she feared their lives literally depended on it. A fact she would very much want to spare Simone.

Chapter 25

She booked a total of three auditions for Peter for that day, starting at twelve thirty. She needed him busy in the studio when Simone arrived. Alex was scheduled to arrive at the same time, which would give her time to get Simone set up in a prep studio. Her mind has made careful preparations for the occasion. She planned to bring Peter some coffee just at the start of Simone's audition, which would conveniently place her in the room at just the right time. She would take the chance to slip into a chair and stay until the end. After her sneak preview over the weekend, she had no doubt that she would capture Peter's imagination.

Danni unlocked the store a little after ten. They weren't officially open until ten thirty, but she often opened early to get a chance to take stock of the shelves and see if any inventory needed to be reordered. She found quite a few items that needed to be restocked and decided to get her mind off the auditions by working on a purchase order to present to Peter for approval. When she finally sat down at her desk to work on the order, she glanced at her phone and noticed the text message alert flashing. She grabbed the phone and read the message from Jake.

"How's my girl?" it said.

They haven't been in actual communication since he left her apartment on Saturday late morning. She has been avoiding him deliberately after the nightmare that played out on Saturday night.

"Not sure where to begin. So much has happened since I've seen you."

"Yeah? Anything good?"

She knew it was the worst time to alienate him. Now that her father has joined forces with her.

"My father will be staying with me for a while, but it's a long story."

"Wow, that is a big change."

"Long, long story. He and my mom are separating for a while," she explained.

"That is horrible news!" he fired back.

"Not sure if it's good or bad."

"I'm off on Friday night." He changed direction.

"How did that happen?"

"Some new hires over here could only work this weekend, so Mark decided to cater to them instead of me."

"You seem unhappy about it," she baited him.

"I'm very pissed. Weekends are the best shifts financially, and he decides to give it to some new guy."

"That makes no sense."

"I know. So I'm free to hang out Friday night."

The one night she was not available. And she hated to have to defend herself to him.

"I'm so sorry, I already made plans with my dad. You usually work on Fridays."

"What kind of plans? Maybe I can join in. Would be good to see him again."

She hesitated. It would be impossible for him to join in with what she had planned. She felt herself squirm, fumbling for a rock-solid alibi.

"We are going to talk to my mom on Friday. To try to talk her out of the separation. I don't think it would be good for you to tag along to that."

He didn't respond right away. She imagined him telling himself to breathe deeply, to keep his nails from digging through the palms of his hands.

"I understand," he finally responded. "What about Saturday then?"

"You're off Saturday too?"

"Yes. Just this weekend hopefully."

She had a hunch that there was more to it than just a new hire wanting a well-paying shift. Her best guess was that Peter had that talk with Mark, which made him wary of having his nephew work the most profitable shifts of the weekend.

"Okay, we can do something on Saturday then. Evening?"

"I'm free all day."

"I'll keep you posted. Let me see how that talk with my mom goes."

"Sure," he said, but she wasn't convinced that he was satisfied.

"I have to get back to work."

"You work too hard. You should look forward to not having to work once we're married."

She despised his words. Always reverting back to the same topic. Laying out empty promises and a lack of understanding that not working would be unbearable to her. He kept rolling over her, breathing life into a dream that had no value to her.

"We'll talk soon. I have a few customers here now," she lied.

She threw her phone down on the table. She wanted to delete the entire conversation with him. At this point, she was merely placating him.

She focused her mind back on the purchase order so she could e-mail it to Peter's before he even made it in.

The first audition candidate arrived around eleven thirty, and Danni walked him back to a small studio with a piano. The man was early and would have a full hour to warm up. She didn't want to make him wait in the store. His nerves seemed frazzled enough.

"Would you like some water?" she asked, knowing that his mouth was probably as dry as a desert.

He nodded and looked relieved, his tongue too dry to speak.

She came back with a bottle from the mini fridge in Peter's office and handed it to him.

"You have ample time to warm up in here, Peter will see you at exactly twelve thirty. I will come get you five minutes before and take you to his studio."

After he gulped down almost half the bottle of water, he finally attempted some audible words.

"Thank you, I'm sorry. For being so early."

"What will you be playing today?" Danni asked, hoping to put him at ease.

"I'm doing a Schubert sonata," he stammered.

"I think Peter usually asks for one of the Beethoven sonatas for piano and violin. Are you planning to play one today?"

"Oh yes, I will do the fifth sonata also, I almost forgot about that."

He finished the rest of the water, probably a feverish attempt to sooth his nerves.

"I will make a note of your choice and let him know," she said right before she left the room and closed the door behind her.

She stood in the hallway and paused. She wanted to hear him play, but no sound came from the room. She leaned against the wall for nearly five minutes, but there was only more silence coming from inside. She pictured him just sitting there on the chair in front of the instrument as sweat dripped off his temples. Eyes closed and breathing long, silent breaths to slow his racing heart. Wondering why he was compelled to put himself through the agony of Peter's judgment.

She headed back to her desk but found a few customers waiting at the counter to get checked out. Her eyes scanned the front of the store area, relieved that there was no trace of Simone yet. She hoped she didn't get the same inkling to arrive early. For her plan to work, she needed Peter safe and sound in the audition studio when she arrived. She checked her watch. Both of her palms were already buzzing like electricity in anticipation of her arrival. She focused her attention on the customer in front of her, slapping a set of guitar strings on the counter.

"You found everything you needed?" she asked her usual question.

"A friend of mine raved about these new Fender Dura-tone strings, and I thought I would come see if you guys carry it."

"We usually keep them in stock. They are very popular."

"Glad to hear. You are very close to me, so it's so convenient to come here."

She helped three others after he walked out, keeping her eyes on the clock.

Peter finally pushed through the door. He looked as if he hasn't slept in days. He certainly hasn't bothered to shave this week at all.

"Hi, Danni," he said, as he approached her at the sales counter.

"Are you okay?" she asked, feeling culpable for the stress he was buried in.

"I had a talk with Mark."

Her hunch was right then. She questioned if Mark would react as patiently as Peter about the situation.

"Was he upset?"

"Very. He knew he was bleeding money from somewhere at the bar, and now he understands exactly where the leak came from. He wanted to fire him right away, but I managed to talk him down."

"Yes, it's important that we get more information first about who we are dealing with."

"I explained that to him. Told him that your father was probably going to be investigating undercover in his bar to help figure this all out. Don't worry, I explained that he was a detective before."

"He was already there a few times, to look around."

"It's good that he can help trying to figure this out. You said it would be good for him too, right?"

"It is. I spoke to Jake this morning and he was upset that he lost his shifts this weekend. Maybe you can ask Mark not to change anything just yet. We don't want to raise his suspicions at all."

"Okay, I will ask if he could consider that. I agree that it would be best if things stay as they are for a little bit longer."

"My dad is looking into the gang there that he thinks has moved into the bar to sell drugs. He wanted to find out how difficult it would be to get them to release their grip on Jake."

"It's just like the trouble we had with his dad all over again. He had to leave in the middle of the night, and we've never heard from him again. What if Jake is forced to do the same?"

"It's better than him getting killed."

"What about you, Danni? If he had to leave?"

"I'm not leaving, if that is what you're asking. My family is here."

"Jake said he wanted to marry you, I'm sure he has told you that."

"I have nothing to run away from."

"Losing you will be devastating to Jake."

She looked at Peter. The pit of her stomach was swirling, making her feel lightheaded.

"You don't feel the same about him then?"

"I used to. Things have just changed. With all this going on."

"I can't say that I blame you, Danni."

She nodded, but she wanted him to be focused on the auditions instead of worried about his nephew.

"Your first audition is getting ready in the prep studio."

"Oh god, yes, it's audition day. How many?"

"Three today."

"I should pick someone today. Get the position filled so we can start prepping for the competitions. Marius has lost his patience with me."

"Let's hope we find someone amazing today then," she said, still bound on keeping Simone's identity concealed to him. The man could use an uplifting surprise today.

"Okay, let's get these auditions started. It would be good to get Jake out of my head for a while."

"I will bring him down in ten minutes. You go get ready."

After the sweaty man finished his Beethoven sonata, Peter thanked him for coming and promised he would get back to him soon. There was no excitement on his face for what he just listened to. Danni watched his reaction when she brought him some water and to inform him that the next candidate was already warming up.

"You didn't enjoy that audition?"

"It was full of mistakes. So no. He is not the one."

"Let's hope the next two will be better then." He chuckled.

"I doubt they could be worse."

"Peter!" she yelled. "You had that man probably so nervous, he couldn't pull off any of the right notes."

"He is not my type, Danni, if you were wondering."

"You have a type? I don't remember you telling me about any types you've been eyeing up recently."

"I try not to mix business with pleasure. It never works."

"Are you referring to Stefan, moving to Seattle? And maybe why you've been dragging your feet to replace him so much this year?"

Peter just stared ahead, but his face was flaming with red heat from ear to ear.

"Is there anything you don't miss, Danni girl?"

"He wasn't that good, but you kept him around. I figured he had to be good at other things you had interest in."

"We do crazy things when we fancy someone. Marius insisted that I pick a woman this year. He doesn't want a repeat of last year's mess."

Peter couldn't stop smiling, as he was clearly reminiscing about the previous year when Stefan was haphazardly accompanying the students while never pulling his eyes off Peter.

"Are you ready for the next one?"

"Yes, bring it on."

Danni went down the hall to let the second candidate know to come to the studio.

It was an attractive man named Robert. His blue eyes were obscured by black-rimmed glasses underneath his stylishly cropped blond hair. He looked noticeably less nervous than the first guy. She imagined him finding Peter, sitting at the piano, scoffing and frantically cleaning the first man's sweat off the keys, while doubting that the next candidate would be any better.

Danni gave him directions to get to the audition studio down the hall, but she was dying to get back to her sales counter. Simone was bound to arrive any minute.

As she walked back to the counter, she noticed Simone already there, waiting and talking to Alex, who must have arrived right behind her. Things were working out exactly as planned.

"You are just in time!" she told Simone, unable to contain her excitement. "The prep room just opened so you can warm up before the audition. Just come back, I'll show you where it is."

"Follow you? No problem," she quipped.

She pushed through the door of the prep studio, and Simone followed her in.

"Are you ready?" she asked as her eyes scanned over how beautiful Simone looked in a printed sleeveless sundress.

"As long as you are there."

"If my timing is perfect, yes."

"I'm sure you have planned it perfectly."

"You know me so well already," Danni said.

She needed Peter's search to come to an end right after Simone's audition.

"I will leave you so you can warm up," Danni said. There was no way she could keep herself from blushing with Simone's eyes burning like fire into her skin.

"I am warming up better with you right where you are," she said boldly.

"I'm sure you don't need this kind of warm-up before your audition."

"It's good to be warmed up for an audition, Danni."

Simone stepped close to her and took both of her hands into hers. They were as soft as always.

"Don't you think you need to warm up on the piano instead? This is an important audition," Danni said with her eyes glancing over to the door.

"You are important to me," Simone said softly close to her ear.

"You are important to me too."

Danni had very little resolve left against Simone's advances. Her scent filled the space between them, drifting into her nose, and Danni desperately wanted to pull her close to her again and recreate the kiss they shared over the weekend. But this was not the time. She needed to hold back and get Simone into that audition studio, prepped to play like she hasn't played in years.

Simone backed away slowly, but kept her smoldering gaze on Danni.

"We never have enough time together," she said as she walked over to the piano and sat on the bench.

Danni tried to find something to say to keep the light in Simone's spirits. Their situation could feel hopeless on any given day, but right before an audition was not the time to think about all the obstacles they faced. In all actuality, what they needed was to find a way to be friends. Deep down, Danni was convinced of that unpleasant truth. They needed to replace the destructive fire between them with something less hazardous. Or they risked losing everything. When she looked at Simone's disappointed eyes, she realized that her thoughts weren't nearly as concealed as she intended them to be.

She walked over and stood behind her. She placed her hands softly on her shoulders. She leaned over and rested her forehead on Simone's head. Inhaled the sweet scent of her hair deep into her nostrils. She could feel her shoulders relax under the touch of her hands.

"Do you know my heart?" she asked softly.

Simone stayed still as if she was trying to hear the beating of Danni's heart so close to her.

Her fingers ran over the keys suddenly, with a series of passionate notes. It sounded like something written by Bach. Her left hand created a rumbling baseline, a rhythmic chord structure to anchor the most beautiful, melodious chord structure flowing from her right hand's upper register. She kept her body close to Simone's as she listened to her heart pouring out.

"Are you going to play that?" Danni asked after Simone brought the music to a sudden halt.

"It's how I feel these days." Danni smiled.

"Who wrote it?"

"Bach wrote this Chaconne for violin, but of course, it has been adapted for the piano, and I have been so drawn to it lately. It matches perfectly what I feel for you. The exaltation of it and despair around every turn. It reminds me of the excitement I feel when I see you and the sadness I feel every time you leave."

Danni knew exactly what she meant, but she would have never said the words so boldly, so loudly. "I think Peter will like it. Even though it's not what he requested."

"I will play it for you."

"I can't wait to hear all of it."

Danni stepped away from her. She looked back before she left the room and saw the shadows in Simone's eyes again.

"Go to room 4 in ten minutes. I'm going to make him some coffee and bring it in just before you start playing. Don't start without me."

When Danni walked into studio number 4, she found Simone already sitting at the piano, waiting. Peter sat amused in the far corner. The small desk in front of him was covered in scribbled notes, most likely beholding his many criticisms of the previous two performances. She walked over to Peter with the freshly brewed coffee and placed the cup in front of him, hoping the sheer aroma of it would keep him from questioning her actions. But he looked up at her, his face perplexed and undoubtably full of questions he intended to ask.

"So are you in charge of orchestrating this unexpected surprise, Danni?"

"Of course," she said. "Doesn't the coffee smell wonderful?" she said as she pointed to the cup with the steam still coming off. She noticed that he was more amused than irritated.

"Billie has never mentioned to me that her mother plays the piano," he said to Simone.

"Billie thinks I wash her clothes and cook her meals. I'm sure she is convinced I was placed on earth for her sole purpose," Simone explained lightheartedly.

"She is still too young to know you have a life of your own, I suppose. What are you going to play today?" Peter asked.

"Do you mind if Danni stays to listen?" she asked. She looked completely at ease with her request. Her eyes had their sparkle back.

Peter frowned in silence for a moment, but then he clicked his fingers and said, "Let's get started. Danni, sit down here next to me so we can both listen."

Danni pulled a chair over next to Peter, and they both focused intently on Simone as she laid her fingers down on the keys of the piano. She took a deep breath and then played the first chords of the adaptation of Bach's Partita. Peter's eyebrows raised instantly when he recognized the piece.

The notes filled the air as her left hand anchored the heavy baseline to ground the countering melodic chords ringing from her right hand. The music told the story of love and yearning. It was rich in emotion, progressing through its many variations on the same theme. It shifted back and forth between two contrasts, singing about its sweet and tragic nuances, over and over. The sound drifted up and lingered as she worked steadily, slowly creating the tension of many crescendos. Danni looked at Peter and saw that he was ready to cry as he latched on to the passion and sorrow of the notes. It was a long piece, but neither Danni or Peter wanted her to stop, both willing to stick with her through the entire journey as her face and hair started to glisten with small strands of sweat.

Simone did not have any sheet music in front of her. She played the entire piece from memory, while engrossed in the emotions of the music. It was as if it were her own feelings bleeding out from the deepest part of her soul.

As the final section of the Chaconne developed into a fantastic climax, Danni noticed that Peter was immersed in the piece. Tears were streaming down his face, and he had finally closed his eyes to focus solely on the sound of passion, loss, and love that swelled forth from the piano.

As soon as the piece came to a final restful conclusion, Peter jumped to his feet and stood with his hands clasped together, staring at Simone. He was awestruck.

"That was amazing," he said as he shook his head in disbelief.

Danni joined in Peter's excitement, and they both stood side by side and finally started giving her a slow hand of applause.

"That is one of my all-time favorite pieces of music. And you have just become my new all-time favorite performer of it."

Simone got up and offered an elegant bow to acknowledge their praise. She remained perfectly human as her face turned red under the onslaught of their accolades.

She finally sat back down and looked over at Peter, her blues eyes filled with light.

"I'm so glad that you liked it, Peter," she said. Her face couldn't stop shining.

"Liked it? You must be kidding me! I was moved by it."

"We can end the search for the position for this year then?" Danni chimed in, trying to capitalize on his favorable impression. She couldn't have scripted it any better.

"Without a doubt!"

"I thought you would consider Robert very strongly," she teased, certain that the handsome second candidate piqued his interest.

"Too timid. Very handsome, but just too timid."

"Are you sure you don't need to think about it anymore?" Simone asked.

"Simone, if you want the position, it's yours. The two of you have conspired and kept me in the dark all this time about your extraordinary talent, but I couldn't be more excited about the surprise."

"Of course, I will accept the position, Peter. I would want nothing more than to work with you and your students."

"All right. I will draw up the paperwork and send you an offer that you would need to read through and sign."

Danni believed they were all dancing on the upmost peak of cloud nine.

Danni led Simone back to the prep studio, floating on air down the hallway. As soon as she shut the door behind them, Simone pushed her up against the door and kissed her, sparking electricity throughout her body. Her mouth was warm, and she could feel Simone's hands slip underneath her shirt, not wasting any time to touch the bare skin of her back. She pushed her body into her and offered her mouth and her tongue as they desperately tried to get more intimate with each other.

Danni never wanted the kiss to end, but she finally pulled away after hearing footsteps coming down the hall. She assumed it was Peter, on his way to his office a few doors down. They held still in their embrace as they listened to the footsteps coming to a halt in front of the door. They held their breath and stood frozen, still clinging to each other, their mouths not even an inch apart. Simone placed her finger on Danni's mouth to keep her from saying anything that would rip their union apart. They both quietly willed Peter to keep moving without intruding on them.

The footsteps finally started to fade away down the hall, and Danni exhaled in utter relief.

"So it will always be like this?" Simone asked.

"Like what?"

"The two of us hiding behind closed doors?"

Danni looked deep into her blue eyes that shimmered like topaz, and she softly stroked the skin on her arms.

"Seeing that you're married and I'm dating Peter's nephew, hiding behind closed doors when we're here is the only option I see."

"I want more than that," Simone protested.

"That is not possible. Let's enjoy what we can. I had chills just listening to you play. You were wonderful."

"You should know I thought about you the whole time."

Danni kissed her again, softly.

"These kisses that we share are amazing. Anything more would make it seem like we were having a full-blown affair."

Danni detected the mischief that popped into Simone's eyes. Danni pulled her close again.

"Is that what you want? An affair?" she asked boldly.

"I would be lying if I said I didn't," she said, kissing her again.

"The thought of an affair with you scares me. It's not that I don't want it. It's just that the possible consequences are terrifying."

"I have no fear when I think about loving you."

Danni's heart melted under all the honesty Simone offered her.

"I have nothing but fear when I think of loving you. I fear loving you only to lose you. I fear what it would mean for my life and your life. Billie's life and Bill's."

"Does all of that fear make you not love me?"

"Being afraid to love you is not the same as not loving you."

"I will take that, Danni. Knowing that you love me, even though you are wise to the many obstacles. I know it has to be enough for me right now."

Danni needed to take a step back. She revered the candor between them, but she wasn't sure she knew how to prepare for its implication on her life. Yet she had to respect the path Simone was on. It would be just as difficult for her to come to grips with their attraction. Probably even more.

"I just seem to need a little more time than you," she said, hoping to keep the ache out of Simone's eyes this time.

She opened the door and steered Simone down the hall toward the front of the store. She held on to the back of her elbow, reluctant to relinquish their connection. She saw Alex helping some customers at the sales counter and getting busy to clear them out was the only remedy she had available to quell her pining heart.

"I promise to text you tonight," she said before Simone pushed through the doors and disappeared out of sight down the street.

After several customers were taken care of, she went to the back office to gather her stuff. Her mind still in in a trance. She wasn't sure if it was from the music or the kiss that followed. Or Simone's confession that she wanted even more. She sank into the chair with her eyes closed, trying to relive every moment of the audition, but her mind willfully drifted to the kiss in the studio after.

"She is something, isn't she?"

Peter's voice called her back to reality.

She looked at him and just hoped he didn't have a third degree planned for her.

She nodded silently.

"Plays beautifully," he said. His words made her smile. She knew he would love her talent as much as she did.

"She is probably way too good for what we need here," he lamented.

"She just wants a chance to get back into it," she assured him.

"Talent like that shouldn't go to waste. I am glad to offer her a chance, but she is meant for much more."

"Maybe on paper, yes. But with Billie to take care of and a husband that just wants a wife, she can't answer a call to anything else."

Peter pondered her words. He, of all people, would be able to relate. Having had to abandon his own musical ambitions in order to come back and manage his father's store. To honor his father's legacy instead of pursuing his own dreams.

"I get it. It will be better than ignoring all that talent. That would be unthinkable."

"She will be happy with this opportunity, I'm sure of it."

"You have grown very fond of her," he pried.

She could see the gears churning his mind into a cluster of suspicion.

"We have grown close, yes. But she is married to a not-so-nice husband."

"And there is your relationship with my nephew," he reminded her.

"Exactly. Some things in life are just better left unchecked it seems."

"Better for whom?" he challenged.

She just smiled, side-stepping the trap he set. Even though she longed to confide in him more. She was sure he would be able to understand perfectly what she was going through. Nearly fifty and still alone, and certainly it was not because he has never loved anyone before.

"I'm heading out. Alex will close the store tonight."

"Thanks for all your help, Danni. You mean everything to me, and it's not just because of Jake."

She smiled at him, feeling the warmth of his words.

"Thank you, Peter. I feel the same way."

She walked away, exhilaration pulsing through her body. The much-anticipated audition was undeniably a success. And as hard as it was to accept, she was overjoyed that she somehow, very unexpectedly, managed to tell Simone that she loved her.

Chapter 26

Danni was back at the store at ten sharp on Thursday morning. Complete with her mind still left in a daze. Still lost in the conversation she had with Simone late on Wednesday evening. She stalled endlessly beforehand, but in the end, managed to quiet her apprehension. Spurred on by the consequential confession she made. She found it difficult to recognize herself. Her interest in women was something she has always chosen to ignore. She brushed it away like a minor irritation. But this time, she has not been able to undermine her feelings in the same way. She used the burner phone to send a text.

"I am so excited about your contract with Peter."

She hoped Simone would keep her phone nearby. She delayed reaching out until well after eleven, trying to map out the best way to navigate their conversation. There was a good chance that Simone regretted every word she said to her. They were understandably on an emotional high after the audition.

The phone rang instead. Danni was surprised that she was able to talk that late.

"The news didn't go over well with Bill," she said immediately. Her voice was strained.

It was deflating to hear, but Danni knew that she would need encouragement from her. Having your dream dismissed as trivial by your husband would be a sharp stab in the back.

"Maybe we shouldn't be too surprised at that. He is obviously coming from a very different point of view," she said. She was grabbing at straws and cringed at her defense of Bill.

"He accused me of having an affair with Peter. Can you believe that?"

That made Danni laugh out loud. His shot wasn't even close to the target.

"Did you tell him the only way Peter would have an affair with you was if your name was Simon?"

"Is that really true?"

"As true as the Gospel."

Her response made Simone laugh, and Danni was relieved to hear some of the tension on the line relax.

"I didn't tell him that."

"Why not?"

"I thought it was better that he accused Peter, instead of you."

"I don't think Peter would agree," she said, still amusing herself with the vision of Bill chasing after Peter with his fist in the air.

Danni was happy for the refuge that the store provided her on Thursday morning. Peter's first scheduled lesson wasn't until two that afternoon, leaving her plenty of time to strategize. She needed to think through some of the suggestions her dad offered about the havoc Jake has managed to cause. He met with a guy named Ruben the day before. He said that he used to work with him at the police department and planned on showing him the sketch she made of the dark-haired Russian. He was hoping that Ruben would recognize him for being on their radar for something.

"Did Ruben recognize our Russian friend?" she finally asked after her dad failed to volunteer any information during their meal when she got home from work on Wednesday afternoon.

"He did," he said and fell quiet again. He clearly wanted to avoid delivering the verdict out loud.

"How bad is it?" she asked impatiently.

"It's not good, Danni. These guys apparently have been operating here for many years. They haven't been caught, because they don't ever leave any evidence. Meaning that people simply vanish, without a trace, when things don't work out as planned."

"So the police have nothing on them?"

He just smirked.

"There's no one ready to rat on them. No one ever made it close to the witness stand."

"Did he say what kind of things they are into?" Danni started to acclimate to the weight of their predicament.

"Gambling, drugs, guns, auto theft. The usual gang type things. They control many parts of the city and apparently have been expanding recently. Which is probably how they ran into Jake. He was most likely just a dumb kid looking for a quick buck. An easy target for them."

"Did you tell Ruben about them moving into Fairmount now? Wait, are you sure you can trust him?"

Her dad gave her a scolding look.

"You haven't been in that unit for ages, Dad. People change is all I'm trying to say."

"Danni, I met with him. I would have picked up if he was compromised."

"So these guys would simply get rid of anyone getting in their way?"

"Yes, and ruthlessly. Ruben showed me a picture on his phone of one of the informants they tried to get wired up to snitch."

"Was it bad?"

"Head beat to a pulp, all the fingers cut off but one, so they could still identify him with a fingerprint. It was a clear message."

"So Jake needs to get out of town. There doesn't seem to be any other option for him, right?"

"It's looking that way. The longer he stays involved, the worst it will be for all of us. They probably keep pretty good tabs on him. Especially since he's an outsider."

"It's not like we can take a whole gang out, right?"

"No, Danni." Her dad couldn't help but grin at her brave naivety. "Like Ruben said, no one has ever survived to testify against these people."

"Jake wanted to come here for dinner on Saturday night, but I managed to get him his shifts back to work at the bar instead."

"He shouldn't come here. Not any night. I don't think it's safe for you to see him here or anywhere."

"There has got to be something we can do."

"Could he go to New Orleans? To stay with Robbie. I could talk to him and see if he would take him in."

"How long?"

"As long as possible. Unless he wants to join this gang permanently and see how long his uncle likes having them sell drugs in his bar."

"It's such a mess."

"He was stupid to think he could get involved with these people. He is not one of them."

"So that's it. I will have to tell him that he either gets out of town or never see me again."

Her father nodded.

"You're very fond of him?"

"This trouble has really changed my feelings for him."

"So who am I cooking for on Friday evening?"

"Just a new friend. Her daughter is one of Peter's students, so we just started getting to know each other during her lessons."

Her dad looked at her, but it felt more like he was squinting at her, trying to peel some of her protective layers away.

"And she is the one that wants us to look into the husband's business, right?"

She nodded.

"And the dinner is to come up with a plan?"

"Her daughter is coming also, so dinner is more just dinner. Friends eating together."

"I see. I will make the shepherd's pie for your friend. It's good for you to have friends. I haven't seen you make a whole lot of them over the years."

"You were in your room mostly, so how would you know?"

"My room had two windows, Danni. And I was distraught, not blind."

"Have you spoken to Mom recently?"

"Yes, because she wanted to know what we should do with the house."

"The house? What do you mean? She is not staying there?"

"She has been staying with Max mostly. She said the house was too depressing."

"Well, I, for one, agree. That house can really suck the life out of anyone."

"You have noticed that also?"

"It's like a hungry vampire."

He smiled at her analogy.

"I told her she shouldn't make rash decisions. There's no telling how serious this thing with Max will turn out to be."

"I thought you knew everything."

"Meaning?"

"They looked serious when I saw them at the bakery."

"So you knew?"

"I see everything too, remember?"

He finished his meal, got up, and started taking the dishes to the sink.

"I'm sorry. That I didn't tell you. I didn't even know what to make of it. She was probably just so lonely. I felt happy for her actually."

He walked back toward her still sitting at the table.

"I feel bad for keeping her in our sick marriage for so long. And when I saw her kissing Max, I was so angry. Not at her. At myself, for stealing her life. I wanted to set her free by leaving. Forever. She deserved it. But I couldn't even pull that off successfully."

"What do you mean, Dad?"

"Instead of just quietly disappearing, I chose to make a show of it. Carrying on and blaming her. There was no way God was going to let me go out like that, leaving her stuck with all the blame."

"Seems like God had her back and yours," Danni said, still feeling nauseous every time she recalled walking in on him holding that gun to his head.

"She deserves to be happy. That is all I know."

"So do you."

"I'm happy to be alive, kiddo," he said with a broad smile. She had to get used to his face with a smile. She hasn't seen one on him for so long.

"I wish there was something we could do about this Russian gang," she said, veering away from the sadness that has engulfed their family.

"Time will tell. If we push too hard, we will just end up getting chased out of this town as well. I doubt your brother would be open to all of us moving in with him down there."

"There is no way I'm moving to New Orleans," Danni said with conviction.

"Not even with Jake down there and out of trouble?"

"Somehow I'm thinking trouble finds Jake, not the other way around."

Her dad smiled and walked back to the sink to wash the dishes.

After he finished, he went to the bathroom to get ready to head back out to the bar. He had been going every night for the past week. She knew that to him, being any kind of detective felt like the most natural thing he could do. She was happy that he slipped so easily back into his old skin. It would be the fastest way to heal for him.

Danni straightened some papers on her desk, waiting for ten thirty to roll around so she could unlock the doors of the store. She ran her mind back over the discussion she had with her father the night before. She tried to get used to the idea that Jake would most likely have to leave town very soon. It would catapult them to the end of their relationship. She wouldn't follow him to New Orleans or to any other place of his choosing. She would choose freedom instead. She wondered if Simone would choose freedom if presented with the option in the same way. She silently held on to the hope for it. Her mind dialed back to the conversation they had the night before.

"I wish you were here with me," Simone said.

"What would we do?" Danni asked.

"You know exactly what we would do."

"I'm not certain I would know what to do," Danni teased.

"That is a silly thing to say, Danni. The love you have will guide you."

Danni was always in awe of her easy honesty.

"Hopefully, we will end all the suspense and find out for sure very soon," Danni said as a playful dare.

"I'm sure we will," Simone assured her. She was the lion between them.

"My dad is on board for Friday night's dinner here."

"I'm looking forward to meeting him. Billie wanted to go bowling with Britton's family, so I asked if they could come pick her up after we finished dinner."

"That would be perfect. It would give us a chance to talk to my dad about Bill."

"I thought so too."

"Where's Bill now?"

She suddenly worried that Bill was listening in on their conversation from the next room over, his ear pressed up against the wall.

"Not home yet. He left angry. See what I mean?"

"You think he went back out to work this late?"

"I'm not sure. But his tantrum only gave us more time to talk," Simone said, shrugging it off nonchalantly.

Danni's mind shamelessly started to plot a variety of ways she could coax her father out of the apartment, after dinner on Friday night.

"Do you have a curfew Friday evening?" she asked, trying to sugarcoat her intentions.

"Only if your father can't get the hint to leave after dinner."

She chuckled, knowing that they were exactly on the same page as usual.

"I'm almost certain I can convince him to go out after dessert."

"I'm sure you'll try your best, Danni," Simone said.

"We better hang up before Bill walks in on you, having this raunchy conversation this late at night."

"I'll tell him I'm on the phone with Peter."

"Let's not poke the beast."

"Okay, okay. I will see you Friday then."

"Friday it is. Hopefully, it won't be a short visit."

"If you talk the talk, Danni."

"I know, I know. I will go read up on how to walk the walk."

"Exactly. I'm going to get busy on Google as well. What should I bring for dessert?"

"Something very quick."

"You're impossible, Danni. Sweet dreams, sweet girl."

Danni remembered every word of the conversation they had. She thought about writing it down so she could savor it for a lifetime.

When she unlocked the front doors of the store, she peered out onto the street. The air felt uneasy and restless. The sound of firetruck sirens screamed through the air, trying to alert her to trouble brewing. She searched up and down the street and then spotted a man standing next to one of the large maple trees that lined the street. He was tall and muscular. His hat threw a shadow across his face, preventing her from confirming her suspicions, but he reminded her of Bill. Simone mentioned that he accused her of having an affair with Peter, and she was almost certain a man like him would waste no time to come sniff around for himself. She went back into the store. She dared him to feel bold enough to come closer. She waited with her eyes fixed to the door, expecting him to barge through them for a confrontation. Ten minutes went by without him showing up. She surrendered to her curiosity and peeked outside again. He has moved about twenty feet closer, taking cover inside a bus stop shelter this time. She was able to get a better look at him this time, and she recognized the blond cropped beard from the two previous meetings they had at his house. It confirmed her suspicions.

She rushed back inside the store. She looked around for something she could use as a weapon and decided on a music stand. She rushed back to one of the practice rooms in the back and dismantled a stand to get to the metal column that she could use as a defense weapon. She set it on the sales counter and refocused her eyes to the door. She could feel her blood pulsing through her chest, injecting adrenaline into her muscles. She expected him to kick through the doors any minute.

He finally pushed the door open and walked in. For a split second, she wanted to reach for her phone and dial 911, but stopped herself abruptly. She reminded herself that he was in a store, open to the public, and technically, he had every right to be there.

"Can I help you?" she asked, when he stood right in front of her with just the sales counter separating them. She kept her hand near the metal shaft of the music stand, her muscles twitching and ready to pounce.

"Danni! Right? You don't remember me?"

"Oh yes, I do now. It was a little hard to recognize you with the hat," she lied.

"My wife mentioned to me yesterday that she will be working here now. I decided to come check it out for myself."

"Same place where your daughter's been coming for music lessons since August," she said sarcastically. She couldn't bring herself to go easy on him.

"With Peter, right?"

"Yes, with Peter."

"Same Peter who just hired her?"

"Same Peter."

He conducted the questions like a cross examination in a federal court room.

"I think I should meet this guy. Since he's injected himself so prominently in our lives suddenly."

"I'm sure he wouldn't mind meeting you at all."

Danni spent a great amount of effort to keep her muscles calm.

Bill looked around the store; she assumed he was trying to find Peter.

"He is not here," she said, saving him the question.

He leaned over the counter and looked straight into her eyes. She could see a red fire glowing in them.

"I just wonder whose idea this all was," he asked, pushing his line of questioning.

"Billie's lessons?" she stalled, aware of what he really meant. She hoped that if she made him spell it out, he would hear how jealous he sounded.

"The audition that she did yesterday. Was that Peter's idea? Or yours?"

"It was her idea. It was open for anyone to apply. She told me she was a very good pianist in college. I figured she must want to get back into it. People usually have a hard time giving up on such profound talent, even years after they abandoned it."

"Is that your theory?"

"I see many people coming in here, eager to start back up where they left off as teenagers. So it's just an observation, I guess."

"And you think you know what's best for her, for our family?"

"It was her choice to make."

"When will Peter be here today?"

"Is there something you would like to discuss with him? He usually sees customers by appointment only."

"I need to let him know that she will not be accepting the position. She will not have time because she's taking care of our child every day. It's her main priority."

"She told me that you are working a lot and don't get to spend much time with Billie. She understands very well that her priority every day is with Billie."

"So how in the hell would she be able to do this job? Can you tell me that?"

She could see his impatience heating up.

"Probably when Billie is in school. Or practicing. She could practice here while Simone is here, just as easy as when she is home. We have quite a few rooms that she could use."

"So you guys had it all figured out? Then you probably know she didn't discuss any of this with me before making this decision."

"She knew that you wouldn't be in favor of her decision."

"And yet you still let her go through with it?"

"Bill, I told you just a minute ago, I don't tell your wife what to do. It seems like you are already doing a good enough job of that."

He suddenly pounded both his fists down on the counter in front of Danni, making her jump back. She quickly recovered and leaped forward to reach for the shaft she placed on the counter. She grabbed it firmly in her right hand and took an offensive stance, hoping he would realize that she would swing if he did not back down.

"I don't like people meddling in my family's affairs," he said calmly, glancing at the weapon in her hand.

"I don't like out-of-control people slamming their fists. I had hoped that you would find a way to support your wife's talent and recognize how extraordinary it is. She said you had no objections to Billie's pursuits."

"So you guys are having late-night pillow talk to discuss the issues in our marriage now? I'm done discussing this issue. Just let Peter know he can keep looking for someone else to fulfill his piano fantasies. My wife is not available to him."

He turned around and walked out of the store gruffly, the tension still visible in his hands. Danni ran to the door as soon as he left, to see in which direction he was heading. Her instincts kicked in, urging her to follow him to see where he was going next. His aggressive demeanor was excessive, and she wanted to piece more of the puzzle together. He reminded her of Jake's Russian gangster. They shared the same brazen bravado. Asserting themselves without any qualms. It was clear to her that he was not just an average real estate broker. He was too hardened somehow. He appeared to be forged from a much darker, more villainous world.

She was parked close to the store, and she realized that if she could keep her eyes on him, she would be able to follow him. She knew it was a shot in the dark, but she had to try. She raced back to the office to grab her keys and purse, and then back out of the store. Her fingers nimbly locked the store behind her, and her legs sprang into action to run to her car. She thanked the stars that there were no customers in the store. She was certain Peter would understand her actions if she explained Bill's behavior to him.

She watched him reach his car, parked about a hundred feet down the street. She would be able to follow him if he didn't make a U-turn in the opposite direction. She was banking on the fact that he wouldn't know what kind of car she drove. He would also not expect her to abandon the store to follow him. She found a baseball cap behind the passenger seat, bunched her hair up, and quickly tucked it under the hat. She reached into the glove compartment and found her sunglasses to complete her makeshift disguise. She noticed his car driving up the street toward her and she turned her head away as he passed her car. She pulled out onto the street a few cars behind him and started her pursuit. She made sure to keep a few cars between them.

She was still blinded by her anger over his outburst in the store. She didn't worry about the consequences of leaving the store unattended. All she focused on was finding out more about the man Simone was married to. A sickening feeling centered in her gut. She was sure that he was dangerous, which only tempted her more to expose him. Her heartbeat quickened as she trailed his black Mercedes. She was launched into yet another pursuit as she stayed on his tail through several neighborhoods. It was as if she moved into an alternate reality. The sky darkened above them as clouds gathered, and she could feel herself pressing over into his world.

He finally came to a stop in the parking lot of a small office building. The sign over the window said, "Olympus Realty." She parked down the street. She was still close enough to watch his every move. He got out of the car and walked over to unlock the front door of the building. There were no other cars parked in the lot. She was determined not to abandon her mission today, no matter how long it took. Her heart finally settled down as she fell into the familiar routine of doing surveillance. She had picked up a level of comfort with it after following Jake. She became accustomed to the mundanity of waiting for long stretches of time, interrupted by the short exhilarating bursts of the chase. She could suspend herself patiently, waiting on the next move. Like a predator waiting patiently before chasing down its prey. And this time, her prey was extra personal to her.

She reached for her phone and texted Peter.

"I'm so sorry, I cannot come to work today. I have a family emergency. I hope you can understand."

She waited in her car for another half an hour before she heard back from him. It was a hot day, but she didn't want to run the air conditioner. Her gas tank was only half full.

"Oh, wow, so the store has not been opened today?" he responded.

"I was there for a short while, but I had to leave unexpectedly. I locked up, but I accidentally took the key with me. Can you use your key to get in?"

"No problem, I'll head over now. Don't worry about anything. I hope everything is okay with your family."

"Thank you, I will keep in touch about tomorrow," she wrote.

She was all in. She wanted to push through this time. Something in her gut told her that something nefarious was brewing with Bill today.

She didn't move an inch and finally spotted him coming out. It felt like she hit the jackpot when she noticed the familiar duffel bag strapped over his shoulder. She sensed that it was time for action and placed her keys back in the ignition, hungry to get the cool air of the air conditioning back on her skin. She ignored her thirst and how unprepared she was for this impromptu mission. But she had to be able to adapt to survive in this business.

He loaded the duffel bag in the trunk of his car. It looked stuffed to the brim and heavy to carry. A minute later, he took off down the street, and she waited for three cars to pass and then pulled out behind him. She was determined not to lose him.

He finally slowed down and parked in front of a house. She followed his lead and parked about fifty yards down the street, making sure she still had a clear view of him. It was a quiet neighborhood, which she assumed was by design. He walked up to the front door of the home and installed a keycode lock on the door. He walked inside, granting her a quick view, and she could see that the place was empty. *Probably a new listing*, she thought.

He returned to his car and pulled the duffel bag out of the trunk. He flung the heavy load over his shoulder and carried it up the front steps. He punched the code in and went back inside. She kept watching and waiting. She was too tense to take any pictures and only had her phone camera to use. She decided to rely on her memory and keep a low profile instead. She had a feeling that it was the wrong type of mission to attract any kind of attention to her. She even doubted the hat and sunglasses and the fact that she didn't have any food in her car to make her look like an innocent bystander, eating lunch while listening to a podcast. She never wished harder for total invisibility, which incidentally, she always thought would be the best superpower to have. But she cracked a smile as she had to admit to herself that it would probably just make things too easy. It would almost be like cheating.

A few minutes later, he came out of the house empty-handed and went back to his car. He drove down the street, only to park again a few houses down. It heightened her interest as she realized that he was in the middle of something more than just listing a vacant house. From where she sat, she had a view of both him and the house simultaneously. He brought his phone up to his ear to either make a call or to answer one. She was sure it involved the duffel bag he left in the house. He just sat in the car, waiting. He opened his car window and lit a cigarette. She slid down in her seat a little more, knowing he would probably scan the neighborhood just to find something to do. He hardly seemed like the type that would be good at waiting. She, on the other hand, could be perfectly still for hours like a stone pillar. She could become very close to invisible on any day.

She waited for about twenty minutes and then saw a dark gray van pull up in front of the house. The sign painted on the side of the van said, "Rocco's Handyman Service." Two men stepped out of the van, dressed in white overalls, as if they came to paint. They teamed up to carry a large trunk up the front steps with them. They punched the code into the key safe and opened the door. Danni tried to get a look at their faces and their features. She challenged herself to recall something about them; it was one of the rules of her game. It was difficult to find something distinguishable with them covered head to toe in overalls. They were each around six feet tall, nothing out of the ordinary. They had bandanas wrapped around their heads. Both their faces were covered in dark stubble. They wore Ray-Ban style sunglasses. They looked inconspicuous. Just two average guys, coming to paint a new house on the market.

They weren't inside for longer than five minutes. Seemed to just drop off supplies, not stay to actually paint anything. They both returned to the van, the stronger one carrying Bill's duffel bag over his shoulder. Their plan was slowly unfolding in front of her eyes. She concluded that it was Bill's job to find a location for the drop, probably always one of his new listings. He was most likely responsible for bringing the money in that bag, and these guys would bring the goods. She had no idea who would come to pick up the goods. Bill didn't seem strong enough to carry the trunk out all by himself.

She had no clue what was inside of it. For a moment, she thought about getting closer to the house for a better look. She looked around for any bushes by one of the windows she could hide herself in. She scrapped the idea quickly though. She wouldn't do anything quite that risky without having her father there as back up. She hasn't made it to the mortal combat part of her amateur detective training and decided that kickboxing classes should figure prominently into her future somehow.

The van pulled away while Bill smoked another cigarette in his car. After he flicked the filter out of the window, he brought the phone back up to his ear. And then they waited again. She assumed another group was on their way to retrieve the trunk. They waited for about fifteen minutes before a black SUV pulled up to the front of the house. The men that stepped out this time were dressed in dark suits and looked out of place in the neighborhood. They almost resembled the Russian man she saw at the park with Jake. Dark features, thick necks and muscles bulging through their suits. They used a similar type of SUV as what she remembered him using. These men were clearly more in the upper rank and file.

The two men bounced up the steps to the porch of the home. One punched the code while the other looked around the neighborhood. Danni sank even lower down into her seat and focused on slowing down her breathing.

They resurfaced about ten minutes later, each carrying a side of the heavy trunk down the steps and lifted it in perfect unison into the back of the SUV. The taller one of the two wiped his fingers over his mustache and then lifted his phone out of the pocket of his jacket. He texted on the screen briefly and then got in the driver seat. After they drove off, she noticed Bill starting his car back up. She followed him as he drove around the block, only to park in front of the house again. She pulled into the same spot down the street again. He pulled a For Sale sign out of his trunk and started working on installing the sign in the front yard of the home. She put the remaining pieces of the puzzle together as she watched him work. He seemed to be the one facilitating the exchange between two different groups, coordinating the location and timing. To make sure things moved smoothly and undetected. With his access to newly listed vacant homes, he was probably an important part of the puzzle to keep things off the police's radar, never tied to the same location twice. And she was sure he took a generous cut for providing them that safeguard.

She watched him go inside the home again. She could see him through the windows, walk through the rooms of the house. Probably now moving on to creating the listing and taking the photos he needed. Whether he sold the house or not, he already made a good bit of money on it. She wondered if the trunk contained drugs or guns. Or both maybe. She was sure they weren't dealing in party supplies.

She followed him again as he finally drove off, heading back in the direction of his office. He ended up passing its parking lot, as if his day at the office was done. Instead, he pulled into the parking lot of a place called Girls Unlimited. She couldn't believe her eyes. She felt like she was caught inside an episode of *The Sopranos*. She tried to push the anger down that welled up in her throat. She choked on the reality of him, storming into the store this morning to accuse Simone of cheating on him with Peter, only to go to the strip club to celebrate his deal with the devil that very same afternoon. She fantasized about taking a steel pipe to his black Mercedes and destroying it in an impressive fit of rage. She knew then why she despised him the moment she met him at their house. She could usually always trust her gut when it came to people, and this time was no different.

She suddenly wanted to talk to her mother. She saw all she needed to see. She turned onto a side street, so she could head back to her childhood neighborhood. Over to the bakery. Maybe she could talk some sense into her mother. Convince her that her father was back to who he used to be. That they should both go back to their home and try again. It was quite evident that people these days had no respect left for marriage.

Chapter 27

Danni stood outside of the bakery with its large glass storefront. She leaned up against one of the parking meters as she watched her mother help customers behind the counter. Her face was different. Glowing and relaxed. She looked happier than a week ago. Her hair was an even softer shade of blond and the blue of her eyes lost all the sharpness that used to pierce through them like ice. She saw her face light up as soon as she noticed her standing right outside of the store. She immediately waved enthusiastically, inviting her to come inside. Danni obliged and pushed through the door. She walked over to the counter, next to the long line of customers, as eager as ever to get their orders of sweets filled.

"If you go have a seat at that little table in the corner, I will bring you a slice of cheesecake, just as soon as I get a chance, okay?"

Danni nodded and walked over to the table her mother pointed to. She hung her purse on to the back of the chair and sat down. She kept watching her mother, who worked effortlessly to get the line of customers served and on to the rest of their days. Once the line dwindled down to the last person, she disappeared to the back into the kitchen. Moments later, Max joined her behind the counter, freeing her up to deliver that promised slice of cake. Danni marveled at the confidence radiating from her.

Her mother placed the slice in front of her on the table.

"Do you want some coffee with this award-winning piece of cake?"

"It looks more like a piece of art. Do you have time to join me for a cup?"

She nodded and went back behind the counter to pour them two cups of coffee to bring over with her. She sat down across from Danni.

"Are you sure you have time for my unannounced visit this afternoon?" Danni asked while her eyes feasted on the cake's swirling strawberry topping.

"For a little while. I'm sure Max can handle the customers for a few minutes."

Danni didn't waste any time and delved in. She immediately savored the sweet flavor that engulfed her mouth. After the day that she has had, the sugar felt as soothing as a bubble bath.

"So what is bothering you today?" her mother asked. As if the sugar came with complimentary advice. Danni gave her a puzzled look. She was not used to her motherly instinct as a child.

"I actually came to see how you were doing. I haven't seen you since that awful night we had with Dad," she said, knowing that it wasn't exactly the whole truth.

"I figured you had your hands full with him. Is he still drinking?"

She took another bite. Sipped on her coffee and tried to mull the words around for the most suitable response.

"I don't know. He does go to the bar every night, so I assume he is still drinking. But he is not anything like how he used to be," she answered, trying to pitch his emotional progress.

Her mother pursed her lips together and just shook her head a little. She couldn't hide her disappointment. His drinking has always been a big obstacle in their lives.

"You're not at work today?"

She sensed her mother changed the subject on purpose. She pictured herself a hooked fish she was trying to reel in.

"Not today. Something came up."

She got stuck again. Instead of reaching out, she opted for more sips of coffee. Her nerves were so frayed, she had to choose carefully to find words that wouldn't cause a complete meltdown in front of everyone at the bakery.

"I can see you are going through a hard time, Danni. I wish you would talk to me. Or maybe we can talk better outside of here. We can go to dinner sometime?"

"That would be great, yes. As soon as I have a chance."

Her mother just nodded and took a sip of her own coffee. She seemed careful not to push too hard.

"How are things with that new girl you met?"

Danni looked up at the ceiling, trying to fight back the tears. After today, she didn't know if things with Simone were good or disastrous. Discovering that her husband was most likely instrumental in a dangerous crime syndicate changed everything. She would have to seriously consider again to step away from her. It's just that she didn't know where to find the strength for that.

"That bad, eh?"

"No, it's good. And it's a total train wreck at the same time. It's her husband, really. He is going to be a real bear to deal with. Actually, he may make the situation completely impossible to deal with."

"That is too bad. It's obvious that you really care about her."

"I do. I just don't know if it's safe. For either one of us."

"Have you told Jake about her?"

"Goodness, no!"

She surprised herself with the overreaction.

"I hardly ever get to speak to Jake these days. We have drifted apart so much."

"And now you have your father to deal with too."

"I don't mind that at all. He's been the best thing out of everything I have going on."

Her mother looked down, unable to hide the guilt she felt.

"I heard you guys are going to talk about the house soon," Danni said, steering the conversation away from Simone.

"We will have to, yes."

"Things with you and Max are serious then?"

"It's going well. We really are good together, Danni. We work together well too. It's been great. I feel like he has lifted me out of a very dark place."

"Your relationship with Dad is really over then?"

She still felt so deflated. Realizing that all their sacrificed years didn't amount to a better outcome for them. She had always hoped that somehow, they would rise like a phoenix out of the ashes. To give purpose to the tragedy they lived through.

"That's been coming a long way, don't you think? We spiraled down far beneath any point of return."

Danni knew it was true. The emotional detachment they have forged for so many years finally culminated into a full-blown inevitable separation. None of them could be too surprised by it. It was a toxic concoction of guilt and blame that neither of them could undo.

It clearly was a welcome change for her mother.

"He is happy for you too," she said, finishing the last bit of her cheesecake.

"Dad?"

She nodded.

"So how does it feel then? To be in love again?"

"Danni!" Her mother protested, but blushed bright red. "If you have to know, I am over the moon about it. I felt for such a long time that I would never have that feeling again. But see, you just never know. Things happen that you wouldn't expect in your wildest dreams. You just have to be open to it. And when it comes your way, you need to have the courage to take it, like you really deserve it."

Danni finished her coffee. Her heart warmed all over, hearing her mother speak so openly about her feelings. They've never shared any conversations like that before.

"Danni, you have to find the courage to go after what you want. Stop hanging on to what you think we want for you and go after what your heart tells you to do."

Danni was tickled by all the advice slipping so freely off her mother's tongue. It was as if a pent-up dam has finally broken wide open.

"And if what you want is not available?"

"Max left his wife too, you know. For us. It can be done."

Danni raised her eyebrows in utter surprise. Her mother noticed her shock.

"Life doesn't always work out for people the way they thought it would. But sometimes, people get a second chance. A second chance at love is always worth it, Danni."

Danni smiled.

"What's his wife doing now?"

"Maybe already sleeping with the next young thing that ended up on her doorstep. From what I understand, she had a real fondness for the young male physique. Just couldn't deal with Max getting older."

"Maybe it's herself getting older she couldn't deal with."

"Perhaps. Anyway, all I'm saying is that it's all right for you to go after someone other than Jake."

"I really thought you liked Jake."

"I do. But I always had a feeling that you saw him more as a friend."

"Maybe."

"Your eyes never lit up quite like when you told me about her. Simone, I mean. I am not blind, you know?"

Danni smiled.

"I should have been there for you more, growing up."

Danni shrugged to let her off the hook, because she saw her finally showing up in a big way now. She would gladly take her up on that dinner invitation.

"You should probably get back to work," she said.

"Probably. Before it gets too busy here again. Thanks for stopping by. It's so good to see you."

"Thanks for the pep talk, Mom. I really needed it today."

"Look out for your father, please. Try to keep him out of the bar."

She nodded. If her mother knew what she and her father were up to, she would probably call five police departments to come deal with them. Playing detective games with gangs and robbers. It felt as if they were galivanting in a twilight zone sometimes.

They got up from the table, and Danni hugged her mother. She held on for a long time, needing to feel her arms tightly around all her scattered emotions.

"I love you, Danni."

"I love you too, Mom."

Danni walked out of the bakery, finally able to breathe deeply. She felt grounded. The anger she felt that morning seemed to be distilled. She was proud that she responded in a healthier way to her emotions this time. Instead of crushing something. Instead of digging into herself with the nearest sharp object she could find. She rubbed over the scars on the inside of her left arm, many times victimized by her own hand. She mostly wore long-sleeved shirts now to cover them. They served as a constant reminder of how she used to lash out at herself and the world around her. She was often tempted to fall back into those old destructive ways. When anger drove her mind to its breaking point and sitting quietly to watch people couldn't lure the poison out of her. Sometimes, her mind shut down to the point that only the sharp sting of a blade could let her know she was still alive. And it was often the only way she could shock her comatose heart back to life.

Chapter 28

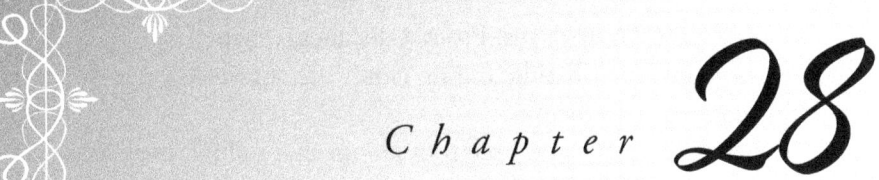

Danni walked into the apartment to find her father at his usual post behind the stove. The kitchen was dressed in the savory scent of meat browning in the pan. She smelled garlic, thyme, and rosemary wafting through the air as he stirred the meat around releasing all the flavors. She was ecstatic about the effort he made for Simone and Billie's visit. She was also nervous about it. She was tempted to cancel the whole ordeal, but as usual, she didn't want to disappoint Simone. She couldn't bear the thought of stealing any of the light out of her eyes. She squeezed in next to her father at the stove and threw her arm around his shoulder.

"It smells mouth-watering in here!"

He kept stirring, but turned his head to the side to acknowledge her presence. She could see his grin. His face was clean shaven except for the mustache that he kept neatly trimmed.

She remembered her mother's concerns about his drinking. She leaned in close again and was sure she couldn't smell even the faintest whiff of alcohol on him.

"I'm going to run through the shower. Do you need any help in here?"

"Yours truly has it all under control, Danni. Go gussy up for your friends," he teased.

"I see you already did," she teased back.

"It's nice to have visitors for a change, don't you think?"

"I never thought I would hear those words come out of your mouth," she said with unabashed surprise.

"Now, Danni, you know how I enjoy watching people," he jeered.

"Out of your window, yes. From a distance, maybe."

"Most people can't handle me up close," he continued.

"But you smell so nice!"

"It's probably the fragrant scent of gloom that follows me everywhere," he bantered.

She hugged him again, throwing in the towel. She wouldn't clinch a battle of words with him. She has worked way too hard honing her ghosting abilities to be a whizz around words.

She left the kitchen, skipping out on the tedious job of peeling potatoes. She stood in front of her closet and agonized over what outfit would be most pleasing to Simone's eyes. That turned out to be a far more difficult problem to solve.

She finally settled on a pair of cuffed skinny black jeans, a flowy white tank top, and a light, khaki green parka to hide her scars. She settled on high-heeled, brown leather ankle boots to add some vigor to her outfit with the hope that it would do the same for their evening. With her mind set on the outfit, she was ready to hit the shower and get the evening rolling.

She told Simone that dinner would be served at seven, which would give them plenty of time before Billie would be picked up at eight thirty for her bowling date.

Her dad was visibly intrigued by her effort once she joined him back in the kitchen. She could see his curious mind linger around the elements of her outfit, along with the lipstick she applied, but he retracted any commentary. He, instead, pointed to the wine.

"Do you think you can open one of the reds, so it has time to breathe?"

She hesitated. With Billie coming along, she questioned whether alcohol on the table would be a good idea.

"I don't think a half a glass each would be such a problem."

He was still so good at reading her mind.

"Half a glass then."

He nodded as they settled the issue without much fanfare. He knew what she meant, and she agreeably opened a bottle of Merlot.

"Where is the pie?" she asked, looking around nervously.

"It's still in the oven. Giving me time to set the table."

He started moving around like an experienced host. Her father never ceased to amaze her.

When the doorbell rang at exactly two minutes before seven, the table was set, the pie was resting, and the wine breathing better than she could have ever hoped for under the circumstances.

She opened the door and drew her breath as she saw Simone, hooked at the elbow with Billie. She was dressed in a long low-cut printed sundress with a short denim jacket. Her delicate feet exposed in ankle-strap, high-heeled sandals. She looked absolutely radiant.

Billie uncoupled from her mother and darted through the door first.

"Hi, Billie, I'm so happy to have you guys here," she said, deciding to shift her attention away from Simone to avoid making everyone uncomfortable.

Billie just nodded with unfocused eyes, but Danni didn't have any loftier expectations.

Simone followed her inside. She boldly reached out and pulled Danni in for a hug.

"Thanks for the invite, Danni," she said as she held her close a little longer than what was custom between friends.

As soon as Danni pulled away, she turned and saw her father looking on.

"I want to introduce you to my father, Matt Whelan. Dad, this is Simone Bradley, and this is her wonderful daughter, Billie."

Her father reached out and held Simone's hand in his.

"I've heard only wonderful things about the two of you. I'm so happy to meet you."

Simone's face was beaming as if it was Christmas.

"I'm so happy to meet you too, Mr. Whelan," she said, keeping her hand in his.

"Please call me Matt."

The introductions and small talk continued as the four of them stood together in the living room, filling the air with a pulsating warmth.

"Billie, I set a few books out for you to look at if you wanted to before dinner. There is one called *Stars and Galaxies*," I thought you would really like."

Making conversation was not Billie's favorite thing to do, and as predicted, the girl wasted no time to slide in next to the coffee table to start paging through the books that Danni left out on display.

"As usual, you think of everything, Danni," Simone said.

"Danni said you aced your audition on Wednesday. Congratulations," her dad said.

The elation in Simone's face faded as soon as her father mentioned it.

"It's been a bit of a sore subject for the past two days at our house."

Danni gave her a baffled look.

"I'm just not sure that I will have time for what the position will entail. Or I should say I'm not able to convince my husband that I will have time," she said, disappointment dripping off her expression, even though she still managed to hold her head up. Danni could tell that she would need more time to absorb the blow of the restrictions placed on her.

"I'm sure you will be able to work something out," her dad said.

"Dad, what do you think? Are we almost ready to start dinner?"

"Yes, just give me a minute to bring the food to the table," he said and disappeared into the kitchen.

Danni looked at Simone, and there was nothing she wanted to do more than to tell her how beautiful she looked. How she made her heart jump and the butterflies swirl in her stomach every time she heard her voice. But Billie was sitting within earshot in the living room, which was enough to make her curb every word she possessed to express her feelings.

"You weren't at the store yesterday or today. I almost thought dinner was cancelled," Simone said, frowning.

Danni skipped work again that day in favor to follow Bill around, even though it ended up being a complete waste of time. The only thing she caught him doing was to spend his afternoon at Girls Unlimited again. She had a feeling that he was a regular there. She could accept that every broker had carved out their own unique niche, but she never thought that strip club dancers would be lucrative for his real estate business. She felt an ache on the pit of her stomach, just thinking about it. She wasn't ready to disclose any of it to Simone. She didn't think she could ever be the bearer of such horrific news to her.

"You went to the store?" Danni asked, surprised.

"Yes, to talk to Peter."

"To renege your acceptance of the position?"

"To let him know I needed a little more time."

Danni was furious but didn't tell her.

"Billie can stay at the store while you are there, there are plenty of rooms she can use to practice."

"I don't think the real issue is Billie."

"So he just wants to keep you locked up like a bird in a cage?" she whispered to make sure Billie stayed out of the conversation. She turned around to look at the girl and was relieved to see that she was still completely engrossed in the books.

"Where have you been though for two days?" Simone asked again.

"I will tell you later. Let's just get to the table and enjoy the shepherd's pie my dad cooked. We will discuss all these other issues when we are less surrounded, okay?"

"Okay," she agreed.

"After dessert, right?"

"After dessert is not going to be the best time for a talk either," Simone said with a randy look in her eyes.

"Maybe after after dessert?" Danni negotiated with a smile.

"Yes, after after," Simone settled and looked over at Billie.

"Are you hungry yet, love? I think we should head over to the table, okay?"

Billie looked up at her mother, closed the book, and followed them to the table in the dining area.

"How on earth did you get her to be so good-natured?"

"She takes after her mother, of course," Simone bantered while they approached the dining table. Her dad was holding a chair out for Simone.

"And see how cordial he is," she continued.

"Ladies first," he said with a broad smile.

He proceeded to hold a chair for Billie, and by that time, Danni had already taken a seat.

She looked at the steam still rising off the shepherd's pie. Her father gestured to the salad he chopped to go with the pie.

"Make sure to get your vegetables," he said.

Danni rushed up from her chair and darted over to the music player on the bookshelf next to the table.

"Everyone okay with some John Denver during dinner?" she asked.

Her dad just threw her a puzzled look.

"I'm good with whatever," Simone answered.

"You like John Denver, Billie?" Danni asked.

"I have never heard of him," Billie said, matching her father's befuddled look.

"I think it's perfect dinner music," Danni said with conviction. She turned his greatest hits on softly in the background and returned to the table to the tune of "Rocky Mountain High."

Her father just shook his head and started pouring wine for the three of them. Each time he stopped as soon as the glasses were half filled and winked at Danni knowingly.

"Our glasses are only half full?" Simone asked.

"Only as long as they are never half empty," he answered, hoping to confuse her out of insisting on more wine.

Danni's dad was first to raise his glass, and they all followed suit to join the toast.

"Wait!" Simone ordered as she interrupted their toast to fill Billie's glass with the iced tea from the jug on the table.

They raised their glasses up again for a toast, this time with Billie joining in.

"Here's to great friendship and hopefully many dinners to come!" Danni offered boldly.

Danni's dad started serving the pie, and they all got busy with filling their plates while John Denver sang about getting his senses filled like a night in a forest.

"So, Billie, what are your favorite thing to do these days?" Danni's dad asked the young girl.

"There are too many to just pick one," she answered without any hesitation.

"Oh, now you have me curious. Can you tell me about a few of them?"

The girl smiled. She didn't flinch from the spotlight.

"I like astrology. And geology. And music, playing piano. And math."

"That is a long list," her dad responded. "I bet you get very good grades in school."

She smiled again.

"Not too bad, but that's only because my mom would be very upset if I didn't."

"That's not true, Billie," Simone argued with friendly protest. "But it's true that we have an agreement that we would visit my parents in Poughkeepsie one full week every summer for every A she gets in school. Luckily, she loves visiting them, and she works hard to get at least six As every year."

"What a perfect motivator for her!" Danni said.

"Yes, and my parents get involved too. They send her a lot of extra reading material on every one of her subjects in order to get her better equipped for those As. It has become quite the family project for us over the years. This is the first year that we have lived so far away from them and so I think she'll be working extra hard this year to get a long stretch with them."

"Where did you used to live?" Danni's dad asked.

"Peekskill. It used to be only an hour's drive for us."

"How do you like Philadelphia so far?"

"It's been so much better since we met Danni. It's good to have a friend in this big city for sure. And of course, since Billie started her lessons with Peter."

"I would say meeting the trombone player would rank higher for Billie," Danni teased.

"Oh yes, Britton and her family has been a Godsend too. To get her away from the piano!"

"A trombone player named Britton?" her dad teased.
Billie chuckled.
"She gets teased all the time for being a girl playing trombone."
"Is she any good?"
Billie nodded as she chewed her salad.
"Does she play in the marching band?"
"No, she plays in the youth orchestra."
"Oh wow, she must be very good then."

Danni and Simone watched elated as Billie and her dad kept their conversation going effortlessly.

The time flew as they kept a steady stream of questions and answers going, getting to know each other while John Denver offered his easy tunes softly as a perfect backdrop.

They finished some apple pie for dessert before Billie started to glance repeatedly at the clock. It was inching close to the time she expected Britton's family to pick her up for bowling.

"What did you think of dinner, Billie?" Simone asked as soon as she watched her take the last bite of her apple pie.

"Thank you, Danni and Mr. Whelan, for the wonderful dinner," she said as if they clearly rehearsed it beforehand.

"You're welcome, kiddo," Danni's father said. "What would you like me to cook next time?"

Billie just shrugged as she glanced at her watch again.

"As long as we finish with apple pie, she will eat pretty much anything," Simone answered on her behalf.

The text came to Simone soon after, notifying her that the car arrived at the entrance of the apartment building. Simone walked out with her while Danni helped her dad to get the dishes piled up in the sink.

"They are so nice, baby. Your friends. I enjoyed meeting them."

"See, you are way less of a hermit than what you've pretended to be all these years."

"I feel like I'm out of the pit where I've been staying for so long. I have more energy to engage with people."

"I'm just happy to know that you are not in a complete crisis anymore."

"So we need to talk to Simone about her husband now? To see what we can do?"

"Yes, to see if she has any extra information to help us figure this thing out."

Simone walked into the kitchen.

"She is so excited about going bowling."

"She was really a good sport for joining the grown-ups for a dinner of shepherd's pie. I don't think many kids would have handled it as well as what she did," Danni's dad praised.

"She is usually agreeable to do things with me. It's only recently that I'm able to have her go out with a friend on her own. She has surprised me actually."

Danni's dad was quietly working on brewing some coffee for them.

Once they all sat back down at the table with coffee being served, Danni's father broke the ice.

"So Danni tells me that you have been concerned about your husband. That you have suspicions about his behavior?"

"Yes. I have been aware for a while now that something isn't quite right. It's been mostly since we moved here from Peekskill. I mean, things may have started to appear suspect there, but it has really ramped up since the move here."

"What kind of things are you noticing?"

"He is working a lot more. He is more stressed. And then, of course, there is the bags he carries in and out of the house. Danni thought it could even be filled with money."

"Bags of money? Have you found large sums of money in the house?" her father asked curiously.

"No. Not in the house. But he buys a lot of things. Lavish things that we don't need. I asked him once point blank what was in the bag he always carries around. He shrugged it off, saying it was things he needed for his business and for me not to worry about it."

"The contents of the bag is speculative then. Other than the fact that he makes and spends more money now than he used to," her dad warned.

Danni stayed quiet. She didn't want to let Simone know just yet what she had found out the past two days about Bill's operation. Not before she had a chance to talk it through with her father.

Simone nodded.

"He is very secretive when it comes to our money. I just have a feeling that something isn't right. He has an account for me that he deposits money into. Gave me a credit card I can use. But beyond that, there is no discussion."

"Has he ever met anyone at the house? People that looked suspect to you?" Danni's dad asked.

"No. Not that I know of, and I'm at the house a lot. He usually meets with clients on the phone or at his office, as far as I know."

"That is good, Simone," he said. "It's best if the people he deals with are not aware of your whereabouts. Or Billie's. He probably stashes the money at his office, if he hides it anywhere."

"I've been trying to convince myself that he would never risk our safety. But of course, I worry that if something goes wrong, they could come after us."

"Does he have a specific routine that you can pick up on?" Danni asked. She didn't want to think about the horrific danger he was exposing his family to.

"Usually leaves our house between nine and ten every morning. Gets back home different times. I think he likes to mix it up to keep me on my toes."

"How often do you see him leave in the morning with that duffel bag?"

"The garage is next to the basement, so I'm not usually down there with him to see when he loads it in the car. Sometimes, he brings it upstairs to his office first. Sometimes, he keeps it in the basement." Danni looked over at her dad.

"We would need to follow him then for a while. See if we can find out what he's up to. At least we know he leaves between nine and ten so it would be easy to hop on his tail."

"How will you do that and be able to go to work, Danni?" Simone asked as the frown lines between her eyes deepened.

"As long as Alex can cover for me a few days at the store, Peter won't mind."

"How dangerous do you think it would be?" she asked.

"He is most likely not dealing with the church, so it's risky. To follow someone who may be involved with criminal activity. They don't usually like to be caught."

"Danni, no need for the sarcasm," her father intervened. "Simone asked a reasonable question about the safety of such a surveillance operation."

"I'm sorry, but I just have a hunch that he is involved with something illegal," Danni said in protest.

"So do you want her to worry more about this than she already is?" her father argued back.

"Of course not, no. Okay, so we try to follow him next week and see what we can find out. And we can try not to worry about it until then."

"Good, let's start on Monday morning then. See what develops from that."

And with that, her father got up from the table.

"I'll be heading out to the bar then."

Danni just nodded. She couldn't shake her suspicion that going to the bar for Jake's surveillance came with strings attached. She had her mother to thank for planting that seed in her mind. But she also couldn't ignore that it provided him with a sense of purpose. If it helped to keep him out of the dark pit of misery he's been hiding in for twenty years, she could not object.

He went to the bathroom to get ready, mostly to change into some version of his disguise. He seemed to be excited about the undercover sting operation he was orchestrating. Danni knew exactly what he was after. She missed the thrill of chasing after Jake. She wondered what other trouble he got into since she has handed most of the project over to her father. He couldn't keep tabs on him after his work shift ended like she could. How many cars has he stolen since? How much money has he lost in bets? How many lies has he told himself about what he was actually doing?

"You can probably take my car tonight, Dad. I'm not going to need it. The keys are hanging by the door," Danni offered.

He usually took an Uber to the bar and back, but tonight, she wanted to give him an opportunity to stay out much later than his usual midnight curfew.

She promised Simone her undivided attention after dessert. Her mother's pep talk from the day before was still loud as a trumpet in her ears. She needed to go after what she wanted, listen to her heart, not waste a second chance at love. Her mother's message registered, but mostly, she wanted to make good on her promise to Simone.

"I don't know that I need to take your car," her dad argued.

"Just take the car, Dad. You never know what trouble he will get into after his shift."

He looked at her, suspicion creeping into his gaze.

She stood strong and pushed back against the growing mistrust in his eyes. She wanted an understanding to take shape between them without needing to say a word. But he has been mostly a stranger to her. Their old connections have rusted over, and they have only recently begun the tedious restoration of their bond.

Still, he finally ordered his suspicions down and agreed to take the car. She could have sworn he flashed her a curious smile right before he walked to the bathroom.

"You guys are quite the pair," Simone surmised as he walked away.

"Just recently."

"You are practically the same person," she continued, still smiling about the sparring that she just witnessed between them.

Danni felt her face grow stark when she thought about the life of her father.

"We are alike in many ways. But I swear, I would have never abandoned my family like he did."

Simone grabbed her hand quickly and looked deep into her eyes.

"I don't think so either. Are we still on for after dessert?"

Danni felt her neck muscles tense under the nerve-racking prospect of going further than a kiss with her.

"Of course, I'm still up for whatever follows after dessert."

She was trying to convince herself more than Simone, who she presumed needed no persuading at all. It wasn't that she didn't want to, but she was filled to the brim with angst about the vast expectations that was tied to such an affair.

"That, my dearest Danni, is music to my ears!"

"Like John Denver?"

Simone laughed.

"No, I think it sounds more like Mozart."

"I hear he was a passionate little bugger."

Simone winked, grabbed her hand, but dropped it even quicker as soon as Danni's father made his disguised entrance out of the bathroom.

Chapter 29

Danni watched her father leave the apartment. Her whole body tingled with anticipation. She kept her eyes on him as he walked down the hall to secure the elevator. She rushed back to the window of her bedroom that overlooked the parking lot of the building. She listened carefully to make sure she could hear her car's engine start. She watched him back the car slowly out of the parking spot and kept her eyes on the lights, fading away as he drove down the street. It was only then that she could take normal breaths and shift her focus back to Simone. She recognized her scent of mixed orange and jasmine and heard her footsteps closing in on her.

Simone's arms reached around her waist. She looked up at the clouds throwing a cover over the night's skylights. The air felt thick with pending rain. She melted into Simone. She could feel the soft mounds of her breasts push against her own rigid spine. She dropped her head to let her inhale the back of her neck. She wanted to exhale, but her ever watchful eyes noticed a car pulling up into the parking lot instead, and she anxiously steered them away from the window. She pulled out of their embrace to pull the curtains shut. Paced over to the bed to turn the small bleaker lamp light on. Her legs felt restless with nervous energy.

"Who else are we hiding from?" Simone asked, approaching her carefully.

"My inexperience, I suppose," Danni said as she stopped her retreat. She went back to the honesty between them.

Simone moved closer again. She brought warmth and a sweet scent rising from her neck as she reached for her hands and pulled her in.

"Maybe you just need to let me take the lead tonight," Simone whispered, and she kissed her neck softly. Danni eased into it. She could feel some of the tension soften under Simone's touch.

Simone gently pulled her toward the bed as she continued to kiss her neck, moving upward toward her mouth. She pulled her down to sit next to her on the bed. Their mouths finally found each other while their arms wrapped around each other, desperately clutching at the moment to keep it from slipping away. She remembered all the times they were interrupted before, unlike this moment, so generously gifted to them. It stretched out as far as the horizon in front of them. They were finally completely alone together, with hours to explore every inch of each other. And inside the room, there was not a cloud in sight.

Danni caressed her soft skin and allowed her fingers to dance through the silk strands of her hair. Simone pulled the parka off her shoulders and flung it to the floor impatiently, just as Danni's fingers started working at the speed of hummingbirds on the buttons of her sundress. Her hungry eyes watched her breasts rise, as she slowly released them from the confines of the fabric.

Their tongues feasted on each other while Simone pulled her shirt over her shoulders and cast it off to join her parka on the floor. Danni pulled the dress over Simone's head, freeing the soft skin of her back and chest. Her fingers brushed across her abdomen, before they finally plunged down to her underwear, lighting a thousand little fires under her touch. Simone's breath rushed ahead, and her moans grew louder in her ear.

They fell on to the bed, stretching out and melting into their soft curves. Their bodies uncoiled to fit perfectly, while their skin started glistening, fusing together like honey.

They couldn't stop kissing. Their hands were electric and intuitive, and they both knew exactly what to do. She finally removed the last of Simone's clothing and gasped at her nakedness, unfolding like a flowering orchid in her hands. They crawled in under the sheets.

Simone rolled on top of her, pressing her warmth into her body. Her arms scooped her up like the wings of an eagle, and they fell into a rhythm, breathing and moving together as if they were making sweet music. Danni could tell Simone played her body as naturally as she played her piano, while she observed every move she made and finally surrendered without any restraints. She let Simone set the pace, stretching every second into a lifetime, still knowing that a million years would never be enough. They merged deep into their desire when their tangled bodies finally drifted off to sleep, drained and spent from the flames that raged between them. Danni felt wide open. Any qualms she had before, any reservations, were burnt to the ground. She felt as free as water running downstream. Her mind was light as she moved with ease down the river which carried them into a new beginning. She felt completely unbound and unrestricted, while all the while never letting go of Simone's hand.

Chapter 30

Danni was lured out of her slumber by the sound of rain doing a tap dance on her bedroom window. She looked at Simone, still naked and dreaming beside her. Her fingers trailed softly down the side of her face. According to the clock on her nightstand, it was just after two in the morning. She was sure that Bill was beside himself that his wife wasn't home yet.

Her sudden concern must have tugged at Simone, and she slowly opened her eyes. She kept still with her eyes focused on Danni, and they both quietly listened to the light patter of the rain. Words would usher an end to their wistful journey. She wanted nothing more than to rewind the clock and go back to the time when they crawled between the sheets and experience it all over again.

"What are you thinking?" Simone whispered finally.

Nothing but the truth, she reminded herself.

"How beautiful you are. And that you probably should have been home hours ago."

Simone's eyes found the clock on the nightstand.

"I told Bill I had a dead battery which we would charge as soon as the rain stops. In the morning. I asked him to stay home with Billie since she doesn't like it when it rains."

"When was this?"

"While you made doubly sure your dad left, right after dessert."

They both smiled.

"You had this planned out perfectly," Danni teased.

"Only from the first time I laid eyes on you."

Danni put a deep frown on her face.

"You didn't know?" Simone asked with feigned shock.

"Of course not."

"It wasn't so much consciously. But deep down, I think every cell in my body knew," Simone explained.

"Maybe we really did know each other in a past life."

"And you finally found me again."

"I think you were the one who strutted into the store like a woman on a mission," Danni said, tickling the skin of her soft spine.

"It does seem that way."

"I have to tell you something," Danni said.

"I know."

She frowned a question at her.

"You told me we would talk about it after dessert, remember?"

Danni agreed. She wanted open lines between them.

"You asked where I was the past two days."

Simone nodded and seemed receptive to an honest explanation.

"I followed Bill around. For two days."

Simone stayed silent, but her eyes widened.

"Your hunch about him was right. He barged into the store on Thursday morning, seemingly ready for a fight. I couldn't let that opportunity go to waste. Something compelled me, and I followed him and watched him work. It was unbelievable."

"What do you mean, you watched him work?" Simone asked, her eyes begging her to elaborate.

"If you can call it work, but I'm thinking it's how he makes most of his money. He arranged for some sort of exchange or trade to go down. They used one of his new listings to host it. He must be the one coordinating it all. I'm not sure what it is that they are dealing in. He carried that infamous duffel bag that we've seen him with at your place into the house. It could only be the money bag. Two big guys came and brought a large trunk inside and exchanged it for the duffel bag. I never saw the contents of the trunk. It could be drugs. Or guns, who knows."

Simone sucked her breath in sharply.

"You think he's in charge of it all?"

"He seems more like a middleman. I don't want to give him too much credit. Which is a good thing."

"A good thing?"

"Hopefully, he's not as intricate to the operation. I don't know exactly where he fits in."

Simone pondered her assessment, nervously biting her bottom lip.

"Tell me the truth, Danni."

"The truth is scary. These people are probably scary, ruthless thugs."

Simone sat up in the bed and turned the bed lamp on. Danni noticed how the shock has darkened her eyes. She took her hand in hers.

"I'm scared that he is the only middleman they want, that he is deeply entrenched in their operation. Or that they would go to great lengths to make him understand that."

"That is not good for me or Billie. I don't want to be mixed up in anything like that. Not now, when I'm trying to realize my dreams again."

Danni nodded. It was the most frustrating turn of events.

"What do you think I should do?"

"Don't tell him anything just yet. Just act completely normal for now."

"For how long?"

"Until we figure something out. I'm hoping that the mere fact of us knowing will redirect everything in our favor. Bringing it into the light might put the gears in motion. We could see where it leads us."

"So you did in fact come to save me?"

Simone turned the light off again and lay back down next to her. Danni slowly rolled on top of her and melted into her body all over again.

"The truth is in the light," Danni said, before she kissed her deeply.

"Have you always been this wise?" Simone asked when they paused for air.

"Not consciously. More in my cells."

Simone reached for her arm. She ran her fingers up and down and found the scars on the inside of her forearm.

"You did this?" she asked softly.

"Many years ago. When I missed my parents terribly and after my brother moved away. I became very lonely and self-destructive."

"What made you stop?"

"I don't know that I have. Meeting you has helped. I'm sure it would be hard for you to believe, but so much has changed for me since that day you walked into the store."

"I know what you mean."

She kept caressing every scar she could find.

"What's the story with your dad? I really like him," she finally asked after she looked satisfied that she has cured every ache in Danni's past with her gentle fingers.

"That's a very long story."

"Tell me."

Danni took a breath a few times to start the story and finally held on to a fleeting moment of courage.

"My little brother died. When he was five. He was thrown off the small boat they were on during a bad storm and drowned. My father was understandably devastated. My mother was angry. My dad blamed himself for that accident, and my mother blamed him even harder. He vanished into his room. It was as if he sank into a coma for years. It was probably the only way he could survive it. He just recently woke up from it. And even that was such a traumatic ordeal. I told you about that craziness when he tried to shoot himself. In the meantime, my mother's anger finally burnt itself out. She simply moved on and found someone else. I'm not sure how long ago that even started, but she has changed into someone I hardly recognize. I feel like I'm getting to know her for the first time."

"That must have been so horrible for you, growing up though all of that."

"I feel like I'm still going through it. We lost everything when my brother died, but we were too broken to help each other."

Simone's fingers caressed her scars again and explored the rest of her arms in search of more.

"It finally looks as if the tides have changed. As if time has finally healed us and given each one of us some renewed purpose."

Simone leaned up to kiss her gently. Danni could feel the passion igniting between them again as their bodies started to fall in sync. Their kiss deepened, and there was nothing holding them back. Until they both heard the apartment door swing open and then closed again. The sound of footsteps echoed from the living room and then they heard the loud thud as something heavy landed on the floor.

Danni jumped up in a flash and rushed to her closet to find something to cover her naked body. She was expecting her dad to come home at some point during the night, but she hoped that he would tiptoe in quietly without waking anyone up. She tossed a shirt and pajama pants over to Simone.

"You can put this on. I'm going out to see what the heck's going on."

She found Jake leaning over her father on the floor in the living room and stopped dead in her tracks. She drew a sharp breath in and then looked at her father on the floor. His face was badly bruised and covered in dried blood.

She rushed over to him.

"Oh my god, Jake, what happened to him?" she yelled out as she kneeled beside him on the floor to get a closer look at the damage.

"Why didn't you tell me you are sending your father over to the bar to spy on me?" he asked, anger escalating in his voice.

"Who on earth beat him up like this?"

"Nikolai."

She shuddered as he said the name and the image of the dark-faced Russian charged into her head. The name fitted his description perfectly.

"Can you be more specific, Jake? I don't know anyone named Nikolai."

"As if!" he yelled with his fists tensing.

"I swear," she lied, pressing him to spell it out to her.

"You know very well that your dad has been coming to the bar to spy. He told me that himself. That it was all your idea."

Her dad tried to open his swollen eyes. He waved his hands up in protest, wanting to explain himself, but his face was likely in too much pain to say anything sensibly.

"Has he been drinking too much over there? He hasn't been himself lately."

"Like a fish. And don't even try to make it seem as if he is crazy. He went right up to Nikolai, asking to buy cocaine. Told him that it was obvious that the Russians owned the drug trade in the place. Then he kindly informed him that he used to be a cop. Threatened to call his friends at the DEA on them."

"Geez, how drunk did you get him over there? That just seems like crazy talk to me. The alcohol has really been getting him so delusional. He sometimes thinks he is still a detective."

Danni didn't know how to come clean to him, and she needed him out of the apartment before he discovered Simone, hiding in her bedroom, wearing her pajamas.

"Help me get him on the couch at least," she asked to distract him from her part in their deception.

They each grabbed an arm and pulled her father up to his feet. They dragged him over to the couch and laid him down. Danni rushed off to the kitchen to get a rag and water to clean the blood off his face.

When she returned, she patted his bruises gently and slowly wiped his face clean.

"I'm so sorry, Jake," she said. "Thank you for driving him home."

"Danni, they would have killed him if I didn't stop them tonight. I had to work a miracle to get them to let up on him. I'm not sure what I said to finally make him stop pounding his fist into his face, but he can't ever come back there. Pretending to be a cop ready to slap the cuffs on anyone coming in for a few drinks."

"How did you know he was my father?"

"They beat that little fake mustache right off his face. And it was easy to put two and two together when he accused me of putting his daughter, Danni, in the middle of a drug ring, which he was furious about. He literally yelled that out loud while he was getting beat up. Talk about crazy. So stupid."

"So are you?" she asked, looking directly at him, curious if he would confess to anything real this time.

"Am I what?"

"Putting me in the middle of a dangerous drug ring?"

"How am I doing that?"

His voice shrieked impatiently as he threw his hands up in dramatic fashion, finding all his old familiar escape routes.

"So you are telling me that a Russian drug ring has not staked a claim to your uncle's bar, relying on you to look the other way?"

He looked at her. She could tell that he felt exposed.

"Where do you get this shit from Danni? Your imagination is really running wild these days."

"Isn't that how my father explained it to you?"

"Your father told you that story?"

They were dancing in circles around each other.

She looked at her father on the couch. She heard his breathing slow down, and he started to snore.

She rushed over and grabbed him by the shoulders. She shook him back and forth to wake him up as soon as she realized that he shouldn't be sleeping after the concussion he most likely suffered.

"Dad! Wake up!" she cried out nervously.

He opened his eyes slowly and smiled faintly when he saw her, careful not to move his face too much. She threw his legs off the couch and helped him to sit up.

"I have to go, Danni. It's been a crazy night! I'm serious, he cannot come back to the bar, so make sure you remind him tomorrow."

"You're leaving without answering me? As usual, when things get uncomfortable for you."

"Can you cut me a break for once? It's the middle of the night! I'm going home to get some sleep," he huffed as he took off toward the door.

"Or are you off to go steal a few cars?" she said boldly, throwing knives to his back.

Her words stopped him cold in his tracks. His body stiffened, and it was as if he couldn't find his breath. He finally gasped and turned around slowly to face her.

"So you have been spying on me too?" he asked with seething eyes.

"You would have never told me on your own. Ever."

"Danni! Your dad is falling asleep!"

They both turned toward the sound of Simone's voice as she ran out of the bedroom toward her father on the couch.

Simone grabbed her father's face in both hands and tapped his cheeks gently to wake him up.

"Matt, stay with us, please. Don't sleep!"

Jake's jaw hit the ground. He stood stunned, with his hands perched on his sides and eyes bulging in his head.

Simone looked at them both.

"You guys weren't paying attention to him. I had to do something. His face was beaten to a pulp, and you decide to argue about the sad state of your relationship. We need to keep him awake."

"I'm sorry, but who are you?" Jake asked with mixed surprise and disdain.

"Maybe it's best that you leave, Jake. It's late, and this is obviously not the best time to sort things out," Simone said fearlessly and walked to the kitchen with the rag in her hand.

Danni was stunned into silence. Simone's appearance in the room has turned the tables upside down. She lost the upper hand she had with Jake instantly.

He looked at her, disgusted.

"You have been cheating on me!"

She couldn't find a suitable rebuttal.

"Spying on me and cheating on me. With a woman?"

Her head swirled around and finally guided her toward a response.

"Mostly spying, Jake. Which is how I know about the cars, the gambling, and the money you owe. What did you call him? Nikolai?"

She was pushed into a corner. Her only choice left was the truth. Things didn't turn out according to her loosely construed plan. Peter was not going to be happy.

"Which means you know what I've been going through then. To make a good life for us. I never thought you'd be lying to me."

"A life built on crime is not the life I want, Jake."

He stayed quiet, but his eyes accused her of a more heinous, more unforgivable offence.

Simone sat quietly next to her dad on the couch, squeezing his hand to keep him from drifting off again.

"It's over between us, Danni. There's no coming back for us from this," Jake said, slinging fire straight to her face.

She offered no protest. He was merely saying what's been written on the wall for a long time.

He walked over to the door slowly.

Danni made one last attempt, right before he reached out to open the door.

"You could leave town, like your dad did. It may be the best way out of this for you."

Her words fell on him like cold water. He turned around and sneered at her.

"See, Danni, you really don't know anything about me. You should know I would never run, like that punk that used to call himself my father."

Danni wanted to believe he didn't mean a word of that, but before she could say anything else, he left the apartment.

She looked at Simone, still stroking her father's arms to keep him awake.

"Do you think now is a perfect time for coffee?" she asked, exhausted by the unexpected confrontation with Jake.

"I do. We could all use a cup," Simone answered.

Her dad opened his eyes as wide as he could.

"I messed up badly, kid. I drank way too much tonight."

"Shh, Dad, it's okay. Jake was probably never going to go down to New Orleans. I think he likes being a gangster too much."

Her dad just nodded, his face in too much pain to express everything he wanted to.

Instead, he looked over to the kitchen. His eyes locked in on Simone, finding her way around the cupboards to find everything she needed to make coffee.

"The girl?" he managed to whisper.

Danni knew he may have looked like he was falling asleep, but he clearly heard every word that was said.

"Yes, Dad, the girl," she whispered back.

He smiled and shook his head in surprise. But his gaze stayed on her, as soft as a summer breeze. Simone finally returned with the three promised cups of coffee. She joined them on the couch, and they each sipped their warm drinks in silence for a while.

"My car battery died, Mr. Whelan. Danni said if I stayed until the morning, she could help me jump it."

He raised his eyebrows and played along.

"No worries, Simone, I don't mind you being here," he mumbled carefully.

She smiled back at him and squeezed his left hand gently.

Danni flicked the TV on so they could stay awake watching a movie. Her father shuffled over to the lounge chair, leaving more space on the couch for the two of them.

"You're never too old for a slumber party," Danni announced as she pulled Simone closer to her on the couch. They threw their legs up to get more comfortable. Danni perked her ears and realized that the rain has stopped.

She settled on *Speed* with Sandra Bullock. They needed a movie with nonstop action to keep her father awake until morning, when the sun could take its turn watching over him.

Chapter 31

Danni woke early on Monday morning with her mind still intoxicated from every minute she spent with Simone two nights ago. Simone planned to take Billie to visit her parents in Poughkeepsie, but she assured Danni she would come to the store on Monday to meet with Peter and Marius. Every fiber in her body missed her. She planned the visit mostly to avoid a confrontation with Bill and his amped-up suspicions. She said he's been watching her phone like a hawk.

Her father slept most of the day on Saturday, and she hovered around him like a brooding hen to make sure he was still breathing. He went to the house on Sunday to pick up some more of his things, while she opted for the park. She tried to zone in on anything that moved, but finally resigned herself to staying still on a bench under a cloudy sky, putting her memories of the weekend on a never-ending loop in her mind.

The early morning sun finally poured through her window that Monday morning, after the unrelenting rain of the weekend finally let up and moved further east. She wanted to pin her father down to discuss a course of action. They had a vague intention to follow Bill that morning, but she was almost certain he wouldn't feel up to it. She got up to go make coffee.

After she poured them two cups, she placed his cup on the end table beside the couch. His face was less swollen but still very bruised, and his hand looked like it could be broken. The knuckles were warm and shiny. He must have at least landed one good punch during the struggle.

He stirred and slowly opened his eyes. She went back to the kitchen to make a bag of ice for him. She handed it to him wrapped in a dish towel.

"You are going to need more ice on your face today to get the last of that swelling down," she said.

"Thanks, baby," he said as he pressed the cool ice into his swollen cheeks.

"Don't worry about the coffee. I will warm it up for you after you are done with the ice."

"'You are too good to me."

"You should rest up a few more days before we tackle Bill's situation."

"I'm so sorry, Danni. I know you really wanted to get on that today."

She decided to come clean. If they were going to be partners, they needed to have full disclosure between them.

"I actually managed to follow him last week."

"What?" he asked, floored by her confession.

"He came to the store. Accusing Simone of cheating on him with Peter, and he just seemed so aggressive. I don't know, I just acted, like it was an uncontrollable reflex, and chased after him."

He smiled and shook his head.

"He got it all wrong, eh?" he said, she assumed about Bill's delusion that Simone was cheating on him with Peter.

"Lucky for me, yes."

"So what did you find out?"

"I watched the whole scheme go down and from what I can gather, it looks as if he uses his new listings as a location for some sort of trade or sale. He opened the place and installed a key code door lock on the door. He left that big duffel bag we talked about there. I'm sure he brings the money for the transaction. Two guys in a van came shortly after and brought a heavy trunk and left with the bag of money. Then two other guys came and scooped the trunk up. And

Bill went on to put the For Sale sign up after that and drove off. It looks like hands off, easy money for him."

"It sounds like he is some sort of middleman."

"As far as I can tell, yes. I don't know if he has more involvement beyond that. With the guys in the van or the other two. I'm not sure whom he answers to."

"Maybe they even buy the homes and use it to launder the money."

"Could be. I mean, how many paintings can he buy to put in his house? He didn't strike me as the type that would just be a middleman. And real estate would definitely be a good way to hide a lot of money."

"Maybe he stashes money into the walls of his basement," he joked.

"Nothing would surprise me with him."

"Did you get pictures of any of the guys who came to the house?"

"No. I was way too wired after the incident in the store with him. And it was broad daylight. They just didn't seem like the type of guys who would go easy on anyone caught spying on them."

"That's good, Danni. You should always ensure your own safety first."

"What should we do next?"

"We should get pictures. Hard evidence."

"You could take it to Ruben?"

"Yes. See what he knows."

"Okay. I was too far away to get a good look of their faces. We can go out to get pictures as soon as you feel better."

"Yeah, I'm sure they don't do these deals every day."

"In the meantime, we could find him at Girls Unlimited. He seems to love that place."

Danni's dad laughed.

"That place has been there for years. It's a hotbed of criminals. Most of the girls are blackmailed and hooked on drugs."

"Why hasn't it been shut down?"

"Cops and robbers, Danni. It's just so hard to know who's who."

"Then why do you trust Ruben?"

"Gut feeling, I guess. Plus, he is all we got."

She looked at him as doubt scurried around in her stomach.

"We just have to go on blind faith here?"

"'So much in life requires blind faith. When you raced after Bill, you showed a lot of blind faith that something would come from it. You trusted your gut, didn't you?"

"I guess so. I had the same feeling when I trailed Jake too. I had the feeling that things were being revealed to me on purpose."

"Isn't life beautiful that way?"

"I'm learning to appreciate that."

"You never know, Danni. Maybe we would make a good team again. Like long ago."

"I remember so much that you have taught me."

"Maybe crime fighting is in our blood. My father was a police officer too, you know? I followed in his footsteps."

He has never mentioned that to her before. He must have regarded himself an even bigger failure, falling so short of his idol.

"Are you ready for your coffee?"

He nodded and handed her the bag of ice that has melted from the heat on his face.

"What are you going to do about your hand?"

"Oh, it's nothing. I'm sure it's just badly bruised. I picked up an ace bandage from the house yesterday, I will wrap it up for a few days."

She left to go warm up his coffee.

"What are you up to today?" he asked when she returned with steam rising off his cup.

"I should get back to work. I haven't been there since Wednesday. I'll have to buck up and tell Peter that his nephew broke up with me and I'm dreading that conversation."

"You don't look too sad about it."

"Things haven't been right between us for a long time."

"Sometimes, it takes someone else showing up to make you see that, eh?"

"Yes."

"It's probably what happened with your mother."

She felt the pain in his voice, as he breathed life into that trying truth. It wasn't the outcome any of them ever expected.

"Max has been good for her. I know it's difficult to hear, but I haven't seen her this calm in years."

He looked down and rubbed his swollen knuckles, as he warmed up his hand with the heat of the coffee cup.

"Why did you get into that fight at the bar?"

"I drank too much, Danni. I started seeing your mother's face staring back at me in that glass. Her image floated in the whiskey. She was happy, with Mattie on her hip. It made me so sad. I sat there, staring down at her, and I wanted someone to bash my face in. For the pain I've caused her."

"When are you going to forgive yourself? God has forgiven you, obviously. Or that bullet wouldn't have malfunctioned like it did. We have all forgiven you a very long time ago. Including Mom."

"Has she? Is that why she is with Max now?"

"She has. If she didn't, she would still have lived with you in that house, punishing you with her anger."

"So I either had her angry forever or not at all?"

"At least you are free now."

He smirked.

"What do they call that? Stockholm syndrome? When someone becomes attached to their abuser?" she asked him bluntly.

He looked down at his hand again, but she could see he was thinking about her words. He slowly sipped the coffee.

"It may take you a while to figure out how to deal with all this freedom, and I'm sure a part of you still wants what was familiar to you. She used to be the one punishing you for what you think you have done wrong. Never mind that it was just an accident. You will have to find a way to forgive yourself, Dad. Or you will keep finding ways to destroy yourself."

"How do you see all of this so clearly. I go into a fog every time I think about it."

"I have been under the same spell for a long time too. They say when you only use your destructive emotions, you forget how to be happy anymore."

She pushed the sleeves of her shirt up and showed him the scars on her forearms.

He looked at her arms and then into her eyes. He showed her a clear understanding of a sadness he could relate to.

"My god, Danni. We have all been through so much."

"But don't you think we are finally coming out on the other side? We just have to get used to the other side first."

"What about Robbie? I miss him. I haven't been there for him at all."

"He managed to get away from here. Probably on blind faith alone. He was barely seventeen when he left, remember?"

"Still just a child."

"I think he lived on the street, when Sarah's dad found him and took him in."

"Minister, right?"

"Yes, I think their church reached out to the homeless a lot. Then they left for New Orleans to lead that church there. It's good that Robbie went with them."

"We should call him sometime. Do you have his number?"

"Somewhere."

"I would like that."

He set the empty cup down on the coffee table.

"I'm going to get ready for work."

"Okay, baby. What do you want for dinner?"

"I'm up for anything you can come up with, Masterchef Whelan."

He laughed as she headed off to take a shower.

"You like frog legs?" he yelled out after her.

She leaped like a frog the rest of the way into the bathroom and enjoyed the laugh that ripped all the way from his belly at her antics.

Chapter 32

Peter rushed into the store with long nervous strides. She checked the clock and saw that it was only eleven, much earlier than he usually arrived for work. She knew instantly that it had something to do with Jake.

"You're early," she said when he stopped in front of her at the sales counter.

"I'm so glad that you are back today. We need to have a talk."

She couldn't read his face to tell if it was about her breaking up with Jake or if Jake told him about Simone sleeping over at her place. Or if he knew about the Russians invading his brother's bar.

"Now?" she asked, looking around the store to see if that one wandering customer was still in one of the aisles.

"Yes," he looked back and noticed the lonely customer lost in front of the sheet music rack too.

"Come back to my office when she is checked out, okay? I'm going to lock the door to keep any more people from coming in for a while."

He was acting completely out of character, making her believe that Jake told him about everything. She wanted to text Simone to find out if she still planned on coming in that afternoon, but her mind warned her with a sharp image of Bill watching her phone vibrate on the dining table. She respected the warning.

She flashed back to her memory on Saturday morning. Simone gave her a ride to where her dad left her car near the bar. They sat in her car, silently fighting against her needing to leave. Simone kissed

273

her goodbye and hugged her tightly. She said she couldn't wait to see her again. Danni didn't ask her about Bill. Things were tough enough already, but Simone assured her she wouldn't let Bill stand in her way again this time.

The girl finally came to the counter, empty-handed.

"Can I help you find something?" Danni asked.

"I have this list of books my teacher gave me, and he said I could find them here."

She handed her a list of early method books for the violin.

"When do you need them?"

"My first lesson with him is next Thursday."

"How about you leave this list here with me, and I will get them all together for you. You should be able to come pick it up by next Tuesday."

"Are you sure?"

"Yes, I will expedite it to have it ready. Who's your teacher?"

"Marius Schultz. He's in the symphony, but he gives lessons out of his home. He said specifically to get the books here."

"He is very good. You are lucky, he usually only takes younger students."

"I know. I'm switching from the piano to the violin, and luckily, my parents know him. They donate to the Symphony. Go to all the fund-raisers," she said it very apologetically.

"I will get the books ready for you, don't worry. Write your number down on this pad here, and I will call you when you can pick it up."

She scribbled her name and number down and then Danni ushered her to the door. The door was already locked by Peter, but he left the keys for her.

"You guys are closing now?" the girl asked.

"Just for a short while. You know how unpredictable musicians are," she said, unlocking the door and swinging it wide open for her to leave.

"Okay, I'll see you next Tuesday then?"

"Definitely, you'll be happy to know that I'm not a musician."

She could tell the girl still wasn't quite convinced.

Danni locked the door behind her again. She walked over to Peter's office, uncertainty obscuring her mind. Her thoughts chased around in circles. She was sure he found out about her and Simone. She could already see the disappointment spelled out on his face.

She pushed his office door open carefully, took a deep breath, and walked in.

"I'm ready," she said, not meaning either of the two words.

He pointed to the chair next to his desk for her to sit down. She complied and wiped her sweaty hands off on her pants.

He looked at her without saying anything.

"What is it, Peter? You are making me more nervous."

"Jake is missing."

"What do you mean, missing?"

"When is the last time you saw him?" he asked insistently.

She braced for the interrogation that was destined to follow.

"Friday night. About two in the morning."

His face hit her with a frown.

"My dad ran into some problems at the bar. He brought him home after a bad altercation with one of Jake's acquaintances there."

"What? That sounds horrible!"

"Surely has a concussion from it."

"You said he was just going to scope things out over there, to see who was extorting Jake."

"He didn't handle it as well as what I expected he would. He is clearly rusty as a detective and apparently also still a bit of an alcoholic."

"Oh my god, Danni. I feel like I'm responsible for this mess. Did his drinking have something to do with the family trouble you had last week?"

"Kind of. We all seem to be in the throes of various meltdowns, Peter. I'm so sorry that I had to miss work."

She crossed her fingers that he that he couldn't see all the way through her lies.

"It's not a problem. Family always comes first."

She looked at him. It was true what he said. His priority truly was his family. She didn't know when that all clicked in for him. After his father's death, maybe.

"Has he not shown up for work the rest of the weekend?"

She steered the conversation back to Jake.

"No, he hasn't. Mark scheduled him for a shift on Saturday night, which he just blew off. We went to his apartment several times yesterday to see if he was home. He wasn't answering his phone at all."

It worried Danni. She had a feeling that it wasn't going to turn out well for Jake. Not after the crazy stunt her father pulled at the bar. He basically blew Jake and the Russian's cover at the bar, and she knew it would cost him dearly.

"So I have to tell you that everything pretty much came crashing down on Friday night at the bar. My dad drank too much and foolishly exposed everything. He accused Jake of looking the other way, while a Russian gang has claimed the bar as their drug territory. He wasn't discreet about it either. He probably made things very difficult for Jake."

"Mark is beside himself. He is too scared to call the cops. He actually said he thought selling the bar was the only solution he could think of."

"It's definitely not how we planned for this to go. I probably shouldn't have involved my father in this."

"Jake hasn't called you?"

"He broke up with me. After I confronted him, I was just so upset about my dad. He really could have been killed."

Peter sat quietly in his chair. She assumed his mind was running through a plethora of equations and outcomes.

"So you confronted him, and he told you that's it, it's over?"

She wanted to keep Simone out it.

"Yes. He wasn't happy that I spied on him. I can't say that I blame him for that."

"Well, we had to find out what he was up to."

"Exactly what I said to him."

He spun his fingers around and around, while his right foot tapped nervously.

"Then he just walked out?"

"Yes, he said my dad should never set foot in the bar again and that our relationship was over."

"I wonder if he skipped town. Like his dad did."

"I asked him to. I told him it may be the safest option for him. Wait, let me check my phone app. I still have that tracker on his car. We can see where his car is at least."

She reached for her phone in her pocket and opened the app. There was no dot showing up on the map. She played around with the settings, but still came up empty. She pictured him, frantically searching every inch of his car, discovering the device, and stomping it into a million pieces, berating himself for being careless enough to get followed everywhere.

"It looks as if he discovered the tracker on his car. He probably put two and two together after I told him that I followed him everywhere."

"Let's hope he tossed the tracker and got out of town in a hurry."

"He told me he would never do that. He wouldn't do what his father did."

"It's by far the best option he has. Why wouldn't he do that?"

"We were going to ask if my brother Robbie in New Orleans could take him in for a while, until things could settle down up here."

"That would have been great. I have a bunch of friends in New York that would gladly have taken him in also. If he didn't want to go as far as New Orleans."

"With how vicious these guys are, New Orleans is probably not far enough."

"So what do I do now, Danni?"

"There is that place in Bustleton where he's been hanging out. If he planned to join their gang in some way, he would probably end up there at some point. Or maybe they would use him in one of their chop shops. He knows a lot about cars, and surely, he would need to become extremely valuable to them."

"What do you mean, chop shop?"

"He has been stealing cars for them."

"Stealing cars? I didn't know about that."

She almost forgot that she never explained the entire truth about his demise.

"Yes, I watched him and another guy work together in perfect harmony to swipe a Mercedes off a driveway and take it to some warehouse, I think. There was just so much going on with him, I didn't really know where to focus my energy."

"Well, he wouldn't have Mark's bar to offer them anymore."

"I don't know how they would handle that situation. I can't see them walking away from that easily."

She watched him wringing his hands again. Trying to piece everything together.

"Do you think you can scope out this place in Bustleton? To see if he shows up there?"

Danni looked at him. She mulled over his request. She didn't want to invest any more time into Jake's problem. She had Bill to worry about. And the safety of Simone and Billie.

"I don't think I can. Not after what they did to my father."

"I understand. Maybe I could get Mark to go with me. If you let us know where it is. I just need to know that he is okay."

"I would, but you should seriously reconsider getting involved with them. Maybe you should let Jake figure this out on his own this time."

"Even with these people as dangerous as you say they are?"

"That's just it, Peter. The best option he had was to get away, and if he doesn't want to do that, he risks the lives of his family and everyone he loves. You and Mark getting involved could even put him in more danger than what he already is. If they're worried that you would involve the police to find your nephew. I can't even imagine what they would do to him."

It looked like he agonized over her words. She could see a sense of defeat crush over him like a six-foot-tall wave. The realization that he may have lost his favorite nephew.

"You are right. I don't want to put him in more danger than what he already is."

"We have to let him choose his own path now. I'm sure he's aware of his options."

Peter rubbed his eyes as if he desperately wanted to see a different outcome than what was presented to him.

"It's still going to eat me alive, Danni."

"We would have to hope that he would make the right decision for himself."

He looked at her with questions in his eyes.

"Do you have faith, Danni?"

"Lately, more so. There's just been too many coincidences for it all to be just coincidences."

He got up from his chair and circled around in the room like he needed to clear his head.

"Marius will be over today around two. To come meet with Simone. Do you know if she still plans on coming?"

"She hasn't called to cancel."

"She came around on Friday, to let me know she had second thoughts. Something about her husband not being a hundred percent on board. I'm not sure how anyone could not be on board with a talent like hers."

"I had the exact same question, after I heard her play for the first time."

"When was that?"

"A few weeks ago. At her house, one afternoon."

"You went to her house?"

"Just for a visit."

"I didn't know you guys were that close back then."

"I took Billie to the movies once to give her some extra time for her music at home. I figured that was the least I could do for her. I was prepared to do that for her on a regular basis, but Billie ended up befriending a trombone player from the youth orchestra."

"Britton?"

'You know her?"

"I know every kid in that orchestra. She just moved here and already got in, I understand."

"Yes, Britton. They hit it off apparently, giving Simone more time at home on the piano. Just another coincidence that happened recently."

"What's up with her husband then? Do you have a theory, Ms. Detective?"

"I think you need a psychologist to figure that one out."

"He's jealous of her talent is the only logical explanation I could come up with. Maybe he doesn't want a wife in the spotlight."

"Maybe he knows for a fact she wouldn't be with him if she became famous and had the pick of the litter," she added to his calculations.

"See, you're more than just a good detective, Danni."

"He gave me the creeps both times I met him." Danni made sure to omit the details of their incident at the store on Thursday morning.

"So you're saying that there is a good chance that she would not make it here at two today?"

Danni remembered that kiss on Saturday morning and the assurances she presented before she drove off.

"If she didn't make it today, it wouldn't be because she didn't want to. She wants this more than anything."

"So here we are again, just needing to hope and trust again?"

Danni nodded.

"Maybe we are mere spectators in a constant series of divine interventions."

"You are getting far too wise for your years. Jake should kick himself for letting you go, because losing you is going to be the biggest mistake of his life."

"Maybe it just wasn't meant to be."

"Why are you so calm about it? I would have been livid about his lies."

He was right. She was far too calm about the loss of Jake. At this point, the friendship she had with Peter meant more to her. She would be more upset about losing that.

"Things didn't mesh between me and Jake all the time. Have you ever experienced that type of cooling off? I hate to be blunt with you, Peter, but even sexually, things weren't as good as what they should have been."

"Really? He always told me he adored you in every way."

"I don't think I was able to admit that to myself for a long time."

"That you didn't have sexual chemistry?"

"Yes. I thought that it would develop later. With more time. But I think it just got worse. I didn't ever tell him that. I didn't know what was wrong with me."

"You sound like me after trying for three years to date girlfriends all through high school."

"Ha. I'm glad you find that you can relate," she teased.

"Are you saying what I think you're saying?"

"That the problem didn't seem to be with Jake?"

"Dear god, Danni. Can you quit talking in circles to me? It's me. Are you saying that you prefer women?"

"It seems that way, yes. It's been on my radar for a while. But more so recently," she said as she watched his face light up like he hit the bonus round on a slot machine.

"Simone?"

"Why would you guess her first?"

"I don't know, Danni. She did turn up on the scene very recently, and I haven't been completely blind to the twinkle in your eyes every time she came into the store. I just figured you really, really wanted a friend."

"So how much would it bother you? If we were more than friends? I mean, now that she may also be working here."

"Is that why you made sure that she auditioned? So that you can see her here, away from her crazy husband?"

"Most definitely. And because I had a feeling that she would blow your socks off."

He stayed quiet, his brain mulling over the bombshell she dropped in his lap. She could see him trying to push his excitement down.

"Are you really planning on having an affair with her?"

"We haven't called it anything yet."

"I've tried a few of those affairs with married people, Danni. They didn't work out. I have to say, you sure are full of surprises today."

"I've been trying this new full disclosure thing out recently. Failing to be honest with Jake was a complete disaster. Not being truthful with myself has cost me even more."

"I get it, Danni. Believe me, I've been there. You're going to go on a journey now. People don't just figure these things out overnight. But there is no easy way to turn back. I worked through so many bad relationships on my journey, and I still haven't found the right guy."

"Have you and Marius ever tried?"

His eyes winced.

"Marius wouldn't leave his wife. He finally got off our midnight train to Blisstown. Unfortunately, he was married to the daughter of the symphony's conductor, and leaving her would have been a kill shot to his career."

"But if it weren't for that?"

He smiled openly.

"We learned to become perfect friends and colleagues. But there aren't many days that I don't think about the memories we had together in New York City We did at least give each other a few trips together to remember."

"So he stayed married, and you moved on?"

"He stayed married. I've been trying to replace him. Not successfully."

"It's obvious. I've watched you work together, you seem really close."

"For as well as we get along, it also aches my heart more than anything. But it's s a tough business we're in. It's more about who you know than what you know. He couldn't burn that bridge and be sure he could ever replace it with another."

"What would you tell me? Willing to get into this crazy affair with Simone?"

He grabbed both of her shoulders softly.

"It's all part of the journey, Danni. And you, of all people, are strong enough to handle it. Maybe it will make you even stronger."

"I don't feel all that strong when it comes to her. In fact, I've been very weak in the knees around her."

"That's how you know it's worth it. So what if you get your heart broken? It would still be better than living with the regret of never trying."

"It sounds like you are giving me a green light, Peter. I was so worried that you would fire me," she said, relishing the relief that washed over her.

"Don't be ridiculous. You are as much family to me as Jake. I root for your happiness one hundred percent."

"I will find out if she still plans on coming then?"

"If you need a reason to text her, then yes, please find out if she is still coming. I need to know if I have to prepare my aching heart for a visit from Marius. The armor I need to deal with him takes over an hour to put on."

She walked out under the bright lights of the hallway, feeling as tall as Mount Everest.

Chapter 33

She reached for her phone as soon as she got back to the sales counter and decided against unlocking the store door just yet.

"Are we sure to see you here at two?" she texted Simone while keeping her fingers crossed.

She waited but did not get a response back. She could sense the knot in her stomach tightening.

She finally snapped herself back to reality and went to unlock the door. She needed to focus on work instead. She studied the list of the books the girl left with her and started working on placing the order from their distributor.

A good twenty minutes passed before she finally received a response back from Simone.

"Call me?"

Danni quickly hit the Call icon on the screen and waited, listening to the soothing sound of the ring tone that promised Simone's voice on the other side of it.

"Hi, Danni. Sorry, I'm just running behind, and I figured it would be easier to talk."

"I'm always happy to hear your voice."

She could feel the brightest light shining through Simone's face.

"Me too," she said.

"Will you be here then? I'm just checking that you didn't change your mind."

"No, no. Bill needed some wifely duties taken care of this morning, making me fall behind. I'm just feeling rushed to get ready."

"Wifely duties?"

She was stumped by Simone's explanation.

"No, no, heaven's no! Not that kind of wifely duties. I'm talking about dry cleaning and laundry, Danni. He wanted me to pick up his clothes of all things. And of course, I got stuck in a crowd of people also needing their clothes picked up today."

"Thank you for the explanation, Simone. You mean, you don't do his laundry at home?" she asked with a chuckle.

"He doesn't trust me with his clothes. I shrank too many shirts years ago and swiftly got kicked off laundry duty."

"Nicely played."

"I know. What a chore! Usually, I don't mind just picking up his clothes, but today was hectic over there. On top of having to do Billie's laundry this morning and getting back from my parents late last night. I took her to school earlier, and I'm still trying to wreck my brain to figure out how I would get her picked up from school at the exact same time as my meeting with Peter. I'm so bad with planning things."

"Bill's not available?"

"No. He said I was on my own with this music gig. He wouldn't help in any way. I had to convince him that I would be able to do that and still take care of everything she needs."

"He drives a hard bargain. Does he not usually help with Billie?"

"He pays for everything, which he considers enough."

"I guess."

"He has been completely immovable on this issue. Won't tell me why. But of course, I now know why. He is probably terrified that I will run into him committing a crime somewhere."

'You are on fire today," Danni teased, as she listened to Simone's rants. She had a suspicion that there were at least three cups of coffee involved to fuel her fire.

"So tell me, how will I pull the impossible off today? Can you tell Peter that I will be late for the meeting?"

"No, that won't be good. He has a full schedule today. I can go pick her up from school and bring her here. Two o' clock, you said?"

"Really?"

"Of course. I can just bring her to the store so she can practice in one of the rooms here. Or she can always help me sell a few instruments. I'm sure she could do a great sales pitch to sell a piano."

"Funny. She does have a good memory when it comes to certain things. You are a life saver, Danni."

"Just get your beautiful self over here. Peter has been so excited to show your talents off to Marius."

"Okay, she is at St. Mary's Elementary School. She would be waiting to the right of the main gate. They would have her with a teacher. I will call over there, so they know it's okay for you to pick her up."

"Yes, make sure, I don't want any trouble with the cops today."

"Just bring her straight to the store, okay?"

"Will do."

"Thank you, Danni. I'm sorry this is such a whirlwind of a call."

"I'm happy to help, of course, but go easy on the coffee until you get here. I will make a note to schedule your future appointments for any time but two o' clock."

"You think of everything. See you soon."

They hung up, and Danni called Alex immediately. She would need him to come in around one thirty at the latest to free her up to make it over to Billie's school.

After she got confirmation from Alex that he would be available for cover for her, she headed back to let Peter know that the appointment with Simone was in good standing and for him to start preparing to face Marius all afternoon.

"That's good news, Danni," he said, combing his hand through his hair and pulling his shoulders back for starts.

"I have Alex coming to relieve me so I can go pick Billie up from school and bring her here during your meeting."

"You think you may be having too many irons in the fire, Danni?"

"I will just schedule her in a different time slot in the future."

"There's no limit to where that woman's talent could take her if she has the right assistant to manage her daily life," he quipped.

"You've been there?" she teased back.

"Of course. It's my lead-off question on every first date. How good they can manage a calendar. No artist wants to be bogged down with something as mundane as scheduling appointments."

"A partner that truly loved you wouldn't mind doing your calendar," she said with a smile, knowing what he was insinuating.

"Women are lucky. Men find it so hard to be the understudy."

They heard the doorbell chime and Danni hurried back to her post behind the sales counter. It was just past one o clock. She wouldn't see Simone until after her meeting with Peter, but she couldn't wait to whisk her into one of the rooms for a kiss. Her body ached for her. It was as if she was going into withdrawal after getting hooked on the most addictive drug.

Danni pulled up to the school. She spotted Billie right away, pacing back and forth in front of the teacher who stood with folded arms against the wall of the school building. She fell in line with the cars taking turns to pick up the various kids who spilled out of the building, crowding the front parking lot of the school. She quickly parked once she made it to the front of the line and rushed over to Billie and the teacher.

"Danni!" Billie yelled out in surprise.

"Hey, kid, your mom got busy at the store and asked me to come get you today," she quickly explained. She was well aware of the line of cars behind her waiting their turn, so she kept it brief.

"Did you guys get the call from her mother?"

"Yes, she said that Danni Whelan was going to pick Billie up today. Are you Danni Whelan?"

"In the flesh. Sorry, do you need some kind of ID?"

"Of course, we do. We don't just give the kids to anyone."

Danni sprinted back to her car and fumbled around in her purse to find her driver's license. The teacher handed Billie over as soon as she was satisfied that she matched the picture on the ID.

She opened the passenger side for Billie and took her book bag to stuff in the back seat, then sped off as fast as she could.

"No wonder they are dealing with such a traffic jam over there," she said as she jammed her ID back into her purse, while she tried to figure out how to backtrack to the store from there.

"Britton asked me to go to her house later this afternoon. I'm going to ask my mom to drop me off there after she is done at the store."

"I'm sure that would be okay. She doesn't usually mind you hanging out with Britton. What about your homework?"

"I'll finish it at the store."

She nodded in agreement as she tried to focus on the traffic to switch lanes.

"She asked me to bring my Ratchet Clank PlayStation game over. My dad bought it for me last week and she wanted us to play it at her house today."

"A video game? Since when are you into playing video games?"

"Since my parents became desperate to get me to stop practicing piano all day long," she said with a playful smirk.

"So they decided to ruin your brain with video games?" Danni teased.

"It's actually quite challenging, and it probably helps make you smarter."

"That is what any kid your age would say."

"Maybe if adults played more video games, they wouldn't always be so serious."

"You think we are too serious?"

"My parents are. And a lot of the teachers at school are."

Danni was amused at Billie's candor.

"Well, adults have tons of worries making them take everything very seriously."

"So can we go by the house first so I can pick up the game?"

Danni pondered her request. Simone would be in the meeting for at least an hour. She would probably not even know if they stopped by their house first.

"She told me that she wanted you to practice piano as soon as you get to the store."

"Our PE teacher was sick today, so I ended up with an extra music class instead. I just had a full hour of practice right before you picked me up."

She did make a good case. She surely could use a break before hitting the piano again. How many hours did she need to practice anyway?

"You have a key to the house?"

"We have a key code on the door."

"And you are just going to run in very quickly, grab the Ratchet game, and come back out?"

"The ratchet game and a different shirt. I spilled my lunch all over this one."

Danni noticed the sauce stain on the front of the shirt as soon as she got into the car, but didn't want to make her feel awkward about it.

"That sounds reasonable. As long as you are quick."

She pulled over to put Simone's address into her GPS app, then went around the block so she could change the direction in which the afternoon was going.

When she pulled up to Simone's home, she couldn't find any parking spots in front of the home.

"Hurry in, I will circle the block until you come out."

She double-parked as Billie jumped out of the car and hopped up the front steps of their home. Danni stayed parked until she was sure she punched in the right code and made it safely inside the home. She then pulled away slowly to circle the block. An eerie feeling settled around her chest.

As soon as she drove a short distance down the street, she recognized Bill's Mercedes parked on the street. A few cars away from him, she noticed the gray van with the familiar Rocco's Handyman Service logo on the side. Her heart froze. It pummeled her like an avalanche. Bill was at his house doing a business deal. Probably because Simone wouldn't be home. Or maybe something fell through at a new listing and using his home was plan B. She went into a panic, knowing that she had unknowingly sent Billie straight into a venomous snake pit. And still, she couldn't find a parking spot!

She wanted to chase into the house after her, but she didn't have the code. She needed to get her dad to come help figure it out what to do, and she needed to let Simone know what happened. She willed herself to take a breath and talked herself off the ledge, hoping that Billie would come out of the house any minute in her fresh shirt and video game in hand. There was still a slight chance that Bill was in the basement with the men and may never even notice that Billie entered the house and went up to her bedroom. She ran that scenario like a broken record in her mind over and over, hoping it would gain strength, but the minutes ticked off and Billie didn't come out of the house. Panic mounted in her chest, and she became almost euphoric when she finally found a parking spot within sight of the van and Bill's Mercedes. She dismissed the fact that it was a handicap spot and sent a tearful prayer up to the sky for having something that afternoon work out in her favor.

As soon as she parked, she reached for her phone in her purse. She scrolled down to Simone's number and dialed it. She listened impatiently as the call went to voicemail. She hung up and called again, tapping her fingers on the steering wheel impatiently. She knew that Simone was most likely already held captive in the meeting with Peter and Marius. She had to dial the number two more times before Simone finally picked up.

"Danni?"

"Simone, I'm in a lot of trouble here. I mean, Billie is probably in a lot of trouble. She asked me to go to the house to pick up a game to take over to Britton's later, and I should have listened to you and not take any detours, but I figured she would be quick."

"Danni, what's going on? Just tell me!"

"She is at your house, but I noticed Bill was home, and it looks like the exact same guys from Thursday's drop is there with him. She has been in there longer than what it should have taken to get that game. I'm not sure what's going on. Can you call him, maybe?"

"Okay, hold on. Are you still over there?"

"I'm parked out front, and I can see the house and their cars."

"I will call him, hold on."

Simone hung up, and Danni waited. Her eyes stayed glued to the front door of the house. There was no way she could watch the garage in the back of the house at the same time, but from where she was, she had a view of their cars at least. Her heart felt like a runaway train. She breathed, imagining she was breathing into a paper bag to keep herself from throwing up.

Her phone rang, and she saw Simone's name pop up on to the screen. She tapped the green icon instantly to answer.

"He is not answering, Danni. I had no idea he was going to be home today."

"Something probably went wrong with his planned location, and maybe the house was his backup plan. Since you weren't going to be home."

"This is not good. What should we do?"

She heard the tears stream down Simone's face and could imagine panic spreading like wildfire all throughout her body.

"Do you think you can go pick up my dad at my apartment? Tell him to bring whatever he has available to take these guys on. I will stay right here and keep you posted."

"I'm not sure that is a good idea, Danni."

"I will feel better if he's here to help me think through this."

"Okay, I'll leave right now, but call me if you see her come out."

Danni could hear her footsteps rush down the hall in the back of the store.

"I will call Peter and let him…"

Simone already hung up the phone. She called Peter's number instead.

"Danni? What's going on?"

"We think Billie's in trouble at the house with Simone's husband."

"I don't understand. What kind of trouble?"

"We are not exactly sure, but I have a feeling they may be held hostage. Simone is going to get my dad and bring him here. As back-up."

"How is that going to help, Danni? Do you want me to call the police?"

"No, Peter! Don't call the police. I will let you know if we need anything else. I have no idea what's going to happen here today. I need to call my dad to let him know to get ready."

She hung up and called her dad's phone. There still was no movement at the house's front door. Still no signs of Billie.

"What's up, Danni?" her dad said after he answered her call.

"Dad, Simone's coming to pick you up. I'm over at her house, and I think Billie must have walked in on Bill doing one of those deals with the guys I saw him with the other day."

"At their house?"

"Yeah. Not sure why he would use his own house instead of a new listing. Maybe something went wrong with the location he had planned to use."

"Probably. When will she be here?"

"She is on her way now. Keep your phone on you, so I can stay in touch."

"Okay, kid. Stay calm and keep me posted."

"Dad, the gun and the bullets are in my safe at the bottom of my closet. The key for it is in the top drawer of the dresser."

"I'll bring the gun and whatever else I can find."

"There's a knife in the top drawer of my dresser as well. And binoculars in one of the other drawers, just check. I think there's a backpack in the bottom of my closet you can use."

"Got it, kid. Tell Simone I will meet her at the front entrance of the building to save time."

She texted Simone with directions where to meet her father as her eyes tracked up and down the street. She finally spotted a group of people coming around the corner. She recognized Bill and Billie immediately and then noticed the two big guys trailing very close behind them. It was the same two guys she saw at the house on Thursday. She noticed Bill had a tight grip on Billie's arm as he steered her down the street, staying very close to her. One of the guys stayed very close behind him, and Danni feared that he had a gun pointed to his back.

Bill and Billie climbed into the side door of the van. One of the men climbed in with them instead of going to the passenger front seat. The second man rushed to the driver's seat and started the van. As soon as they pulled away, Danni saw the man cover Bill's eyes

IN THE SCATTERING OF LIGHT

with duct tape right before he pushed him down out of sight. They pushed Billie down right after.

Danni pulled out into the street behind them to follow, realizing that the situation was far worse than she could have ever imagined.

She called her dad's phone.

"Simone just picked me up, what's going on there?"

"They are on the move, Dad. Those two guys have Bill and Billie in the van with them. Their eyes were covered with duct tape and I'm sure they probably tied their hands up too. We are going east down Queen Street."

"I'm guessing they are heading to the I-95 to go north. I'm going to have Simone go east on Route 30 so we can join you on I-95. Just don't lose them, Danni."

"Can you stay on the phone with me?"

"Sure. Simone, can you plug this phone in your car somewhere? I don't want to lose power to this thing."

"I don't have a charger for that type of phone. Tell her to call my phone, and I'll keep it on the charger." Danni heard Simone's voice, panic-stricken, in the background.

"Did you hear that, Danni?"

"Yes, I'll call her phone."

Danni hung up and called Simone's number as she stayed close to the van after it hopped on the I-95, just as her father predicted.

"Can you see Billie in the van?" Simone asked.

"No, only the driver is visible. He must have them on the floor in the back. It's a cargo van, so there probably aren't any seats back there. Dad was right, they are going north on I-95."

"Okay, we are not too far from you then. Traffic is going to start to get heavy, so just make sure you keep them in your sight."

It was comforting to hear her father's voice guide her through what felt like a battering storm.

She received a phone call from Peter again, and she clicked over to it.

"Danni, what's happening? We are beside ourselves over here."

"We are following them now."

"Who?"

"Two men put Bill and Billie in a van, and they're driving up north somewhere. We're on the I-95. Simone has my dad in her car, and they are following not too far behind me."

"Are you sure we shouldn't call the police? That sounds like a kidnapping!"

"No, Peter. We can handle this better than the police right now. We are at least familiar with the situation and the people involved."

"I hope you are right, Danni. It sounds like a nightmare. We can't lose Billie!"

"I know."

She hung up and crawled along the highway behind the van, with the traffic jam packed on all sides.

They finally exited off onto Route 63 and wound their way through the neighborhoods of Byberry and Normandy. It looked as if they were moving toward Somerton. She called Simone's phone again. Her dad answered quickly.

"I think they are heading over to Somerton. How far behind me do you think you are?"

"I'd say ten, fifteen minutes at the most. You are doing good, kid. Keeping close to them all this time."

"I could follow anyone in my sleep by now with all the experience I picked up with Jake. How's Simone holding up?"

"White knuckles on the steering wheel kind of thing, but she's managing."

"Simone?" Danni asked, wanting to hear from her that she was okay.

She didn't respond back.

"We're dealing with it, kid," her dad said, "but she is scared, understandably."

Danni imagined the only sound that would come from Simone at that moment to be gut-wrenching sobs.

They made a left turn and then turned off onto Byberry Road. They followed that for a couple of miles and then finally turned left on to Bustleton Avenue.

She texted the directions to Simone's phone as she drove. They finally turned left on to Somerton Street and pulled into the driveway of a detached two-story home. Danni parked in the street a few houses across from it. She texted the final destination to Simone's number.

The two guys dragged Bill and Billie out of the side of the van. There was no tape applied to their eyes and hands, most likely to get into the house without attracting any attention to them. She could tell that Bill still had the gun pointed to his back. He did exactly what he was told. He steered Billie by the arm, and she stayed close to him. She was still wearing the stained shirt, which meant that she was probably ambushed as soon as she walked into the house.

Danni's mind tried to conjure a plan to get them out of the house safely. She was sure they would be watched like hawks. The two men would not willingly let them get away. One of them stayed on the porch, looking up and down the street, casing the neighborhood. The other man pushed them inside the house. He had a roll of duct tape in his other hand.

Simone and her dad pulled up less than fifteen minutes later and parked behind her. Her dad jumped into the passenger seat beside her. His eyes zoned in on the house with the van parked in the driveway.

"They went in about fifteen minutes ago. No one else has shown up yet," Danni explained to get him up to speed.

"They were probably instructed to either take care of the problem or wait for someone else to come to take care of the problem."

Danni couldn't hold the tears back as the reality of her father's words knocked hard against her.

"I think we have to do something fast here, before someone else shows up. You're going to have to keep it together, Danni, we don't have much time."

"I'm listening, Dad. How are we going to pull this off?"

"Okay, listen. That guy on the front porch is our first target. You need to go up there and engage him. I'm thinking we can stage your car having a flat tire or something. Go up to him and ask him if you can use his phone. I'll ambush him from behind."

She looked in disbelief at her father.

"We have to act fast, Danni. And handle this head-on. We can't solve this problem from out here."

"I understand. Okay, let's do it."

She punched her fear down.

"Once we are in the house, we will have to take the other guy out. Is he as big as this guy on the porch?"

She nodded. "They are about the same size."

Her father got his gun out and made sure it was loaded and tucked it back into the waistband of his pants.

"Text Simone to stay in the car. No matter what."

Danni complied. She followed every instruction her father gave her, putting her trust in him completely.

"Okay, now, let's drive around the block."

She started the car and drove off. Once they circled the block and approached the house, he told her to stop the car.

He got out and crouched over to the passenger's side wheel. She could hear him stab the tire and then heard the loud swish as the air escaped. The car quickly kneeled toward his side. He popped his head up and signaled for her to open the window.

"Okay, it's go time, kid. Pull over at the house like you hit something. Then go talk to the guy. I'm going around the back, so I'm going to be right there, okay? Lure him over to the front part of the porch."

She just nodded and watched him take off. He walked down the street like he was simply out taking a casual walk in the neighborhood. She followed his instruction and rolled down the street with the flat tire until she brought the car to a halt in front of the house, next to the sidewalk.

She got out of the car and walked up to the man, who was still standing guard close to the front door on the porch.

"Hi there," she said as she approached him.

He just looked at her, not responding.

"I'm so sorry to bother you. I got a flat tire," she said as she pointed back to her car.

He peered out at the car and walked over to the front of the porch to get a closer look at the car. He looked back at her, clearly annoyed.

"I see that," he said gruffly.
"Do you have a phone I could use to call triple A?"
He rolled his eyes.
"What, you got no phone?" he asked, and she immediately picked up an accent. He sounded Russian, or something similar.
"Today would be the day that I didn't bring it. And then this happens."

Out of her periphery, she noticed her dad climbing over the porch railing on side of the house and snuck in quietly behind the man. He moved without making a sound, like a cat on the prowl. It was imperative for her not to lose the man's focus on her.

"I have a friend I can call to help me change the tire too."

Before the man could respond to her, her father reached up and knocked him hard over the back of the head with a retractable stick. He tumbled over instantly, and her father kept hitting him over the back of his head a few more times. He placed his finger over his mouth, instructing her to keep quiet. He fumbled around the waist of the guy's pants and pulled out a gun from a holster. He checked the magazine and saw that it was fully loaded.

"Help me pull this guy over to the side," he whispered to Danni.

They each grabbed a leg and dragged his heavy body over to the side of the porch, behind the half wall and out of sight.

Danni's father came down hard on the man's head one more time with the retractable.

"To make sure he stays out."

Danni's heart pounded in her chest. She could barely feel her legs, but she forced her mind to focus on every follow-up instruction he gave.

"Okay, stay right behind me, we are going in. Here, take my gun."

"What?" she whispered, shaking her head.

"Take it, Danni!" he whispered insistently "You may need it. Just don't shoot the two we came to rescue. Anyone else inside is out of luck today."

Her father pushed the front door open carefully, and they tiptoed in. She repeated every step he made behind him, holding the gun out in front of her. She curled her finger securely around the trigger.

They walked through the empty living room. Moved on to the dining room which was empty too. They reached the kitchen and scanned the room, guns pointed out and ready to fire.

"They are probably upstairs. Relax your elbows holding that gun," her dad whispered.

He pointed for them to move up the stairs. She relaxed her elbows and took a deep breath.

She stayed close behind him on the stairs next to the wall. They moved slowly, going up one step at a time, careful not to make a sound.

At the top of the stairs, they scaled the wall of the hallway to inspect the rooms, but they both heard footsteps in the first room at the top of the stairs, and her dad pointed to the room and then for her to follow him.

He took position right next to the door, his gun pointed directly into the path of the opening. Danni stayed a few feet behind him, with her back pressed against the wall. He took his retractable out with his left hand and tapped the wall. They could both hear someone's footsteps coming toward the door. Her dad dropped the stick to the floor and reached around to add his left hand on the gun. He took a ready stance, and as soon as the man's head appeared in the doorway, he fired the gun without any hesitation. Blood shot out of the man's head and sprayed the door jamb behind him. He instantly collapsed into the door frame and then slid down the wall on to the floor, blood still pulsing out of his head and staining the carpet scarlet red underneath him.

Her father leaped closer to him and fired one more shot into his head as if he needed to make sure that the threat of him was eliminated. He proceeded to search around his clothes and found a gun in a holster under his arm. He checked the magazine again to count the bullets and then slapped the magazine back into the grip. He handed Danni the gun.

"Use this one instead of mine now."

They both looked up from the lifeless man and saw Bill and Billie, tied up, sitting next to each other on the floor, against the back wall of the empty room.

Her father lunged over to them. He took the knife out of his pocket and, without saying a word, cut the tape around Billie's wrists to free her hands. He left the tape over her mouth.

"It will hurt too much to rip that off, Billie," he told her kindly.

Danni held the gun her father handed to her and pointed it at Bill. He looked baffled that her dad knew Billie's name.

"Is this house one of your new listings?" she asked him, without expecting an answer, since she had no plan to remove the tape from his mouth. She would spare him from having to explain himself in front of Billie.

"Who else is coming here, Bill?" her father asked as he hunched down in front of him. He clearly had a different strategy in mind regarding Bill's questioning. He reached for the tape over his mouth and ripped it off in one swoop. He watched him flinch from the pain without showing him any sympathy.

Bill's eyes were filled with tears and panic, as her father took a threatening stance, pressing Danni's knife into his neck.

"Who were they waiting on?" he screamed loudly, into his face.

"I think they called Rafael to come."

"Do you know him? This Rafael?"

Bill nodded skittishly.

"Does he work alone?" her dad asked, pressing down harder on the knife.

He shook his head quickly.

"He usually works with a guy named Aren."

"So there are at least two more people on their way here to come take care of you, is what you are saying?"

He closed his eyes and nodded slowly.

Danni noticed that Billie was quietly rocking back and forth against the wall. Her breathing was shallow and her face as white as a sheet.

"They don't sound Russian," her dad continued his interrogation. "What nationality are they?"

Bill kept his eyes closed and didn't answer.

Her dad pressed the knife into his neck again, and Danni noticed a small trickle of blood as he refused to let up.

"I asked you a question, Bill. Where are these people from?"

"They're Armenian," he finally confessed.

With that, her dad seemed satisfied and lifted the knife off his neck. He smirked as he kept his eyes on Bill.

"Jesus Christ, Bill. You are crazy to be going into business with Armenians. Stir fucking crazy."

He circled around the room a few times, collecting his thoughts.

"Let's get this guy out of sight, Danni," he said, pointing to the man on the floor.

They each grabbed an arm and dragged him out of the room and down to the end of the hallway. Danni fell out of breath from the weight of him and the shock of seeing all the blood still draining out of his wounds. They walked back into the bedroom.

"Text Simone to tell her Billie is okay. But we are going to need a little more time in here."

Her dad's face stayed hard as steel as he kept an unwavering focus to get them through the afternoon alive.

Danni reached for her phone immediately and started texting the message. She was certain that Simone was very close to losing her mind out there waiting by herself.

Bill's eyes widened as soon as her father mentioned Simone's name. Danni used the phone's camera to take a picture of Bill, dry mouthed and fear stricken. She added his picture to the text for Simone, with the caption, "He's not feeling too good right now."

Danni didn't feel like talking to him at all, but she wanted to make sure he remembered his bravado in the store last week.

"What's going on today, Bill?" she asked. "You don't seem as cocky as you did when you came to see me at the store last week."

He stayed quiet and just turned his eyes away from her.

"It looks like the tables have turned," she sneered.

Her father approached them with the roll of duct tape he found on the windowsill.

"Don't waste your breath with scum like this, Danni."

He covered his mouth, wrapping the tape around his head twice.

"Hold his legs," her dad directed.

He wound the tape around his ankles at least five times while she kept his legs still.

"Just in case you had any ideas about running off, tough guy."

Her father pushed him over onto his side, then went to the bedroom across the hall that had a view out over the front yard.

"No one's here yet," she heard him call out.

Danni squatted down in front of Billie, who looked at her, clearly terrified.

"I'm so sorry, Billie. We are trying to get you out of here safely, okay?"

She nodded but kept rocking. Danni knew this nightmare was going to do a number on her psyche.

"Your mom is out there waiting for you, and as soon as we can, we will get you to her."

Billie kept nodding and rocking. Danni reached for her hands and squeezed them tightly.

Her father came back into the back bedroom, looking determined.

"Danni, let's go downstairs and talk through this."

He looked over to Billie, rocking continuously and then back at Danni. His eyes begged for an explanation from her.

"I'll tell you downstairs."

She followed her father down to the dining room and tucked both guns back into the waistband of her pants.

"I think Billie has some form of autism, so let's not be too hard on Bill in front of her. This is probably really hard for her deal with," she whispered.

"Jesus, I'm sorry, Danni. It's just, this is a real mess. I had to find out what we're dealing with."

"Apparently, we are dealing with Armenian gun smugglers. What do you think?"

"I think so too. This is the big leagues, kid. It's going to be ugly today, there will be no mercy from them, and there can be no mercy from us."

She nodded and felt for her gun again to keep her heart from chasing out of her chest. She followed him out on to the porch. She looked over to where Simone was parked. Their eyes locked, and Danni could tell she was at the edge of her emotions. She feared that Simone would abandon her car and run straight toward them. She couldn't even imagine having to worry about Simone stranded in the house as well. She waved at her just briefly, but then signaled for her to stay in the car.

She turned her attention back on the man, lying on the porch. Her father found the keys of the van in his pocket and held on to them.

"Let's get him inside," her father instructed.

They each grabbed a leg and struggled to pull the heavy man inside the home. They pulled him all the way through the living room into the front corner of the dining room. Her dad sat him up against the wall. He picked up his wrist to feel for a pulse. He dropped his arm and then reached for the gun he used on his partner upstairs.

He pointed the gun to the left of the man's chest.

He looked at Danni, staring at him. She was dumbfounded.

"I'm sorry, kid, but I told you this was going to be ugly today. We cannot have any loose ends."

He fired a single shot straight into the man's heart. Danni heard a high-pitched shriek coming from upstairs. It was Billie. She ran upstairs to check on her.

She found Bill still lying on his side, his eyes closed as he was probably reluctant to face his daughter and the mess that he created. She kneeled in front of Billie and squeezed her hands again.

"It's almost over. I promise. Then we'll get you over to your mom. Just hang in there a little longer, okay?"

She nodded again, her wide eyes seemingly stuck, unable to blink.

She passed Bill and walked to the bedroom across the hall again. She found her dad there, standing next to the window.

"No signs of any visitors yet," he said impatiently. "Can you go see if Bill has his phone on him? Make sure he isn't pulling any shit, like calling to warn Rafael about what's going on."

Danni rushed back over to where Bill was lying. She stuck her hands in both of his pockets to feel for a phone. Felt in all the pockets of his jacket. She couldn't find a phone anywhere. She lifted his pants legs to see if he had anything hidden in his socks.

"No phone?" she barked at him.

He wildly shook his head.

She walked back to see her father.

"Nothing on him."

"Good, the last thing we need is for him to sabotage this."

"So what now, Dad? How do we get Billie out of here? I mean, what if a whole team of people swarm down on this place?"

"We shoot them all."

"Gun smugglers will surely be armed too."

"We'll have the advantage, being in here already. We're going to surprise them."

"Do you really think it's going to be that easy?"

"I told you, honey, it's going to be ugly. But you don't go into a gunfight thinking you're going to die. You have to hold your head up and ditch all the fear. We have to get Billie out of here, and we have to eliminate these people from her life forever. Just focus on that. Don't go soft on me now, kid."

Danni looked at him. His face was still so bruised up from the beating he got in the bar. It seemed to her as if that beating unleashed something fierce in him.

Her muscles suddenly tensed as they both heard a car door being shut. Her dad leaned into the window, just enough to get a slight glance of what was happening outside.

"It's time, Danni," he whispered. "Get your gun ready."

She cocked the dead man's gun to push a bullet into the chamber, while keeping her dad's gun tucked away in the waist of her pants as backup.

"I'm going to the front door. I want you to go wait right next to the dining room entrance and back me up," he whispered.

She peeked into the bedroom where Billie and Bill were held and placed her finger over her mouth as a warning to them to be quiet. She closed the door quietly and darted down the stairs.

She took her position on the left side of the front wall of the dining room. She stayed close to the doorway and could jump into the living room within a split second. She squeezed both hands around the grip of the pistol and focused on breathing as quietly as possible. She took a quick peek into the living room and saw her dad standing next to the front door. He would be obscured behind the door as soon as it was opened. He raised two fingers up to her, and she assumed that he meant there were two people getting out of the car to approach the house. She took cover right behind the dining room wall again and waited. A sense of calm washed over her, knowing that her dad was leading the charge, and that all she had to do was follow his lead.

She focused intently with her ears and heard someone fumble with the doorknob. She could hear the door being swung open slowly. Her hands gripped tighter, and she curled her index finger around the trigger of the gun.

The deafening sound of a single shot echoed through the room. It rang as a signal to her that her father stepped out from behind the door. She lunged out into the living room and saw the second man draw his gun and point it straight at her father. Danni aimed at his chest and pulled the trigger instantly. She heard him fire a shot, then watched his gun-slinging arm jerk back as soon as she pulled her own trigger. The blood gushed out of his shoulder, and she pulled the trigger again and again, until he finally dropped to his knees, toppling over, face first onto the floor. She looked at her father and saw the blood stain spreading around his shoulder as he stood doubled over at the waist, wincing in pain. He pressed his free hand into the gaping wound. She ran over to him as he sank to his knees. She pressed both of her hands over the wound to stop the bleeding, but realized that she needed something more substantial. She ran into the kitchen and found a dish rag in one of the drawers, then rushed up the stairs to grab the roll of duct tape.

After pressing the rag into the wound and wrapping the tape around it, it looked as if they had the bleeding under control. She stared at the two lifeless bodies sprawled out on the floor in front of them. She was stunned that the house wasn't surrounded by the police yet, considering the amount of gunfire that rang out from there that afternoon.

Her dad grew more antsy, and she was sure he had the exact same fear flooding his mind.

"We have to get out of here, Danni. We don't have time for this wound right now. Hand me that gun and then go get Billie."

"And Bill?"

"Just untie him and give him the keys to the van. We're going to have to trust that he will keep his mouth shut about all of this," he instructed, reached into his pocket and handed the van keys to her. She gave him the gun and he limped toward the kitchen.

"I'll wipe these clean," he said, grinding his teeth.

She ran back upstairs. She cut the duct tape off Bill's arms and legs and handed him the keys to the van.

"It's time to go," she announced.

She watched him run out of the room like a coward, without once looking back at Billie.

She went over to Billie and slowly pulled the tape off her mouth.

"Come quick. We have to hurry."

Billie followed her down the stairs. At the bottom, she tugged her arm to guide her out of the front door as quick as possible, praying that she wouldn't register the details of the two dead bodies on the floor.

Once outside, she led Billie straight over to where Simone was still waiting. She flung the back door open and pushed Billie inside.

"Get her out of here as quick as possible, okay? I'll be in touch later."

"What's all that blood on your hands from?" Simone shrieked.

"It's okay, it's okay. Nothing to worry about."

"Where should we go?"

"Don't go to your house. It would be best if you get a hotel for tonight."

She nodded, still wide eyed.

"I'll call you as soon as I get a chance."

Simone sped off, and Danni ran over to her car, still parked in front of the house with a glaring flat tire. She waited for her father as she paced around the car, wondering how far they could get on three good tires.

Her father made it to the car and jumped into the passenger seat. She followed suit and started the car up.

"How are we going to deal with this tire situation?"

"Just get us away from this house for now. We will need to put the spare on."

She looked around again, still baffled by the absence of the police to the neighborhood.

"Maybe they are used to gun shots around here," her dad answered before she could even ask it.

She drove away slowly on the flat tire. They managed to get about two streets over and realized that was as far as they could take it without ruining the wheel.

Her father was still clutching his shoulder to keep the wound under control. She needed to get him to the hospital as soon as possible.

He wasn't much help to her while she struggled to change the tire, but he supervised and instructed as she changed her first tire ever. When she finished securing all the lug nuts and sank back into the seat of her car, her dad asked her to wait.

"I have to give Ruben a call."

He climbed out of the car slowly and made the call. She watched him pace in circles while he talked on the phone. She was glad to have a moment to breathe, to retreat from the chaos she was whisked into for the past few hours.

When he got back in the car, she looked at him. Something was different about him. Or she looked at him differently.

"All good?"

"Yes, he is going to come over and check it out."

"Check it out?" she asked.

"To make sure things check out for when the Somerton police comes over. He also gave me the name of a good lawyer. Just in case we need it."

She stayed quiet while they drove off, but the tightness around her chest came back with a vengeance.

"Where's your phone? I have to put an address into your GPS."

She grabbed her phone out of her pocket and handed it to him. He typed an address into the GPS app and clipped the phone into the dashboard stand.

"Where are we going?"

"A nurse practitioner. It's a friend of Ruben's. I have to get this bullet out."

Chapter 34

Danni was awakened by the incessant ringing of her phone next to her on the nightstand. She fumbled around for it in the dark and looked at the clock, telling her it was just shy of midnight. She focused on the screen, flashing Peter's name. She decided to answer, knowing he was probably worried sick.

"Hi, Peter," she answered, still half asleep. She scooted herself up in bed.

"Hey, Danni. I'm glad you answered. I'm sorry I'm still calling you this late."

"Did you try me earlier? I was probably out like a light."

"I'm sorry, but I've been freaking out, not knowing if you were all okay. I haven't heard back from you since this afternoon."

Danni stayed quiet, as she tried to recall everything that happened that day. She had to think quickly to comb through the facts and sort through what she could realistically tell him.

"I'm sorry. I haven't been able to organize my thoughts yet."

"But Simone and Billie? Are they okay?"

"I think they went to a hotel. Things were out of control with her husband. I was going to call her, but I fell asleep by the time I got my dad back from…" She stopped herself. There wasn't much she could divulge. She felt pushed into a corner.

"Okay, I'm sorry to bother you so late, Danni. Call me in the morning?"

"I will. Sorry, Peter. It's been an ordeal, but we are all okay."

"That's all I needed to know," he said.

She hung up the phone, then wiped more of the sleep out of her eyes.

She wanted to call Simone, but not if she was already asleep. She was sure they were exhausted by the time they made it to a hotel somewhere. She was still a wreck herself and not up for a long conversation yet. She opted for a quick text instead.

"I hope you were able to find a hotel. I can call tomorrow if you want?"

She didn't get a response back right away and laid back down. She closed her eyes and heard her father snoring softly on the couch. The practitioner gave him a good dose of pain medication to help him sleep. Even asleep, she felt comforted by his presence in the apartment. She was unable to keep her mind from racing through the events of the day again. It hovered over her, spreading through her like a heavy cloud. She tried to push it away, but it buckled down and crowded her mind. She couldn't get back to sleep.

She finally heard the buzzing of her phone. It was a call from Simone.

"Hi, where are you guys?" she answered quickly.

"We found a room at a hotel in Center City. Billie was finally able to fall asleep after I gave her some Tylenol PM. We stopped at the drug store to get some things."

"Today was not a good day. I'm so sorry, Simone."

"I feel like our lives fell apart today. I haven't really absorbed all of it. But I am just happy that I have her back."

"Having her back is all that matters."

"I have no idea what to do now. I'm so rattled. I can't think straight enough to come up with a plan."

"Can you go to your parents for a while again?"

"I thought about that. But what would I tell them? Do you think it will be safe?"

"Safer than going back to your house. And you need a place from where you can sort things out with Bill."

"Yes. I am too scared to go back to the house right now. And taking Billie there would be impossible too. I'm not sure she could handle it."

"Just get to your parents in the morning. I'm sure Bill will contact you to talk through what to do next. He is the one that got us into this mess."

"I am getting a divorce, Danni. There is no doubt about that. I could never forgive him. He probably ran all the way to New York by now."

"Maybe your parents know a good lawyer?"

"I'm sure they do."

"Have you tried to call him? Bill."

"It goes straight to voicemail."

"He probably didn't go back to the house either. He didn't have his phone on him when I checked him at that house."

"I watched the news earlier. They didn't mention anything about a shooting in Somerton."

"That is good news."

"How could something like that just blow over?"

"It won't. I'm sure it's just the start of this mess. For all of us."

"You and your dad were so brave. I want to ask what happened inside, but I'm too afraid to hear. I know if you didn't intervene, there would be no chance that I would have her back now."

"It's going to be difficult for Billie to work through. Things didn't go smoothly in there. She is going to need help. To process all of it. I can't talk about what happened there myself yet."

"Oh my god, Danni. I'm so sad for you and your dad. And Billie."

"We did what had to be done. But she is too young to understand."

"I was beside myself out there, waiting. Not knowing."

"I'm sure," Danni said.

"I don't know where to start, how to talk to her."

Danni didn't respond. She thought about the blood on the carpet underneath the man she shot. His lifeless eyes, glazed over. The three other men whose lives they took. She knew damn well there was no other choice, but she expected the devil would come around quite often to tell her that wasn't true. They couldn't risk the life of

Billie in order to save the lives of four gutless criminals that would sink as low as to kidnap a child.

"Give her some time first. She will tell you when she is ready to talk. And promise me you will go to your parents tomorrow."

She pulled her overwhelmed mind out of its destructive spiraling.

"All right. We will get on the road first thing in the morning."

"I'll be in touch tomorrow then."

"I wish you could come with us. To help me get through this."

"I wish I could too. I will come visit soon."

"I'd like that. I won't forget about us, Danni."

"I won't either. I promise."

It would take a long time and conversation for all of them to work through the tragedy. She felt brave for her part in saving Billie. But she knew mentally, they all paid a steep price. And she questioned if they would ever really be able to bear the cost.

Chapter 35

Two weeks later

The doorbell rang, and Danni rushed over to open the door. Her father was busy in front of the stove as usual, this time making her mother's favorite spicy meatball soup with Italian bread. He was counting on her mother to bring the bread from the bakery, along with that chocolate cake that her bakery was so famous for. The days had become shorter in the weeks that passed since that horrific day in Somerton. Leaves were starting to turn into a bright display of reds and yellows, changing the color palette of the season and preparing them all for a period of renewal. This year, her family couldn't wait for winter to arrive.

"So good to see you, Mom," Danni said as she gave her mom a close hug.

"You too, darling. Did your dad really turn into the cook of this household?"

"It seems like it. I have gained five pounds since he's taken over the kitchen here. Not that I'm complaining."

"We used to fight over the kitchen when we were first married. He liked to cook, and I wanted to bake, so you can imagine."

"I am just glad he never lost his skill. Everything coming out of there is mouthwatering."

"When he invited me over for my favorite meatball soup, I couldn't resist."

"Did he say what he wanted to talk about?"

"No, but I know what we should be talking about. Where should I put the bread and cake?"

"Let's take it to the kitchen."

They walked in just as Danni's father tested the soup and appeared satisfied with the taste. He kissed his fingertips and called out boisterously, "Magnifico!"

"Hi, Matt. It smells terrific in here."

"Hi, Sandy. Dinner is just about ready. Danni, can you set the table?"

"Already done, Dad," she boasted.

"So I will just bring the soup to the table then. Let's cut the bread and bring some butter."

Danni started slicing the bread, placed it on a plate, and brought it to the table. Her mother brought the butter. They each picked a seat and started serving the soup.

"Ladies first," her dad bantered, as he watched them each take their turn first.

Danni thought about how long she has waited for a dinner together at a table with both her parents. It seemed like a lifetime.

She reached each of her hands out to them.

"I would like to say a prayer, okay?"

"Sure, Danni," her father said and placed his hand in hers.

Her mother followed suit and reached for her other hand.

"Lord, thank you for bringing our family together for this meal. Thank you for keeping us safe, and thank you for continuing to guide us in love. Amen."

"Amen," her mother and father repeated, both their eyes filled with light.

They started eating, and all of them were quiet as they experienced the full array of flavor that her dad had carefully developed into the soup.

After a few minutes of eating in silence, her father finally spoke.

"I asked you to come over, Sandy, because I wanted to talk to you about the house."

"No sense in wasting time," she said as she continued eating, clearly not able to get enough.

He put his spoon down and looked at her mother. His face was filled with kindness, but Danni could also sense the worry in his eyes. They have become so in tune to each other since he has moved in with her.

"I think that we have to sell the house. But I first wanted to tell you the story of the house."

Danni and her mother questioned him with baffled eyes. He continued to eat again.

"That house does feel like it's alive. Like it has a long, complicated story," Danni added.

Her father poured water in a glass and looked at them as if he didn't know where to start. He squeezed a fresh lemon into the water, while his mind sifted through the words.

"I was a young detective when that house came on the market. I remember, it was my first year on the job. I told you that I found the house through a realtor because I was ready to buy a home for our family."

"I remember very well," her mother said. "You surprised me, telling me we were going to a Phillies game, but instead, you took me to that house and said you thought we hit a home run with it."

"I wasn't exactly telling the truth."

Danni frowned and noticed her mother's equally puzzled face.

"I told you that we got the house for a steal, because the people who owned it had to move to California for a new job offer the man accepted."

"I remember that."

"It wasn't true. The truth is that the house became available, because of a horrific crime that was committed there. The home was on our radar frequently in the department."

"What kind of a crime?" her mother asked carefully.

Her dad looked at them, his eyes filling with more trepidation.

"The husband killed himself in that home. He hung himself from one of the attic rafters."

"Oh my god!" Danni's mom yelled as she held a hand over her mouth. She placed her spoon back down in the bowl.

"The wife was left with three very young children. She tried for a while to raise them, but I suppose, ultimately, it just became too difficult for her."

"What do you mean?"

"She drowned them, Sandy. All the kids. In the bathtub. And then she killed herself, slicing her wrists open on the bathroom floor."

Danni could barely draw another breath. Her mother stared at him, her eyes as wide as saucers.

"So the house was taken by the state, and when after a few months, it came on the market, I jumped at it. It was priced way below market value. I couldn't pass it up. Plus, I didn't believe in ghosts then, so I saw no trouble with the history of what happened there."

Her mom stayed quiet, pushing her last remaining meatball around in the soup.

Danni's appetite left completely, and she pushed her bowl away.

"Thinking back about it now, of course, I see things differently."

"You think?" her mother said sharply.

"I think that the house, I don't know, I spent a lot of time there, and it was wringing the life out of me, day after day."

"I agree, Dad," Danni said. "That house definitely tried to snuff the life out of anyone that lived there. Robbie told me how relieved he felt the moment he moved out. I felt the same way."

Her mom took the last bite of her soup and pushed her bowl away.

"I felt it too," she said softly. "A weight has been lifted off my shoulders ever since I left and moved in with Max."

"And the same with me. Since that night I left and moved in here with you, Danni. I could finally breathe again."

"Are we saying that the house is some sort of living, angry, cruel place, feeding off the misery off its inhabitants?" Danni asked her father.

"Yes, I do. And not only that. I'm convinced that it perpetuated the misery, like an endless curse getting passed on."

"So how could we ever sell it, Matt? How could we sell it and let it go on to terrorize another family?"

"I have struggled so much with that too. I suggest that we don't sell it."

"We don't sell it? I don't intend to move back into it," her mother said adamantly.

"I mean we don't sell it and we leave it empty. Leave it to starve. Maybe the ghosts will wither away and finally end their reign."

"How would we afford that?"

"I will make payments on it as soon as I get my business up and running," he said calmly.

"What business?"

"Private detective. I have applied for my license and business name."

"That is awesome, Dad!" Danni said as her heart warmed for the path her father embarked on.

"Ruben said that the force often contracts out, they have been so overwhelmed, and they use private companies quite often. He could throw me some business to get started."

"And you think we should pay for an empty, abandoned house?" her mother asked, still seemingly in disbelief.

"I just don't see how we could sell that house, knowing what we know about the place. After what it has put us through."

Her father seemed settled about the issue.

"You blame it all on the house?" her mother continued.

"Maybe so. Who knows how things could have been different if we never moved in there?"

"I'm willing to help any way I can to make the payments," Danni offered, looking at her mother with pleading eyes.

She finally caved.

"If we all pitch in together, I guess. I should have a little extra money to give for a while, now that I'm staying with Max."

"And Dad can stay here for as long as he needs, as long as he doesn't mind the couch," Danni added.

"We will see how the business takes off. I will find a place of my own as soon as I can, Danni."

Her father held his glass of water up to them. Danni was surprised to see that he has been able to stay away from alcohol these days.

"So we are all in agreement? We won't sell the house, and we'll pitch in to pay the mortgage?"

"How much do we still owe on it, Mom?" Danni asked.

"It's not that much. We have about five more years to go on it, I think."

"That's not bad. That should be long enough for that house to die," her father said.

And with that, they settled the issue and raised their glasses to toast their commitment. Danni knew they could have never come to that agreement, had all of them not escaped the wrath of the structure that ruined all their dreams.

Danni's mother got up and walked over to the kitchen.

"Let's have dessert to celebrate," she announced.

Once back at the table, she served the decadent cake with coffee. Her eyes were filled with pride for her creation.

"Is Simone still in Poughkeepsie?" her mother asked, eager to change the subject.

"Yes. She filed for divorce. She will be staying with her parents until that is finalized."

"Do you think she will ever come back here?"

"I hope so. Once the divorce gets settled."

"I'm sure you miss her. You liked her so much."

Danni looked at her mother. She recognized the woman in front of her even less these days. But she loved her infinitely more.

"I do. I miss her. But we talk often on the phone."

"I liked the kid. Billie," her dad said.

She and her father never told her mother about the kidnapping. They agreed that no one else should know about that violent day. She gave Peter a watered-down version of it. He was not told about any casualties or struggles. Simone told him that she had to leave for New York to file for divorce with the help of her parents. There was no benefit to him knowing any more. Danni trotted that lukewarm version of the events out so often that she almost fooled herself into believing it. She considered it a much more bearable version of the truth.

"She is a great kid, yes. I love them both," Danni confessed.

"They will be back some day, Danni. I know it," her dad assured her.

"You know it?"

"Yes, for many reasons, but Billie made a good friend here, and I think she will want to come back for that friendship. I don't think she makes friends easy."

"My hope hinges on Billie's friendship with a trombone player?" Danni said, laughing.

"And Simone wanted to work with Peter and his students."

"He found a replacement."

"That he would ditch the minute she walked back into his store."

"He does complain a lot about the new guy."

"Danni, love doesn't happen according to your timeline. You have to be patient. And wait. Wouldn't you think she was worth it and wait?"

She knew he was right.

"I would. I would wait a very long time."

"That's my girl. You will be rewarded with a love twice as good."

Even in matters of the heart, her dad could coach her along, and she hung on to every word the same as she used to when she was barely old enough to remember.

"I can't believe how everything has changed for all of us," was all she could think to say.

"Change is good. Who thinks we should call Robbie?" her father asked with a courageous smile.

They tossed more curious looks in his direction.

"Call Robbie? What has gotten into you, Matt?"

"Our family is healing. He should be a part of that. I am going to call him now, okay?"

They threw their hands up, convinced that there was no stopping him.

He scrolled down on his phone and pushed the little green Call icon. He placed the call on speakerphone and set the phone up in the middle of the table.

"Hello?" Robbie answered.

Danni could hardly recognize his voice. She couldn't remember the last time she spoke to him.

"It's your family, Robbie. Danni and me and your mother," her dad said.

"Wow, it's great to hear from you guys. What a surprise!"

"You won't believe how much has happened up here, son," her dad continued.

"Hi, Mom! How are you?" Robbie asked, delight ringing from his voice.

"I'm good, Robbie. I miss you! How's things down in New Orleans?"

"So good, Mom. I'm still here with Sarah, and we're working with her father at his church. I'm doing some of the youth counseling and outreach. I guess he thinks I have a lot of experience with that sort of thing."

"I think you do too, Robbie. I'm so happy for you! You will be good at that."

Her mom's face beamed as bright as the sun at the sound of her son's voice.

"It's so strange that you called. But since I have all of you on the phone, maybe it's a good opportunity for me to tell you something else," he said somewhat hesitantly.

Danni immediately thought it was bad news, but she corrected herself quickly. Scolding her first instinct to jump to a dark place.

"Sarah and I are getting married down here. On the eleventh of November."

They were all stunned into silence.

"We would understand if you couldn't make it. It's just around the corner. But it would be wonderful for me if any of you could come."

They looked at each other, wide-eyed. Danni could see her father's excitement getting close to boiling over.

"I'm down for that!" he shouted out.

Her mother hesitated longer, but then her face softened.

"I would love to make it too, Robbie. Let me see if I can get away from work."

"How about you, Danni? Can you come too?" Robbie asked.

"I'm definitely in," she said gushingly.

She could never pass on the chance to have her entire family together in one room again.

"That is wonderful, I will let Sarah know to get a few more tables set for you guys. Let me know how many will come in total."

A sudden burst of rain started outside. It came out of nowhere, surprising them. Danni noticed the clouds gathering earlier in the day, but she didn't expect it to storm like this. The rain started to pepper the roof and windows harder, and it became almost impossible for them to hear Robbie.

They ended the call, and Danni rushed to the windows to pull all the curtains shut. She always felt uneasy with lightning around the windows. She would never forget her classmate in elementary school who was struck by lightning and died while doing homework in front of the window of her bedroom.

They saw the lights in the apartment flicker as the storm must have threatened the power lines in the area. They huddled around in the living room, waiting it out. It was as if nature had forced them all into a room and wanted to take full advantage of it. The storm didn't relinquish its rage for close to an hour, and they waited and listened. The hammering raindrops finally tempered down on the windows.

"I hope that's the end of it," Danni's mom said.

"It sure has been a rainy summer this year," her father added.

Danni looked at her watch. It was just after ten o'clock.

"I'll turn on the news," she offered and reached for the remote.

She found the channel that would have the ten o'clock news on, and they all sat and waited for the weather report to come on.

They stared at the television just as a breaking report was announced. The screen offered a video of a house engulfed in flames. The reporter boasted that they were first on the scene and that it was still unknown whether there were any victims in the house. Multiple fire trucks with bright, flashing lights were staged in front of the home, and they showed footage of the firemen fighting to extinguish the raging fire to prevent it from spreading to the neighboring homes.

It suddenly dawned on all three of them at once. It was their house. Their street name and house number flashed in bold letters across the screen. They saw their angry, dysfunctional home completely engulfed in flames. The reporter stated that the fire started right after a series of lightning strikes were observed in the area, but that the exact cause of the fire was unknown.

Danni looked at her parents. She was in total shock as she looked at them and then back at the television screen.

"That is unreal," she finally said.

"Our angry house erupted in flames. Like a dragon," her dad explained as the blood drained out of his face.

Her mother threw her head in her hands, and tears started streaming down her face uncontrollably.

They were stunned. Glued to the image of the flames burning through all their memories. All their heartache. To Danni, it felt like watching a brush fire, a cleaning of a worn-out landscape to make room for new growth.

"I guess its reign is finally over," Danni announced softly.

Her father got up and motioned for the two women to join him in the middle of the room. They stood in a circle and joined their hands together. They watched the tears stream down her mother's face. The color returned to her father's face. He raised his eyes up to the sky and smiled, and Danni pulled them closer to her as she felt the burden of the house fall away from all of them.

"I don't know why, but God has been so good to us," her father said quietly, like a prayer of thanksgiving.

"I'll be back," Danni said, as she left her parents standing in the living room with their hands entwined.

She went to her bedroom and dialed Simone's number. She was overcome with emotion and needed to hear her voice.

"Hi, Danni," she answered in a sweet cantabile.

"Were you sleeping?"

"No, not yet. Relaxing in bed."

"I felt like talking with you all of a sudden."

"About anything in particular?"

"About a crazy storm here. It came out of nowhere, pounding down just like a sudden scolding of the earth."

"I think the earth is going to get a beating over here too pretty soon," she said, and Danni could hear the warmth of her smile.

"I had dinner with both my parents tonight. My mom actually came over."

"What did your dad cook this time?"

"My mother's favorite. Spicy meatball soup."

"That sounds delicious."

"We called my brother. In New Orleans."

"That's amazing. Was it a good conversation?"

"Yes. He told us that he is getting married next month down there and invited all of us to come."

"That will be a wonderful reunion for your family."

She fell quiet. Her courage jumped ship just for a moment. She took a deep breath and snatched it back quickly.

"Danni?" Simone asked patiently.

"How…would you like to go with me?" she asked, as if she leaped off the highest bridge with only a flimsy piece of rope tied to her ankle.

It was quiet between them again. Danni willed her mind not to spiral down. She kept her head up while she waited, envisioning herself sitting at the table in the wedding hall with Simone next to her.

"I wouldn't miss it for the world, Danni," Simone finally said.

Tears gushed down her face as she felt the thrust of ten thousand fireworks explode inside her heart like the brightest, scattering light into the sky.

About the Author

Charlotte Geringer is a first-time novelist who decided to trade in her healthcare career for a chance to chase her dream of writing. Born and raised in South Africa, she moved to the United States as a young, adventurous occupational therapist and worked in many different cities and towns around the country. She finally settled down in Pittsburgh, Pennsylvania, where she lives with her partner and two French pointers. When she is not dreaming up stories, she likes to listen to classical music, play the violin, hike with her dogs, and arrange backyard barbecues with her friends.

CPSIA information can be obtained
at www.ICGtesting.com
Printed in the USA
BVHW071009240123
656981BV00001B/102